MW00527653

"Kate Flora has done it again with her gripping new thriller, *Teach Her a Lesson*. When Alexis Jordan, a well-liked high school teacher, is accused by one of her troubled students of having seduced him, her life spirals out of control. No one believes she's innocent—not her school, the police, her cheating husband, or even her friends—and it's up to her to prove she is. This draws Alexis—and the reader—into a suspenseful journey that doesn't stop until the harrowing end. Bravo."

—**B. A. Shapiro**, *New York Times* bestselling author of *The Art Forger*

"Infatuation, threats, and lies are all on the menu in this thriller from Kate Flora. When high school teacher Alexis Jordan becomes the focus of a disturbed teen, things quickly spiral out of control. And as the danger intensifies Alexis learns that not all of her friends are allies. With more twists and turns than a mountain highway, *Teach Her a Lesson* will keep you turning pages late into the night."

—**Bruce Robert Coffin**, award-winning author of the Detective Byron Mysteries

"With her marriage failing, Alexis can at least take satisfaction from her teaching. But when popular teen Evan fixates on her, insisting they are having the affair that he's fantasized about, Alexis's liberty as well as her career are threatened, and Alexis learns quickly how deep and twisted loyalties can be in this devious, all-too-believable thriller. Seasoned author Kate Flora knows how to depict the slow tumble into the depths of despair—and how to craft a driven female character who can fight her way out. *Teach Her a Lesson* is timely, scarily real, and impossible to put down."

—**Clea Simon**, author of the Massachusetts Book Award Must Read, *Hold Me Down*

"…a tightly woven tale of suspense… This well-written and fast-paced drama kept me in the game, and I could not put this book down until all was said and done. …a great read that had my heart pumping as I had to know the outcome. Good job."

—**Dru Ann Love**, Dru's Book Musing

TEACH HER A LESSON

KATE FLORA

Encircle Publications
Farmington, Maine, U.S.A.

TEACH HER A LESSON Copyright © 2023 Kate Flora

Paperback ISBN 13: 978-1-64599-438-1
E-book ISBN 13: 978-1-64599-439-8

Library of Congress Control Number: 2023936648

ALL RIGHTS RESERVED. In accordance with the U.S. Copyright Act of 1976, no part of this publication may be reproduced, distributed, or transmitted in any form or by any means, or stored in a database or retrieval system, without prior written permission of the publisher, Encircle Publications, Farmington, ME.

This book is a work of fiction. All names, characters, places, and events are either products of the author's imagination or are used fictitiously.

Encircle editor: Cynthia Brackett-Vincent

Cover design by Deirdre Wait
Cover photographs © Getty Images

Published by:

Encircle Publications, LLC
PO Box 187
Farmington, ME 04938

info@encirclepub.com
http://encirclepub.com

EVAN – ONE

Today was it.

He would speak to her today, tell her how he felt. He'd been watching her, waiting for the sign his attention would be welcome. Last Friday, he'd gotten it. The briefest of touches, her hand on his shoulder, her body close to his. He'd known then she was ready to stop pretending she wasn't interested. Ready to stop treating him like just another one of the guys who vied for her attention, and finally acknowledge he was someone special.

He'd about run out of patience. She was tough. Cool. Reserved. Shyer than she let on. He thought her surface confidence was only that—a gloss she put on the face the high school world saw. She was always so popular, always surrounded by people clamoring for her attention, always careful not to play favorites, guarding against someone who'd take advantage of her. The pretty ones had it hard that way. Underneath, she was like anyone else. Longing for someone who'd appreciate her specialness, but afraid to let it show.

He wanted to be cool, but this was a big deal. He'd fantasized about the two of them and now it was going to happen. Beneath his tight Under Armour shirt, he was sweating. Alone in the high school bathroom, he moved closer to the mirror and lifted his arms. Navy was good. Sweat didn't show. He sniffed. Some guys thought sweat was manly. He thought the smell was meaty. Animal. Playing soccer, he'd bump against people and carry their smell the rest of the game. He liked using his body, checking their progress, pushing them out of his way. When the game was over, though, he couldn't wait to get home and shower.

He checked his hair in the mirror. Girls told him he had nice hair.

1

Curly, dark blond, a little long. Lighter after a week in Florida. His last girlfriend liked to touch it. Been a little jealous, saying his hair was nicer than hers. Which was true. Carrie's hair was wispy and pale. Except for those dumb flares of temper when she'd get mad and pound on him, her personality was pale, too.

Screw Carrie. She knew he wasn't interested any more, but she wouldn't go away. Hanging around, texting him, saying how much she still loved him. How mean he was being. She was acting like he owed her something for sleeping with him.

He rubbed the stubble on his chin. He hadn't shaved since Friday and he liked the way the blond stubble looked against his tan. He stepped back and studied himself in the mirror. At 6' 2", he was big for sixteen. He thrust his pelvis forward, admiring the way his athletic shorts draped. Nothing too suggestive. Just confirmation, in case she was wondering, that he wasn't just another pimple-faced Junior, but a man with something to give her.

Thinking about her brought a responsive stiffening. Shit no! He didn't want his body to give him away before he got a chance to say what he wanted to say. He wasn't going out there to fly the flag, get her nervous about sex right away. Sure there would be sex. But he wanted to make a connection first. She needed to understand they were meant to be together.

"Vaunting aloud, but racked with deep despair."
—John Milton, *Paradise Lost*: Book I

CHAPTER ONE

Alexis Jordan shut off her "clean" rap playlist and got out of the Jeep, leaning against it as she watched the students stream off the buses and climb out of parked cars, heading into the high school. Clean-cut guys, girls in skimpy clothing looking like baby hookers, androgynous ones in oversized shirts, boys in baggy jeans with crotches to their knees, showing a wide swath of boxer. Kids of both sexes in plaid pajama pants and flip flops, looking like they'd rolled out of bed and right onto the bus, complete with bed head and half-opened eyes. Oblivious to the lovely April day, the majority of them clutched electronic devices, like robots with their controllers. On the Monday after spring vacation, none of them looked happy to be there.

Wave after wave of their parents' pride and joy, slouching, marching, striding, and sidling through the schoolhouse door. She empathized with the slouchers and sidlers, the boys disappearing into their hoodies, girls who weren't part of laughing cliques and who were practiced at being invisible. Getting through adolescence unscathed was like surviving Baghdad outside the Green Zone. Electronics made everything more complicated. They lived in a world of texting, Instagram, Snapchat, and selfies. Carried toys that amped up their narcissism and made getting and keeping their attention difficult.

Her challenge today would be settling them down and focusing their energies on something besides sex, the fun they'd been having, and what were bound to be endless discussions of a party at the Rinaldis that had gotten totally out of control, resulting in serious looting and vandalism. After a week of cleaning closets and having too much time to notice how often her husband had to "work late," Alexis had started researching hip hop. Now she was eager to be back in the classroom, though she could already picture their eye rolls when she uttered the word 'poetry.' Eye rolls she hoped to turn into stares of surprise when she showed them the "Rap or Shakespeare?" video that would lead off their discussion.

She lingered in the parking lot, face turned toward the sun, grabbing a few more breaths of fresh April air. Spring in Massachusetts was a fleeting and changeable thing, reminding her of Frost's observation about April that as the clouds and wind shifted, you could be one moment a month ahead in May, the next a month behind in March. Robert Frost. Poetry. She'd spent some crazy hours putting together material she hoped would capture their interest, so of course she'd think of Frost this morning. Frost and Wu-Tang Clan.

Time to leave sunshine behind and enter the cave of Crawford Valley High. Alexis took a deep breath and mounted the steps, preparing to check her personal life, and her husband Micah's ominous, "we need to talk," at the door. For the next eight hours, her life would be herding the hearts and minds of horny teenagers, restless juniors, and ready-to-check-out seniors toward an understanding of the English language. In her classroom, that understanding included conforming with the sign over her desk that read: **I don't like *like*. Kindly check it at the door.**

Air rushing toward her carried familiar smells: lunch cooking in the cafeteria. Strong old coffee. Paint from the art department. Pine-scented cleaner. And everywhere, the clashing apple, coconut, vanilla, exotic flowers, musk, tobacco, and herbal scents of laundry detergent and fabric softener, hair products, deodorant, and aftershave. A veritable bazaar of the scents that broadcast clean. She was only two steps in before someone stopped her.

"Morning, Mrs. Jordan. You got time for me after school today?" The nervous student loomed over her, grinning self-consciously, tanned, and reeking of Axe.

Alexis hesitated. She needed a long run this afternoon to plan her response to Micah's, "It's not working out." She was helping the boy with his part in *Death of a Salesman* because the drama coach was overwhelmed by the arrival of triplets. But this student was frustrating to work with, not understanding the part or responding to her suggestions.

"Please?" He hunched his shoulders, giving her a mock-hangdog look. He could be charming—and knew it. "I almost have it, I think."

Reluctantly, she said, "I can give you thirty minutes."

"Thanks," he mumbled, and fell into step with his three buddies. Athletes all, the uncrowned kings of the school. Kids forgiven too much because of their skills. Arrogance. Bad manners. Drug and alcohol use. It was lousy preparation for life.

Aiming for the teachers' room and a second cup of coffee, she headed down the hall into the land of artificial light, chessboard floor tiles, and dully soothing paint, a world of bulletin boards scaled with overlapping posters, swirling bodies, and voices rising and falling like verbal electrical surges.

She was almost at the door when she heard a small mewling sound. Not a lost kitten, a lost student. A sound she couldn't ignore. Around the corner she found a senior girl, shoulders shaking, trying to muffle her sobs in an open locker.

"Gretchen, what's wrong?"

The girl turned, tears running down her face. "Oh, Mrs. Jordan. I didn't get into any of the schools I really wanted. Now I have to make a decision about the others and I don't know what to do." She pressed her knuckles against trembling lips. "I never thought none of them would want me."

She looked so wretched Alexis wanted to hug her and tell her it would be all right, but hugging students was a no-no. "Have you revisited the schools that did accept you?"

The girl nodded, overwhelmed by her dilemma.

"Visiting didn't clarify things?"

"They're all nice... but, I don't know. I feel so rejected, and everyone else has gotten in where they wanted. I mean, you know, Mrs. Jordan.

You know. I remember you telling us once about not getting into the college you wanted."

To hell with the rules. It was idiotic to stand here, hands at her sides, with this girl in such pain. She put her arm around the girl's shoulders.

"It hurts. Big time," she agreed. "But it worked out. I ended up at the right school, found out I wanted to be a teacher. And met my husband. Have you talked with your guidance counselor?"

"No."

"Played pin the yes on the map?"

Gretchen raised her head, surprised. "How do I do that?"

"Like pin the tail on the donkey. Put up a map. Mark the schools where you've been accepted. Then take a bright piece of paper, write yes on it, put on a blindfold, and pin that paper to the map." She smiled. "Who knows? You might stick the pin in, look where it went, and realize you'd love that school. Or that you'd hate it."

Alexis handed the girl a tissue. "Let's walk down to guidance and find you some help."

"I guess." Gretchen gave her a faint smile. "I kind of liked pin the yes on the map, though."

"You can do that when you get home."

Too late for coffee. She walked Gretchen to the guidance office, grabbed her mail from the box, and went to her homeroom. As soon as they saw her, the students around her desk started chirping like hungry little birds. "Give me a minute," she said. They fell silent, shifting restlessly while she skimmed her messages. The silence didn't last. They started talking again, to each other if not to her, about the party that had gotten out of control over the weekend.

"So I heard they took all of Mrs. Rinaldis' underwear. And the knife collection."

"And all the liquor. Hard stuff, too."

"And now her parents are talking about sending her away to school, when, like, it wasn't her fault. It was those senior—" The girl who'd used the word "like" sent her a glance to see if she'd noticed. Alexis nodded.

"It was all the guys. The athletes."

Nothing urgent. She stuffed things into her bag and looked up. "Who's first?"

"I am." Carrie Canavan leaned in, her narrow shoulders twitching with anger. "I want to know where you think you've got the right to make my boyfriend break up with me?"

Where was this coming from? She never gave dating advice. She wouldn't. She wasn't even sure who Carrie was dating these days. "Carrie, I don't know what you're talking about. I haven't discussed your relationship with anyone."

"That's bullshit!" Carrie's small face was tight with outrage. Being aggrieved and outraged—complete with shoulder and butt twitches— was part of Carrie's adopted persona, but today she was really amped up. "He said we were breaking up because of you."

"I have no idea why he would have said that." She had no idea who "he" was.

"Of course you do!" the girl insisted. "You told him to—" Carrie swung to face her clustered girlfriends. "Can you believe that bitch would lie about this?"

No way was she letting that pass. She cut them plenty of slack, but this was not negotiable. Using her 'don't mess with me' voice, she said, "Carrie, that's enough! That language has no place in my classroom."

Carrie whirled back around. "I wasn't talking to you."

"Well, I *am* talking to you." She had no patience with this. Getting students back under control after vacation was hard enough without having to deal with blatant misbehavior. Letting it go would give other students license to act out. "Detention this afternoon, Carrie. Anything further and you'll go to Mr. Clemente. If something's bothering you that you'd like to discuss in a civilized manner, find me during C-block."

"I've got class then."

"Or after school."

Lowering her eyes, Carrie mumbled, "I'm sorry, Mrs. Jordan," and swept away, her sympathetic friends buzzing around her like disturbed bees.

That set the tone for the day. Alexis wanted to teach. That was what she

7

was here for. Poetry. *A Separate Peace. All the King's Men.* She wanted to keep her mind off her husband's words. But getting her students focused today was like arm-wrestling an octopus. Give them a moment's slack and their hands would fumble for forbidden devices, the *sotto voce* chatter would flip from classwork to the Rinaldis.

"Today we're going to talk about poetry," drew a chorus of groans. Her eyes traveled the circle of desks, looking for a responsive face. Nothing. Say "poetry" and the lights went off. Some days, Alexis could have scripted everything. What she'd say, what they'd say. She wanted to be the teacher who helped students like Gretchen, not the one who fended off Carrie's furious attack. She decided to get a little controversy going. "Do you like it? Eliza?"

"I hate it."

"Why do you hate it?"

"I just do. It's boring."

"Tommy? Do you like it?"

The boy ducked his head, turning a little pink, and said, "I'm just not sure I get it. You know?"

They weren't getting off that easily. "How many of you have heard of the favorite poem project?"

One hand went up. Evelina Gonzalez. Evelina rarely spoke. "The Poet Laureate of the United States. He started it. I forget his name. Pisky? We did it at my church. My mother read a poem in Spanish. I never saw her speak in public before."

"Do you remember what poem she read?"

Evelina shook her head. "Someone named Lorca, I think. It was nice. All kinds of people were reading poems. The guy from the bodega. This fat old lady in black with a gravelly voice. There was even a cop." She pushed her sprawling hair back. "I didn't think cops knew poems."

Evelina's shining eyes and rare enthusiasm caught the other students' attention. Someone raised a hand and asked if poetry was harder to write than fiction. Alexis asked what they thought. The responses were divided between those who thought it had to be easier because it was shorter, and those who thought it must be harder to make every word count. Haji

Hassan, who was a Somali Bantu refugee, then asked about Countee Cullen's poem, "Incident," and talked about Black on Black prejudice in Somalia, and the way Cullen's poem captured a child's discovery of prejudice in such a few lines.

That certainly got the discussion going. She hated to interrupt it to show the Ted Talk about Hip Hop or Shakespeare. But that really had them sitting up and taking notice. They were still discussing it when the bell rang. She knew they'd be carrying away Evelina's images of the old lady in the black dress and the cop and Haji's real-world experience.

Tomorrow they would be talking about Eminem and Gerard Manley Hopkins, and her hours of prep while they were vacationing were rewarded by the expressions on the faces of those who looked at her handout.

There was a commotion of colliding chairs and scuffling feet, voices and zippers and rustling clothes as they swarmed her with questions about their weekly writing quotas, offering up excuses, explanations, and pleas for mercy, shoving papers at her and grabbing the ones she passed back. Like a subway prophet, she dispensed judgment, decreed fate, prognosticated imminent doom, and urged reform. Then, with a last shuffle of feet and the thudding of the door, she was alone with Micah's voice in her head and a stomach-knotting worry. What if his comment wasn't an opening salvo, but a parting one?

No time to worry about that now. Her next class was junior honors. A class that would have been best controlled with a whip, if such things hadn't been forbidden. Classes had personalities. Since kindergarten, this one had earned a reputation for trouble. Despite all the changes over the years, with new students coming in and others moving away, this group remained difficult. So bad some teachers speculated there must have been something in the water that year.

This late in the term, revved up from vacation, their brains a jumble of college visits and getting ready to replace the seniors, these juniors were a handful. They seemed to get up in the morning primed to argue. She pushed away her own concerns, arming herself with a metaphorical whip and chair as the door burst open and a wave of students flooded in.

"To sorrow abandoned, but worse felt within,
And in a troubled sea of passion tossed..."
—John Milton, *Paradise Lost*: Book X

CHAPTER TWO

Three giggling junior girls sprinted for seats on the far side of the room, one of them immediately pulling out nail polish, shaking it, and starting to unscrew the top.

Alexis imagined a deft flick of her whip snatching it from the girl's hand. She gave an inward sigh. "Put it away, Shireen."

The girl's chin jutted. "It's not class yet."

Alexis wasn't arguing about the folly of trying to write with wet nails. "Put it away."

"I don't see why." Shireen gave her a poisonous look and put the bottle away. She never saw why. Alexis didn't know whether the girl would be a corporate CEO or a career criminal. Shireen was smart, capable, and insightful. She was also self-centered, manipulative, and mean. In a Lord of the Flies world, Shireen would eat a classmate without compunction.

The rest of the class watched, eager for a confrontation. Alexis wasn't taking the bait. "Okay, people. Free reading time, remember?"

They knew, but about to be seniors, they were testing her, trying on attitude and independence. Something they could try out in another classroom. "All right." She raised her voice. "Settle down."

There was a collective giggle from the three girls, and an audible, "Mrs. Jordan's got PMS."

"Shireen, that's disrespectful to me and everyone else in here. Keep it to yourself."

Shireen leaned back in her chair, inspected nails painted the brownish purple of dried blood, and said, "Hey, you're the one who's always crabby. What's your problem?"

As if discipline was debatable. "You're not reading." Shireen had gotten a poor grade on her last paper. Maybe that's what this was about.

But Shireen wasn't done. She tossed her hair, a shiny confection of waves that must have taken an hour to create, glanced at her friends, and said, "Do you hate us or what, Mrs. Jordan? You sure act like you do."

No way, Alexis thought. She crooked her finger at Shireen and gestured toward the door. "Outside."

To the class, she said, "I want it quiet in here, and I want you reading." She spotted two troublemakers winding up for something. "This isn't kindergarten. You, Sam, and you, Kris. Go to the board and write down four things you learned from today's reading." She looked from one to the other. "Four different things."

As the red-faced pair lumbered to the board, she added, "And make it thoughtful, okay?"

Sam, who was really quite sweet when he wasn't infected by group testosterone, grinned at her, then wrote: *There are 437 pages in the book.*

Shaking her head, she followed the girl out, closing the door behind her. Shireen, her face blotched red, stood with her arms folded, swinging one foot like a pendulum. Clearly spoiling for an argument. "All right," Alexis said, "What was that about?"

The girl gave an insolent shrug. "Jeez, Mrs. Jordan, lighten up, will you? I didn't mean anything."

She did, though. Shireen had been working up to this for a while. Sneaking sarcastic comments into class discussions, arguing her points long after the conversation had moved on. Maybe there were problems at home and she needed to blow off steam, but the classroom wasn't the place.

"I think you did mean something, Shireen. You think your PMS comment was acceptable?"

Shireen studied her swinging foot, stubbornly silent.

Why did they do this to themselves? All the girl had to do was take responsibility for being rude and apologize. Sometimes they let their stubbornness dig them into such unnecessary holes.

Shireen blew out a sudden breath, like a bull about to charge. "You used to be so nice and now you're such a bitch."

Stung, Alexis took a step back. The accusation stunned her. She tried to teach the canon while also meeting them where they lived. Dystopia. Graphic novels. Their movies and music. Books that addressed their issues. She worked hard not to become the kind of teacher she despised, indifferent to their students, treating the job like a walk-on part. Was she wasting her time?

She could ponder that later. Right now she had to deal with Shireen.

"I ask you to explain an inappropriate remark, and your response is I'm a bitch?"

"You used to act like you cared," the girl said. "Now you treat us like morons, always do this, do that. Nothing's any fun. You *are* a bitch. Everyone's noticed it. It's time someone told you."

Escalation instead of apology? Shireen was friends with Carrie Canavan. Maybe this was connected to Carrie's outburst this morning. "Should I send you to the office? To Mr. Clemente?"

Shireen's swinging foot accelerated as she gave herself permission to lose control. "Like I give a shit. Then I can tell him what a bitch you're being. What you did to Carrie. And you gave me a C on my last paper. A fucking C. I'm a junior. You know I can't get C's."

"It was a C paper from an A student, Shireen. As for Carrie? I have no idea what that's about, but it doesn't have anything to do with your being rude."

She hated confrontation, and this was the second one today. Now she'd have to spend the rest of the week hyper-vigilant. This class was like a shark tank. But that wasn't Shireen's business.

"You need to get your mouth under control before you return to class," Alexis said. "Can you do that?"

"I don't want to be in your stupid class."

Enough. Alexis had done everything but say, repeat after me: *'I'm sorry.'* "Have it your way, then," she said. "Go to Mr. Clemente's office."

The swinging foot stubbed against the floor as Shireen's words exploded. "Ohmygod, no, Mrs. Jordan! Wait! You can't do that to me. You can't. He'll call my mother."

"You did it to yourself, Shireen. Now go."

The girl headed off down the hall, head hanging. Suddenly, she swung around. "I meant what I said, you know. You are a mean old bitch. Bitch. Bitch. Bitch." She turned and ran.

Alexis sighed. A certain amount of conflict came with the job. Adolescents could be pretty volatile. But they were supposed to be rested and restored. She didn't like the look of this restoration. She sent the assistant principal a quick text, explaining Shireen's behavior.

She was relieved when she got back to the room and found the class was engaged in suggesting ideas to Sam and Kris, who were writing frantically to keep up. She took a seat at an empty desk and let the discussion go on. She'd worried that *All the King's Men* might feel dated, but recently politics had gotten so fraught and public figures were behaving so badly that it was feeling relevant to them.

Shireen's outburst was forgotten and the rest of the hour—and the day—flew. Finally, the last bell rang. Thirty minutes with an adolescent Willy Loman and she'd be shedding her serious teaching clothes, climbing into black spandex, and running along the river, music blasting into her skull, awash with the endorphin surge.

She waited in a small room off the library where she could keep the door open and use the librarians as chaperones. A teacher couldn't be too careful, especially in a town with entitled kids and even more entitled parents. It was so easy for these kids to take things the wrong way. Look how her day had gone so far.

Usually, he was there first. Today, when her time was tight and she was impatient to be gone, he was late. He wasn't a good actor. He couldn't let go of being himself to become the character he was playing. She'd tried role-playing and suggested he see the movie. It didn't help. He remained a slightly awkward kid named Evan Palmer, wearing a big man's body that didn't quite fit, reciting an adult's lines. This week she'd brought a recorder, thinking hearing himself might help.

She worried about Evan. Narcissism was the name of the game with so many of these kids. Lately, though, he'd shown a disturbing, extremely self-centered edge. The way he treated Carrie was dangerously physical. Grabbing her, shoving her, walking past like she didn't exist. He'd been combative with teachers—arrogant and refusing to listen. She blamed athletics, concerned about steroids and his mental health. She'd mentioned her concerns to guidance, but in a school where someone was always spinning out of control, it took a conflagration to get noticed.

He flew in, slamming the door behind him. Ran a hand through his hair and over his bristly cheeks as he apologized for being late. The stubble made him look like one of those Chris's—Pratt, Hemsworth, Pine—and he knew it, enjoying the way the girls fawned over him.

She walked to the door and opened it again. Never be alone with a student in a room with a closed door. The precaution had become as natural as breathing. He pulled out a chair and perched on the edge of it. Jumpy and agitated, which didn't bode well for their session. "Time's tight today, Evan. Shall we get started?"

"Sure. Sure. That would be great." He pulled out the script and pushed it across the table.

She turned on the recorder and fed him his first line. He started off sounding better than usual. The emotion was there, the intensity, the strain in his voice. This was a different Evan. More mature. More Willy Loman. He flew through without hesitation, finishing with a triumphant smile.

She clapped her hands. "Evan, that was great. Just great. You're really getting a feel for the character." She turned the page. "You're on such a roll. Let's do the next part."

He checked his watch and shook his head. "You said thirty minutes, right? We've only got a few minutes left and I need to talk with you about something."

Looking up, she saw he'd come around the table and was standing quite close, his face terribly serious. Was he about to confess to some crime? Had he been at the Rinaldis' party? Maybe taken something and didn't know how to give it back? He slid into the chair beside her. "This is so important I don't know how to begin."

14

She waited. Usually, if they were determined to speak and you kept quiet, students managed to get the words out.

"I know…" He swallowed. "I know you probably think of me as just another awkward high school boy."

He pulled his chair closer to hers, leaning back and hooking his thumbs into the elastic waist of his oversized shorts. "I mean, I don't blame you for thinking that way. Why wouldn't you, right?"

Did he have an erection? She looked away, embarrassed for him, as his hand came out of the elastic, slipped quick as a snake across the tabletop, and grabbed her arm.

"Evan. Don't!" She tried to pull away but his fingers tightened, holding her there.

"Listen," he said. "Let me say this. I think we could be something to each other, Mrs. Jordan. I've seen the way you look at me. The way you smile. I know you don't think I'm just any student. You think I'm special."

Embarrassment stung her face.

He bobbed his head. "You *know* I'm special. And I know you're lonely. Your husband doesn't appreciate you. You aren't getting what you deserve at home."

What on earth was he talking about? He didn't know anything about her marriage or her husband. Shock clenched her chest as she tried again to pull away.

His grip was too strong.

He flattened his hand out, caressing her arm from her wrist to her shoulder, an unfocused, almost blissful look on his face. "Mrs. Jordan, I could be someone special to you. I'd like to be, if you'll give me the chance."

"Evan. No. Stop that!" She jerked her arm away and stood. She'd been hit on before. High school boys got crushes. But she'd never been cornered like this. Or touched. He was standing, too, physical and aroused, backing her toward the corner of the room farthest from the exit, his brawny 6' 2" looming between her and the door.

He'd actually touched her! And if she was reading him right, he wanted to do it again. She needed to establish the inappropriateness of the situation without humiliating him or escalating things. Teenage boys did really stupid things sometimes. But he was tense as an animal about to spring and she couldn't seem to catch her breath.

"Evan, I'm your teacher." She heard the tremor in her voice. "It's against rules and policy and... and... against plain good sense for there to be any relationship between us other than student and teacher."

"No!" The word exploded in the small space. His face was a map of emotions—anger, confusion, determination. He towered a full head over her, a volatile male animal, violating her personal space. "No," he gasped. "The rules don't matter for us!"

She'd always counted on the librarians to come if she called for help, but she wanted to defuse this without exposing Evan or herself to embarrassment—if she could. A teacher was supposed to be able to handle her students. "Evan, listen, you must understand—" As if this was a moment for reason when she was talking to a broad male chest less than a foot away, to someone on a mission whose ears weren't tuned to receive.

"No, Mrs. Jordan. *You* listen. It's okay, you and me. Don't you see? We're special. We're not like everybody else."

Trying to get his attention, trying not to sound as scared as she felt, she said sternly, "Be sensible, Evan. There is no special—" She was having trouble breathing.

"Look!" He closed the space between them until his body was touching her, his eyes wild.

No way would she reach him with reason. She pressed her back against the wall, trying to create space between them, looking for a way to escape.

"Look—" He grabbed her arms, sweaty fingers digging in as his voice dropped into a deep, intimate register. "You think I haven't known what you were doing? That I didn't get the messages you were sending with your smiles, your touches? Giving me rides home. This special time we've spent together. Our special time." His voice caressed the "our."

One ride, she thought. One ride. A car full of students. And some tutoring sessions. He'd made that into *this*? Into an invitation?

"Evan. No. For heaven's sake. You can't think I wanted this?"

But he was all output, no receptors.

He released her arms, but quickly planted each of his hands against the wall beside her, still trapping her. "Look, you can't lead me on like this and then pull back with some 'Oh no, no, this can't happen, I'm your teacher' bullshit."

Her heart pounded. Iron bands tightened around her chest that wouldn't let it expand. Special messages? Leading him on? Where was this craziness coming from? She tried to duck under his arm. His arms closed tighter. She felt his erection press against her. She'd never been physically scared of a student before.

"Evan, I'm sorry if you misunderstood, but I have never—" Her brain was a jumble, but this was dumb. She's worrying about embarrassing him while an obsessed male is trapping her and rubbing his erection against her? "Evan..."

"Don't!" he exploded, closing the trap with his body, pressing her back against the wall. "You can't brush me off just because I'm younger. Because of some silly rules. Rules don't matter for people like us. People attracted to each other, like we are. Like you *know* we are."

So fanatically certain.

Her mind raced. How long had he been misreading what she'd meant as kindness and building this fantasy of mutual attraction? She had to get out of this too-small room before he acted on what she was reading in his eyes.

"Evan, listen," she said, her voice emerging small and uncertain. Who needed the speech coach now? "You misunderstood. I never suggested that anything inappropriate could happen between us. It can't. Cannot. This is not going to happen."

He stared as if she spoke a foreign language, half-moaning as he pressed himself against her.

Foolish to worry about embarrassing him. Or herself. She had to end this. The situation was out of control. Making her voice more forceful, she commanded, "Evan! Stop this, Evan. Let me go!"

He didn't move. Her feet were jammed against a box of books, her shoulders against the wall. She couldn't breathe. Things like this wrecked teachers' careers. Innocent teachers' careers. Under her loose jumper, sweat trickled down her spine and between her breasts. "Evan, listen, there is no way—"

"Stop it!" His voice was thick with anguish. "Don't talk." He pressed against her, pinning her there. She felt the sweaty heat of his body. The force of his hands behind her, pressing her into him. His obvious arousal. He groaned as his chest touched hers, as he rubbed his erection against her. Shock closed her throat, paralyzing her as his frantic fingers tugged at her buttons, ran up her skirt.

Fear and outrage gave her strength. She put her hands against his chest and shoved hard, pushing him away. "Stop it! Take your hands off me. You cannot behave like this."

She raced toward the door, putting the table between them, but he came around the other side faster, still between her and the door. He shuddered, his eyes sweeping her with a glance so intimate she felt he was seeing through her clothes, appearing more puzzled by her response than angry. Sweat-glistened skin trembled over his well-defined muscles. He talked fast as he edged toward the door.

"I guess this was a shock to you, wasn't it?" His forced, toothy grin recalled King Kong grinning at Fay Wray. "I didn't mean it to be. I thought you wanted it. But you need time to absorb it. Sometimes women need time. I know. And you're right. We shouldn't do this here." He swung his pack onto his shoulder.

She'd almost started to breathe again when he said, "We can talk Thursday. Our usual time. But Lexie, uh... Mrs. Jordan, you've got to give me a chance, a fair chance. I deserve that. You've promised me that."

As Evan strode through the door and disappeared, she sank into a chair, rearranging her clothes with shaking fingers.

"Thou never from that hour in Paradise
Found'st either sweet report, or sound repose…"
—John Milton, *Paradise Lost*: Book IX

CHAPTER THREE

"I promised you nothing," she told the empty room. "Never." Shaking as she absently rubbed her bruised arms, stunned by how frighteningly physical he'd been. She swiped at tears as she tried to restore her breathing.

Oh, God. God. *God!* How could she have let this happen? Careers were ruined by events like this. And what should she do now? Go tell her boss, that bureaucratic cold fish Dr. Huston, how she'd been unable to handle a pass from a sixteen-year-old? That Evan had cornered her and rubbed himself all over her, fully believing it was what she wanted?

What was going on today? She stared at the wall, seeing Evan's obsessed face. Carrie Canavan's pinched anger. Shireen O'Reilly's blotchy red rage. This morning she'd been so happy coming through the door, so excited about ways to make their classes relevant.

The smells of that terrifying encounter lingered in the room. Evan's powerful cologne, the reek of his acrid sweat, the hot odor of testosterone, the pungency of his lust and the curdled stink of her fear. She put her head on the table, ignoring the recorder as it tumbled to the floor, and banged her head, softly and steadily, against the cool, hard wood.

After a while, she stopped. Head banging was a sign of pathology. Undoubtedly, the DSM enumerated the disorders associated with head banging. She was certainly suffering from a disorder—one of perception for not seeing this coming. A disorder in her heartbeat, racing and erratic. A disorder in her lungs as if she'd just run ten miles and couldn't catch her breath. Her foot knocked against the tiny recorder, sending it spinning into the wall. She shoved it in her jumper pocket and hurried from the building.

Her shaking hands were trying to unlock the Jeep when her friend and colleague Dan Morgan took the key away and pressed the unlock button.

"What's happened, Lex?" he said.

"Nothing."

"And I was born yesterday. You're obviously upset. Put your things in the car and come sit with me." He waited while she dumped her bag in the Jeep, then steered her to his truck.

From the window, she watched the wind blow an empty Coke can across the asphalt, something to concentrate on to hold back tears as she gave him an edited version of what had just happened.

"I feel so stupid, Dan. I can't believe I didn't see it coming." All her runner's fitness had deserted her. She had to keep stopping to breathe. "The scariest thing is how sure he was I'd been sending him all these covert messages, which he read as signals this is something I wanted. Truly," she shook her head in disbelief. "I hadn't a clue."

Dan pushed up her sleeve, exposing bruises. She was a pale-skinned redhead and bruised easily.

"Did Evan do that?"

She nodded. "He was very physical. But I'm more scared by what was in his head." Was she? Her stomach churned at the memory of how he'd pinned her to the wall and forced himself against her. "Why didn't I see this building?"

"Lex, don't do this to yourself!" The sharpness in his voice surprised her. Dan was normally so gentle. "Don't blame yourself for missing this. There may not have been anything to see. This is about what he imagined, about him seeing what he wanted to see, not about anything you did." He shifted so his back was against his door, focused intently on her face. "I don't like this at all. I know you. You're not easily shaken. So what really happened with Evan? The whole story, not some edited version."

She described how Evan had trapped her, how he'd pressed his body against her. His sexual excitement. The look in his eyes as he'd forced himself against her. His hands under her dress. Retelling brought back her overwhelming sense of violation. She finished, expecting some comforting words.

Dan only stared into the distance, frowning. Eventually, he said, "You're going to hate me for this, but I've got to say it." He hesitated. "Even though you didn't do anything, even though you're the victim here, you still have to be prepared to defend yourself."

"Defend myself? Against what, Dan? I'm the victim here." But hadn't she had the same thoughts herself? That situations like this wrecked careers? That Evan might be the instigator, but what the world would see were a high school boy and an adult woman. She didn't want to defend herself. She wanted to go home. Go for a run. Forget this ever happened.

He held up a hand, blocking her protest. As though he'd read her mind, he said, "Listen, Lex. You can't just forget this happened, because given what we both know about Evan, it isn't over. When you get home, write everything down. Every detail of what happened. Then write down every contact with him you can remember. Any time you might have been alone with him, like those hours you spent working with him on the play."

"You really think this is a big deal, don't you?"

"You were sexually assaulted by a student who genuinely believes you invited it. That's a big deal."

"It wasn't a—"

"Sexual assault? What would you call it if it happened to someone else? It happened, Alexis. You have to take it seriously, and you have to act fast."

Her heart sank. This was not her easygoing friend, someone who'd say what she wanted to hear—that she should shake this off and forget about it. That Evan would come to his senses. This was a Dan she'd never seen before, scaring her silly. And he wasn't done.

"Talk to the union representative," he said, "and yes, he's an asshole, but also talk with Dr. Huston. Be sure he hears your side first."

"But I don't have a side. And I don't want to talk to Dr. Huston about this. It's humiliating." She felt shaky. Disoriented. Her bruised arms stung.

She'd been a lot more scared in that small room than she'd admitted. Evan's scent and sweat had transferred to her clothes. She wanted to rush home and change. Put some distance between herself and what Evan had done. Dan's attitude wasn't helping.

"Better humiliated than out of a job." His ominous tone chilled her. "I couldn't be more serious, and trust me, I *know* what I'm talking about. Something like this happens, you've got to cover your ass."

A light dawned. "It happened to you?"

"Something pretty similar. A crazy girl with a wild imagination, who could read something into nothing like you wouldn't believe. She came on to me. I told her no way. Next thing I knew, she'd flipped it and I was the aggressor. The worst of it was, when she told her story, it sounded so damned plausible I almost believed it myself, and I *knew* it wasn't true. I still get a sick feeling when I think about it."

His eyes roved the lot as if he were scanning for spies. "I hope that's not what's happening here, but these days, with parents seeing predators behind every tree and screaming bloody murder at the slightest threat to their precious darlings, you can't take chances."

"But I haven't done anything." A tiger had her stomach in its claws. She pressed a fist against her abdomen. "It's Evan who's done something. To me."

"Neither had I done anything," he said. "But you're an adult. He's sixteen. A kid. That's how the world will see it. I know you didn't invite this. And yes, it's horribly unfair, but back in that room, your life changed."

Surely, because of his own experience, he was blowing this way out of proportion. "Come on, Dan. He's a screwed up kid with a hard-on and a crush. When he's calmed down, I'll talk to him, make him see how he's misread things."

"Goddammit, Alexis," he exploded, "don't be a simpleton! Are you listening? Look what just happened. He cornered you and wouldn't let you leave. He had his hand under your skirt and was trying to unbutton your clothes. He restrained you while he rubbed his erect penis against you, believing that's what you wanted. That's not just some misguided kid with a crush."

She'd never seen Dan so upset. She turned up the collar on her coat and zipped it. She was freezing, and not from the weather.

He started the engine and turned on the heat, then took both her hands in his and met her eyes, his face lined and ominous. "You think you can get him alone and talk sense into him, don't you?"

She nodded.

"Well, excuse my bluntness, but he thinks he can get you alone and talk his way into your pants. He already believes you want him there. In my book, Lex, that's a recipe for disaster."

Gently, he released her. "I know you're frightened and I'd love to comfort you and say don't worry. But I'm trying to make you see the reality here. You can't just brush this off. I know how much you care about these kids, how willing to go that extra mile, but they're not all wide-eyed innocents. There are manipulative kids. Self-centered kids. Crazy kids. And once in a while, there's a kid who's downright evil."

"Evil?"

"Yes, evil. Destructive. Bent on having his way and never mind who's hurt. I've been there, Lex. It's like going to hell. When it happened to me, there was still some presumption that teachers were honorable. These days there isn't even healthy skepticism working in your favor."

He sighed. "I know. It sounds awful. It's unfair. But you have to protect yourself. For starters, don't ever, ever let yourself be alone with him again. He comes into a room, you leave. He calls, you hang up. He approaches you on the street, you walk away."

He waited for his words to penetrate. "You've got to get out in front of this. Get the assault on record right away, when it's just happened. Before he has the opportunity to spin it his way. You can't take any chances. Ask Micah how much trouble a teacher can get into if he's accused of fooling around with a student."

Micah. Oh, god. Micah. "Thanks, Dan," she said, her mind spinning. "Advice taken."

"I hope so," he said. "Ask Maggie what it was like. It got so bad she had to shop in the next town. She couldn't stand the looks, the trial by innuendo. And you know what a stoic my wife is. Even though I was ultimately vindicated, I had to leave that job. Everything was tainted."

She didn't want to hear this. She needed to hear this.

"I feel like this is my fault," he said, ducking his head like a guilty kid. "I'm the one who asked you to work with him."

Another time, she would have followed up on that. She knew she should explore this further, ask more questions, but she was too shaken. She needed to exorcise the memory of Evan's rough hands and the intrusive heat of his body, his look of crazy certainty, and her pervading sense of violation. To run until she'd sweated it all out.

"Should I talk to the police?"

"You could. They're going to cut him a lot of slack, though. He's sixteen."

So she'd work within the system. She might prefer to downplay it to herself, and to avoid the embarrassment of discussing it with the principal, Dr. Huston, who was a fat, bureaucratic martinet—but it *had* been a sexual assault. And Dan was right. What if Evan did it again? To another teacher or a student? It needed to be on record. Evan should be watched.

"Okay. I'll make those notes. Report the incident to Dr. Huston and call our union president. Who is that, anyway?"

"Jim Fisher."

That was bad news. Fisher was Evan's soccer and lacrosse coach. Notorious for playing favorites with his athletes. He wouldn't want to hear this. "Will he be helpful? He thinks Evan walks on water."

"Regardless of his relationship with the boys on his teams, he has an obligation to you." But Dan's tone echoed her uncertainty. He looked around, making sure they were alone. "Here's one reason this worries me. Evan specifically asked for you as his drama coach. I talked you into doing it after he talked me into asking you. Why not? Your students love you and you're good at this. But now it seems deliberate. Like you were targeted."

The students didn't love her. Wasn't that what she'd been hearing today? What else might she be missing? Was she being paranoid because two students gave her an unusually hard time? Or was it all connected to Evan?

She felt her head might explode. She pulled out her keys, wishing they unlocked a time machine she could crawl into and do this day over. "You've scared me, Dan."

"I wish I didn't have to, but you can't just tough it out. You need to be proactive." He shook his head, frowning. "There's something disturbing about that boy. And tenacious. I don't think he'll let this drop."

"Go in thy native innocence, rely
on what thou hast of virtue…"
—John Milton, *Paradise Lost*: Book IX

CHAPTER FOUR

At home, she stripped off the dowdy stuff she wore to work and dressed for running. She'd started wearing shapeless clothes—nothing short, nothing tight—back when she was only a few years older than her students. Now it was a habit. Feeling a little like Superman in the phone booth, she transformed back into herself. She pulled on sleek black tights with narrow white stripes and a black and white jacket, grabbed her iPod, and headed out.

She had a three-mile loop for her daily run, five for when she had serious kinks to work out. Today was definitely a five-mile day. Exercise as exorcism, casting out the lingering shock of being pressed against Evan's aroused body, trying to clear her head for tonight's conversation with Micah. It took three miles to stop obsessively rerunning the scene with Evan. By four, endorphins had kicked in. Coming into the home stretch, she was simply filled with the joy of running.

She threw her jumper and blouse—tainted with Evan's scent—in the washer and started dinner. Almost six and Micah wasn't home. According to the calendar, he didn't have a meeting or an evening class. She called his office and his cell and got no answer. She looked at the neatly sliced vegetables, ready for a stir-fry, the bluefish marinating in soy sauce, ginger, and vermouth, the steamy pot of bubbling rice and the waiting salad. He'd better come soon. She was starving.

While she waited, she wrote up the incident with Evan. Describing it was like a second violation. She kept playing the game Dan had warned her about, asking what she'd done to bring this on and why she hadn't seen it coming. When she hit print, it was seven-thirty and Micah still wasn't home. *Keep busy*, she thought. She carried her school bag into the study and took out student papers. Picked up her red pen. Got up again. Dammit! She'd run five miles. She was hungry. This wasn't a play and she wasn't waiting for goddamned Godot. She marched into the kitchen, put the food away, and made a grilled cheese sandwich. Still holding Micah's parting words at arm's length. "It's not working, Lex. We need to talk."

At nine-thirty, anger at Evan and her missing husband having eclipsed embarrassment, she called the teachers' union president, Jim Fisher. Coach Fisher. She heard loud sports on a TV in the background and his impatience to get back to it came through more clearly than his slurry voice. He only focused once she explained she was calling because he was their union president and she had a problem with a student and needed his advice.

Because of his relationship with Evan, she didn't use names. She described what had happened—the edited version without erections and intrusive hands—said she'd written it up because she understood she needed to be extremely careful about such things, and she'd put a copy in his box in the morning.

"Am I overreacting, Jim?"

"Ten years ago, I would have said yes. These days, I'm not sure you can overreact."

Exactly what Dan had said. The crowd roared and she felt him drift away. "Jim?" She waited until the noise died down. "Jim? What else should I be doing?"

"Talk with Dr. Huston. Be sure you give him a copy of that thing you wrote. Excuse me." The roar from the TV was loud enough to hurt her ears. "Man, what a game!" he said. "Look, you gotta go through the steps to cover your ass, but I wouldn't lose sleep over it. They're kids. They get crushes, read too much into a situation. Then it all blows over. Just stay away from him. Don't give him a chance to make any more of it than he already has, you know? If he won't stop, come see me. That's why I'm here."

She wasn't reassured. He'd said the right things, but she knew how guys were when they watched sports on TV. Aliens could abduct their wives and children and they wouldn't notice until they went looking for something to eat.

After a restless night and awful dreams, she woke to smooth sheets and an empty pillow on Micah's side. Her husband, the man who'd told her they needed to talk, hadn't come home.

Unwillingly, she recalled Evan's words. "I know your husband doesn't appreciate you. You aren't getting what you deserve at home." As though he'd overheard Micah talking to another woman on the phone, like she had. How could he know? She'd told no one, not even her closest friend. She'd been raised in the proud old New England tradition where one maintained privacy at all costs. Things were always *fine* even when everyone had cancer, including the cat, and bill collectors camped on the sagging porch.

Outside, it was gray and rainy. She wanted to pull the covers over her head and stay in bed, avoiding Evan and Dr. Huston, Dan's worried look, the students' prying eyes. But she had to heed Dan's and Jim Fisher's advice, and talk with Dr. Huston about Evan. Get her version of the story in first, like this was some kind of contest.

She shouldn't have to do this. They should know she'd never do what Evan fantasized she'd done. Her record spoke for itself—her teaching and all the extra hours she put in—special projects, tutoring and mentoring, never mind being the universal shoulder for all to cry on, students and faculty alike. Was she a big dunce to believe all that mattered? A bigger dunce to think she'd get through this without feeling utterly humiliated? Getting her "he trapped me, he groped me, he pressed his erection against me" on file before Evan told them she'd wanted him to? It was so degrading.

She put on underwear and studied her rack of baggy, boring clothes. Clothes designed to avoid any suggestion she was sexy or provocative. Fat lot of good they'd done her. Maybe she'd go to school like this. Leave her bright red hair loose and wild. Go in green satin underwear that matched one of the colors in the tattoo just below her navel.

In college, she and some friends had gone up to Maine and gotten tattoos. She'd picked the "M" for Micah, getting through the discomfort by imagining his pleasure when he saw it. Instead, when he discovered the emblem of her affection, he was shocked. For all his show of counter-culture style, her husband turned out to be pretty traditional. It had been a damned hard way to find out, and made her wonder if she did tend to misread other people's signs. Not a place she wanted to go this morning.

Amusing as the underwear image was, meeting Dr. Huston in anything but her usual dull garb wouldn't help her "side." She chose a jersey the bright blue of her eyes, and a black jumper. Locked her hair back with a barrette. Fifteen minutes later, at her favorite coffee shop, the proprietor, Ollie, whose smiles had been a fixture of her mornings for years, fixed her coffee and bagged her muffin as soon as she came through the door. Handing it over the counter, he said, "Something is wrong, Red? You are not well?"

"Couldn't sleep," she said, thrusting her money at him. She grabbed the coffee and the bag and left without her change. She had a pretty good buzz of self-pity going already. Sympathy was the last thing she needed.

Dr. Huston, his face as blank as a Monday morning blackboard, gave her only a few minutes and barely seemed to be listening. "Thanks for bringing this to my attention, Mrs. Jordan," he said, dismissing her. A teacher gets assaulted and he seems more concerned with arranging the forms on his desk by color.

She wished she felt reassured by his casual manner, but for numerous reasons—craftiness, laziness, or manipulation—Huston often didn't respond, so she persisted. "What about my request to move Evan to another English class, Dr. Huston?"

"Let me worry about that," he said. "I'll have a chat with Mr. Clemente, and we'll decide what course to take." He shifted his attention to a waiting stack of papers.

Seething, she considered rolling up her sleeves and showing him her bruises, but his assiduous attention to paperwork made it clear the interview was over. Had Huston been too indifferent? There was something studied in his non-responses. Her anxiety level, already high in anticipation of encountering Evan, rose as she tried to figure out what the principal was up to.

That early morning interview with Huston set the tone for the day. Her students were jumpy as crickets. Damp clothes made the air smell like wet dog. It was a universally bad hair day. The discussion of Eminem and Hopkins roused them for a while. Impossible not to. But the students who'd volunteered to read poems chose dull old chestnuts like Longfellow and mumbled utterly predictable reasons for picking them. The class nodded and yawned through their presentations. At least she was spared *By the Shores of Gitchee Gumee.*

She'd been so excited planning this project. Now, nodding off with the rest of them, she felt dismal. "My turn," she said, opening her book with a thump. She read them Mark Strand's poem, "Pot Roast," watching the puzzlement on their faces, and the beginnings of understanding on some, and pleasure. Coming to the end, she read, "I raise my fork in praise, and I eat."

"Does it seem like an odd thing to you," she asked, "to write a poem about a pot roast?"

One of the boys raised his hand. "I liked it. When my mom went back to work she was too busy to cook anymore. Sometimes after sports, I'm hoping that when I get home, she'll be making dinner like she used to and the house will smell real good again."

Alexis smiled. "One of the things this poem is telling us is that to be meaningful, poetry doesn't have to be about grand themes or elevated ideas. It's about things that matter. It's about how the poet uses ordinary things to touch us, stir our memories, or create longings." She gave them a second for that to sink in. "Have you ever longed for something particular to eat because it was comforting? Because it was associated with a special time?"

Hands popped up, students reporting their stories of holiday food, or soothing food, things they ate only at a relative's house, or when they were sick, or what it felt like to eat a whole bag of Doritos. She sat back, pleased, and let them talk.

When the bell rang and they streamed out, she wanted to put her head on the desk and rest, like she'd done in first grade. But the classroom had a glass door. It would have been like sleeping in a fishbowl.

Instead, she tried to call Micah—no answer—then went to the teacher's bathroom to splash cold water on her face.

Claire Simkoff, who ran the computer lab, paused behind her, smeared on a streak of glistening scarlet lipstick, and patted her shoulder. "Honey, right now you look like I feel, you know? Some days I feel more like a lion tamer than an educator." Claire was six feet tall, part African-American, and a former basketball star. As far as Alexis could tell, Claire wasn't afraid of anything. When she grew up, she wanted to be like Claire.

"I thought vacation was supposed to return them revitalized and refocused," Alexis said.

"They are, honey. Refocused on having fun. Seeing what they can get away with. Refocused on relationships and their sex lives and other people's sex lives. The desire for academic achievement has been suctioned right out of their little heads."

"You're such a cynic, Claire."

"I prefer realist."

"Nah. If you were a realist, you wouldn't be working here. Not with marketable computer skills. You'd be out there in the business world, making money."

"And miss all this? Where else would I have to purge the temp files of dirty pictures every night and get to read lurid messages all day long? Did you know there are women out there with breasts bigger than our heads?" Claire snapped her purse shut. "Gotta run before one of those little darlings messes with one of my computers."

Alexis walked to Junior English, head high and determined to handle whatever happened. But Evan wasn't in class. Billy reported he was sick. Thank goodness something was going right. Though Shireen spent the entire period staring daggers at her, the class managed to have a pretty good discussion of *All The King's Men*. Sure, she cheated and gave them an extra-long free reading period. And used the set of canned questions she kept for days when she felt brain-dead. She still got them thinking.

Plenty of other teachers gave a lot less on a regular basis.

She was heading to the teacher's room for coffee when she ran into Ruth Bauer, the department secretary. "Excuse me, Lex. I'm afraid I blew it." Ruth bobbed her head apologetically. "It's Mrs. Findley. When she asked when your free period was, I said C-block without thinking. And now she's here."

Alexis suppressed a sigh. She wasn't up for someone as demanding as Lauren Findley's mother today. Ruth meant well, even if she didn't get that part of her job was to protect them from moments like this. And Ruth was staring at her with spaniel eyes. "Put her in the conference room and explain I have only twenty minutes."

Mrs. Findley was stabbing at her phone with a red-tipped nail. Matching lipstick had begun to creep up the lines around her mouth like a blood sample up a pipette. As Alexis pulled out a chair, the woman's head snapped toward her.

Alexis smiled. When they left this room, Lauren's mother should think she was sweet as pie. "We have twenty minutes. How can I help you?"

"It's Lauren's last paper. That grade you gave wasn't a fair measure of her ability." She reached into a Vuitton bag and drew out the paper, pointing at the grade, B minus. "Lauren is a junior," Mrs. Findley announced. "A critical year for grades. She's getting a B minus in English."

Alexis leaned away from the woman's asphyxiating perfume. She always let students rewrite their papers to improve their grades and gave clear and precise comments to guide them. Lauren was a sweet, contented girl who rarely rewrote. "You read my notes?"

"Of course, but I don't see—"

"Has Lauren read them?" Alexis asked. "Have you discussed them? Is there something I might clarify for you?"

"I'm here to discuss them with *you*," Mrs. Findley said. "No. To discuss her *grade* with you. I don't think the grade fairly reflects Lauren's writing ability."

"Her ability, or her performance on this paper?"

"What's the difference?"

Alexis wanted to roll her eyes and flip her hair, sigh and wriggle on her chair, giggle and make stupid faces—all the responses her students gave when one of them said something utterly moronic. She earned $55,000 a year doing a job that drained her daily. Mrs. Findley probably pulled down well over 100K, yet she was unembarrassed about giving such an idiotic response. Maybe she gave Lauren idiot advice as well. It would explain why her daughter couldn't follow directions and rewrite a paper.

She smiled. "Lauren has the potential to be quite a good writer. She has a rich vocabulary and a good understanding of the concepts. But good writing doesn't happen at the first draft stage. That's why I encourage them to write their papers early, so they'll have time for revision."

Mrs. Findley opened her mouth to interrupt.

Alexis raised a hand. "You know I also let them redo the papers, based on my comments, and resubmit them for a better grade?" She flipped to the last page and turned it to face Mrs. Findley, running her unmanicured finger down her long hand-written paragraphs.

"If you sit with Lauren and review these so she clearly understands the points I've raised and can answer my questions, she can rewrite this paper and substantially improve her grade."

"She's going to do that," Mrs. Findley said, shoving the paper back into the bag. "But if she starts with a B minus, the best she can do is a B plus. That's not good enough. She needs to start with a B plus so she can bring it up to an A or an A minus."

This conversation sounded like they were haggling over the price of a car. They were supposed to be talking about training a mind, about instilling habits of discipline and analysis. Actually, only Alexis was. Lauren was content to be a B-minus student. Mrs. Findley just cared about winning.

"It isn't a B plus paper, Mrs. Findley."

"It's what you asked for. Six pages long. It's typed. It has footnotes."

Lauren could have copied text from Wikipedia to meet those criteria. Alexis checked her watch, and stood. "Lauren's paper is a good start. The point I emphasized was her failure to analyze. Maybe you can work with her, help her with the rewrite. She has until Friday."

"Lauren has a terrible week," the woman said. "She doesn't have time to rewrite." Saw that argument wasn't a winner. "You're so demanding. You hold them to an impossible standard."

Alexis forced another smile. Mrs. Findley wasn't the only one who wanted to win. They were just fighting different battles. "I like to think it's a *possible* standard. Your daughter is a lovely girl with great potential. Our challenge is to help her be more ambitious for herself. And thank you for your concern. There's nothing we teachers appreciate more than an involved parent."

Back in the hall, she ran into Mark Clemente, the assistant principal in charge of discipline.

"Oh, good, Alexis," he said. "I was looking for you. Got a minute?"

"Sure thing," she said. "I was just going to grab some coffee."

"I've got coffee. And donuts."

"How can I resist?" She followed him into his office and sank into a comfortable chair. The chairs in Huston's office were cheap vinyl and hideously uncomfortable. "Nice chair," she said. "So I guess Dr. Huston talked to you about Evan Palmer?"

"No." He hesitated as he poured her coffee. "Cream or sugar?"

They'd shared hundreds of cups of coffee together and he didn't know? "Both, please." She gave him a copy of her memo about Evan. "I thought this was what you wanted to talk about."

"Donut?" He held out a bright Dunkin' Donuts box. She shook her head.

He tipped back in his chair and read her memo through. "Something's going on with that boy," he said. "I've been watching him for a while now. He's pushing a lot of limits. Coming in late, skipping class, little temper flares. Maybe working himself up to this?" His eyes were somber and probing. "Was this really the first inkling you had that he felt this way?"

Since when was a full-on groping an inkling? "It was a complete surprise. If there were clues they were so subtle I missed them."

He set her memo down and tented his fingers. Usually, their interactions had a light, bantering quality. Today, he seemed distant and reserved.

She thought hard. "Well, there was something Carrie Canavan said yesterday. Yelled, actually." She told him about Carrie's outburst and her accusation that Alexis had meddled in their relationship.

"I tried to think what I might have said that he could have misunderstood as dating advice. There's nothing. You know how it is. You try to be so careful, but with a dozen of them at a time asking questions, something might slip out that could be misconstrued. And working with Evan one-to-one on the play, sometimes he tells me things about his personal life."

"I do know how it is."

It was quiet here, isolated from the noise and chaos of the corridors and classrooms. An oasis of calm. But something was wrong. "If you didn't know about Evan, why were you looking for me?"

He straightened a stack of papers on his desk, a classic stalling technique. Her stomach twisted. Huston indifferent. Mark evasive. Something was up. "Shireen O'Reilly says you're being unfair. She says she tried to explain that she wasn't being rude and you wouldn't listen."

What was this? Mark didn't usually second-guess her discipline decisions. "We went over that yesterday, Mark. Swearing and screaming that I'm a bitch isn't explaining. I gave her multiple chances to apologize and she wouldn't take them."

"I know. Her father called, all bent out of shape because she got a detention yesterday, ruining her perfect record." He paused. "He mentioned that another girl had called you a bad name and she didn't get detention. I assume that would be Carrie?"

"He might have meant Carrie. But Carrie apologized and stopped being disruptive, while Shireen blew up and called me a bitch. And Carrie did get detention, remember?"

"That's pretty much what I told Mr. O'Reilly. Just wanted to be sure I had that right."

And if I believe that, you've got beachfront in Kansas to sell me. The chair was feeling a lot less comfortable as she tried to parse Mark's odd behavior. "Shireen's been a walking time bomb for weeks. You know that. What's going on? Something I should know about?"

He shifted uneasily in his chair. "No."

"You're not being straight with me, Mark."

He stared out his window at a mesmerizing view of a brick wall. "Lex,

I'm sorry. Dr. Huston wanted to keep this under wraps until we could get to the bottom of it. I probably shouldn't be telling you."

"Keep what under wraps? Get to the bottom of what?" She gripped the sticky wooden arms of the chair, nervous and damp-palmed, and felt a sudden, disturbing connection to the sweaty kids who'd sat here awaiting discipline.

"Yesterday, after I spoke with Shireen, I spoke with Carrie." His sad eyes were the color of sweet sherry. "She says they broke up because you're having an affair with Evan."

For a moment, she was speechless. Then her words exploded as the acid sharpness of adrenaline surged through her. "She said what? That's outrageous! That's libel or slander, or whatever it's called. I'd never even consider something like that. You know what being a teacher means to me."

Stop sputtering and get a grip. But she couldn't, god help her. She couldn't. "Mark. I can't believe... I mean, you don't think... You *can't* think... Dr. Huston can't possibly think—"

Was that "methinks she doth protest too much" on his face? She didn't see understanding or sympathy. He acted like he was taking this crazy allegation seriously. As if he thought there was something to get to the bottom of.

"You know we have to look into it, Alexis. It's far too serious to ignore."

There was no 'it.' She was half-surprised her hands didn't snap the arms right off the chair. If he was giving Carrie's bitchy rumor credence, what did that tell her about his reaction to her memo? Did he think it was a cheap attempt to protect herself from Carrie's accusation by claiming Evan was the aggressor?

"Look into what, Mark? Carrie's belief is not an allegation, it's a rumor. You look into rumors now? Do you investigate Mr. French every year because the girls in the chorus get crushes on him? Did you investigate the rumors that Mr. Atlee downloads child porn on his home computer and has pictures of naked boys in his dining room? That Rosie Risoli keeps medicinal sherry in her desk?"

He wouldn't look at her.

"The whole idea is ridiculous. Do you try to get to the bottom of "it" every time Coach Chambers slaps an athlete on his rear?"

"Then you don't have anything to worry about, do you?"

Shock socked her like a fist to the chest. He *was* taking it seriously. *Of course, I do* was on the tip of her tongue. Luckily, her internal cop, trained by years of instant self-censorship in the classroom, held her back.

"What am I supposed to do, Mark?" she said. "How do I defend myself against such a ridiculous accusation?"

Like someone chasing a runaway kite, she grabbed her flaring temper before it escaped. She lifted her coffee, willing her hand steady, and took a sip. She needed to act confident. Point out the absurdity of the accusation. She gave him her best smile. "I know you don't believe this," she said. "You know me too well and you know how unstable Evan is. So how do we deal with this?"

He spread his hands out on the blotter and studied his stubby fingers like a man discovering starfish. Silence hung heavily between them. "Maybe it will blow over," he said. "Most of these things do. For now, let's wait and see."

Most of what things? Assaults on teachers? He didn't sound like he expected it to blow over. Hadn't he said he'd have to look into it? What about the presumption of innocence? What about fair play? She studied his blank face. Of course he could be calm. No one was saying *he* was having sex with a sixteen-year-old. He wouldn't have to go through every day with a killer pain in his gut, trying to act normal while watching his back. All he had to do was sit and listen to their lies.

"Wait and see doesn't sound right, Mark. I'm very concerned about having slanderous rumors circulating about me." She put particular emphasis on *slanderous*. She gave it a beat and said, "I'm even more concerned about having been the victim of a sexual assault. That's what you should look into."

Even as she stepped on her anger, she felt something else—pain at Mark's betrayal. Five years of friendship and now, in minutes, he'd morphed into an officious stranger. When she first met him, she'd found the way he combed his hair over his bald spot pathetic. When they became friends, she'd stopped noticing. Now she was mesmerized by the sheen of sweat under those crisply sprayed strands. It *was* pathetic.

"I'll be looking into it," he repeated, his fingers dancing some papers around on his desk.

There was plenty to look into. Like Evan's dangerous instability and lack of boundaries. The risk to her and others. She didn't think that was what Mark meant. "You'll keep me informed?"

"Of course," he said.

Her anger almost got away from her again. She didn't deserve this. "Thanks for the heads up," she said. "I appreciate it. One thing we need to be clear about." She pushed herself up, wondering how many of her predecessor's sticky hands had been clenched in righteous anger.

Sweet as pie, she reminded herself. "Consider my stellar record. My honorable character. Compare it with what you know about Evan. Consider how you'd want people to behave if this were *your* life. Your career."

With an effort, she kept her voice level. Unhurried. "Evan Palmer attacked me. Physically. Sexually. If he was that brazen, it's probably not the first time, and it's unlikely to be the last. I'm certain you'll regard *that* alarming behavior as something worth looking into."

EVAN – TWO

He watched through the small window in the garage loft as the vintage BMW pulled in. What the hell was this? Her husband never came home during the day. Neither of them did. He'd been here often enough to know that. Leaving school in the middle of the day was laughably easy. His mother, the controlling bitch who thought she knew everything about him, had "signed" a few notes getting him released for doctor and dentist appointments. Other times, he simply took off.

Sometimes he only drove by or parked across the street and watched. Sometimes he came on his bike, lingering on the lawn fiddling with his spoke wrench or drinking some water or playing with his tire pump. When he wanted to go inside, like today, it was different.

He'd planned today carefully, trading his car for his best bud's truck, a nondescript vehicle Billy drove that would be invisible on her nice suburban street. Wore his jeans and the navy Cooper Brothers Carpentry T-shirt he'd gotten at Goodwill. Timing it for mid-morning when there was little traffic, and a man walking around with a clipboard would seem innocuous. That setup had worked fine. He'd gone around the house checking windows and doors, taking the occasional measurement, and marking his clipboard. But all the damned doors and windows were secure.

Last time, he was able to get inside. Today, he could only get into the storeroom over the garage, where he'd left the window open last time. He'd propped the ladder he'd brought against the garage, hoping they'd neglected to lock the door connecting the storeroom to the house. No luck. Locked tight.

He shrugged. Who knew what he might find in these stored boxes? Old love letters? Some of her old papers? He snickered, imagining recycling her words into a paper of his own. Would she notice? Feel the familiarity? Take it as another sign of their compatibility?

He felt so close to her sometimes, almost protective, despite the difference in their ages. She was such a cautious woman, taking pains not to reveal herself either through her words or her clothes. God. The ugly stuff she wore! Baggy sweaters and lumpy skirts. Prim blouses and shapeless jumpers. He knew she had other, sexier things in her closet.

In class, and when they worked on the play, she'd listen, smile, sympathize, but she rarely spoke about herself. They must teach them that, because other teachers were the same. But sometimes she let something slip. Some small thing. They were always small things. A lot of what he knew he'd read off her face. Like yesterday, when he'd done Willy Loman so well. Her pride and pleasure had just glowed. He could be something to her, be what she needed. He knew it. He just had to take it slower, not spook her like yesterday.

Lately, he wanted to kill her jerkoff husband. Take a knife, or maybe a baseball bat, and put the sucker out of his misery. It bothered him the way the guy was cheating on her with a student almost every goddamned day. Evan knew. Between school and sports practice, he'd drive by the campus, see the guy come out with that girl. They'd get in their cars and the husband would follow her to her apartment. The affair had been going on for months.

He wondered if she knew. He spent a lot of time studying her, observing her moods. Before vacation, she'd seemed unhappy, so maybe she'd figured it out. At school, she tried to be "on" for everyone. Worked harder than they deserved. Mostly her students took her for granted. Like he had. Until he'd seen her out running one day and oh man, that body!

Then, in one of their conversations about his acting and his character, she revealed something about her childhood. He'd been talking about his mother, how she didn't listen, was so distant, always lecturing him about her expectations and how he disappointed her. That was when Mrs. Jordan had said, "It's so hard, isn't it, when others don't see us at all? When we want so desperately to be known and understood?"

When he heard the Beamer and saw the slimeball husband pull into the driveway, he was looking through a box labeled "high school." He shoved the stuff he'd found into his pockets and listened. As soon as he heard the door into the house open, he skittered to the window, down the ladder, slipping now that it was really raining, and dashed for the truck. He'd have to come back for the ladder, but he'd bet his ass the jerk wouldn't even notice it. Too stuck on himself.

Evan knew, from going through their drawers and closets, that the husband had all the nice stuff. The cashmere sweaters. Silk underwear.

He'd been through her underwear, too. Unlike the clothes she wore, it was colorful. Everything matched and she kept it in sets. He'd taken one black set from the back of the drawer. Size 6 panties and a 36C bra. He liked it that she didn't wear a thong.

He started the truck and pulled away from the curb. Thinking about her underwear had given him a boner and made him all jumpy. One time he'd gotten right into her bed, put his head on the pillow, and jerked off. Another time, he'd jerked off in her panties and rubbed the cups of her bra all over himself. Sometimes it seemed like he spent half his life jerking off. His mother—The Witch—in one of her rare attempts to talk about sex, had told him jerking off was disgusting and if he kept doing it, he'd have to wash his own underwear and sheets. He didn't know why she cared—the maid did the laundry and changed the beds anyway—but since then, he'd tried to do most of it in the shower. But he didn't want to take those nice lacy panties into the shower. He kept them under his pillow except on cleaning day.

Turning onto Main Street, he saw her car coming the other way. Man, something really strange was going on. Her husband at home. Mrs. Jordan leaving school in the middle of the day. Instinctively, he reached up to pull his hat down to obscure his face. The damned thing wasn't there. He must have left it in the storage loft.

So what? It was only a hat. It wasn't like it had his name on it, like when he was a little kid. Still, he'd better get it when he went back for the ladder. Not smart to leave things behind.

"And each the other viewing,
Soon found their eyes how opened, and their minds
How darkened."
—John Milton, *Paradise Lost*

CHAPTER FIVE

Fellow teachers had warned her. When the chips are down, the administration never backed you. She hadn't believed them. Now, after her unsettling conversation with her former friend Mark, she did.

Grabbing her coat, Alexis told Dr. Huston's secretary she was sick. She needed to talk to her friend Lori, on leave this year with a baby. Her best friend, a teacher a couple years ahead of her who understood the politics better. Plus Lori was married to a lawyer. She'd be sure to have some good advice. Just the idea of having someone to confide in made her breathe more easily.

The relief was slight, though. Teaching was her life. Her calling. Was she really at risk of having it taken away from her because of a student's lies?

She drove home on autopilot, rerunning the conversation with Mark. Had she handled it right? Besides Lori's advice, she had Micah. She wanted Micah to guide her through this scary situation. But given their situation, could Micah, the one she relied on for the sage advice of a more experienced teacher, help her now? Before she could turn to him for this, they needed an open and honest conversation about why he hadn't come home and what that meant. She shook those thoughts out of her head. He'd be in class and unreachable right now anyway.

Except that he wasn't. As the garage door rose, she saw his car. Her cowardly husband had come home in the middle of the day, probably to change. He might abandon her without a qualm or a phone call but Micah was too fastidious to teach his afternoon classes in the clothes he'd worn yesterday. Well, like it or not, he wasn't getting away without talking. She parked the Jeep right on his bumper and went inside.

In their upstairs bedroom, her handsome husband stood before the mirror, holding up two shirts. He turned at her footsteps, shirts suspended in mid-air, looking like one of her freshmen caught lying. His lips moved as he fumbled for words.

"Alexis, what are you doing here?"

"I live here." She took a moment's mean pleasure in the foolish, flapping lips. "Isn't the important question where were you last night?"

"One of my students was having a crisis. I had to stay with him."

Him? "You could have called me."

"He didn't have a phone, I'd left mine in the car and I was afraid to leave him."

Everybody has a phone, she thought. And he'd recently bought a new, expensive phone that did everything, a toy he was never without. At this moment, it was half out of the pocket of the jacket he'd tossed on the bed. "But you *have* left him."

"Her father came to stay with her so I could leave. I have classes to teach."

Her. Okay. So he was moving closer to the truth. "How did you reach this father? Telepathy?"

She wished she could believe him. But what really mattered was what he'd do now. *Utter an abject apology and take me in your arms, dammit. I'm an easy mark. Despite my efforts to harden my heart, I still love you. Declare your love and comfort me. I am so in need of comfort after two horrible days and a night alone.*

"Okay. So I was caught up in the moment and I forgot." He glanced impatiently at his watch. "I've got to go. I have a class. Can we talk about this when I get home?"

Her temper started a slow boil. "Are you coming home?"

"Of course I'm coming home." He tossed the rejected shirt on the bed and started unbuttoning the other.

"This *girl* in crisis, what's her name?"

"Yvonne. Yvonne LaCroix."

Gotcha! "Are you sleeping with her?"

"Of course not."

She replayed the words she'd overheard two nights ago. Micah on the phone saying, "You know I love you, baby." They'd weathered his previous affair. But another one? She wasn't sure she wanted to hear the truth right now. After her little "chat" with Mark, she felt pretty ragged.

Micah was so damned handsome. She'd never gotten over her pleasure in looking at his smooth tan skin and his incredibly dark eyes, at his sculptured cheekbones and his sexy mouth. Often people looked like they'd been made by a committee that couldn't quite agree, while Micah had been assembled by experts. Looking at him hurt. Right now, everything hurt. Her world felt disrupted. "Micah, we can't..."

"Why is there a ladder up against the side of the garage?" he interrupted. "Are you having work done?"

Was *she* having work done? On *their* house. On *their* budget, without discussing it first? How likely was that? "There's no reason a ladder would be there. I didn't call anyone."

Having raised the question, he went on dressing like it didn't matter.

"Micah! Someone must have tried to break into the house."

"Don't be silly," he said. "No one's trying to break into our house."

The word silly fanned her anger. She crossed to the low door that led from their bedroom into the loft over the garage, undid the locks, and flung it open. She stared in dismay at the open window, overturned boxes, the floor littered with scattered papers. At rainwater pooled on the floor. "Did you do this?"

He came through behind her. "Boy, someone's made a heck of a mess. Luckily, there's not much of value here."

She looked at the spilled boxes. It was old high school and college stuff. Old papers, letters, pictures. Why would anyone bother? But someone had. The unfastened window moved slowly back and forth. Goosebumps crawled up her arms. She turned away, feeling vulnerable and scared and angry that someone had been here, pawing through their things.

"I'm calling the police," she said. "I want you to stay with me until they come."

"I told you, Lex. I have a class."

Her anger at him was no less intense, but now fear eclipsed that. She didn't want him leaving her to deal with this alone. Irrational, maybe, but somehow it would seem a worse betrayal if he were to leave now. "So cancel it. What's the big deal? Someone has been in our house, Micah. Going through our things. That doesn't bother you?"

"You can handle it."

She wasn't letting him off that easily. "No, Micah. I can't." She reached into his jacket pocket, grabbed his phone, and dialed 9-1-1. After exchanging a few words, she said, "They're sending someone over."

She saw him eyeing the bedroom door, assessing his chances of escape. "I came home because I felt sick," she said, kicking off her shoes. Her stomach did feel unsteady. "Now I'm feeling worse. You'll have to deal with the police." Still holding his phone, she went into the bathroom. He wouldn't follow her—the possibility of someone being sick would send him into cardiac arrest—and he couldn't leave. Her car was blocking his, her keys were in her pocket, and he didn't know where she kept the spare.

She sat on the edge of the tub in queasy limbo, trying to breathe through her stomach's unwillingness to commit. Eventually, her stomach quieted. Micah's phone sat beside the sink. Quietly, she opened the bathroom door. Downstairs, drawers opened and closed as he searched for the spare key.

Through the window, she watched a Crawford Valley police car turn into the driveway. A tall officer in a leather jacket got out and started up the path. Now Micah would *have* to deal. She picked up his sleek black phone and scrolled through the speed dials. First, his department number. Then their landline. She took a deep breath and tried the third.

After two rings, a girl's slightly breathless voice said, "Hello?"

Putting on her best fast-talking, high school girl gush, Alexis said, "Yvonne. Hey. It's me. Did he actually spend the whole night with you?"

"Yes." The answer was followed by a hesitant silence. Then the girlish voice said, "Hey. Who is this?"

"His wife," Alexis said and disconnected.

She looked in the mirror at her pinched face and angry eyes. She could put on make-up. Comb her hair. Do something to look more—more what? Cheerful? Respectable? Pleasant? "Screw it," she said. She shoved her feet into shoes and went downstairs.

Micah was in the kitchen, talking with the officer. Next to the stolid, beefy man in uniform, he appeared small and dapper. He looked up with relief when she came in.

"Here's my wife. She'll be able to help you better than I can." He held out his hand. "Why don't you give me your keys, honey, so I can move your car? I'm late for class."

To the officer, he said, "She was so startled, driving up and seeing that ladder, she parked right behind me."

Like a little dummy, he might as well have added. Keys wouldn't do him any good. The patrol car was right behind hers.

"Honey," she said, handing them over. They never called each other honey, except in irony. "I wish you'd stay."

He was already out the door. She looked at the officer, sitting calmly at the table, pen poised, watching her. "Would you like some coffee? I could make a fresh pot."

"No, thanks, ma'am, I'm fine." He tapped the paper. "If you could tell me what happened."

"I don't really know what happened." She caught herself. The officer only wanted to know why they'd called.

"I'm a teacher at the high school," she said. "I'm never home during the day, but I wasn't feeling well, and when I got home…" She swallowed, surprised to find herself at a loss for words.

"Take your time, ma'am."

He had a wonderfully ordinary face, middle-aged, slightly fleshy, eyes a blue that was almost gray, and short, graying brown hair. His calming manner suggested he'd probably done this many times but hadn't forgotten how upsetting it could be.

"Thanks," she said. "My husband was here, and when I came in, he asked why there was a ladder up against the side of the garage. There's a loft we use for storage, like an attic, that connects to the house."

He nodded encouragingly.

"When I unlocked the connecting door, I could see that someone had been in there. The window was open. Some of the boxes had been knocked over, stuff dumped out on the floor."

She took a breath, annoyed that talking to a police officer upset her. She was an adult. He was a public servant. Her public servant. No reason to feel like an eighth grader caught smoking behind the school.

"It's not that… I mean, it doesn't look like anything has been taken. We don't store valuable stuff up there. Just old school stuff, photographs, out-of-season clothes, camping gear. It's the idea that someone was there. That someone came with a ladder when they knew—well, I mean, when we weren't home—and was in our house. Going through our things. I'm home alone a lot. It makes me feel unsafe."

"I understand."

She disliked the way his cool eyes seemed to be studying her soul.

"That's not your ladder?"

"No. Well, I don't think so. We have a ladder in the garage, but the garage was locked. I guess I should go and look, shouldn't I?" Boy did she sound like a ditz.

"You said you aren't home during the day. Is your husband usually home?"

"No. He's usually at work." Alexis felt a hot blush steal up her face.

"Mrs. Jordan, are you all right?" The matter-of-fact question caught her off guard. Not that it was any of his business, but she was pretty far from okay right now.

Before she could answer, Micah returned, the skin around his mouth and eyes tight. His shirt was splotched with rain. Raindrops clung to his spiky black hair. He tried for nonchalant. "Forgot my coat. Lex, did you put my phone back?"

No, asshole, after I called your girlfriend I flushed it down the toilet. "It's on the bathroom sink." She caught the cop's curious eye and wondered what showed on her face. She was used to reading faces, not being read. But so was he.

"The ladder that's up against your house, Mr. Jordan," the officer said. "Is it yours?"

Micah shook his head. "Our ladder's newer than that. And it's in the garage."

"Probably gypsies," the officer said.

"Gypsies?" She had a vision of horse-drawn caravans and people in colorful dress. "Are you serious?"

Coming from the PC high school world, she was surprised he was even allowed to use the term. But he was saying something.

"Guess you don't read the paper," he said. "We've been getting a lot of that. This time of year, people start working outside, leaving doors and windows open. These gypsies come up here to Massachusetts from New York and cruise around, looking for houses to burglarize. A man, maybe a couple women. They look for empty houses, but if someone's home, one of the women will engage the homeowner while another sneaks in and steals stuff. We had two last week. Both times, they were in and out in a flash, took the silver and jewelry."

He smiled. "You read the weekly police report, you'd know. The chief's asking everyone to pay close attention. You'd better check carefully. See if anything's missing. Ladder's a new touch, though."

He pushed back his chair and got up. "I'm gonna look around outside, and then you could show me the storage space? Mr. Jordan?" He swept a hand toward the door.

Micah nodded. "I'll get my jacket." He pounded upstairs, then came back down wearing his sports jacket, shoving the phone into his pocket.

"Micah?" His dark eyes glared at her. She felt torn between her own anger and her need for reassurance, but even if she kept him here, he wouldn't be reassuring. "Don't forget to bring back my keys."

She stayed at the table, staring at her fingers as they rested on the deep indigo tablecloth. It wasn't such a big deal, really. People got their houses broken into all the time. At least the burglar hadn't gotten into the main house. But had he taken some things? She thought about what was in those boxes. Just old stuff. Memories. Nothing anyone would be interested in stealing. Maybe they tried to get inside, got frustrated, and vandalized instead.

Tremors ran up her arms. Her chest felt tight. Sitting in her pleasant kitchen on a mild April day, listening to the rain splattering against the window, she thought how strange everything suddenly seemed. While she was preoccupied with her marriage, her students, her job, her normal life had been taken away, leaving her with a disturbing jigsaw puzzle of assault, betrayal, and accusation. And she didn't know how to put it back together.

"There is a fatality, a feeling so irresistible and inevitable
that it has the force of doom..."
—Nathaniel Hawthorne, *The Scarlet Letter*

CHAPTER SIX

Gypsies. Colorful clothes. Quick hands. Predatory strangers. Alone in the loft cleaning up the boxes, Alexis couldn't banish these thoughts. It was so creepy. If the intruder had put the boxes back and taken the ladder, she and Micah might never have noticed. She closed and locked the window. Found their intruder's calling card—a Red Sox cap she knew wasn't theirs. Then she dried the floor and locked the door connecting the loft to her bedroom.

The officer hadn't offered much in the way of comfort or consequences. Since nothing of value had been taken, there would be no action other than a report. The officer and Micah had put the ladder in the garage. She wished the officer had just taken it away with him, and then wondered why the intruder hadn't taken it. What if he—they?—meant to come back for it? What if they *did* come back?

She tried Lori and got the answering machine. "It's Lex," she said. "Something really strange and creepy going on at school. I need to talk it out. Call me."

She couldn't sit around jumping at every bump and creak. Rain or not, she had to run. Otherwise, she'd only watch the day get darker, wondering if Micah would come home tonight, if their intruder might return. She changed into her rattiest running gear, laced on her old shoes, and grabbed her iPod. After checking that all the windows and doors were locked, she headed out.

Two miles in, she was ready to quit. Running on too little sleep and too little food, she hit the wall. But if she believed in quitting she would have fled from teaching her first year, so she challenged herself to try half a mile more. Then another half. It was rocky going. At four miles, she threw up beside the path. At four and a half, a killer pain slammed into her side. But she finished the full five miles, soaked with rain and sweat, feeling almost normal for the first time all day.

She walked the last quarter mile home. Pumped with endorphins, enjoying the cooling rain on her face. A silver Honda CRV came racing toward her, steered sharply across her path, and jerked to a stop. Her progress blocked, she veered toward the street, then froze. Evan Palmer. He got out and hurried toward her, his eyes sweeping her appreciatively from head to toe.

"Hey, lookin' good, Mrs. Jordan, lookin' good."

His intrusive gaze recalled yesterday's fear and revulsion, and made her aware of how she must look to him, wet Lycra clinging like a second skin. She started running again, making a wide detour around him and darting into the street.

"Hey," he said. "Hey… hold on. Don't run away. I just want to talk to you."

Dan Morgan's warning echoed in her head. Don't talk to him. Don't be alone with him. If he comes near you, leave. "I can't talk now." She kept moving away from him. Accelerating. Calling over her shoulder, "You'll have to see me at school."

All 6' 2" of him loped easily after her. "Look, I just want to say I'm sorry." He spread his hands wide. "I know I startled you yesterday, upset you by what I said. What I did. I didn't mean to."

Had he come to his senses? Hopeful, she slowed her pace. Then, as he drew closer, she saw his eyes. Excitement. And lust.

"I shouldn't have rushed you," he said. "I realize that now. Look, can we go have coffee and talk about this?"

He couldn't be serious. She's soaking wet, he's just scared her out of her wits, and he thinks they're going to have coffee? "No, Evan." Nervousness made her voice sharp. "I've just run five miles. I'm wet and tired. We can talk tomorrow."

As soon as she heard her own words, she wanted to call them back. She shouldn't have used the word "we." She couldn't meet him tomorrow. Or any time ever again. She couldn't even linger to explain. He wasn't listening anyway, only waiting for her to finish so he could speak. As soon as she paused, he jumped in.

"Look," he said, his tone aggrieved, "will you stop a minute and listen? Just listen."

"Evan, do you understand how inappropriate you were yesterday?"

"I said I was sorry, didn't I? Mrs. Jordan, I think *you* don't understand. You can't do this to me, you know. Lead me on like this, then act like I'm not supposed to have noticed, saying stupid things about what's appropriate, like it doesn't matter. Look, it matters to me, okay? It matters."

She kept moving, trying to put space between them. But she'd run five miles. She was tired. However fast she went, he kept up, talking faster and faster, like running wound him up.

"When you gave me a ride home… the way you dropped me off last so we could be alone together. You think I didn't notice? The way you put your hand on my shoulder in class? The way you say my name. How excited you are when I get things right?"

This boy was seriously scaring her. Once she'd given a bunch of them a ride home. Once. Turning, Alexis saw the playground ahead. She could cut through it—there were people there—but it was out of her way. Instead, she sprinted for home.

He kept talking, jogging easily beside her, while she was stumbling on exhausted legs. "Mrs. Jordan, it's been killing me. The nights I've sat in my room, reading books you've assigned, imagining I was with you in your blue kitchen, in your yellow living room on the big white couch. In your bedroom, the two of us together on that fluffy white rug? Mrs. Jordan, Lexie," he said, anguish in his voice. "You've kept me waiting so long."

Don't call me Lexie, she thought. And how the hell would he know about her bedroom rug? Her heart skipped. This was not a teenager misconstruing things. This was someone crazy enough to have gone around her house looking in the windows. She never entertained students at home. Home was her sanctuary. Maybe crazy Evan had brought that ladder. But no. She'd seen his car in the lot when she left. Now her chills weren't just from being cold and wet.

She slowed. "Evan, what are you talking about?"

"I'm talking about us," he said.

His hot eyes, and her sense that any moment he might grab her, got her moving faster and scared her past any attempt at tact. "There is no us."

He blew off her harsh denial. "Of course there is. You can't fight it, Mrs. Jordan. Some things are meant to be. To hell with the rules. I heard you say it. To hell with the rules, sometimes you have to follow your instincts."

Goddammit, what universe was he living in? "I said that about writing, Evan. About creative writing." Could she get away from him? What if he followed her home?

She kept trying to move away from him. He stayed beside her, easily keeping up, matching whatever pace she set.

"But I understood what you meant. What you were *really* saying."

Two more blocks. One block. He would have touched her, but she reached down for a last burst of energy and pulled away from him, unzipping her pocket for the key as she reached the steps.

"Evan, I have to go in. I'm cold." She sensed his bold eyes tracing her body revealed by the form-fitting running clothes. She shoved the key in the lock and turned it, throwing herself through the door and slamming it behind her.

So much for a cool down. This one went right to her bones.

"But all was false and hollow; though his tongue
Dropped manna..."
—John Milton, *Paradise Lost*

CHAPTER SEVEN

She fumbled off her wet clothes and jumped in a hot shower, scrubbing herself frantically, as though soap and water could erase the taint of Evan's lust. The way he'd looked at her, like he was peeling her clothes off right there on the street. The things he knew about her house. Goddammit! The boy was out of his mind. Boy? Hell, this wasn't some teenage crush. He was a creepy stalker. How could she make him understand his behavior was way out of bounds, when he'd stored up all these twisted and misremembered things and ignored everything she said?

What if he kept following her? Should she go to the police? Would they believe her if she said her stalker was a sixteen-year-old boy? Would they help or give her queer looks and assure her, as Jim Fisher had, that the boy would get over it? They hadn't seen Evan's eyes. Hadn't had his hands tearing at their clothes.

When the hot water ran out, she pulled on sweats and forced herself to sit down at the little desk in their bedroom and write up the incident. She was bent over the page, engaged in a struggle with language as difficult as a mediocre student trying to write an English paper, when Micah stormed into the room. "What the hell did you do that for?" he demanded.

"Do what?" she asked, pulling her attention away from teenage lust and potential violence and the challenge of describing fear. "What time is it?"

"Six-thirty. You haven't even started dinner. So what the hell did you do that for?"

"What? Not start dinner? I'll do it now."

"No, dammit! Call Yvonne. You fucking called Yvonne on *my* phone."

He'd left her here to deal with that cop and gone to see Yvonne? Anger brought her into the moment. "What upsets you? That I called her? That I used your phone? We were dealing with an intruder in our home, remember?"

His look declared her somewhere below a mushroom on the intelligence scale. "You know why I'm upset."

"Like hell I do." She thought about her own situation when they first met. How he'd told her he wasn't married. She'd believed him until a friend clued her in. "She didn't know you were married?"

"She knows. But she was still shocked. Suppose, back when you and I were first together, if my wife had—" Seeing that example wouldn't work, his mouth shut like an invisible hand had smacked him. "Lex, we need to talk."

They sure did. Among other things, about why *she* should be considerate of Ms. LaCroix's tender feelings.

"You said we had to talk yesterday morning on your way out the door, remember? That's what I was thinking of last night while I made dinner. While I watched the rice congeal, waiting to cook the fish. While I stood in the empty garage wondering if you were all right, and lay in our empty bed. I kept thinking Micah's right, as soon as he gets home, we need to talk."

She waited, but he didn't initiate conversation.

"So talk," she said. Sheer bravado. Who wants to hear from a husband about another woman? What would he do now? Declare he was leaving, describing all the ways she had failed where Yvonne succeeded? Or say it was all a mistake and beg forgiveness? How had things gotten this bad without her noticing?

The tiger had her stomach in its claws again, her mother's scornful voice in her head, *Alexis has such a weak stomach.*

"I never meant for this to happen," he said. He stopped. "Let's go downstairs, fix ourselves some drinks, get some dinner going. It's been a hard day."

"You don't know the half of it," she said.

"What do you mean?"

"I mean, you've had a hard day, we've had a hard day, and I've had a hard day."

He was right. Their bedroom was the wrong place for this. This was where they made love, or at least had sex. Micah, with his lithe and elegant body, was a profoundly sexual animal. They didn't want the air in here full of hurtful phrases and painful confessions. She headed for the stairs, still a little bit hopeful.

In the kitchen, he was suddenly all bustling domesticity. Trying to placate her. Distract her. Make peace. After his words upstairs, after his recent behavior, she wasn't sure peace was on the agenda.

Putting ice into glasses, he asked, "We got any limes?"

"Lower right vegetable drawer," she said. Where they always were. She lifted out the marinated bluefish she'd planned to cook last night. Snapped on the broiler. Started some rice. Began tearing up salad greens. Trying to let the pleasing motions of cooking distract her from the emotions that were choking her.

He squeezed lime into a gin and tonic and slid it toward her. "You said you'd had a bad day?"

"I have a problem," she said, which was a ridiculous understatement. Obviously, she had several problems, one of which was here in the kitchen with her. Maybe it would help to start on more neutral ground. An area where he could advise her. That might ease her back from her anger and remind them both how much they had in common.

She began with Carrie Canavan's outburst yesterday morning, then told him about that afternoon's session with Evan and the awful encounter today while she was running. Harder, she found, to tell her husband about a sexual assault than describing it to Dan Morgan. He tried to hide it by bending over his drink, but there was even a hint of titillation on his face as she described Evan's actions. She hadn't been thinking clearly. Micah was more like Evan. He saw something that attracted him and went for it.

Feeling like she was in a play—the loving wife going through the motions of domesticity, making dinner while chatting about being sexually assaulted with her cheating husband—she spread mustard on the bluefish and slid it under the broiler.

But she wanted his advice, so she soldiered on, telling him about the meeting with Mark Clemente. "I thought Mark and I were friends, Micah, but he treated me like a dangerous stranger. Like there might be something to this. Why would he do that?"

"Fact of academic life, Lex. When the chips are down, the administration is not your friend. They're trying to cover their own asses, not worrying about yours. Another harsh fact of work life—you think they've got your back, but where their own interests are at stake, your co-workers are not your friends. Associating with you may be detrimental to them, so they'll distance themselves. I don't want to alarm you. Stuff like this happens, kid with a crush letting his imagination run wild. The administration will try to put a lid on it, especially if they know the kid is a troublemaker. It's only if it all blows up that you have to worry."

Probably right, but he sounded so clinical and disinterested. She repeated his words, "'Try to put a lid on it. Try to distance themselves.' It sounds so cold and heartless, Micah. This isn't about me. Obviously, Evan needs to get help. That's what they should be worrying about."

She turned down the burner under the rice. Despite her delicate stomach, she was starving.

"That's what *you* would worry about. Almost six years of teaching, Lex, how can you still be so innocent? The world *is* cold and heartless. Don't you see how awkward it would be for them to tell his parents their son is crazy and needs to get treatment? Parents are a school system's clients, not the teachers."

"But we're all on the same side," she protested, bouncing between anger and her need for his advice. "We're a team. About Evan. What should I do? Should I see a lawyer?"

He shrugged. "What's a lawyer going to do for you?"

"Give me advice about how to handle this. How to protect myself. My job."

"What's to handle? Nothing's happened, has it?"

What was that supposed to mean? Plenty had happened—to her.

Nothing had happened to Evan. "They're acting like I'm a child molester."

"If they really thought that, they'd call the police. They'd have to." Her panic must have been obvious because he made a calming gesture with his hands. "First they'll look into it themselves. Schools like to keep things close. It doesn't look good for them, either, you know. Guess you'd better watch your back on this one, Lex."

She'd expected him to be helpful, not scare her more than she already was. "Watch my back? But I haven't done anything." Being told to watch her back invariably called up images from "The Exorcist" and Linda Blair's head turned around backward. How else could you watch your own back?

"Then you've got nothing to worry about."

"I wish I believed that." She flashed back to the end of her run. Evan didn't have a crush. He was crazy. Obsessed. And willing to act on it physically. She thought she had plenty to worry about.

Micah had disappointed her on this front. The harder was still one ahead. She took a deep breath. "We have to talk about Yvonne," she said.

"Look, Lex… this isn't easy for me. I never wanted to hurt you."

Was that supposed to make it better? She should whack him with her carefully seasoned cast iron frying pan. But they needed to have this conversation. To keep from throwing something, she got out olive oil, vinegar, and mustard, and made the salad dressing.

Ice clinked as he fortified himself to go on.

"She was one of my students, back in the fall. Very talented. Extremely insecure. She was always hanging around after class, asking questions. One day, I invited her for coffee. No sense in standing around talking when we could be comfortable."

Almost the same thing he once said to her. That's what finally sunk her, back in college, their intertwined hands, the beautiful contrast of milk white and café au lait. He'd reached between two cups of coffee. Thick white mugs. Creamy brown coffee. Thin white hand, creamy brown one. Hers nervous and chilly; his warm and reassuring. She'd been so insecure and miserable after being raised by a mother who could never be pleased. He made her feel special, and safe, like the world might be all right after all. He'd said he was single.

"She was so eager and sweet," he said. "So grateful for my help. We got in the habit of having coffee. Then, one night, you were at school late for parent conferences. You know how you are, how much time you give them, how you're always talking about them, always planning great lessons, always running late."

Like doing her job well was a fault. God was he good at shifting blame. What was he saying exactly, that if she cared about teaching and that took time away from being attentive to his needs, he was entitled to screw a student?

He finished his drink and crossed the room to make another. "She asked if she could cook dinner. We drank wine. She looked so pretty by candlelight. I kissed her, and one thing just led to another." He gave an almost imperceptible shrug.

Alexis grabbed a warm, plump tomato from the window sill, named it Yvonne, and hacked it into juicy bits. So vigorously she sliced through her finger. She bit her lip as blood welled, the pain breathtakingly sharp. Balancing her internal and external pain.

Ice cubes clinked. Glass clicked against his teeth. She squeezed her wounded finger, trying to ward off the pictures in her head: his body, which she knew so intimately, coupling with another woman's. The hacked-up tomato Yvonne swam in a pool of blood. She dumped all of it into the salad, wanting to hurl the bowl at his head.

"I thought it would be only that once," he said. "I never meant for it to happen again."

He sounded like he expected her to be sympathetic. Poor baby. The helpless victim of women's rapacious appetites. What's a man to do? "Micah." Her voice was unsteady as she swept the knives into soapy water, putting them out of sight. "I don't want to hear any more of this. What I need to know is where things stand with you and me."

She gulped some of her drink, trying to wash the tightness out of her throat and still her growing temper. This was her love life, her marriage. Maybe about to end? He could still do the right thing. *Take me in your arms, you idiot. Tell me it's over with this Yvonne. Tell me you're home and you'll keep coming home and we can work this out together.*

59

"I don't know," he said. "This is all so sudden. I haven't had time to think about it."

She'd struggled to keep an open mind, an open heart. To put love before pride. Why did he have to say such dumb things? Lie to her? Sudden? This had been going on for months.

Her temper flared. Her hair was Scots red, not Irish. She had a slow fuse—a necessary trait to survive life with her domineering mother—but given adequate provocation, her core ignited.

She checked the rice, slammed the cover back on, and snapped off the burner.

"Please don't insult me, Micah. What's so sudden? *You've* known you had two women, two lovers, two sex partners for months. What haven't you had time to process? My knowing about Yvonne? Yvonne knowing that I know about her? Or how you're going to balance two women in your life now that it's out in the open?"

He didn't answer.

She sounded like a mother and he acted like a ninth-grader. And oh god, she wondered if he'd used a condom with Yvonne. Her gut filled with revulsion imagining Micah coming from Yvonne's bed to theirs. She banged the cupboard open, slammed the mustard back on the shelf, and shoved some rolls into the toaster oven to heat. Going through the routines of cooking as though her life was still normal and orderly even if the words flowing between them were so at odds with that. She poured dressing on the salad and tossed it. She'd made the kind of dressing she liked—eye-openingly strong. Micah would complain and she didn't give a damn.

"It seems to me," she said, "that if you've been sneaking around with Yvonne this long, you've had plenty of time to think."

He gulped his drink and shrugged. "I was just going with the flow."

"Out of respect for our years together, please don't lie to me. You and Yvonne must have discussed this." She looked at him, leaning against the counter. The blue silk shirt, elegant black slacks, expensive loafers. His artfully styled hair. She'd always taken pride in his appearance, in the way women stared at him. Now she wanted to dump oil and herbs over his carefully spiked hair, rub mustard into the expensive silk shirt.

"I'm not—" His eyes fell. "All right. Of course, I've been wondering what to do. What I meant was that I haven't made any decisions. I feel like a guilty schmuck, but frankly, I'm torn. I love you, Lex. You know that. But we've become—" He searched for the words. "It's all so mechanical between us. We're just walking through it because it's easy and familiar, but we're not really connecting. Yvonne and I, we connect."

"Fuck you," she said. "I'll bet you do. I'll bet you connect real good in bed, just like I delude myself that we do."

She wondered how Yvonne would feel if she knew that Micah still had sex with his wife. He'd probably told her his wife was a cold fish who wouldn't give him sex and didn't understand him. The same things he'd told *her* back when she'd discovered he'd been lying to her about being single. She'd refused to see him again until he left his wife, but she had still been the "other woman." She wished she didn't know Yvonne's side of this so well.

"How can we connect when we're not talking? Not spending time together? When you're with her instead of home with me?" Why was it only his decision, anyway? Pick Alexis? Pick Yvonne? She slid the perfectly cooked fish onto a plate. The rice needed a couple more minutes. She grabbed plates, napkins and silverware and held them out. "You can set the table."

He took them reluctantly, the boy who never got over being his family's darling, who thought he shouldn't have to be bothered. She hated the way he turned her into his mother and the way she played into the role again and again. Did making the same mistakes year after year make her a slow learner or an impossible optimist?

She removed two wine glasses from the cupboard, pulled the bottle of white from the fridge, and poured. She carried them to the table, went back for the salad, and put the rice in a bowl. Last came the rolls, crisp and hot, and butter. This conversation should have ruined her appetite, but this was her first meal today unless a muffin counted, and after running five miles she was ravenous.

Two people at a table always seemed like too small a number. And how many times had she done this over the years? She was almost twenty-seven, and had met Micah when she was twenty. For nearly a quarter of her life, he had been a constant. Her focus. Her companion. How was it that she wasn't bored with him but he was so bored with her?

The strong flavor of bluefish went well with the dry vermouth, fresh ginger, soy sauce and a touch of garlic marinade. Perfect. She looked over. Micah had put food on his plate but he wasn't eating. "Try the fish," she said. "It came out really well."

"I already ate."

Why did he have to make everything so damned difficult? She was only cooking and sitting down to a civilized meal because they needed to talk. "Then why did you complain that I hadn't started dinner? So you could be on the attack? Or so I wouldn't know you'd already dined with your lover?"

"Yes," he said.

She wrestled with her urge to throw things until she'd subdued it. She seemed to be subduing an awful lot these last few days. "Have you discussed the situation with Yvonne? Before today?"

He ate a bite of fish. "This is good. Really good."

She'd already finished her fish and reached for a small second helping, aware that his comment about the fish was meant to distract her. But nudging the reluctant to answer was what she did every day. Keeping her tone level, she repeated, "Have you discussed the situation with Yvonne?"

"She wants me to move in with her."

"Has she known all along that you're married?"

"In the beginning?" He shrugged. "She didn't ask and I didn't mention it. Later, when she complained that I never saw her on weekends, I had to tell her." Absently, he started eating.

It would help if you wore your wedding ring. The conversation kept getting more and more bizarre, but she persisted. "What have you told her about our situation? Did you say you were unhappily married, just waiting for the right moment to end it, or that you were in a reasonably happy marriage and your wife had no clue you were screwing around?"

He served himself more fish. Watching him eat, she wondered if Yvonne was a lousy cook. She sure hoped so. But she didn't want to hold onto a loveless marriage with a husband who enjoyed only her cooking. She ate some salad. Drank some wine. Wanted to drink more but then her temper would certainly get away from her. She waited for his answer.

Finally, he lowered his fork. "I told her I was waiting for the right moment."

She'd known what he'd say, but hearing it was like being slammed in the chest with a 2x4. Sticks and stones may break my bones but words can never hurt me?

When she could speak around the pain, she asked, "Did you mean it?"

Micah's soulful brown eyes stared at her across his empty plate. Eyes that had first stared at her across those thick white crockery mugs. Eyes that had gazed at her from the adjoining pillow. Meeting hers over candlelight dinners. Peeking into the shower to see if she'd like company.

"When I said it, I was just trying to keep her happy. Now, I'm not sure."

A sudden burst of wind slammed rain against the window like a janitor slinging a wet mop. Her thoughts jumped to some stranger out there in the dark, scheming to get his ladder back. She shivered. "I keep thinking about someone being in our house."

He pushed back his chair and walked away.

She followed him into the entry. He was putting on his coat. *They* weren't done talking, but it looked like *he* was. Right now, she didn't like him much, but she didn't want to be here alone.

"Are you going out? It's raining cats and dogs."

He smiled. "I think you need a hot fudge sundae. I was going to run out and—"

Like chocolate was all it would take to get them through this. Wishing that was the case, she reached past him and grabbed her coat. "I'm coming with you."

"Afraid your bogey man will come back for his ladder?"

Like it was a joke. "Yes, Micah, I am."

Giving him a look that dared him to make further fun of her, she snagged her purse and followed him. Did he not understand that she knew his errand wasn't about chocolate? He'd been looking for a chance to sneak out and call Yvonne. Now he'd have to wait 'til she was asleep.

"...none, whose portion is so small
Of present pain, that with ambitious mind,
Will covet more."
—John Milton, *Paradise Lost*: Book II

CHAPTER EIGHT

Pulling out of her driveway the next morning, she noticed how many of her neighbors were also leaving for work. The place must be deserted in the middle of the day. No wonder her burglar—her gypsy?—had chosen that time. Had anyone been home who might have seen something? This afternoon she'd ring a few doorbells. The police might not care, but she did. She'd also connect with Lori, who'd texted to say the baby was teething and fretful and she'd call tonight.

She was heading into school when a deep voice said, "Mrs. Jordan?" Evan Palmer, once again pungently doused in scent, quickly closed the gap between them, towering over her, an odd expression on his face.

She sprinted for the door. "I'm in a hurry, Evan."

He came after her, covering the distance easily with his long legs, getting to the door in time to open it. He followed her inside and down the hall, staying oppressively close. "Something wrong, Mrs. Jordan? I was wondering if you'd thought any more about... about what we discussed on Monday during our session. I mean, yesterday you seemed like you were spooked or something."

Discussed? Since when was a male rubbing his erection against you a discussion? And was she spooked? He nearly runs her down, then chases her and utters crazy things. He's scoped out her house and created a fantasy relationship and he's surprised she's spooked? She had to set him straight. Right now. There'd never be a time when what she had to say could be said more privately. She felt safer here in a corridor teeming with students.

"Evan, I'm in a hurry," she repeated, slowing slightly. It didn't look good to be seen running from him.

Taking a deep breath, she plunged in. "You did scare me. You acted too aggressively and not respectful of my personal space." Acutely aware of his eyes fixed hopefully on her face, of the curious stares around them, she felt as tongue-tied as some poor freshman.

"Look, Carrie has been telling people we're having a relationship, which we both know isn't true. Rumors like that, even if they're just talk, can damage my position as a teacher."

He shifted his shoulders restively, clenching and unclenching his large hands. Waiting to hear what he wanted to hear, ignoring everything else. He seemed to have grown several inches overnight. She couldn't let him intimidate her, yet menace hovered in the air.

"Since I was eight years old I've wanted to be a teacher. Getting to do this every day is the most important thing in the world to me. I'm sure you understand that we, your teachers, walk a delicate line every day, trying to be available to you while maintaining an appropriate distance. Even the suggestion of something between us is a serious problem for me."

"Okay. I get it." He nodded. "We need to keep it our secret."

Her chest constricted. Was he hearing anything she said? "Evan. No. You're not listening."

His expression changed. Not the dawning of understanding, as she hoped, but frustration. Anger. He didn't care about any of this. He only wanted to hear yes.

"I know you've developed a special affection for me, Evan. That happens. It's very normal. But it is not appropriate for me to reciprocate your feelings."

"But you do! You know you do." He raised a hand to stop her. "Not now. Not here." His voice was tight with emotion. "Tomorrow. At our regular time."

"Evan, that's impossible. Surely you can see—"

He grabbed her arms and jerked her to him, his clutching hands like vices. "Don't do this to me, Mrs. Jordan." He was oblivious to the students surrounding them. "Don't try to blow me off like I don't matter. Like *we* don't matter."

"Evan. Let go. You're hurting me." She wanted to scream at him to stop this nonsense and slap him silly. Keeping her voice firm and professional she spoke slowly. Loudly. "There is no we except in your head and there never will be. Now let go of me."

He stared with surprise at his own hands, clutching her to him in a fierce grip, and released her. "We'll talk about this later. In private. I'll find you."

"No, Evan. We won't."

But he'd stopped listening. His gaze swept the curious eyes surrounding them. Everything that happened in school happened with an audience. Arguments, fights, discipline, hugs and kisses, tears, breakdowns, all grist for their evolving gossip mills.

"I'll find you," he repeated. He pushed his way through the crowd and disappeared.

She hurried into the teacher's room and dumped her stuff on a chair. *Breathe.* But she couldn't. Her chest was constricted.

Claire paused, packet of coffee in mid-air. "Lex, is something wrong?"

"I'll say something's wrong." Might as well tell. It would be all over school anyway. *Breathe.* "Monday afternoon, when I was working with Evan Palmer on his part for the play, he made a pass at me." Pass? "Cornered me. Groped me..." *Breathe.* "He kept talking about how he knew I wanted him and we should have an affair. It was clear he'd been working himself up to it for quite a while." She dropped into an armchair, still having trouble breathing.

Claire shook her head, her big tortoiseshell earrings jangling. "That kid's wired funny. He's felt like a ticking bomb to me for a while. I mentioned it to Mark, but he blows me off. Says they're all like that, it's testosterone. Well, I've got two boys of my own, plus one husband. I know about testosterone. Some days, the air in my house gets so thick with it, I'm afraid I'll grow a beard. And this ain't that. This is pathology."

She put a hand to her lips. "Oops. You did not hear me say that. I'm not qualified to diagnose psychological problems. Nor, I might add, to comment on the boy's toxic mother." Her eyes dropped to Alexis's fingers, massaging her new bruises. "Did he hurt you?"

"I'm okay."

"And I'm the Queen of England. Better get an ice pack from the nurse. So, that was Monday. What happened today?"

"Make the coffee," Alexis said. "I still have to tell you about yesterday. And that's not even all that happened Monday."

She described Carrie Canavan's outburst, then the meeting in Mark's office. She described Evan swerving across her path when she was heading back from her run and then chasing her home.

"It's not enough that he scared the heck out of me yesterday. This morning, he comes after me in the parking lot, moving into my space like a heat-seeking missile. I can't be seen having a tete-a-tete in the parking lot, not with rumors flying around, so I book it for the door. He follows me into the building, demanding an answer. Then, as I'm explaining—for the third time—there could never be anything between us, he grabs me in front of half the school and loudly insists we meet in private later."

She was talking too fast. Other teachers were staring. She lowered her voice. "You know what this place is like. We're surrounded by students and he's yelling that I can't blow him off like 'we don't matter.' And he won't let go of me."

She pulled her sleeves down. "I told him there was no *we* except in his head. I don't know what to do. I can't reason with him."

"God, that's a bitch, isn't it?" Claire clucked sympathetically. "Look, I wish I didn't have to say this, Lex, but listen to Auntie Claire, because I've been around. First thing, you have to see Dr. Huston, tell him what happened, and show him those bruises. Things like this have a way of spinning out of control. You think you've taken care of it and suddenly it rises up and bites you on the ass. Excuse my language. It's all those swearing menfolk. Then—"

"What?" Alexis felt the sharp teeth of fear bite into her. "Then what?"

"Get yourself a good lawyer."

Breathe, she told herself. *Breathe.* "A lawyer? That's ridiculous, Claire. This doesn't deserve that kind of attention. Yes, he scares me. He seems so off balance about this, so obsessed. But I should be able to handle it."

"Listen to yourself, Lex. You think you can handle it because you're a rational person. But what if he's not? Look what you just described. What if he persists? What if he claims that what he's wishing for is true? How do you deal with that?"

Claire dumped coffee in the pot and poured the water. As the machine began hissing and whooshing like some diabolical engine, she pulled out a sheet of paper, scribbled something, and held it out. "Lawyer. This woman is very good. Comforting, sensible, and tough as nails. Call her and arrange to see her. Sooner rather than later. She who hesitates is lost."

"But I'm the innocent party here. I haven't done anything wrong."

"Honey, I know that. You don't need to have done anything wrong for all this to blow up in your face. Someone merely has to believe you have. Look, I'd rather see you scared than fired. Gotta have someone around here to talk to. Someone who's retained her sense of balance and irony. What you have or haven't done may not matter if a lynch mob is after you."

The tiger sank its claws. "A lynch mob?"

"I've been around too long to look at the world through rose-colored glasses," Claire said. "It's an ugly fact of life—people are far more ready to think the worst of you than the best." She held out the coffee pot. "Want some?"

Alexis shook her head. Her stomach felt like squirrels were clog dancing in there.

"Thing is," Claire continued, "little Evan gets upset, even though he hates her guts, he's gonna run straight to mama. And Dinah Palmer, despite her blond curls, pastel suits, and designer accessories, is actually Satan's mistress." She made shooing motions with her hands. "Now scoot along, dear, and see Dr. Huston before the day gets rolling and his pomposity becomes overweening."

"People don't actually say overweening, Claire." Trying to keep it light, when she wanted to crawl under a chair.

"I thought I just did. Now go." She fluttered the piece of paper with the lawyer's information. "Don't forget this. I've got an unhappy feeling you're gonna need it."

Alexis was in her classroom, using her free period to grade some papers, when Lauren Findley rushed into the empty classroom. "Mrs. Jordan, you have to come. Kyle and Jesse are fighting."

She found a group of students bunched around Kyle Vonmering and Jesse Pelletier. Kyle was a senior and captain of the wrestling team, Jesse a junior on the football team. Jesse's nose was bleeding and Kyle had a split lip. Fighting in school was an automatic suspension, but the boys in the crowd hadn't intervened. An unspoken rule of the gender. A stupid, stupid rule.

Teachers develop acute peripheral vision, along with the ability to multitask. As she approached the group, she was already counting heads and taking names. She pushed her way through, hearing the meaty smack of fist on flesh, a cry of triumph, a grunt of pain. "Lauren, go get Dr. Huston and Mr. Clemente. Tell them it's a fight."

Blood flung by their fists splattered the wall and glistened in bright drops on the polished floor. The heat and sweat of anger had accelerated the pungency of aftershave, the earthy funk of their sweat.

"Stop this!" she said. When she got no response, she stepped between them, holding up her hands. "All right, you two. Stop. This. Now!"

Kyle's fist, already launched, slammed into her shoulder, sending her staggering back against Jesse. There was a collective gasp as the combatants, panting and wary, moved away from her and each other, faces scarlet with anger, embarrassment, and blood.

She'd never been hit before. The speed of the blow and the sharpness of her pain gave her a sudden, shocked insight into physical violence.

Around her there was total silence. Getting caught fighting meant a mandatory suspension; hitting a teacher could get you expelled. "Everyone except Kyle and Jesse, you have places you're supposed to be, so take yourselves there. Now!"

Reluctantly, students shouldered their bags and shuffled away.

She wanted to rub the pain out of her shoulder but forced her hand to remain at her side. She wanted them focused on her message, not on her. "Okay," she said. "Now what's this all about? You both know the rules about fighting."

Where were Mark and Dr. Huston coming from? Siberia?

Kyle, short and square and every inch muscle, blinked back tears. His jaw trembled as he muttered a panicked, "Jeez, Mrs. Jordan... jeez... I didn't mean to hit you. Honest. I would never... you gotta believe. You shouldn't'a got in the way like that. I was just like... like not seeing anything but what was happening with me and Jesse, is all."

"So I should have let you and Jesse keep hitting each other?"

The boy's big shoulders hunched. "Aw... Mrs. Jordan, gimme a break." He shuffled his feet like he could dig his way through the floor. They could hear the commotion of Dr. Huston and Mark approaching. "Jeez..."

Kyle lifted pleading eyes to her face. "Jeez, Mrs. Jordan. You know I didn't mean to. If I get expelled, my father will kill me. Four years he's been telling me I'll screw up and never make it. I've only got, like, a month to go. Please."

He swiped at his nose, leaving streaks of blood across his cheek and up his arm.

"Yeah," Jesse said. "Please, Mrs. Jordan."

Too bad they couldn't have thought of this before. "All right," she sighed. "I know you didn't mean to hit me. But it's bound to come out. You better bring it up yourself. And if we all agree it was an accident? I think the penalty for fighting is punishment enough."

She handed them off with a quick summation, as cold to Mark today as he had been to her yesterday.

The rest of the day, the students were hyped over the fight and her part in it. One of the reminders they were still kids was their questions. Often, with genuine, wide-eyed innocence, they asked astonishingly intimate things. Today they probed with frightening accuracy the very things that had gone through her mind. Did it hurt? Had she been scared? Had she seen it coming? What did it feel like to be punched? Did it leave a mark?

Did she think anything was broken? Was she mad at Kyle? Should he be kicked out of school?

She managed to connect their curiosity to a discussion of *A Separate Peace*, thereby not wasting the hour, but by the end of the period, she'd been ruthlessly scoured. When the bell rang, she put her head down on the desk and closed her eyes, perilously close to tears.

When she felt the warmth of a comforting hand on her undamaged shoulder, she assumed it was Claire, the likeliest person to come and comfort her. Grateful, she opened her eyes.

Evan Palmer bent over her, an expression of deep concern on his face. "Mrs. Jordan, Lexie, are you okay? I heard what that asshole Kyle did. I'll kill him for you if you want. I will. I swear."

At least a dozen students clustered in the doorway watching Evan's impassioned offer of vengeance and his inappropriate caresses.

She jumped to her feet. "Don't touch me, Evan! Don't ever touch me." The words came out before she could think.

He reeled back, stricken. She cleared her throat and tried again. "I appreciate your concern, Evan, but this has to stop."

He got that hopeful look again. "But Mrs. Jordan... I can't let him do that to you and get away with it. Not the way I feel about you. With all that's between us." His hand stayed with her, continuing its painful rhythm on her shoulder.

She backed away, anger eclipsing discretion. "Stop it! Goddammit, Evan, get real! There is no *us*. There never can be. There never will be. Now take your hands off me and don't you ever touch me again."

He pulled his hand back, his face flushing scarlet, and stared at her, stunned. Then his face twisted in horrible anger. "You led me on," he said, "and now this. You are going to be so sorry, Mrs. Jordan." His voice shook with fury. "I am going to make you so sorry." He dropped his voice to a whisper. "I *am* going to touch you again. And whether you want it or not, we *will* be together."

EVAN – THREE

Still shaking with anger, he peeled out of the parking lot, leaving a streak of rubber and a cloud of swirling sand behind him. He was doing fifty before he even got to the main road.

Goddamn that bitch! How dare she treat him like that! He'd gone to offer her comfort, revenge if she wanted it. Commitment. Jesus, wasn't that what women wanted? He'd humbled himself before her. Tipped his hand in front of those stupid idiots in the doorway. Now it would be all over school. And what had she done? Blown him off again. Like he was nothing.

He didn't even slow at the stop sign but pulled out onto the road in front of a goggling old fool who kept blasting the horn.

"Go ahead, jerkoff," he muttered. "Blow it out your ass." He stepped on the gas, leaving the old fart in his dust.

No, she sure hadn't been grateful. What does she do when she realizes who's patting her shoulder? One minute she's making this humming sound, like she's so happy to be touched. The next she jumps up like she's seen a rat and squeals, "Evan, don't do that. That is so inappropriate!"

Like he was just anyone. Some dumbass student trying to get over on a teacher. Fuck that. Like she ever cared about appropriate before. Making extra time for him when she didn't for anyone else? Giving him rides home when his mom got tied up? All those special smiles, touches, looks, the way her eyes kept sizing him up, like she knew what he had to offer? Leading him on for months, and when he reciprocates, she acts like she's shocked. Another damned cockteaser. No different from Carrie or any other bitch. Get you where they want you, what do they do? Start jerking you around.

He floored it, flying up the long hill to the highway. He was going to have that bitch. Prove to himself—prove to her—that she wasn't anything special. And he wasn't going to beg, or crawl, or be nice about it, either. He was going to take what he wanted and to hell with how she felt. Goddamned Carrie had made him beg and plead and practically crawl before he could get in her pants. And then, once they'd done it, it didn't make them like a couple so they could keep doing it. Every time she'd make him repeat the same stupid fucking dance. Like screwing her was so great? Screwing Mrs. Jordan—Lexie—*would* be great. Was great.

He was so caught up in imagining himself with Mrs. Jordan, nothing but creamy naked skin and her gorgeous red hair down, he totally forgot about Officer Collins, who liked to hide just over the top of the hill. Forgot until he saw the blue lights in his mirror. He was a sitting duck. For a second, he considered giving the cop a run for his money, but he hadn't been driving that long. Wasn't sure he was the better driver. Cursing, he pulled over and got out his wallet. As he looked up into Collins' smirking face, he decided she owed him for this, too. Owe him big time.

He'd see that she paid up in full.

"...high passions, anger, hate,
Mistrust, suspicion, discord, and shook sore
Their inward state of mind..."
—John Milton, *Paradise Lost*: Book IX

CHAPTER NINE

Friday morning as she hurried into the teacher's room for coffee, she saw Evan Palmer and his mother coming out of Dr. Huston's office. Her stomach twisted into a hard knot. It didn't take an oracle to read this. Something brown and smelly was about to hit a fan, and it looked to be aimed in her direction.

Breathe, she told herself. *Act normal. Get your morning coffee.* She gave a quick greeting to Claire as she zeroed in on the coffee pot. Empty. Charles Avon was heading for the door, clutching the last cup, the pig.

"Charlie," she said, "You know the drill. You take the last cup, you make the next pot."

"I'm in a hurry," he said.

"Me, too." She forced a sweet smile and a voice to match, when she wanted to bump his cup and spill coffee down the front of his spiffy white shirt. Displaced anger, she knew.

Other teachers in the room watched like this was a play staged for their benefit as he hesitated, then set the cup down hard on the table and returned to the machine, making a major production out of a simple act. Dumping the soggy grounds with a loud splat, noisily adding water, and slamming the empty pot back. "Satisfied?" he asked, stabbing the button. Juvenile behavior. She got enough of that outside this room.

Alexis got to be the enforcer because she wasn't a wimp, but being

75

the stand-up gal got tiring. Right now, she didn't feel tough. She felt like cowering in a corner and whimpering like a kicked puppy, waiting for the summons to Huston's office that would put today, and possibly the rest of her life, into a tailspin.

"What's his problem, Claire?" she said, watching Avon's huffy departure.

Claire grinned. "I dunno." She looked at May Englehart, who was studying her tiny feet. "May, is he old enough to be in testopause?"

May's hands gripped the edges of her beige cardigan like a lifeline. "In what?"

"Never mind," Claire said, shaking her head so her big gold hoops glittered. "Joke's no good if it has to be explained. Oh hell. There's the damned bell. I swear he sets it earlier every day. The old fart loves to make us miserable."

"The old what?" May asked.

"Exactly," Claire agreed. "The old what."

Alexis waited for enough coffee to accumulate, savoring this last moment of quiet, then grabbed a cup and headed to her classroom.

She started right in answering their questions. Had she written the letter one of her students needed? Yes. Did she think it was worth taking an SAT prep course? Sometimes. Did she think it was important to have summer jobs for the college application or was it okay to bum around in Europe? Depended on how the bumming around could be characterized. Had she watched TV last night? No. Josh asked if he'd handed in his paper. No. Back when she was young, had she been a Beatles fan or a Stones fan? God. Twenty-six or sixty-six, it was all the same to them.

Then the intercom did its obnoxious crackle and hum and summoned her to the office. She watched twenty-five curious faces. Could they tell her heart was doing flip flops? See the jazzy flashes of anxiety? Did her face only feel like the color had drained away?

She still wanted to drink her coffee, but if this was what her gut said it was, she'd probably spill it and that would be taken as evidence of guilt. So would breathing, no doubt, or even being upright. The only way she could prove she was not guilty was if she let them throw her in the pond and she didn't come up. Rather a hard way to make a point. *Get a grip*, she told herself. Whacking yourself upside the head, like watching your back, was difficult and ungraceful.

No flippant or ironic remarks, she reminded herself as she walked to the office. She had to take her situation seriously. It affected her life and her livelihood, and the Administration didn't exist to make the teachers' lives easier. Yet she had a hard-earned competence and confidence in herself and her performance that made it hard to believe anyone would give Evan's accusation credence. After nearly six years of being friendly, clean, loyal, brave, and reverent without a glimmer of trouble or suspicion, surely it should be implausible that she'd suddenly become a predatory teacher who seduced her students? That she'd suffered a sea change into something wicked and foul?

She hadn't gotten through the office door before she got the message things had changed. Dr. Huston's secretary, Donna, with whom she ordinarily shared jokes and smiles, stared through her. "You can go right in," she muttered. "He's waiting for you."

A cold prickle hovered over the surface of her skin, like the touch of an ice-feather duster. Her forearms pocked with goosebumps. At the same time, she was sweating. Maybe malaria? Maybe she was simply scared. She straightened her shoulders and walked into Huston's office.

He didn't even wait for her to sit before damning words started pouring from his liver-lipped mouth. "Mrs. Jordan, it is my duty to inform you that a student and a parent have just been in my office making a very serious allegation against you." He spoke like a preacher warming up for the hellfire and damnation phase.

She wanted to say, "It's all a damned lie and you know it," but if it was all a lie, how would she know what he was talking about? Her former friend Mark, like some chicken-hearted granny, had pulled his chair away from hers.

Ignoring both Huston's lack of manners and Mark's plague-fearing avoidance, she settled herself in a chair and waited. Eventually, her silence unnerved Dr. Huston. "Well?" he said.

"*You* called *me*," she said calmly. "I'm waiting for you to explain what we're doing here."

"I thought I just told you that, Mrs. Jordan."

She wanted to say she didn't read minds. "No, Dr. Huston. You said there was a very serious allegation. You didn't say what that allegation was, nor who made it."

"Yes. Well..." He cleared his throat and looked at Mark. "As I said. A serious allegation of misconduct... and I'm wondering how you'd like to respond."

"Respond to what, Dr. Huston?"

She was amazed at how calm she sounded despite hosting an acrobats' convention in her stomach. She wished she'd brought a recorder to memorialize this idiocy. What could he have been thinking? That she'd break down at once? That she'd throw herself at his feet, confess, and beg for mercy?

"Of course," he said, making little sputtering noises with his mouth like an engine that wouldn't catch. "Well, these allegations are serious, Mrs. Jordan, very serious indeed."

Did he think this was easy for her, being the victim of his rude eyes and obvious disapproval while she waited for him to spit it out? He was probably struggling to translate the Palmers' complaint from English into his native language, Bureaucratese. But he was devious. This might be a deliberate attempt to frustrate her into saying something incriminating.

The rivulets of sweat under her jersey made her thankful she'd worn all black today. What Micah called her "Italian widow" look. Huston probably thought it exemplified evil. She sure was feeling evil, more so by the minute. She looked pointedly at her watch and then at the clock on the wall. Almost time for A block. How long, oh Lord, would it take this mealy-mouthed asshole to get to the point?

Perhaps exacerbating her nervousness *had* been part of his strategy, because now he grimaced in satisfaction. "Evan Palmer says you initiated a sexual relationship with him which has been going on since the beginning of the year."

After a brief pause, he sputtered out citations to the various rules which forbade such conduct, as though she had them all on file in her brain and could flip through them as he spoke, highlighting with a mental marker.

Okay. Here it was. The thing she'd feared. She had to keep it off her face. She wouldn't give him the satisfaction of seeing how scared she was.

"I have no idea why he'd say such a thing," she said, "but I am a professional educator with a clear understanding of the appropriate boundaries as well as the applicable rules and laws. I have always maintained them with Evan as I have with all the students."

He actually looked disappointed, the prick. He studied the sheet of paper on his desk. Even upside down, she recognized Mark's handwriting. "You have never had sexual relations with Evan Palmer?"

"No."

"Have you ever touched his genitalia?" Huston barely got his mouth around that word. Men of his generation, growing up before the ubiquity of sex education, always found the word "genitalia" caught in their throats and stuck to their tongues.

"No."

"Have you ever touched other parts of his body while he was unclothed?"

"No. Absolutely not."

Who wrote this script? Well, she knew who'd written it. Mark. Maybe bureaucrats consulted a book called *How to Question Teachers Accused of Sexual Misconduct*? No matter. The list of questions was long, their content intrusive and damning, and she was alone with two men who had no intention of playing by the rules. Nothing about this situation felt right.

She made a time-out gesture. "I'm sorry. We're going to have to stop."

"Stop, Mrs. Jordan?" Dr. Huston said. "We've barely started."

She shook her head. He wanted to quote rules at her? Two could play that game. She wasn't submitting to this inquisition without someone from the union with her.

"Dr. Huston, I'm not comfortable with what is happening here. I know we both want to have this discussion in accordance with all the proper rules and procedures. I'll have to consult with the union about my specific rights, but I know our contract defines the procedures to be followed in a situation such as this, where a professional teacher's ethics and conduct are being questioned. They include the right to have a witness present to protect my interests. I would prefer to not be adversarial. I like to think we're all on the same side here." She forced a smile. "But as you have stated, this is a very serious accusation. Evan is lying, but if you find it necessary to ask these questions, I find it necessary to protect myself. Any reasonable person in my position would do the same."

"If it's all a lie," Mark said, "what's your problem with answering a few questions?"

You miserable little worm. "I have no problem answering your questions, Mark." She gave him her sweetest smile. "That's what I just said. But we all know the reality here. I wouldn't be the first teacher to have a career damaged or ruined by false accusations. I have to protect myself. I'll answer your questions with a witness present, according to contract procedures."

She made her voice deliberately soft, forcing them to lean forward to hear. "I would imagine at the very least, given my excellent record, never mind applicable law, that I'm entitled to a presumption of innocence. Now, if you'll excuse me, I have a class to teach. You can let me know when you'd like to reschedule this meeting. And not during the school day. That would make it difficult to arrange to have my union rep present."

While they shuffled papers and exchanged looks, something else occurred to her. "Also, it would be to everyone's benefit—and well within my rights—to insist you transfer Evan to a different English class. I request that you do so immediately. Do you need that in writing?"

When they didn't respond, she stood and turned to leave. Like an accident victim learning to walk again, she made her way out of the office by forcing each leg in turn to lift, move forward, and set down again. Past Donna, who pointedly ignored her, and out into the hall. Did it look as choppy to them as it felt to her? But it wasn't time to collapse yet. While her legs still held and her breath flowed, she had to start working on a defense.

Neither her own nervous anticipation after her "chat" with Mark nor her friends' warnings had truly prepared her for this—Evan's damning accusation and the administration's abrasive questioning of her integrity. She understood their position—a student makes a serious allegation, it has to be followed up. But they hadn't been gathering information, they'd been seeking confirmation, certain that the accusation must be true. She was unhappily aware of how hard it was to fight assumptions. It was time to talk to Jim Fisher again.

She returned to the office. Ignoring Donna's mixed disapproval and unveiled curiosity, she said, "Can you check Jim Fisher's schedule and see when he's free?"

Reluctantly, Donna pulled out a notebook and ran her finger down a chart. "C block." Good. They had the same free period.

She left the room and stood in the hall, looking quickly up and down the corridor to see if she was being observed. Had it really been less than half an hour? It seemed like a day-long marathon. She felt beaten up and degraded, yet consumed by the wicked urge to find a mirror, imitate Dr. Huston's prune face, and repeat the word "genitalia."

During C block, she tracked down Jim Fisher and described what had happened. Instead of responding with a statement of her rights, he shook his head dismissively. "That doesn't sound like Evan."

She wasn't letting him blow her off. "Jim. It happened. We talked about this on the phone the other night, remember? You have my report describing the incident. And the second incident with his car. Now he's made this damning allegation. So what do we do next?" Deliberately using "we."

Another shake of his head. "If you say so. What do you want me to do about it? You want me to talk with Evan? Set him straight on this?"

"If *I* say so? It's Dr. Huston who says so. And with his next breath, he started asking me if I had ever had sex with Evan, and if I'd ever seen him naked. And no, I don't want you to talk with Evan. I want you to talk about strategy. About my rights under the contract. About what happens when a student lodges such a complaint after I've reported two assaults which Dr. Huston has ignored."

This guy was supposed to be on her side, her liaison to support, advice, and legal counsel, yet he was offering to talk to Evan as if he were simply a confused student who'd done something he hadn't meant to do. What did he think Evan hadn't meant? Hadn't meant to come to school with his mother and meet with the principal? Hadn't meant to say she'd seduced him and they'd been having an affair all year? As if any of Evan's actions could be inadvertent. Evan had sworn he'd make her sorry and that's what he was trying to do.

"I thought you'd come to me because I'm Evan's coach."

"Jim, we spoke about this Monday night, remember? I gave you a written description of his first assault on me." Her smile felt like a lopsided smear drawn by a clumsy child. "I'm facing a potentially career-destroying situation and I'm coming to my union for help."

She wanted to do what she sometimes did with distracted students: hold her finger in front of her nose and say, "Focus."

"Oh," he said. His eyes searched the empty classroom, a prisoner looking to escape. The only door was behind her. Finally his eyes returned to her face, understanding—and resistance—on his.

"Come on, Jim. Tell me what to do."

"You seem to know," he said, throwing up his hands. "You asked for another meeting, right?" His eyes shifted to the window, following a passing phys ed class. "And asserted your right to have a representative there? So what do you need from me?"

"Support. Advice about how to handle the meeting. I've never been in a situation like this. I need to know who the union reps are. I want someone official. Somebody tough, who isn't going to back down if the administration starts playing hardball."

His eyes came back from the window. "Oh. Someone official. It isn't really necessary… under the contract, I mean. Except in the most serious cases, we usually don't bother."

She couldn't keep her anger in check. "Are you saying being accused of sexual misconduct with a student isn't serious?"

"You're blowing this way out of proportion, Alexis. Kid probably has a crush on you and took a smile or pat too seriously. It'll blow over."

"Dammit, Jim, you aren't listening." Alexis pressed her fists against her stomach. "Evan came in with his mother. Dr. Huston said Evan alleged a sexual relationship. Not a pat. An ongoing sexual relationship. It's a lie, and a terribly damaging one."

At least he was looking at her now. "If you were in my place," she said, "what would you do?"

He shrugged again, but whether he really didn't believe the situation was serious, or he didn't want to take her side against one of his athletes, she had no idea.

"Take Claire with you. She's a union rep and she scares the crap out of Huston."

He patted her shoulder clumsily, using the gesture to edge past her. "You're overreacting. You'll see. The whole thing will blow over. Huston's just being a bureaucrat. If he leans on you and you tell him what he wants to know, his job's easier, right?"

She didn't care what made Huston's job easier. The issue they should be talking about was an effective defense, at least she was. "Jim, wait. What if they try to force me out? What if I need a lawyer?"

"You'll have to clear that through me," he said, jerking the door open. "We'll discuss it when the time comes. Whether we provide a lawyer depends on the charges. Whether it's within the scope of your employment. One step at a time, Alexis, okay?" He stepped through the door and was gone.

Goddammit! Depends on the charges? Scope of her employment? Was he trying to duck that, too? A coward and a jerk. She kicked his wastebasket, sending it spinning into the wall, and walked out without bothering to pick up the trash. If a student did that she'd give them detention.

"...fairest unsupported flower,
From her best prop so far, and storm so nigh..."
—John Milton, *Paradise Lost*: Book IX

CHAPTER TEN

She needed Lori's take on this, but when she called, Lori answered but immediately said she couldn't talk, she was trying to rock the baby to sleep. "Just you wait and see, Lex. People think babies are a piece of cake but they're not. Sorry I'm being such a bad friend. I know you need to talk. Call me after school. She usually sleeps around then."

So much for confiding in her best friend. There was still Claire, and she needed to talk to Claire anyway about being her union rep.

In the computer lab, Claire was bent over the shoulder of a slight Asian girl, their eyes glued to a screen on which strange 3-D objects slowly rotated. "Anita and I were trying out a program she wrote," she said. "Come on into my office."

Claire's office was even more of a fishbowl than most classrooms since she supervised both students and expensive machines through its glass walls, but it had a door, and no one was around except Anita, who was lost in techie heaven. Claire closed the door and leaned back against her desk. "I hear they tried to put you on the grill this morning but you wiggled off and stalked away."

"Heard from whom?" Too jittery to sit, Alexis stood.

"I have my sources. What's up?"

"Evan Palmer and his mother." She felt herself choking up. She opened her purse and fished for a tissue.

"Here." Claire plucked one from a box and handed it to her.

"Evan is claiming... he told his mother, and Dr. Huston... that I—"

All this morning's bravado deserted her. "He told them I seduced him, Claire. That we'd been having an affair since the beginning of the year. They asked me all these intimate questions—had I ever been alone with him, had I touched his genitals, had I ever had sexual relations with him. Huston had this whole list. At first, I was so dumb I tried to cooperate."

Claire patted her shoulder. "Until you realized they were violating your rights under the contract?"

Alexis nodded.

"And that it was a goddamned witch hunt, and that even people you thought were your friends were willing to turn on you at the drop of a hat?"

"Exactly. How did you know?"

"Huston's an asshole. A bureaucrat's bureaucrat. And Mark? Well, on a good day, you might say he's a nice guy. But he's ambitious. Shallow. And a coward."

"Why didn't I know that?"

"Because you thought he was your friend. We're less critical of our friends."

Alexis felt off balance, as if the ground underfoot had turned to quicksand. She was a teacher, not a litigator. She didn't know how to handle this. "How can this be happening to me, Claire? I've worked so hard for these kids."

"This isn't about you, you know."

"How can it not be about me? I'm the one who's accused."

"I mean it's not about your behavior. It's about Evan's craziness. You aren't accountable for what goes on inside the heads of others. For who they are when they come through that door. What life has made them."

"That's so discouraging, Claire."

"Realistic. You do your best. We all do. But we have to work with what we're given. A high head and a confident attitude are no match for a diabolical mind bent on your destruction. So now..." She shook her head sadly. "You can't wait around to see what happens next. You need to start acting defensively." She grabbed the phone. "I'm calling the lawyer. Maybe she can see you this afternoon."

Alexis wanted to believe, as Fisher had said, that this would blow over, but it wasn't blowing anywhere. "They really haven't given me any choice, have they?" She pressed her hands hard against her stomach. It was all so ugly. So unfair. So wrong. She sank into a chair and sat, numbly, as Claire made the call.

*   *   *

"Tell me what's going on," Janice Trustman said, picking up a pen.

Alexis liked the slightly chaotic lawyer's office with its piles of papers, framed kids' drawings on the wall, and a serene photograph of a still lake. Trustman had a warm, firm handshake—Alexis hated damp, dead-fish limp hands—an attractive, smart face and no-nonsense brown hair.

"I'm not sure I know myself." It wasn't what she meant to say.

"Something scared you enough to make you call me."

"My friends kept telling me..." That was dumb. "It was Claire who..." Dumber. She clenched her hands in her lap. She was so angry about having to be here.

"Your friends didn't put you in the car and drive you over here." Trustman's tone was neutral as she looked at her notes. "You teach with Claire, right? She said something happened at school today, a run-in with the administration. Start by telling me about that."

Trying to keep outrage from her voice, Alexis described the meeting in Dr. Huston's office. "I've taught there five years, this is my sixth, and they acted like they didn't know me. Like I was someone capable of doing those things. All those questions about what I'd done to, or with, Evan. I even tried to cooperate, until I realized how wrong the questioning was and made them stop. I thought Mark was my friend. I—"

She had to curb her impulse to editorialize. She couldn't afford to pay Janice Trustman to listen to her anger or fear, only to the facts. Lawyers were expensive. She fumbled for a coherent version of the story.

"I understand how hard it was for you to come here," Trustman said.

The sudden kindness put a lump in her throat. Despite support from Dan and Claire, the world didn't feel kind right now.

"I didn't believe I needed legal support, but everyone is reacting so dramatically. It frightens me. The accusation frightens me." She hesitated. "I love my job, Ms. Trustman. From the tone of that meeting, it feels like I've already been tried and convicted, even though no hearing has been held and no investigation conducted. I'm pretty sure they'll try to force me to go on leave, and I'm equally sure that will be perceived as guilt—when I haven't done anything wrong."

"Let's back up a little. The allegation is that you've been having an affair with a student?" Trustman clicked her pen open and shut and poised it over the yellow legal pad. "Tell me about this boy who made the accusation."

"Evan Palmer," Alexis said. "He's one of the golden boy athletes. Soccer and lacrosse."

"How old?"

"Sixteen."

Trustman made a note. "One of your students?"

"He's in my junior English class."

"When did you become aware of this boy's interest in you?"

"Monday." Feeling embarrassed at having to reveal how scary and sexual it had been, Alexis described Evan's proposition during Monday's coaching session and his certainty that she'd invited his attention. "The worst thing is that I usually see it coming. This one caught me completely off guard."

"Usually?" Trustman's eyebrows rose. "This sort of thing happens often?"

"This sort of thing? No. But crushes do. Not often, but it happens," Alexis said quickly. "When I started teaching I was only a few years older than they were. And teenagers, you know, they're such masses of emotion that their crushes are often inappropriate." She shrugged. "You get used to firmly but kindly clarifying the boundaries. We teachers all live pretty defensively. Never be alone with a student unless there's a door open and someone nearby. Have conversations about discipline in the hallways. Be careful of any contacts with students outside of school. I always thought it sad having to be so guarded, so careful about what I wear, do, say. But this is different. This isn't a crush. It's an obsession."

Trustman nodded. "So Evan Palmer made a pass at you, and you turned him down?"

"If pinning me to the wall, grinding his erection against me, putting his hand up under my skirt, and trying to unbutton my blouse is a pass." She hadn't meant to be so blunt. Telling brought back how badly it had shaken her.

She took a breath and tried to unknot her clenched hands. "I wrote it up immediately, and gave copies to our union president and Dr. Huston. I brought you a copy of what I gave them." She passed it across the desk. "Then I learned that Evan's girlfriend had already told Dr. Huston that Evan and I were having an affair. So Dr. Huston, instead of reacting appropriately to a student committing a sexual assault on a teacher, merely thanked me and dismissed me. Maybe he thought I was trying to shift the blame away from myself by labeling Evan the sexual aggressor in case the so-called affair came out."

She shoved up her sleeves to show her bruises, still livid purple against her pale skin. She bruised easily and they took forever to fade. "Evan grabbed me hard enough to leave these."

"We'll want to get pictures before they fade." Trustman made another note. "So then he came on to you again while you were walking home from a run, is that right?"

The bruises were ugly. She tugged her sleeves down. "Came on to me? He swerved his car off the road right in front of me and blocked my path."

"And that scared you?"

"You bet. He was grinning, so I guess he thought it was funny. The whole situation—using the car, the way he acted, the way he looked at me, felt like a kind of sexual aggression."

"And then?"

"He jumped out of the car and started talking."

"Back up," the lawyer said. "What did you do when he jumped out of the car?"

"Made a detour around him and started jogging away. I wasn't letting myself be alone with him. He came after me. Said something apologetic. I thought, good, he's finally getting it. He understands. Until I saw his eyes."

"His eyes?"

"The look in them. It was pure, predatory lust. Like I was something he wanted to grab and savage. Something, not someone." She could still feel that fear. "He was talking about how I'd led him on. Acting like we had a relationship."

"Have you done things to encourage that thinking?"

"Of course not."

But there was no reason to snap. A lawyer was supposed to ask questions. "Never anything other than listening and being kind. I wouldn't."

"Do you know what behaviors he might have misunderstood?"

It was hard to tell these stories about herself. She put a hand to her neck, trying to massage away the tightness in her throat. "I've been searching my memory for anything he could misconstrue. Last spring I was an advisor to the committee for the sophomore semi-formal dance. We—the whole committee—met after school and once I gave some of them a ride home. Evan was on that committee. He happened to be the last one dropped off. He claims I did that to be alone with him. Once I was talking to a group of students and I inadvertently put my hand on his shoulder as I leaned in. He says I was sending him a message."

She looked at Trustman's eyes. So opaque. She couldn't get any feel for what the lawyer was thinking. "Could I have some water?" she asked.

Trustman picked up the phone and made a quick request. "Go on," she said.

"When Evan jumped out of the car, he was babbling about wanting to be with me in all these different places in my house. Describing them in detail, which was creepy since he's never been in my house. And during that first assault, when he made his move, he said my husband doesn't understand me. Like he knew things about my marriage. Like he's been spying on me. Stalking me. Building up to this. Dan Morgan, the drama teacher, told me that Evan specifically asked for me to be his drama coach for an upcoming play. He thinks Evan was looking for a way to be alone with me. And now Evan's twisted that in his mind as one more sign of my interest in him."

Trustman's assistant entered quietly and handed Alexis a cup of water. She gulped it down. No difference. She still felt like someone's hands were closing around her throat. She hated disclosing such personal things about herself. Hated being scared. Hated not knowing what this lawyer thought.

"Yesterday, when I finally made it clear to him that there was not going to be any relationship, he became so angry he exploded. He said he was going to make me very sorry I rejected him. And today, he came to school with his mother and made his accusation."

"How was the accusation made, and to whom?"

"Evan and his mother came to see the principal, Dr. Huston."

Feeling way too close to tears, she shifted uncomfortably. "I don't know what you must think of me, coming here with this lurid tale of an obsessed teenager. I don't normally go around claiming boys are lusting after me." She shook her head. "It's just, now that they've taken it to another level and gone to Dr. Huston, I don't know what to do. There's this crazy thing happening and I can't defend myself against it because no matter what I say or do, everyone's going to think I'm the one who's either bad or crazy. Do *you* think I'm overreacting?"

"Not at all. You're a teacher. Being accused of sexual misconduct with a student is a very serious matter. I wouldn't be honest if I didn't tell you your situation is potentially very grave. On the other hand, it's sensible of you to involve me early in the process. I wish more people had your foresight. As for being crazy and hysterical, if your assessment of the situation is correct, I think you're wise to perceive this boy—young as he is—as potentially dangerous."

Just as Alexis was feeling reassured, the lawyer's voice and demeanor changed. "Before we go any further, we need to talk about why you're here. What's your goal in coming to see me today?"

Alexis studied the woman across the desk, so calm and kind, yet so professionally distant. What was Trustman looking for? Were lawyers like teachers in the way they watched for voice and behavior changes and read nuance?

"My goal? To keep my job. I love teaching. That means protecting my reputation. To prevent these lies, this poor boy's obsession, from ruining a life I've worked hard to build."

"You said 'this poor boy.' Despite what he's doing, you still feel sympathy for him?"

Did she? "I've always seen my role as helping my students. Being there for the ones who don't have other people on their side, being someone who'll take the time to listen."

She hesitated, wondering if she should say what else was on her mind.

Trustman caught the hesitation. "There's something else, isn't there?" she prodded. "You've got to be open with me, Alexis. I have to know all your thoughts about this."

True. She nodded. She needed to tell someone. "Okay. My automatic reaction to my students is one of understanding that they need me to be there for them. But with Evan, something else is going on. I'm a little afraid of him. I think he could be dangerous."

"Tell me more about that."

"Despite his age, I sense a real potential for violence. The way he's invaded my space. The obsessive quality of his attention. The fact that he has no hesitation about touching me, doesn't respect age or authority or sexual boundaries. Twice he's grabbed me hard enough to leave bruises. He's rough with his girlfriend. And there are the lies, fantasies really, that he's telling to Carrie, to his mother, to the administration, to himself. And to me."

She swallowed. "The way he looked at me when he said I'd be sorry. There's something abnormal about all of it. Kids bluster and threaten. Their emotions are all over the place. But this was cold."

She stared at the lawyer. "Am I making sense here?"

Trustman's pen clicked. "He trapped you. He was sexually aggressive. He left you bruised. And you were frightened. But you didn't go to the police. Why?"

"I asked another teacher, someone who's been in a situation like this, and he said because Evan was sixteen they probably wouldn't take it seriously. And then I thought... I don't know, that I'd look pathetic as a teacher if I couldn't handle the situation myself. And I didn't want to damage his..." She fumbled for the right words. His what? Future? Reputation? She sighed. "I thought he'd come to his senses. I had no idea he'd be so persistent. So delusional."

"Let me be clear," Trustman said. "It wasn't because the two of you were having an affair and on that particular day, he just lost it, forgot about the boundaries and the necessity to keep it secret, and tried to have sex with you at school?"

"Their inward state of mind, calm region once
And full of peace, now tossed and turbulent . . ."
—John Milton, *Paradise Lost*: Book IX

CHAPTER ELEVEN

"My God!" Alexis stared at the lawyer. "You think I could? You think I would even consider?" Her voice climbed half an octave. "Ms. Trustman. He's sixteen. I'm his teacher. I'm responsible for setting and enforcing boundaries."

This was hopeless. She'd bared her soul. To Dr. Huston. To Jim Fisher and Mark Clemente. And now to this woman. What do you do when you are innocent and no one believes you? She fumbled for her bag and stood.

"Sit down," Trustman said. "We're not done."

"I'm done."

"Sit down, Alexis, and listen to me. I had to ask. I had to know. I thought you were being straight with me, but in my business, I see a lot of liars. If you were having an affair with this boy, you might have come to me looking for the best result. A quiet exit. A record that would allow you to get another job somewhere else. And you might begin by protesting your innocence."

She clicked her pen. "What else should I know?"

Alexis's hands had gathered in a tight, white-knuckled ball. Her stomach hurt and her throat felt like she was trying to swallow a rock. She felt unsteady as she dropped back into the chair. "There are notes in his file—other teachers have noticed a change in him, gotten a sense there's something off balance, something explosive about him. Maybe I'm just being paranoid... but now that he's made this accusation, I worry that everyone will assume this imaginary affair explains the change in him. I worry those notes—the official record of teachers' concerns about his erratic behavior—will disappear. And the teachers, the ones who've wondered but haven't made notes, will find me—find this—a convenient answer."

She forced her fingers to uncurl. "I don't know how to protect myself. I feel like I'm in a room with moving walls and they're closing in around me."

Trustman's smile was quick and reassuring. "I don't think it's that bad," she said. "Let's take this a step at a time, okay? Let me get some basic information, and then I'll give you your homework."

They walked through a list of names and addresses of people already involved or knowledgeable about the situation. Then it was Alexis's turn to get out her pen and paper.

"I want you to make a list of all your contacts with Evan, in chronological order, for the past year. You said he claims this affair has been going on for some time?"

Alexis nodded.

"Consult your daybook, diaries, notes, calendars, anything or any place where you might have written things down. Be as specific as you can, although—"

The lawyer's pause, and her direct gaze, signaled she was about to say something particularly important. "I tell you this now so you'll be prepared if you are questioned by the police or have to testify about any of this. Use the same precaution in your hearing with Dr. Huston. If asked about a particular incident or occurrence, you will always say 'approximately,' or 'on or about such and such a date.' Because god forbid you should be too certain about something and then be proven wrong. It will make you look like a liar."

Alexis, fixed on that single phrase, felt like she'd been plunged into ice water. "The police? Do you think it might come to that?"

"I hope not, but I wouldn't be doing my job if I didn't advise you that it's a possibility." Trustman leaned forward. "Now, about your homework. You need to search through all those contacts—in and out of class—

and identify anything you've done that he could have misconstrued. Things you've said. Have you ever sent him a note that he might have misunderstood? Anything at all—"

Alexis started to protest.

The lawyer held up a hand. "I said things *he* might have misinterpreted. I know right now you're feeling like you're under attack, but I'm on your side."

Trustman waited for her words to sink in. "This is hard for you. I understand that. But you are an experienced teacher. You may not feel it right now, but you are well-schooled in self-control. In hiding your emotions. If this doesn't blow over quickly, if he doesn't retract his accusation, the school will have to take it seriously, and you'll have to respond seriously. There could be some tough times. You need to keep your cool, hold your head up, and calmly and firmly refute the accusations against you without appearing angry or defensive."

Trustman set down her pen and tented her hands. "You came to me for advice, right?"

Alexis nodded.

"So I'm going to give you some. We will be working closely together preparing you to defend yourself against Evan Palmer's accusations. Right now, things are at the informal stage. They're trying to conduct an investigation, you're trying to protect yourself by exercising your rights under your contract. How will that play out? Well, you've already seen the first round."

"What do you mean?"

"The meeting this morning. What happened? They caught you off guard and tried to get you to admit you'd done something wrong without telling you what the accusation was, right? Then, when you insisted on a hearing with a union representative present, what did they do?"

"Nothing."

"Exactly. They're letting you stew. Trying to make you lose your temper, make you anxious enough to lose your composure, hoping you'll make mistakes, blurt things out, make it easy for them so they won't have to conduct a full investigation."

Trustman smiled wryly. "They don't know much more about handling this than you do. The one thing Dr. Huston is better at is manipulating people. Manipulating you. Your job is to keep that from happening."

"That's so ugly. I guess I thought—"

"What? That all you'd have to do was invoke the rules and they'd play fair?" Trustman shook her head. "People only play by the rules when they have to. That's why you're here. Because you don't believe they will be fair and you need a team on your side, too. To protect you when they play dirty. Isn't that right?"

"I guess." She felt sad. Flattened. Crushed. She'd come for help only to be told things were worse than she imagined.

Trustman tapped some keys. "The weekend enough time to put some stuff together? Meet again on Monday?"

They chose a time. Alexis asked, "What if he schedules a hearing?"

"You're taking Claire as your union rep?"

Alexis nodded.

"She'll be good. Insist on a written statement of any charges or complaints against you that are to be the subject of the hearing. Insist on your right to record the proceedings. Keep it simple. Yes and no answers. Be cooperative. Be responsive but don't volunteer anything. Don't get defensive. Don't get angry. If you feel you're losing control, ask for a break. If something comes up you can't deal with, or you're really over your head, call me."

"Shouldn't you be there?"

"If you want, but it's expensive, makes you look defensive, and probably isn't necessary. Once it's scheduled, call me and give me a head's up though."

"What if they try to force me to take a leave of absence?"

"Then we need to evaluate that and discuss your options. If they bring it up, ask if they have a written policy setting out the process for investigating matters like this. Get a copy of it. If they suggest a leave, ask them to put their specific request in writing. What the terms are. How your explanation will be handled. If you'll still be paid. Ask if there's a written policy for when teachers can be placed on leave without their consent. Then tell them you need to consult your lawyer and come see me."

Alexis pressed her hands against her stomach. All so logical. So orderly. So why should she feel sick? She didn't have time to feel sick. She had to start defending her life in bullet points and checklists.

"I'm sorry," Trustman said, checking her watch. "I have another appointment. Is there anything else?"

Alexis shook her head.

"You're tough," the lawyer told her. "You've had to be, teaching high school for six years. You can get through it. Hopefully, it will all be over soon with a finding in your favor. If not, we'll fight."

"Thank you." Alexis shook the lawyer's hand and crossed the room on uncertain legs. She hurried through the waiting room and into the hallway, wanting to throw herself down on the utilitarian brown carpeting, scream, and pound her fists like a cranky toddler. Instead, she leaned against the wall and forced herself to take three deep, calming breaths.

Lawyers saw people in trouble every day. People in trouble saw lawyers perhaps a few times in a lifetime. Then she pulled away from the wall and hurried down the stairs, the lawyer's last words echoing in her head. "If not, we'll fight."

That's when another of Trustman's possibilities returned, striking her with the harshness of rock against rock. "The police. Police. Police." Images of being arrested battered at her as she drove the few miles home, oblivious to the glorious spring afternoon.

What if Evan went to the police?

EVAN — FOUR

He stripped to his boxers and lay on his back on his unmade bed, ignoring the wad of the duvet beneath him. He felt only the pleasure of her black panties draped over his face. Holding them by the edges, he moved the silky fabric across his lips, wishing the pair he'd taken weren't from her drawer but from her laundry, so they would smell of her. That would be even more exciting. Continuing to brush her panties across his mouth, he closed his eyes and visualized her naked. Her nipples would be small and pink and her bush a true red like her hair. Red would be nice against all that smooth pale skin. Carrie's bush, what she hadn't waxed away, was thin and brownish and looked like one of those faggoty little soul patches. But he didn't want to think about Carrie. He wanted to think about Mrs. Jordan. Alexis. Lexie.

He had tried to get a glimpse of her naked, but even in winter, when it got dark early and he could move more freely without worrying about her neighbors, he hadn't succeeded. Her bedroom and bathroom were upstairs, where he couldn't see in without a ladder. Once he'd almost worked up the courage to hide in her room and wait, lying quietly under her bed while she changed for her afternoon run, but when he tried to let himself in, the window he'd been using was locked. The best he'd been able to do was see her walk through the kitchen in a bra and running tights. She was so hot.

She also looked hot the day she was out running in the rain, too, those wet clothes clinging to her, cold little nipples poking right out at him. He'd wanted to take her right there.

Why was he doing this, dreaming of her, after the way she treated him? Because it was what he did every afternoon while he waited for The Witch to come home and fuck up the rest of his day. Until Alexis Jordan proved she was no different from other women, she'd been his refuge. The one woman who seemed to like him not for his looks or his sports abilities, or because he was tall, but because he was a nice guy. He'd come home, fantasize about her, jerk off, then shower and make his bed. The Witch liked things clean and neat.

She might be his mother, but he knew The Witch didn't like him. She didn't like men, and he had become one. A big, hairy, muscular, sweating, shaving adult-bodied man. Once or twice, passing her in the hall with his morning boner, she'd turned an ugly purple and looked like she might heave. Except for one bizarre lecture about masturbation, delivered coldly from the opposite end of the kitchen, The Witch never mentioned sex. Never.

Some days, when she made him feel particularly useless and incompetent, he felt like whipping it out and laying it on the table, the way a character in a movie would lay down his gun. A quiet statement. Look at it, lady, I'm not a helpless little boy anymore.

Unlike a lot of his friends, whose mothers didn't work, The Witch ran her own consulting business. He didn't know much about what she did— the few times he asked, she blew him off. All he knew was she must work too hard because it made her uptight and bitchy. She always rushed in late and slammed around getting dinner on, insisting on a home-cooked meal every night. Then she was crabbier because she'd had to cook. He'd given up saying he'd be happy with Chinese or pizza. She'd wrinkle her nose like the idea had a bad smell.

He checked the clock. She was later than usual tonight. Like the other night, when he told her about his dilemma. His sad treatment at the hands of his beloved teacher. He waited 'til she'd worked herself into a frenzy, trying to get a nourishing meal on the table in ten minutes. That was her timetable—ten minutes. The Witch was an awful cook. He'd always eaten her cooking, so it wasn't until he ate at friends' houses that he'd realized what a bad cook she was.

The Witch had a talent for sucking the flavor out of everything she served. Salt was bad for you. Spices disguised the natural goodness of food. Basic foods were best. She didn't like fish—it smelled up the house. Instead, she cooked liver, which smelled even worse. The Witch had the same talent for sucking the flavor out of life.

No wonder he'd been drawn to Mrs. Jordan, with her vibrant red hair and super warm smile. Mrs. Jordan had the opposite talent—she put flavor into life. But not for much longer.

The other night, as soon as The Witch had worked herself up to a fevered pitch, he dropped his bombshell. She'd been at the stove, shrouded in an apron, busy hands trying to stir three pots at once. He said, just as he'd practiced, "Mom, listen. I have to talk to you. I don't know what to do. I'm so confused and ashamed and I need some advice. Ever since she seduced me last fall, I've been having this affair with one of my teachers."

She had taken that and run with it. He could always count on her to take his side, no matter what he did. Now he had that pompous ass Huston on his side, too, Huston and his little ass-lick sidekick, Mark Clemente. Shit. Their faces when he'd told them about Mrs. Jordan. Huston practically drooling, while Clemente doodled on a pad. He could tell from Clemente's face that the man wished he'd been the one boning Mrs. Jordan. But he was sure Clemente had never fucked anyone that hot.

It was only a matter of time before Alexis Jordan found herself fired. He would not be at all sorry. People ought to understand—sooner or later, he always got his way.

He rubbed the panties over his face again. First, he'd get her fired. And then he had another idea.

> "All the elements
> At least had gone to wrack, disturbed and torn…"
> —John Milton, *Paradise Lost*: Book IV

CHAPTER TWELVE

It poured all weekend, the skies a dismal gray that turned the world to perpetual dusk. The old promise of April showers bringing May flowers failed to console Alexis as she graded papers, searched for rap and hip hop lyrics she could use, and toiled over her plan book, her calendar, and her personal files. Reconstructing more than a year of her life as it related to Evan Palmer made her feel trapped and crabby and miserably sorry for herself. Even her cheerful yellow living room wasn't sunny enough to lift her mood.

She did finally catch up with Lori on Friday afternoon. Her friend's sympathy was comforting, her take on the situation similar to Claire's. This was not something Alexis had done, it was Evan Palmer's adolescent craziness and the school should know that. "We should have lunch tomorrow," Lori said. "Ned can watch the baby for that long." She sighed. "It's hard to say this, but back when I had stars in my eyes, falling in love with him, I didn't see how selfish he could be. He's the one who couldn't wait to have a baby and now I have to practically twist his arm to get him to do anything for her. Because he's the big shot working man while I'm on maternity leave."

Her friend sighed. "He doesn't want me to go back to work while honestly, I can't wait. I miss teaching so much."

Alexis thought about how much she wanted a baby, and how things with Micah made that look impossible.

"We're not exactly living the dream, are we? So, lunch tomorrow? That would be so great."

"Plan on it," Lori said. "Maybe Ned will have some good advice for you."

Saturday, just as she was working herself up to tell him about the lawyer, Micah grabbed his car keys, gave her a distant air kiss, and went off to the mall. Spending money she needed to pay her attorney. Through the window, she watched the departing taillights of the Beamer with clenched fists. She needed a hug, a sympathetic ear, and some comfort. All the things Micah used to be. Today she got an empty house with sudden startling splats of wind-driven rain smashing against the windows. Tired eyes and black-smudged fingers. The growing sense that her life was going to hell. A stocking full of coal and it was only April.

Lunch with Lori—her one thing to look forward to—got scaled back to a quick coffee in a noisy shop where it was too loud to talk. Still, seeing her friend helped remind her she wasn't alone, and Lori brought her a beautiful pink and white azalea and a package of bath bombs. "Because you need something to lift your spirits. I didn't get a chance to talk to Ned about your situation." She tried to hide it but Alexis could see tears in her friend's eyes. "He was such a bear about having to watch the baby. He's…" Lori hesitated. "He's not a very nice person these days." A pause. "Before he went off on his rant about me messing up his day off, he did say that your lawyer is very good."

She shrugged. "I guess that's something."

Sunday, Micah went to his office early, claiming he needed to do research. Researching Yvonne, she assumed, but challenging him would have been futile. Since that conversation over dinner, they'd danced around each other with elaborate politeness but not exchanged a single authentic word.

Sunday afternoon, explosive with frustration, she said to hell with the rain and went running. She didn't mind running in rain as long as it wasn't too cold, though lately, she was nervous about another encounter with Evan. They were all five-mile runs now. It took that long to work the kinks out. Friday during her run she'd had an unnerving sense of being watched, but today had been fine. Coming back, she was thinking of a thick steak and a funny movie, a total escape from all this. Maybe she could persuade Micah to go out.

When she reached the house, feeling alive and energized, an unfamiliar car sat in the driveway and a strange man stood on the front steps.

"Alexis Jordan?" he asked, stepping into her path.

She didn't like the deliberate way he positioned himself between her and her door. She didn't like the look on his face, either. He wasn't unattractive, but his eyes were eager and greedy. He looked at her boldly, as if she was on an auction block and he was considering his bid. He had the rumpled air of someone who slept in his car.

"Dave Hovarth, *Crawford Valley News*." He stuck out his hand. "I was hoping I could ask you some questions."

She felt a stab of panic. She'd never thought about reporters.

"Excuse me," she said, keeping her voice calm, "you're in my way." She was acutely aware of their physical disparities, that she was alone, that recently someone had broken into her house.

He shifted slightly, barely enough to let her get her key in the lock but not enough to let her open the door. This dance was about control and power.

"What did you want to talk about?"

"Evan Palmer," he said. "I'd like to hear your side."

There was only one side, and that was in Evan's head. She hadn't discussed the media with her lawyer and didn't want to make any mistakes. She forced a smile. "I'm afraid this isn't a good time, Mr.?"

"Hovarth."

"Mr. Hovarth. Do you have a card? Maybe I could call you?" Whatever would get him off her doorstep.

He made an elaborate show of producing the card, running his finger along a string of numbers. "Home. Work. Cell." A pause. "When can I expect a call? I'm on a deadline."

She took the card. "I'd like to get into my house, Mr. Hovarth."

He looked from her to the doorknob, his smile predatory. "You know a story is always better when it has both sides, when the viewpoints are balanced."

Her story. As if, even if she had one, she'd tell him. The way he looked at her, she knew anything she said would be twisted and perverted. If he were genuinely interested in balance and fairness, his approach would have been different. He would have called first instead of showing up, introduced himself politely instead of eyeballing her like a piece of juicy meat.

"I can expect that call when?" he said.

She was soaked to the skin and getting chilled. She relocked the door, pulled her key out, went down the steps and around to the side door. Hovarth followed.

"I hear you've been having sex with Palmer. Maybe you'd like to respond to that."

She didn't look back.

"You can't run away from it," he said. "Sooner or later, you're going to talk to me. Evan's friends have talked to me. I'm writing a story about this. I should think you'd like to tell your side. 'No comment' or 'she refused to talk' looks bad in print."

Willing her hand steady, she let herself in, jerked the door shut, and turned the deadbolt. How had he heard this? She couldn't imagine Evan going to the papers. He wanted to hurt her, not himself. Not his mother. Then it came to her. Hovarth didn't say he'd talked to Evan. He'd said "Evan's friends." Friends like Carrie, angry and vindictive, not caring who she hurt. She could picture Carrie picking up the phone. Her breathy little girl voice, "My boyfriend's having an affair with our teacher."

She sat on a kitchen chair and unlaced her soggy shoes. She should have gone to the mall with Micah and gotten a new pair. Running was her therapy, and for a serious runner, good shoes were important. But then she wouldn't be ready for her meeting tomorrow with Janice Trustman. She was about to strip off her wet things and dump them in the laundry room when she remembered Evan's remarks about her yellow living room, her couch, the color of her rugs. No privacy even in her own home.

She looked out the window. Hovarth's car was still there. What was the man waiting for? Micah to come home? She'd better warn him. Micah should be more savvy about this than she was, but she didn't want to take the chance. She dialed his office. Then his cell. Then she called directory assistance and asked for Yvonne LaCroix's number.

Blocking caller I.D., she dialed and got the same fluttery voice she'd heard before. "Micah Jordan, please."

"Hold on." She heard the words, "It's for you," spoken in a puzzled voice.

Micah's hello was cautious. "It's Lex," she said, rushing before he could hang up. "I wanted to warn you there's a reporter sitting in our driveway. Waiting to talk about my imaginary affair with Evan Palmer. If he's still here when you get home, don't talk to him." She hung up, stung by the irony of warning the man who *was* having an affair about a reporter interested in his wife's fictitious one.

Feeling under siege, she closed the upstairs blinds and stripped off her wet clothes. After showering, she pulled on black yoga pants and an oversized sweatshirt. When she looked out, Hovarth was still there. On the internet, she found a movie near her favorite steak house that sounded interesting, and got her purse and her raincoat. She went through the connecting door to her car, opened the garage door, and backed out, missing his car by inches. When their windows were parallel, she lowered hers. "I don't know what you're waiting for, but you have no right to sit in my driveway. This is a private house. If you're still here when I get back, I'm calling the police."

She rolled up her window and headed down the street. At the first stop sign, she looked in her mirror. He was right behind her.

Two could play this game. She called Claire. "It's Alexis. I need advice." She explained about the reporter. "Can you think of a way to get him off my tail?"

"Pull into my driveway," Claire said. "By the time you get here, I'll have something figured out."

Claire opened her front door as soon as she saw the Jeep pull up, motioning Lex inside. "This is my niece, Charlotte, who's visiting for the weekend," she said. "Alexis, give Charlotte your coat and your car keys."

A minute later, they watched Charlotte, hood up, go back down the walk, get in the Jeep, and drive away. Hovarth followed.

"Half man, half pit bull," Claire said, watching them depart. "Hope you don't mind my being peremptory. I didn't want to give him time to think."

"I wouldn't mind if you took a bazooka and blew him to Boston. This is so maddening."

"You see Janice?"

She nodded.

"Like her? She's very good, Lex."

"She scared me, though, talking about the police."

"She really thinks it might come to that?"

"Just trying to warn me about possibilities. But after finding that creature on my doorstep, I'm feeling even more nervous. It means people are talking. It means the media may get hold of this."

"Hovarth's hardly media, Lex. He's a second-rate reporter for a small-town weekly. He covers the zoning board and the conservation commission. Writes flamboyant pieces about the danger of rabid animals. Mostly he sits home, drinking himself into a stupor, and mopes because his wife left him for another man."

"Means he's got a thing against straying wives, doesn't it?"

"Which is not what you are."

"You're right. It's just, I feel... I don't know. Like everything's going to hell. Like one day I'm a respected teacher trying to do her job and the next I'm a suspected predator. Those assholes Mark and Huston acting like they believe it. Now reporters on my doorstep."

"You haven't heard any more about a hearing?"

"Not since Huston's attempt at interrogation. I think they're letting me stew and Trustman agrees. How do you know her, anyway?"

"My older son, Brendan, the one who's at Connecticut College, was out with a friend on New Year's Eve. The usual story. Beer in the car. Driving around doing stupid things. The friend was driving but they were both arrested. Naturally, being parents of a high school senior, we panicked. We found Janice, and she calmly and competently sorted it, and him, out. I don't know." Claire made a face. "Maybe we could have achieved the same thing ourselves, you know, small town, user-friendly police department, but Janice was so cool about it. Kept us from blaming and accusing each other. I liked her commonsense approach and the way she kept us all calm. I thought she'd be good for you. And I know she's done work for other teachers."

Claire looked at her watch. "So, it's a rainy Sunday in April. My husband's working. And Charlotte has borrowed your car to go meet some friends. Instead of borrowing my car. What do you want to do? Steak and a movie?"

"You read my mind."

"There's nothing better for a case of poor me blues than a good, thick steak and a baked potato. You look like you could use a hot meal."

"That bad, huh?"

Claire gave her a frank look. "Yes, dear. That bad. You have a pale, slightly spooked look. Guess I would, too, if our positions were reversed. Well, not the pale part. So we'll go eat rare meat and get your blood built up, then laugh our asses off at some dumb movie. Sound good?"

"My treat."

It was late when they got back to Claire's house. The Jeep was out front, her keys on the hall table, and the tireless and tiresome Hovarth parked across the street.

Walking out to her car, it was all she could do to keep from giving him the finger.

She tried to distract herself from the lights on her tail by listening to loud music, jumping when a gust of wind slapped rain against the car. When she saw a silver CRV like Evan drove. A Crawford Valley police car. By the time the garage door had shut behind her, she was shaking.

Micah still wasn't home.

She wanted to march out to Hovarth's car and smash all his windows. She dropped first her keys and then her purse onto the wet garage floor. *Get a grip, Jordan.* If she let one lousy reporter for a sleepy local paper unnerve her, how would she handle the situation if it got any worse?

"...a universal hubbub wild
Of stunning sounds and voices all confused
Bourne through the hollow dark, assaults his ear."
—John Milton, *Paradise Lost*: Book II

CHAPTER THIRTEEN

"Have you ever touched his body while he was clothed?"

What's the matter with you? I never touched his body. I wouldn't touch his body. She wanted to shout it into Huston's fat, self-satisfied face. This had been going on for an hour and a half. One offensive question after another. Her self-control and acting skills were taxed to the limit. Huston seemed to thrive on the process. Claire sat quietly beside her.

The room was hot. After a day of verbal tightrope walking with stirred-up classes, she had to fight her desire to rest her head on the conference table and doze. That wouldn't be good. She'd read somewhere it was the guilty who fell asleep. Innocent people were too nervous.

She ran her lawyer's advice through her mind for the zillionth time. Don't volunteer anything. Just answer the question. If you don't understand it, ask for clarification. If you don't like the way it's phrased, rephrase it and answer your own question instead. Don't get mad, be impulsive, or blurt things out. Don't be defensive. Above all, stay calm and cool. Remember you are the innocent party here.

"I can't recall an instance, but it is possible that at some point, in the course of teaching or coaching him, I might have touched his shoulder."

Dr. Huston looked like he'd just found the Holy Grail. "Have you ever been alone with Evan Palmer here in the school building?"

"I coached him for his part in *Death of a Salesman* in that small room off the library. There were always librarians in the main room and the door was always open."

"Have you ever been alone with Evan Palmer outside of school?"

This was a tricky one. "It's possible, when I was advising the dance committee and drove some students home, Evan was dropped off last." At the time, she'd been aware of the risk of being alone with any student but it had seemed so petty. Teachers occasionally drove students places. And someone always got dropped off last. She didn't like their smug looks, so she said, "We've all done it. You remember, Mark, last month you had to drive Shireen O'Reilly home when she got sick, and just last week I saw Dr. Huston with two female students in his car."

"Yes. Well." Dr. Huston stabbed the list with a plump finger, ran it down the questions, and asked, "Have you ever been alone with Evan Palmer in your house?"

She bit back an angry *of course not*. "No."

He lit up at that and made a note. "You've never been alone with Evan Palmer in your house?" he repeated.

"I said no." A little too snappish. Beside her, Claire raised a finger and then lowered it. Alexis put her hands on the table and pushed her chair back. "Excuse me," she said. "The ladies' room." She didn't ask permission. That would concede too much power to Huston.

She was braced against the sink, doing some calming breathing, when Rosie Risoli came in. "You're working late," Rosie said with a malicious smile. Rosie didn't like her. One of the sets of feathers she'd ruffled, alas, with an unguarded speech about deadwood. Rosie, two years from retirement, was as dead as they got. She did as little as possible and made no bones about it. It was odd to find her here this late. Usually she was right behind the students.

"Meeting," Alexis said.

"Me, too." Rosie's brows lifted. "I hear you're having trouble with one of your students."

Alexis shrugged. "I hope not." She returned to the conference room.

As soon as she was seated, Huston cleared his throat loudly and repeated his question. "Have you ever been alone in your house with Evan Palmer?"

"No."

"Has Evan Palmer ever been in your house?"

"Not that I recall."

"Can you explain how he knows what color your kitchen is?"

"No."

"Your living room?"

"Maybe he looked through a window."

They went on like that for another ten minutes. Evan had alleged he'd been alone with her in a hell of a lot of places, had sex with her in all of them. To every question, however offensive, she squelched her angry retorts and simply answered no. No. No. No. Like a broken record.

"Is your pubic hair red?" He had almost as much trouble with pubic as he'd had with genitalia.

She almost laughed. She was a milk-skinned woman with vibrant red hair. And yes, she had what Micah had affectionately termed a burning bush. "I expect," she said, suppressing humor with an effort, "that you, Mark, and ninety-nine percent of our students could answer that question by using common sense."

At this, Huston gave up. "You're not helping," he said unhappily.

"Of course I'm helping," she said. "I'm telling the truth. How would it help if both Evan and I lied? I should think one liar was enough."

Mark gave her an angry look she didn't understand. Guilt for putting her through this, when she'd given him so much help? Then it came to her, the way things do when you stop seeing people through the lens of friendship and just *saw* them. Mark was angry because she'd embarrassed him in front of his boss. Because she hadn't cooperated and admitted she was a vile child molester. He'd probably hoped to be finished in time to get in some golf. The big jerk.

Dr. Huston glanced down at his papers again, then dusted his hands together like he was rubbing off crumbs. "Yes. Well. We have a difficult situation here. Difficult and sensitive."

He made a series of little chugging sounds, then tented his hands. A power gesture. She planted her elbows and tented her own hands a few inches higher. He pulled his elbows in to make his tent higher. His arms were longer, so she gave up the game. "Naturally, we will be conducting a full investigation and we expect your cooperation."

"Naturally," she echoed.

He hesitated, looking down again at his papers. "Given the serious nature of the allegations, I would request that you take a paid leave of absence, effective immediately, until the matter is resolved."

Not based on anything he'd learned today. He could have said the same thing two hours ago. She asked, "Is there a written policy about teachers and leaves of absence?"

He made more puffing noises. "Mark?"

Mark was fumbling through the book. They had been so sure she'd fold they hadn't prepared. He found what he wanted, stabbed it with his finger, and turned the book toward her. "It's right here." He sounded inappropriately triumphant.

With a calm she didn't feel, she pulled the notebook closer. "This is the policy for processing a teacher's request for a voluntary leave of absence."

"Exactly," he agreed, stabbing it again.

"Perhaps I misunderstood, but I thought Dr. Huston was suggesting an administrative action. An involuntary leave of absence. It's that process I was inquiring about. I'm being victimized by a student who assaulted me and made a slanderous accusation. Why would I request a voluntary leave when that could so easily be misconstrued?"

It took willpower, but she managed wide eyes and a baffled smile. "And given the, as you put it, serious nature of the allegation, I would be ill-advised to take any action inconsistent with the presumption that I'm innocent."

The silence on their side was absolute. Surely they'd expected her to fight? She was a bold, innovative teacher, always top in student reviews. How could they mistake her for some guilt-ridden little wimp who'd fold at the first sign of pressure? But that wasn't the only thing they'd mistaken her for, was it? They'd also mistaken her for a dangerous predator.

She drummed her fingers on the table, wondering why they'd think a woman bold enough to prey on her students would fold her cloak and slink away at the first threat of exposure. The answer gave her a sudden, stabbing pain in her chest she identified as emotional heartburn. Because if she *were* guilty, she wouldn't want the exposure. She *would* want to quietly resign and leave the district.

Dr. Huston cleared his throat again. "Yes, well, we really think it would be best... for you, and for us, if you would leave..." he struggled with the last word, "...voluntarily."

She wished Janice Trustman was here. She didn't know what to do. She only knew that if she let them push her out the door, she might as well start wearing a scarlet A on her chest, or whatever the modern equivalent was. She repeated her earlier question. "What is the process for an involuntary leave?"

Mark had been thumbing noisily through the book. Now he shot her an unhappy look. "I'm afraid we're going to have to look that up."

"As soon as you find it, I'd like a copy. I assume, knowing how well our union has negotiated on our behalf," she smiled at Claire, "that there are fair procedures for the process."

She stood, working on the breath control necessary to keep her voice strong and level. "It's dreadful enough to be an innocent person facing such ugly accusations. It would be unwise to agree to *anything* that might give such accusations any credence. I know you understand."

Better leave the window open. "Of course, once you've clarified the leave policy in writing, I will discuss the possibilities with my attorney."

She looked at Claire to be sure the recorder was still on. Claire, following her eyes, nodded.

She said, "Something I don't understand. You said you'd be conducting a full investigation?"

"That's right," Dr. Huston said.

"So far, you've interviewed a sixteen-year-old high school boy whose student file is full of notes from his teachers expressing concern about his attitude and behavior, and a popular, innovative, hardworking twenty-six-year-old professional teacher?" She waited for the nod. "And based on that, you're trying to rush me out the door? Why?"

Huston's face assumed its most pompous expression. "Mrs. Jordan, we are required to take matters concerning sexual allegations between students and teachers very seriously."

"We all do, Dr. Huston," she said. "We also know what teenagers are like, and that anyone can say anything about anyone. Maybe I wasn't clear. What I'm asking is why, if your investigation is at such an early stage, you're trying to force a step so detrimental to me?"

"Our first duty," he said sententiously, "is to our students."

"I believe…" She hoped she wasn't wrong, "that under the terms of our contract, in fairness, *and* in law, you also have a duty to me."

She picked up her bag. "Is there anything else?"

She knew she was late to meet her lawyer. Very late. But she didn't check her watch. She must appear to have all the time, and ease, in the world.

Huston shoved back his chair with a clatter. "Not today, Mrs. Jordan. Thank you for coming in." He inclined his chins at Claire. "Mrs. Simkoff."

Claire stood so she towered over Huston, then inclined right back. "Dr. Huston." Mark, she ignored.

*　　*　　*

In the school parking lot, Alexis found the driver's side window of her car smashed. On the seat sat a brown paper grocery bag with the top folded down. Even from several feet away, Alexis smelled the awful stink. She held her nose and went closer to see what was written on the bag. The Magic Marker scrawl read: *A Sack of Shit for a Sack of Shit.*

Today she'd borne the students' stares and curiosity, Huston's intrusive questions and ugly judgment. Yesterday filthy, insinuating Hovarth on her doorstep, but this was a piece of pure nastiness. Sickened, she turned away, feeling totally violated. *Now it begins*, she thought, as a knife of pain stabbed into her stomach. *Now it really begins.*

"Behold alone the woman,
opportune to all attempts..."
—John Milton, *Paradise Lost*: Book IX

CHAPTER FOURTEEN

"You have to call the police," Claire said.

Alexis turned, surprised to find Claire beside her. Claire's face was fierce with anger. "This is vandalism. This is outrageous. Besides, your insurance company will need a police report before they'll pay for the damage."

"I'm late for my appointment with my lawyer."

"Call her. She'll understand."

Alexis punched the buttons with uncertain fingers. When Janice Trustman answered, she said, "It's Alexis Jordan. I'm very sorry. Something's come up. I need to reschedule."

Trustman's voice sliced through her explanation. "You sound upset. Something about the hearing?"

"My car's been vandalized."

"Vandalized how?"

Alexis steadied her voice, hoping her lawyer wouldn't catch the tinge of tears. "Someone smashed my car window and, and..." How could she describe this without descending into language she never spoke aloud? "And they left something nasty on the seat. From the smell, I assume it's a bag of feces."

"Have you called the police?"

"I'm about to."

"Good. Be sure the administration knows about it, too. Now, how about tomorrow afternoon? Four-thirty?"

TEACH HER A LESSON

"That's fine. I'll be there."

"Anything about the hearing I should know?"

"They tried to make me agree to a voluntary leave. I said I didn't think it would be wise in my situation because it could be seen as a sign of guilt. I asked them about the policy and process regarding involuntary leave, which, by the way, they didn't know. And I said I'd have to consult my lawyer."

"So we'll talk about that. Anything else?"

"Just what you'd expect. It was ugly. Claire came with me. It's all recorded."

"You might as well bring that along, then. And Alexis? Some advice, okay? You don't deserve this. Don't let anyone treat you like you do. Not the administration, your fellow teachers, or your students. And don't start acting like you do, either. Understand?"

Trustman's words put some strength back into her spine. She didn't deserve this. "I understand. Thank you."

Next, she called the police. The same officer showed up who'd come to her house about the ladder. Officer Collins. Once again he was calm and matter-of-fact, yet with a comforting undercurrent of compassion. "Kids," he said, when he'd taken her statement. "They'll do anything for kicks. Don't give a damn who they hurt. Especially this time of year. They get restless." He gave her a sympathetic look. "Not easy keeping a lid on 'til June."

She realized she'd seen Collins around the school, meeting with Mark or Dr. Huston. He seemed so calm and nondescript that he hadn't stuck in her mind.

"You can pick up a copy of the report at the station tomorrow, in case you need one for your insurance company. I'll get photos first. You called them, yet?"

"No." She looked from the key in her hand to the mess on the driver's seat. "I was going to call when I got home, only…"

"I know," he said, "it's kind of ugly. Why don't you make that call while I clean up?"

"Really, you don't have to."

But he'd already opened his trunk and gotten out gloves and a sturdy plastic bag. She supposed police officers needed sturdy plastic bags. For roadside trash and dead animals and stuff. For times like this. She couldn't imagine a life where this became routine.

"I'm heading out, Lex," Claire said. "Will you be okay?"

"It's just a window, Claire." A window and a gross insult. But she was hardly the helpless type, even if she did feel ragged just now.

"Right. Good. See you tomorrow."

Watching Claire's tall figure walk away, she felt bereft. Not looking forward to the evening ahead. She'd be brooding about her car. Waiting to see if Micah showed up. Replaying the hearing in an endless, painful loop.

"That should do it," Collins said, closing up the plastic bag. "If you scrub the seat with some fabric cleaner and leave the windows open overnight, it should be fine tomorrow."

"It was kind of you to do that," she said. "I never expected... well, I guess I never expected that the police... that you did this sort of thing for people."

He smiled. "No problem, ma'am."

No problem, ma'am. Reducing her to a generic citizen. One of many messes Collins cleaned up on his rounds through town. Roadside trash, rabid raccoons, fender-benders, and a slightly vandalized car. No big deal. No emotional connection to the cause or the outcome, while this felt like a big deal to her. She'd like to see this as a teenage prank but she knew better.

She stood in the empty school lot and watched his car until it was out of sight. Whoever did this had achieved their purpose—they'd made her feel assaulted and vulnerable. She turned in a slow circle, unable to shake the feeling that someone lurked nearby, watching. Gloating. That feeling ruined what could have been a peaceful moment. The slanted afternoon light tinted everything a rich gold. Damp earth scents mingled with the subtle perfume of some early-blooming bush. She leaned against the car and closed her eyes, in no hurry to get in and drive.

*   *   *

Leaving the Jeep in the garage with its windows open and the garage door up, she went inside and got a can of air freshener. She sprayed about half the can into the car and left the car doors open, but she closed the garage. Still spooked by last week's intruder, she wasn't leaving the house open. She got into running gear and headed out, knowing not even five miles of churning muscles and burning lungs could scour away the emotional residue of this day.

She had to push herself again, exhausted from the meeting with Huston on top of too many sleepless nights, the unsettled state of her marriage, and the emotional toll of teaching in the face of her students' relentless questions. She ran awkwardly at first, stumbling and tripping along the path. But she didn't give up, not when the sick feeling in her stomach reminded her that she hadn't eaten all day; not when the pains in her legs reminded her that she wasn't used to running this much. If she pressed on, she'd hit her stride. She closed her mind to everything except the driving music and the physical effort of running.

She got so completely into what she was doing she didn't see the figure lurking in the bushes until he grabbed her. For a few seconds, she was blinded by panic, aware only of strong, rough hands clamped around her arms. Then the lessons from her self-defense course kicked in, actions she'd visualized many times in preparation for a moment like this. Instead of fighting the hands that gripped her—a grip too strong to break easily, she grabbed the man's arms, pulled herself closer to him, and brought her knee up hard into his groin.

Unlike her instructor, this man wasn't wearing a padded protective suit. He gasped and groaned. As he instinctively leaned forward, bent by the pain, she slammed her head into his nose, then, as his head flew back, she jabbed the pointed spear of her fingers into the base of his throat. He made an ugly gurgling sound and collapsed onto the ground.

She heard her instructor's voice *Run, Alexis. Get away. Don't stop to see if he's okay.* She accelerated, leaving her attacker thrashing and cursing on the path, outrage pouring from his lips. She was two hundred feet away, running like the devil was on her tail when she recognized the man. The reporter. Hovarth.

Not that she cared. Bruised and angry, she was purged of any vestigial instinct to see if he was hurt. A man jumps out and grabs you, you owe him nothing.

"Goddammit," she yelled back. "Goddammit, you bloodsucker, you stay away from me. Stay away, you hear!"

She took off.

His car pulled in as she was crossing the lawn, his door flying open as he rushed toward her, bellowing her name. She dashed inside, slammed the door, and dialed 9-1-1. "A man jumped out at me while I was running. Please," she said, "he grabbed me. I fought him off and I ran. He followed me home and now he's downstairs banging on my door. Please! I'm scared. Can you send someone quickly?"

Hot from exertion and from anger, she pulled off the light jacket she'd worn, pacing the bedroom restlessly as she waited and Hovarth pounded on her door. Hovarth had been rough when he grabbed her. New livid bruises bloomed on her upper arms.

The cruiser was there in minutes. She hurried downstairs and pulled the door open. Hovarth was gone and the young officer on her doorstep seemed more interested in her tight top than her bruises or her story.

She paced the kitchen restlessly as he took her statement. Reporting the incident was almost as brief as the attack had been. And as disturbing. The officer was perfunctory. Seemingly unconcerned when she pointed out that this was an attack on a female runner in a public park. She tried to keep her voice calm as she asked what they would do. Tried not to yell, "I want him arrested!" when he said they'd locate Mr. Hovarth and speak with him. She was not comforted, reassured, or expecting that anything would be done.

Until today, she believed she lived in a nice, safe community. Sure, the cops were too lenient with teens who caused trouble, bowing to pressure from overprotective parents. She'd never paid much attention to that. She was beginning to suspect the police were too lenient, or lazy, with everyone. What if Hovarth approached her again? More worrisome, what if Evan acted on his threats?

Standing bare-armed in the fading afternoon light, bruised and scared, exhausted from her trying day, she felt deeply discouraged. Where do you go for help when the cops don't care?

EVAN — FIVE

He couldn't stand the waiting. It knotted his guts like a twisted Slinky. Every morning, he had to watch her cross the parking lot, head high, like nothing happened. Like she hadn't led him on, then screwed him in a major way. Like he didn't lie here every night and hear her smarmy voice, sweet and oh so serious, the way teachers talked when they really wanted you to get it, telling him he'd simply misunderstood. Saying how much she loved being a teacher.

Well. Not for long, lady.

Last week, he'd dragged The Witch into Huston's office and put on his best abused innocent act, unleashing The Witch in all her ghastly protective glory. Watched the fat man cross his chubby legs to protect his nuts from her. The way she acted, any man would be afraid. If The Witch had her way, all the cocks and balls in the world would be harvested, boiled, and fed to wild dogs.

Things were moving too damned slowly. Mrs. Jordan should have been fired by now. Bounced out on her tight little ass. How long did it take to ask a few questions, decide she was a liar, and terminate her? That asshole Huston didn't get it. Procedures, Huston had explained, because of her contract. He'd been sympathetic to how hard it was for Evan to attend school, knowing he might run into HER. How impossible to concentrate. The only thing he'd gotten out of this so far was not having to do his homework.

How could he, when he had to sit outside her house, watching? He knew which nights her husband didn't come home, and where he spent the night instead. Couldn't understand it, either. The girlfriend was much less attractive. She had big, floppy tits and made little grunting sounds during sex. Mrs. Jordan wasn't like that. She was smooth and sleek and really hot.

Stop that, he commanded. He had to stop thinking nicely of her. She wasn't nice. Look what she'd done to him. Only fifteen when she'd first seduced him. Little more than a kid. He'd practiced this story so often that he almost believed it. He'd been visualizing the whole thing until it had become part of his adult sex life. What he'd done to give her pleasure, what she'd done to him. What they'd said. Which sheets were on the bed. How her skin felt. How she smelled. How he'd loved sucking those tight pink nipples.

Smashing her car window and leaving shit on her seat had been fun, but her reaction—which he watched with binoculars—had been disappointing. He'd wanted to see her extremely upset. Instead, like always, she'd stayed calm and handled it. Even handled that asshole Collins, even though the cop was checking her out when she wasn't looking. He sort of admired the way she held it together. But his goal was to make her lose it. Grind her down until she understood the depths of rejection. Whatever it took.

He studied himself in the mirror. Did he look boyish enough? Vulnerable? The baby blue shirt did make him look younger. But young enough? Did he look too much like a kid for that reporter to take him seriously?

In half an hour, he would meet Hovarth at the coffee shop. He couldn't wait to see how his story played. And wasn't it time to get The Witch all fired up for a visit to the cops?

"...she perchance underwent an agony
from every footstep of those that thronged
to see her..."
—Nathaniel Hawthorne, *The Scarlet Letter*

CHAPTER FIFTEEN

Alexis didn't need a mirror to tell her she looked like hell. She couldn't bear to top it off by dressing in her usual frumpy clothes. Passing up shapeless jumpers and baggy tops, she pulled a slim black skirt off its hanger, added a soft gray-green jersey, a silver necklace, and big silver earrings. She clipped her hair back with silver barrettes. The mirror shrugged, liked the little black booties and tights, and said *better*.

The momentary surge of defiant energy she'd gotten from dressing like herself instead of boring Mrs. Jordan lasted until the first whiff of that odor. Her car smelled like an elementary school bathroom. She gave the upholstery a few spritzes of fabric deodorizer and went back inside to call a repair service to fix the glass. She felt vulnerable enough without being unable to lock her car. She told them the car would be in the school lot all day. They said it would be fixed before school got out.

She grabbed her bag, hit the door opener, and headed out into the cool spring morning with all the fresh air she could ask for pouring in her open windows.

By the time she got to Ollie's lot, half-frozen from all that fresh air, she was looking forward to wrapping her hands around a hot cup of coffee. She paid her respects to Mr. Riley and baby Emily—their smiles a part of her morning routine—and dashed up to the counter. Ollie paused with the cup in mid-air. "New job?" he asked, his bushy eyebrows rising inquisitively.

"Same job." She shrugged. "I got bored with looking like a frump."

"You look good," he said with a firm shake of his head. "You should do this every day."

"Yeah," a familiar voice behind her said. "You should."

Hovarth stood behind her, an ugly smirk on his bruised face. His nose was swollen. When he spoke again, his voice was low and smarmy. "Evan Palmer says you have pale yellow sheets with deeper yellow lemons on them."

She froze.

"He says you keep an assortment of condoms in the drawer on your husband's side of the bed. And Anais Nin's soft porn on your side. He says your bush is thick and curly and a paler red than your hair."

Her stomach twisted at this invasion. At the truth in what he'd said. She snatched the coffee from Ollie and wheeled on him, keeping her voice low enough so others couldn't hear. "Evan's a filthy liar and you're disgusting. There's never been anything between us except in his twisted mind. I told you to stay away from me. I mean it." She brandished the cup of steaming coffee. "You back off or I'll throw this right in your ugly face."

Hovarth stepped back, forcing a laugh as his words chased her out the door. "You can't run from the truth, Mrs. Jordan."

She was struggling to unlock the car door when she realized how dumb she'd been to lock it in the first place. The window was missing, for goodness sake. She'd also forgotten her muffin and left without paying for the coffee. The hand holding the cup shook.

"Alexis, are you all right?" The big man looked a little sinister with his long dark hair gathered into a ponytail, dark beard, and intense dark eyes. She braced for an outburst or another accusation. Instead, he paused before he got too close, like he understood her need for personal space. On his shirt pocket, white embroidery spelled "Peter."

From the look on his face and his calling her by name, she knew he hoped to be recognized. But it was his deep voice and polite manner, not his looks, that stirred recognition. She'd never known him as Peter. Back in high school, during the brief time they'd dated, he'd been Ev.

"Peter Everett. Is that really you?" With him between her and Hovarth, she felt instantly safer.

"I didn't expect you to remember," Everett said.

"Sometimes I think I remember too much about high school," she said. "Maybe because I'm still there every day. I'm more surprised that you remember me. I no sooner find a guy who can dance and he moves away, right? You live around here?"

Making small talk. Like her life was normal instead of in shreds.

"Eldon," he said. "Been there about five years. But lately, we've been doing a lot of jobs in Crawford Valley. Always plenty of work for an electrician. What about you?" He rocked back and forth. "You look great."

"Thanks." She lowered her eyes as if she was still a dorky high school girl. She'd never been good at taking compliments. As a kid, her mother had only dished up criticism, making clear that compliments were reserved for herself. And today, Alexis knew, it was such a lie. "I teach at Crawford Valley High. English. Been there almost six years."

She liked his respectful distance. Remembered how he had always been kind. Another time, another life, catching up would be nice, but she was already late and that bastard Hovarth was watching.

"Gotta run, I'm late," she said. "It's great seeing you."

She drove away too fast. When she looked in the mirror, Peter Everett was standing where she'd left him, staring after her. No way to explain that it wasn't him driving her away but Hovarth. But she'd already moved on, or back, to things Hovarth had said. How did Evan know the color of her sheets or the contents of her bedside drawers?

*   *   *

She was taking the class through one of her personal passions—vocabulary building—when they came for her. First class after lunch. Not that she'd had lunch. Responding to the needs of her body, she'd gotten a sandwich, but hadn't been able to eat. There were two cops, bristling with equipment, looming big and authoritative as they towered over her in the hall. Dr. Huston was with them, and if he wasn't kind, he at least had the grace not to look triumphant.

It was Dr. Huston who came into the classroom and asked her to step outside, but after that, the cops did all the talking. The shorter and slightly older of the two stepped up to her and read aloud from a paper: "Alexis Stewart Jordan, 7-15-96?" She recognized her name but not the numbers, then realized it was her birthday. She nodded, preferring gesture to speech, unsure she could speak around the knot of fear lodged in her throat.

"Detective Sergeant Paul Green, Mrs. Jordan. This is Officer Kennedy. We have a warrant for your arrest. I'm afraid you'll have to come with us."

She closed her eyes against a sudden rush of dizziness, knowing anything she said or did that wasn't absolutely neutral might be interpreted as a sign of guilt, aware of the classroom full of curious faces behind her. "Will you take over, Dr. Huston? They're doing vocabulary," she said, hoping she didn't sound as scared as she felt. "It's a game. Everyone writes down three words and passes them to the next student, who writes three sentences using those words. Then the list of words and the sentences move on. Do that three or four times, then they read them aloud. Could you take over?"

She turned to the officer. "May I get my purse?"

"Yes, ma'am. Where is it located, please?"

She pointed. "Across the room in my desk."

"Is this the only entrance to the room?" he asked Dr. Huston.

Huston looked at Alexis. "Mrs. Jordan isn't going to run away."

The first acknowledgment of her professional status from a school official since this nightmare began. Absurd as the notion was of her trying to run from two armed police officers, she felt ridiculously grateful. Huston could have simply told the truth—there was no other exit. The officer nodded at her. "Go ahead."

It was terribly hard opening the door and walking across the classroom. Her feet felt distant and clumsy. Twenty-five pairs of eyes followed her. The room was more silent than she'd ever known a high school classroom to be. As if no one was breathing. She went behind the desk, used the key from her pocket to open the drawer. Pulled her purse from her tote bag. Normally she would have taken the tote, which was full of planners and schedules and other important papers. But it also held the detailed list of all her contacts with Evan Palmer over the last year. She wasn't handing *that* over to the police if she could help it.

She relocked the drawer with clumsy fingers. Forced herself to look at her class. "I have to leave," she said. "Dr. Huston will be taking over."

She recrossed the room and went out the door, walking past the officers and around the corner on treacherous Gumby legs. Whatever was coming, she wanted to do it with the smallest possible audience. Glad during her sartorial rebellion this morning she'd picked simple wedge booties, not the stilettos that looked so good with this skirt. The man who'd identified himself as Detective Sergeant Green reached for her purse. "I'll take that," he said. "Is there some identification in here?"

She handed it to him. "My driver's license. In my wallet."

The other officer produced a set of handcuffs. "Put your hands behind your back," he said.

Panic surged through her. They wanted to put her in handcuffs? She looked at Green. "Is this really necessary? Here, where I work? Where I teach. I'm not going to give you any trouble. Couldn't you wait until we're outside?"

"Afraid not, ma'am. It's procedure." There was a hint of satisfaction in his voice.

She realized she hadn't asked about their warrant. What authorized this arrest? What was she charged with? Demeanor mattered. If she wasn't curious, would they think she knew what this was about? Would an innocent person understand this? Someone who'd already been grilled by Dr. Huston and Mark Clemente? Would the police know she'd been grilled by Huston and Clemente? For that matter, she was innocent and she *didn't* know what this was about. Given Evan's lies, what possible crime could she have committed? She'd failed to ask her lawyer.

"I intend to cooperate," she said. "But before you put those things on me, humiliating me in front of my colleagues and students, I'd like to know why I'm being arrested."

The detective nodded. Absolutely calm. Totally cool. In no hurry, which she appreciated. Despite her best efforts at self-control, she was having trouble breathing. The sudden rush of fear made her lightheaded.

Evan must have gotten frustrated waiting for Dr. Huston to act and gone to the police.

"Indecent assault and battery," the detective said, "and statutory rape."

"But that's ridiculous. I didn't. I'd never. My God!" The words burst out before she could stop herself.

"Your hands, ma'am, please," Kennedy said calmly. As though she wasn't shaking and stunned and this was an everyday occurrence in both their lives, instead of only in a cop's. "Ma'am?"

She leaned against the wall, both hands pressed against the blooming pain in her stomach. What on earth could that boy have told them? Once, perhaps twice, she'd touched him on the shoulder. *Indecent assault and battery. Statutory rape.* It was the stuff of the six o'clock news. *Lustful, predatory teacher seduces innocent male student.* Her life crashing and burning as her imaginary sins were paraded before a rapacious public.

"Mrs. Jordan?" The officer's hand on her arm was firm and steady. So was his voice. The voice of authority. "We need you to cooperate with us now, please. This will all go much easier if you do."

Cop bullshit. Nothing would make this easier, but his message was clear. Cooperate or they'd use force. They were comfortable either way. No sense in making this a bigger circus than it already was. With an effort, she stepped away from the wall and put her hands behind her back. Wanting to resist, argue, run like hell out the door and away from all this. Knowing it was futile. To them, she was a predator. A vile woman who'd seduced her student. They couldn't wait to lock her up.

She felt the cold touch of metal on her wrist. Then the circle closed, digging into her skin.

"Let me know if that's too tight," Kennedy said, snapping it around her other wrist, locking her hands together. The second band painfully tight. She didn't want to delay this by complaining. Just get this humiliating perp walk over with. Except for the bite of the cuffs, having her arms pinned behind her wasn't as uncomfortable as she'd imagined but she was overwhelmed by helplessness. What if she fell?

"Let's go." He placed a hand on her arm just above her elbow as they headed off down the corridor, one officer on either side, Kennedy's grip

127

unnecessarily tight. She fought the urge to shake him off. To complain that she was already bruised. Evan. Kyle. Hovarth. Now the cops. All these males leaving their marks on her.

She stumbled slightly going down the inclined ramp toward the front door and the hand on her bruised arm tightened, steadying her. She kept her eyes down, avoiding the ranks of watching faces, certain Evan stood among them, gloating. This was too humiliating. Among the many pairs of feet they passed by one stood next to a bucket on wheels and she heard a soft voice say something in Spanish. "*Que Dios te cuida.*" May God watch over you. Carlos Rivera, one of the janitors. His gentle words carried her out the door and toward the waiting police cars.

Two cars. Light bars flashing. Right in front of the door. Everything calculated to maximize her shame. They'd done everything but sell tickets. Why not just put up a banner? Fly a flag? Tar and feather her, carry her out on a rail. Avoid clichés like the plague.

Her stomach flip-flopped. Bile, unbidden, rose in her throat. She couldn't be sick. Not in front of the entire school. Not right at the entrance, knowing every eye with a view to the front was glued to the windows. Needing to breathe to settle her system, she paused.

Kennedy tugged on her arm.

"Please," she said, "I'm only trying not to be sick. Here or in your car."

The pressure on her arm slackened as he rocked to a stop. "Take your time," he said.

For a second, they were on the same page. Probably the only time that would happen. She took a deep breath in and slowly let it out. And another. Then she gave him a slight nod.

He put her in the car just like on TV, with the careful hand on her head. "I'm afraid it's not the most comfortable ride," he said. Not that her comfort was high on their list of priorities or they would have done this quietly. At home, not out here in front of the whole school. They could have called and asked her to come in. Her comfort? The back seat was a plastic bench, like a lunchroom chair only wider, with holes for the seatbelt. Easy to clean up if she was sick, which was still a distinct possibility.

"I'm going to fasten your seatbelt," he said. "Turn your head to the left and keep it there." She heard the click, then he moved back past her. "All right."

He started the engine and the radio came on. Talk radio, those rabid hate-mongers pandering to people's worst instincts. "You mind the radio?" he asked.

"I'd prefer music."

Such an odd interchange under the circumstances. Was it because she was still a member of the public, despite the stigma looming over her? Innocent until proven guilty? Because he was a nice guy? Because they're taught to be courteous? He switched the station.

Before they moved, he communicated with the dispatcher, giving the time and his location. Then they pulled out with the other car right behind them.

The ride to the police station seemed much too brief. She wouldn't mind remaining in this limbo forever. Always in transit, never arriving. Arriving would have a frightening finality, forcing her to face the fact that this nightmare was really happening.

They drove into something that looked like a small garage, the door coming down behind the cars, shutting out the daylight. Claustrophobic. Locked in a car, locked in a box, unable to use her hands or move. Completely at the mercy of others.

Kennedy spoke on his radio again, then got out of the car. Green got out of his and the two of them walked to the front of the garage, took off their guns, and shut them inside little boxes on the wall. Then Kennedy opened her door.

Getting out was awkward. No hands, watching her head, worrying about catching her foot. If she fell, she couldn't stop herself. Kennedy stood there, always anticipating, taking her arm and leading her through a sliding, locking door. "This is the booking area," he said.

It was gray, sterile, and empty. To her right, she saw a window with a slot to hand things through, like a ticket window. In front of the window a thick metal bar, two chains hanging from it. At the end of each chain, a single handcuff.

KATE FLORA

Kennedy handed her purse through the slot and steadied her in front of it. "I'm going to take the cuffs off now," he said, "one hand at a time. When I release your right hand, I want you to put it on your head."

This felt ridiculous, like a kid playing Simon Says. But there was nothing of a game about this. Not with Kennedy and Green standing solemnly behind her, and another, older officer staring at her through the glass. Thinking, perhaps, so this is what a female predator looks like.

"Are you right-handed?" Kennedy asked.

"Yes."

"Lower your left hand, then, please." He fastened the hanging cuff around her left wrist, chaining her to the bar like a leashed dog or a tethered horse. She wished she'd spent more time exploring arrest possibilities with her lawyer. Maybe she'd feel less panicked if she knew what was coming. And when did she get to call her lawyer? Explain that, ironically, she'd be missing this appointment, too.

Her wrists hurt, a bone-deep ache that made her want to rub away the pain where the tight handcuffs had left deep grooves. She saw that the cuff around her wrist was too big. She could slip her hand right out. Be free if she wanted. Free.

The man behind the glass pulled a form in front of him and started asking her questions. Name and address. She had to think before responding. Fear had slowed her brain. She could hear that fear in her answers, in her voice. Felt the distant throb of a headache. She never got headaches. Between her head and her stomach, it was hard to concentrate. She had to concentrate.

An abrupt movement behind her, the creaking of a cop's leather jacket. "Hold on," Kennedy said. He grabbed her wrist and checked the cuff, sliding it easily over her hand. She gritted her teeth against the pain of his pinching fingers. In a motion so fast her eyes couldn't follow, he had his own cuffs out again, snapped one end onto her wrist, and the other onto the chain.

She bit her lip and blinked back tears, reduced to the status of a child. She'd been a child in a household where only her mother mattered. Learned early the skills of being invisible and not making waves. She

130

heard her mother's scornful voice: *Alexis is such a baby.*

The man behind the glass resumed his questions. He fumbled her address. People often fumbled her address. She was used to smiling and making a joke about her number being a palindrome. There was no joking here. She might be desperate for reassurance that things would be all right, but these men were in the business of being intimidating. These were not the nice police officers you were told to find when you were a child in trouble. These were the stern, punitive police officers who preserved society's order by taking bad guys off the street.

A second wave of panic swept over her. She was here because these police officers believed she was one of the bad guys. They had taken *her* off the street. They believed she'd done something unthinkable and were preserving society's order from a sexually perverted woman who'd seduced an innocent boy. Someone's child. Despite some fundamental courtesies they'd extended, when they looked at her, they did not see a respectable citizen, a dedicated teacher. They saw a predator.

The tiger that played with her stomach was again flexing its claws. She needed to sit down. Lie down. Any minute now she was going to throw up. Couldn't do any of those things. Not chained to this bar. She looked at Kennedy's cold face. At Green's. How could she ask them for help?

"How old are you?" the man asked. "How tall?" She gave her age, twenty-six, which suddenly seemed very old. So many years had passed. Her optimism had faded. *Oh dear,* she thought, *this is no time to get philosophical.* She needed to concentrate. Her weight? Hair color? Obvious. Her eyes? Blue. Did she have any scars or identifying marks? Defiantly, she didn't mention her tattoo.

"Do you have any personal property?"

Reluctantly, she handed over her necklace and the big silver earrings. Awkward to take off, especially the earrings, chained to a bar. He made her take off her watch and pass that through the window. As she removed it, she saw the marks the tight cuffs had made had become a livid red. They hurt. She kept her face blank, determined not to give them the satisfaction of seeing how miserable she felt.

Item by item they inventoried the contents of her purse, laying things out on the counter in front of her. Brush and chapstick. Tampons. They laid out her credit cards and counted out her money like a grocery store clerk would. Not very much money. Put her stuff in a clear plastic envelope, in plain sight like those unfortunate clerks at Lord & Taylor, forced to carry a transparent purse. She'd always wondered about the indignity of carrying tampons and prescriptions for everyone to see. Then there was all the ratty stuff from the bottom of the purse. Both mints and breath spray. Would they assume she had awful breath? Was that box cutter for coercing innocent boys to have sex?

Only it wasn't funny. It got less funny when they handed her the Miranda form and asked if she could read it. She read slowly, losing her place and having to go back and restart each paragraph, her brain jarred by fear. Her stomach in the clutches of the tiger. The words pounded into her throbbing head. No way to pretend this wasn't really happening. She'd been arrested. She had the right to remain silent. She had the right to stand chained to a bar like a dog or a slave when she felt desperately sick and dizzy with such a roaring sound in her head she couldn't hear what the man was saying.

She gripped the bar with her free hand. Imagine having only one free hand. The word *free* had never taken on such resonance before. She was an English teacher. She loved language. With her *free* hand. She closed her eyes, willing her sickness to pass and not mortify her in front of these unsympathetic men.

But acid burned the back of her throat. Her stomach twisted.

Kennedy, icy and expressionless, grabbed her elbow. "What's wrong?" His harsh tone implied her pain was a stalling device, a ploy for sympathy, when what she was focused on was trying not to be sick. The man behind the window, older, heavier, with a gentle face, watched.

"Sorry," she said. "I'm feeling sick." Apologizing to them for the inconvenience. How pathetic was that?

Kennedy unlocked her hand and turned her toward the cell behind her. More cinder block, more utilitarian gray. Asphalt tile. A stainless steel combination sink and toilet. Taking her elbow, he led her to the door, waited while it slowly opened, then propelled her through it, standing calmly beside her while she ran for the sink and was violently sick. The acid burn left her throat raw and her sinuses stinging. Tears streaked her cheeks. The pounding in her head was worse.

She wanted to wash her face, wipe her nose, brush her teeth, sit down until the shaking stopped, the usual things a person needed to do after being sick, but Kennedy led her back to the bar and chained her up again.

She signed the Miranda form with a shaking hand. Then it was on to a different place for fingerprints. She couldn't get it right. Her cold fingers kept curling, bungling, getting in the way. The booking officer told her to relax and let him do it all, "like we're dancing," his instructions calm and detailed, his warm hands unintentionally reassuring. To the right, to roll the recalcitrant fingers on the pad, to the left to roll them again on the form. Two copies. One for here. One for the FBI.

The idea of her prints going to the FBI filled her with horror. What about her lawyer? Wasn't she supposed to be able to make a phone call? When did that happen?

The fingerprint cop told her to be careful with her blackened fingers. Not to touch anything. She imagined a defiant criminal stamping black prints on all the dull gray surfaces. She noticed a slot in the wall, like a night depository at a bank, with the word NARCOTICS etched in stainless steel. She felt like she'd been here all day and all night. She swung up her wrist to check the time—forgetting they'd taken her watch—and both officers were instantly alert. She dropped it. Dropped her eyes.

"Wash your hands," he ordered, pointing at a nearby sink. She scrubbed three times, trying to get the black off, feeling like a child under the supervision of a disapproving relative. Black clung to the cracks around her fingers.

Dumb as a dog she waited. Kennedy told her to sit on a bench. Grabbed a camera and snapped her picture. Told her to turn her head and snapped again. Asked if she was wearing a belt. Asked her to remove her boots. She unzipped them and slipped them off, wondering what on earth she was going to do with plain wedge boots that posed a danger to herself or others. A female officer came and searched her, impersonal hands running over her body, feeling around her breasts and between her legs.

Then Kennedy took her to her cell and the door slammed shut.

"Wait," she said. "What about my phone call? I need to call my lawyer."

Kennedy walked away without answering. How could she tell someone she was here, ask someone to get her out? What were the chances that Claire had made a call? She sat down on the metal bench. It was dusty around the edges, the surface mottled with spilled paint. Beside her lay a whitish-yellow crescent of fingernail, looming large in a room with nothing else to look at. She wrapped her arms around her legs and pulled them in to her chest, wondering how long she'd have to sit here with someone's nail.

Dammit! If they were going to inflict this kind of indignity on people at least they ought to keep the place clean. In a rush, she swept the offending article onto the floor. Then she curled up on her side and pulled her knees into her chest. It made her stomach hurt a little less.

The place hummed quietly. No one came or went. There were no other sounds except distant voices and energetic drummers practicing inside her head. Suddenly, Kennedy appeared at the cell door, gesturing for her to come forward. "I have to read you something," he said. He unlocked a slot in the door. It fell open with a horrendous crash, reminiscent of the clanging cell doors in old prison movies, that hurt her tender head. He read to her about her right to make phone calls, then asked if she had anyone she wanted to call.

"Do I get just one phone call?" she asked.

"If you act like a lady, you can make all the calls you want."

She appreciated what he was saying, and resented it. Why should anyone, innocent and exposed to these indignities, act like a lady? How did ladies act, anyway? Surely, under traditional rules, ladies never got arrested. Women, maybe, but not ladies. But he was still talking. "We'll get you to the phone pretty soon. Officer Collins has a few questions."

Collins again. The man who was everywhere.

Kennedy unlocked the door and motioned for her to come out. She moved hesitantly out of the cell, waiting for orders—a quick study in the cooperation and humility department. Hoping a move within the police department wouldn't require handcuffs. She hurt enough already.

He led her to a small box of a room with a table and a couple chairs. Tapped the closest chair with his hand. "You sit here."

Carefully, she lowered herself into the wooden chair. There was nothing in the room except the table and chairs. Nothing but herself and Officer Collins, who was wearing his kind cop's face. She wasn't fooled. If they were going to be kind, it would be for a purpose. The timing of the arrest and everything since told her that.

She sat in the chair, trying not to rub her throbbing wrists, waiting to see what Collins would do.

He opened a manila envelope and tipped out a black bra and panties onto the table. "Recognize these?" he asked.

"...what malicious foe,
Envying our happiness, and of his own
Despairing, seeks to work us woe and shame."
—John Milton, *Paradise Lost*: Book IX

CHAPTER SIXTEEN

She did. They were the missing set she'd looked for several times over the past two weeks. The set that had disappeared from her drawer. What was Collins doing with her underwear? Could he tell she recognized them? "Looks like women's underwear," she said. "Aren't I supposed to be able to make a phone call?"

"Don't worry. You'll get your phone call." He leaned forward, a concerned look on his face. "Are you all right? You look a little pale."

She'd tried to be as formal as the situation called for but this was ridiculous. She needed a touch of humor, whether he liked it or not. It was debilitating, being this scared, and she didn't believe his sincerity for one second. He'd been kind, if perfunctory, with her damaged car. But everything that had happened today had been cruel, calculating, and manipulative. If he cared how she felt, he would have asked that first, instead of dumping out the underwear. That was what civilized people did. People who didn't have an agenda, like getting an innocent person to confess to a crime. He probably considered himself a guardian of civilization.

"Officer Collins," she said, "I was born pale. Look." She shoved up her sleeves to show her arms. Hovarth's bruises, Evan's bruises, the marks from Kennedy's firm grip, and the marks the cuffs had left were striking against the whiteness of her skin. She skipped removing her top so he could see the bruise left by Kyle's fist. "And no, I'm not feeling all right."

"Would you like a Coke or something? That might help."

Wanted? Sure. Wouldn't dare drink with her stomach in this state. "I'd like to make a phone call."

"You know, Alexis… a case like this can get pretty messy, especially when the defendant doesn't cooperate. You sit down and talk to us, explain why you did it, how it happened, and everything can be handled. No need to play hardball." His face was solemn, as if he really believed what he was saying. Maybe he thought, like Huston, that a guilty woman would jump at an easy way out. As if any of this was easy. "And believe me, we can play as hard as we need to, if that's what you make us do. You're always better off if you cooperate."

Collins waited for that to sink in, like she had an impermeable layer in her brain. All she had was the mother of all headaches. He stirred the lacy underwear with his finger. "Any idea why Evan Palmer might have had these?"

Why Evan might have had them? What about *how*? She wanted to bat his hand away. She didn't like him handling her underwear. Her very nice underwear. She imagined an attorney holding them up in court, giving the jury a good view of the sheer mesh cups with just a tracing of embroidery across the nipples. What a predator wore to seduce an innocent boy.

It put a such knot in her stomach that it took all her willpower not to double over. That would bring her closer to the table. Easier to bang her head. Would that make it feel better or worse? *Get a grip, Jordan.*

"You're asking me why a teenage boy might have women's underwear? I should think, having been yourself once, you could answer that question better than I."

Collins poked the bra again, the metal hooks clattering against the wood. He made a show of reading the label. "Thirty-six C. Is that your size?" When she didn't answer, he shrugged. "We're going to search your house, you know, so we can confirm that."

She wanted to raise her eyebrows, drawl Collins' first name, if only she'd known it, and ask what it could possibly prove if Evan Palmer had a bra in his possession that happened to be the size she wore. Millions of women wore that size. Carrie Canavan probably did.

"Come on, Alexis, we both know this is your underwear."

Only one of them knew that. She wanted to grab his arm, dig her nails in, and tell him to stay away from her goddamned house, her personal things. The thought of cops rooting through her drawers and closets was repulsive. Yet another violation. His expression told her he knew he'd upset her and was pleased.

She looked at her hand, which was absently rubbing at her wrist. The chair was hard and the too-bright lights hurt her eyes. She was so very tired. "Look, I know I have the right—"

"Oh, I'll bet you do know your rights," Collins interrupted, "but what about your responsibilities? What about your responsibility to keep those fine white hands off that poor boy? Jesus Christ! Only fifteen years old, Alexis, when you started. Fifteen. What were you thinking?"

Don't call me Alexis, she thought, staring at his ugly, competent-looking hands. *We are not friends. It's part of some power game, isn't it? Well, forget it. I may not be at the top of my own game today, but if you want to play dodgeball, I'm going to just keep dodging until we're both sick of it.*

She tried to remember what she knew about Miranda. "Look," she tried again, "I don't want to talk to you. I want to—"

"Listen to this, Alexis," he said, interrupting again. His interruptions were deliberate. Everything he did was deliberate. He was doing whatever he could to trick her into saying something incriminating. He reached into the manila envelope again and pulled out a plastic envelope with a card inside. He held it so she could see the card—a cheerful yellow "Thank You" note. Hallmark cute with plaid flowers. "This your writing?"

She reached for it to bring it closer.

"Just answer the question," he barked, laying it on the table and pushing it toward her. "Is that your writing?"

"Don't yell at me," she barked back. A mistake. He wanted her losing control.

It was a short note in blue ink. She stared at the words, not reading them, looking at the handwriting. It was similar to hers. "I don't know," she said. "It might be. I can't tell."

"That's no problem," he assured her. "Our handwriting expert can tell. Let me read it to you." He put on a pair of glasses and picked up the note:

> *Dear Evan,*
>
> *I can't believe that last night almost didn't happen, that we almost let our shyness and our differences get in the way. If we hadn't spent the evening together, I would have missed out on one of the most wonderful times of my life. How could you be so good when you said you'd never done that before? Usually, I feel so clumsy but last night everything worked just right. Now you'll probably retreat in embarrassment and I'll never get to do it again. Don't be shy. Please. You were wonderful.*
>
> *Alexis*

"So," he said, laying down the letter. "You want to explain that?"

She stared at him in astonishment. It looked like her writing. But she'd never written any note to Evan, never mind one that could be so badly misconstrued. You don't spend all these years wearing dumpy clothes, going out of your way not to turn on teenage boys, and then do something like that.

It would have been ridiculous. She wasn't ridiculous, or stupid, or a danger junkie. She'd take risks to challenge students' minds. But this cop actually thought she'd taken risks to challenge their bodies. She felt sullied just sitting in the room with him.

"Well?" Collins looked smug. "Where's your glib answer this time, Mrs. Jordan?"

She couldn't explain it. Maybe a handwriting expert could. Maybe Evan had learned to imitate her writing. Goodness knows she gave them enough samples, with the copious notes she scribbled on their papers. She reread it, staring at the slightly smudged "Evan" as if it might be a clue. Nothing changed. It still looked like her writing and she still had no idea what it was or where it had come from.

At the bottom of the page, even seen through the thick plastic, it looked like something had been erased. She started to bring it to Collins' attention but changed her mind. This was something for her lawyer to deal with. She didn't trust people interested in convicting her not to make those marks disappear.

What would he pull out of that envelope next? A used condom with her alleged secretions and Evan's sperm?

Pretty good guess. Collins turned the envelope upside down and shook it. A condom—fortunately unused—dropped onto the table. Collins picked it up delicately by one corner. "Your favorite brand, right? If I go to your house, I'll find these in the table by the bed, right?"

Alexis had had enough. Enough surprises. Insinuation. Badgering. Enough of this cop's ugly mind sifting through her personal life. Enough of trying to be cooperative and having her right to make a phone call ignored. Of Collins' deft interruptions every time she started to assert her rights. Between her headache and her wonky stomach, she was a mess, but her brain was working again. "I would like you to stop asking me questions now, Officer Collins. I am represented by an attorney and I'd like to call her."

Collins stared at her like a kid stared at an empty cone and the scoop of ice cream on the sidewalk. Probably thought he was on the verge of getting some admissions. Why did people assume she was stupid and easy? Did she look like some fragile blossom who'd wilt at the first threat? Didn't these guys know being a high school teacher was hard? Alexis Jordan could tap dance on a rolling barrel in a lake full of alligators while reciting poetry. She was used to being bullied and badgered, sworn at and yelled at, regularly tricked, lied to, sweet-talked, and cried at. Collins hadn't tried double-teaming, yet, like Huston and Clemente or Carrie and her coterie of buzzing friends, but she'd had plenty of that, too.

She put her hands on the table, the livid marks on her wrists reminding her that these people didn't care about her rights or her comfort. They cared about trapping her into admissions they could use against her. They cared about punishing her for the bad things she hadn't done, maybe things that their own forbidden desires, fantasies, and prurient imaginings needed a scapegoat for.

Hadn't that form Kennedy made her read say she had to be allowed a call within an hour? "How long have I been here?" she asked.

Collins looked at his watch and shrugged. "All right. You can make your phone call. Just remember, we gave you a chance to cooperate and you shot us down."

"No more Mr. Nice Guy?" she said.

Collins shoved back his chair and walked out of the room.

It seemed like a long time before Kennedy came and took her to a phone. Another deliberate delay. She called Janice Trustman's office and told the secretary it was an emergency. When Janice Trustman came on the line, she explained what had happened.

"You've gone through the booking procedure?" Alexis made an affirmative sound. "All right. I know it must be terrifying, but I'm sure you did a great job. Now keep your head. Don't answer any questions they ask. Don't volunteer anything. They'll be bringing you to the courthouse soon. I'll meet you there."

"You done?" Kennedy asked coldly. Leaning into her personal space, using his body to diminish her. As if she wasn't small enough already.

She thought about calling Micah. Too awkward on the phone. She'd rather tell him in person. She nodded. "What happens now?"

"In a while, we'll take you over to the courthouse. You'll be arraigned. The judge will decide about bail." She wanted to ask how long a while was, but Kennedy was too intimidating. These cops weren't in the business of answering questions. That was the business she was supposed to be in. Tell us all about that sex with a fifteen-year-old that never happened. Tell us how you did it and where you did it and why you did it so we can use that against you. Forcing her to look at people and see the word "pervert" written all over their faces. Sick. Twisted. Depraved. God. All she'd done wrong was to be kind. Proof, if she needed it, that no good deed goes unpunished.

Kennedy led her back to the cell. She bent over the sink and rinsed out her mouth. Then she sipped some water. It hit her stomach and bounced back up, leaving her bent over the toilet bowl until the retching stopped and nothing remained but the pain. At least her head was finally clear.

She wiped her tears and wrapped herself in the rough wool blanket. All alone in a cold gray world with a writhing stomach and a stranger's fingernail, trying not to think about how the cops had her underwear and an incriminating note.

Trying not to think about bad results and helplessness.

Trying not to imagine the possibility that Evan might win.

"In darkness, and with dangers compassed round, and solitude."
—John Milton, *Paradise Lost*: Book VII

CHAPTER SEVENTEEN

The sun was still shining and it was still the same day when she and Trustman left the courtroom, but Alexis felt a decade older. Animal instinct made her want to crawl somewhere safe and dark to lick her wounds. Instead, she kept her head high as she walked past a mass of reporters shoving mics and cameras into her face. Their looks were salacious, the questions vulgar and ugly. She barely made it to Trustman's car before collapsing in a shaking heap.

"They're like a pack of hungry animals," she said.

"That's right." The lawyer found a sweater and handed it to her. "Head up," she commanded, starting the car and driving out of the courthouse lot. "And keep it up. They're still watching." Alexis wrapped the sweater tightly around herself, her shaking hands jumping like scared mice. She welcomed Trustman's being tough on her when she wanted to wimp out, but right now, she needed kind words and sympathy more than at any time in her life.

At the thankfully almost deserted high school, they retrieved her bag and her car. Still shaky, she followed her lawyer back to the office, barely able to keep the Jeep on the road. She wanted to rush home, lock the doors and climb into a hot bath. Sip tea. Scream. Storm around. Throw things. Run ten miles. Anything to stop this awful shaking. She was tired of answering questions. But she knew she and her lawyer had work to do.

When she was settled in a chair with a cup of mint tea, still huddled in the sweater, Janice Trustman sat down and clicked her pen. "How did they behave?" she asked. "Was it very bad?"

Alexis stared at her.

"The arresting officers," Trustman explained.

"It was totally humiliating." She fumbled for a description. "They were so cold and unfriendly. They really believe I've done something bad. I feel like I ought to just go shoot myself or something. How can I—" She rubbed her aching wrists as she searched for words.

"Hold on." Trustman came around the desk. "Pull up your sleeves." She studied the ugly red grooves the too-tight cuffs had left. "That was completely unnecessary," she said. "Kennedy, right, the big, cold one? I think he gets off on stuff like this." She headed for the door. "I'll be right back. I want some pictures. It makes me so angry. He snaps 'em on as tight as he can and then asks if they're too tight, knowing you won't dare complain. It's part of the games they play."

She took a dozen shots of the bruised wrists. "It's such grandstanding. If they have to arrest you, then arrest you. There's no need to do it like this. That's Chief Wexler playing to the media. I know the police have their job, but most of 'em act as if they've never heard of the presumption of innocence."

She set the camera aside. "Sorry. Guess we've all got our pet peeves. You don't need to be listening to mine right now. How are you doing?"

"I was sick to my stomach." Her face flamed at the memory. "A couple times. In front of Kennedy. He watched like I was doing it to annoy him. It was humiliating. The whole thing was humiliating."

"You feel all right now?"

"I don't. My stomach is… it hurts. I still feel pretty rocky."

Trustman made a note. "You told them you felt sick?" Alexis nodded. "Did they ask if you needed anything?"

"No."

"Offer you the opportunity to take a break, lie down?"

"No." Alexis thought of her shaking legs. "They wouldn't even give me a chair."

"Ask if you needed a doctor?"

She didn't want to remember Kennedy's cold eyes and heartless efficiency or being in the cell with that fingernail. "After I threw up they just chained me back to that bar and went on with the process." She stared down at her plain black boots. Boots so dangerous they'd had to confiscate them. Would she ever get this day out of her head?

"Do you need a doctor?"

Alexis shook her head.

"Did they make any attempt to question you, other than the necessary information for the booking form, while you were in custody?"

"Yes."

"Yes?" Trustman exploded. "Grant Collins, right?"

She nodded.

"I'm not surprised. Usually, Collins is down a suspect's throat the minute she opens her mouth. They boxed themselves in going for the grandstand arrest like that. Been a whole lot better off if they'd simply talked to you. Non-custodial. Just a friendly little chat. But the chief jumped the gun, going for the big news splash, and then sent Collins in to make nice to see if he could get you to talk. You didn't talk, right?"

Alexis shrugged. "I tried not to. They kept asking questions and I kept asking about my phone call. Trying to ask."

"Good girl. Who else was there?"

"Detective Green and Officer Kennedy came to the high school. And there was a booking officer. Older man. I don't know his name."

"Oh. Green. He's not a bad guy. Did they ask if you had an attorney?"

"No."

"No?" Trustman looked surprised. "Maybe they thought they were getting in on the ground floor, catching you off guard. In that case, though, I'm surprised they didn't try to interview you first, instead of going straight to an arrest. Oh well. They have their ways. Their reasons. So," Trustman looked up expectantly, "you did your homework?"

"Yes. But we need to talk about Collins first. About what he said. What he did."

"You said you didn't tell him anything."

"I said I *tried* not to tell him anything." She hated how pathetic she sounded, the shudder that announced she was close to tears.

"Sorry. I rushed right through that, didn't I?"

"You see, they did try to interview me. I did pretty well, I think. But Collins had these things. Things he said he'd gotten from Evan."

"What things?"

"Underwear. A bra and panties. Black lace."

"You think they're yours?"

"Not for certain. But some of mine are missing, and these look the same."

"How would Evan Palmer have gotten them?"

"I don't know. He must have been in my house, but I have no idea when, or how. And a condom. Like the ones we use. Like ones they'll find if they search my husband's bedside table." She pressed her fists against her stomach. "Are they going to search my house?"

Trustman clicked her pen. "We'll talk about that. Was the condom a common brand?"

Alexis nodded. "But it's the third thing that's really got me stumped. It's a note that begins "Dear Evan" and is signed "Alexis" and thanks him for a special time. In what looks like my handwriting."

"The kind of note that looks like you and he—?"

She nodded again. What could she say?

"So, how do you explain it?"

"I can't. I've never written anything to Evan except notes on his English papers." She stared helplessly at her lawyer.

"All right." Trustman sighed. "There's always an explanation. Maybe he forged it. Let's get on to your homework."

Alexis pulled out the notes she'd made over the weekend, and passed them across the desk. But she had more to say. "Look, something really strange is going on here. Creepy, skin-crawling, watch-your-back strange. Not that getting arrested isn't strange enough, or that the accusations themselves aren't horrible, but it's what Evan is telling them. What he knows. About my house. About our relationship, Micah's and mine. About my personal things."

"What do you mean?"

146

The pain in her wrists was a bone-deep ache. She couldn't stop rubbing them, as though if she could erase this pain, she could erase the day. "This morning I was waiting in line at Ollie's... and there was this reporter behind me. Dave Hovarth. He's been following me. The other day when I was running he jumped out and grabbed me, trying to make me talk to him."

"Jumped out and grabbed you? And you didn't call me?" Trustman interrupted. Then her tone softened. "You do understand that I'm here to help you? That's my job."

"I thought I could handle it. I called the police when he followed me home and they sent someone to take a report. Was that wrong?"

"No. That wasn't wrong. That's what I would have told you to do. Look, I'm not trying to make you feel bad. But you're supposed to bother me. I'm your lawyer. I'm supposed to be protecting you."

"No one's protecting me." She started to cry, which made her furious. She grabbed a handful of tissues from the box Trustman pushed across the desk. "I can't stand being helpless, Ms. Trustman. And I don't cry."

"Call me Janice," Trustman said. "If I'd been through what you've been through, I'd cry, too."

Alexis just shook her head.

"I'm not just saying this, Alexis. I know how you feel. I was arrested once. I was humiliated and brutalized. I felt terrified and helpless. It's one reason I became a lawyer. To help other people survive that ordeal. Believe me, I wish I could send you home for a warm bath and a glass of wine. But we can't just sit here and feel sorry for you—we have to work on your defense."

The attorney leaned back in her chair. "Talk to me about what Evan Palmer knows."

"Evan knows things about me that he can't possibly know. He told Hovarth the color and pattern of my sheets. He knows what brand of condoms my husband keeps in his bedside table. He knew my husband was cheating on me before I did."

"Has he ever been in your house? Have you ever had a gathering of students, something he might have slipped away from and snooped around?"

"No."

"These aren't simply good guesses? He couldn't have seen your sheets on the line?" Alexis shook her head. "What about looking in the windows?"

"Our bedroom is on the second floor."

"These aren't things you might have inadvertently told him?"

"The color of my sheets? Of my bedroom rug? About my husband's condoms? Come on. I suppose you think I gave him my underwear, too?"

"Look, I have to ask. Sometimes people talk too frankly. They get carried away and talk inappropriately, even if they don't behave inappropriately."

She felt ravaged. She'd been shaking since she left the courthouse, and neither the sweater nor the tea was helping. Didn't Trustman understand she couldn't do this right now? "I've got to go," she said. "I'm sick. It's been a long, horrible day."

"No." Trustman shook her head. "What you've got to do is work with me on this. You can't run away from it, Alexis. None of this goes away because you feel shaky and sick and it's going to get worse. People will treat you badly. You need to be prepared for that. We need to be prepared. We need to start figuring out what's going on here and how you defend yourself against it."

"No," she said stubbornly. "I have to go."

"Look," Trustman raised her voice, her face fierce, "the first time you were here, I asked what you wanted to get out of this. You said you weren't going to let this boy ruin your life, you wanted to fight. Now things have gotten tough and you want to run and hide. If you hole up at home, feeling sorry for yourself, instead of crafting a defense, you let him get away with this. You let him be in charge. I would have thought this would make you madder. More determined."

She tapped the pen on the desk again, two hard, sharp taps. "This isn't fiction, Alexis, something you assign to your students, the trials and tribulations of some fictional heroine. This is your life, your reality now. People *are* going to stare and talk. Deal with it."

Alexis dropped her head into her hands. "I'm sorry," she said. "You're right. I'm not a quitter. I'm just so humiliated. I feel... I don't know. Broken."

"Which is exactly why they arrested you when and how they did. They want you scared and humiliated. On edge and doubting yourself. It's happening, it's going to keep on happening, and it's very serious. We don't want to let them win, do we?"

Alexis shook her head.

"Now, tell me about Evan."

"He's lived here for two years. He's a junior. Good soccer and lacrosse player. It's a single-parent family. He lives with his mother, who is a hateful woman. He's never mentioned his father. He says he was abused by an uncle when he was very young. That's about all I know... except that he scares me."

"Scares you how?"

"His intensity, and the abnormal quality of his behavior. It's frightening. There's both scary obsession and cold calculation in his need to punish me, in the lengths he'll go to. Like getting his way is irrationally important."

"Has he ever done anything overtly violent, to you or anyone else, that you know of?"

"Grabbing me hard enough to leave bruises, and that thing with his car blocking my path. I call that overt violence. I heard he's been abusive toward his girlfriend, Carrie. But I'm sure she'd deny it."

"What else should I know?"

"What he said when I finally got through to him that there wouldn't be a relationship. He said I'd be sorry, he'd make me so sorry. And then..." She had to force the next words out. "He said he *was* going to have me. That we would be together. On his terms."

"Were there witnesses when he threatened you?"

"There were students watching, but I don't know if they heard anything."

Trustman looked down at the list of Alexis's contacts with Evan. "I'm going to make you a copy of this so we're both working from the same list. Go back over it, see if you can add the names of people who might have been present at these times, these places. Witnesses for your version of things. Part of my job will be to find out what he's said to the police. What his story is."

The lawyer took her quickly through the hearing process with Dr. Huston, said she'd review the tape. Made her list the people who would be on her side, her support team, the people who'd be against her, people she'd pissed off. Like the deadheads. Students who felt she'd been unfair. "It's just as important to know who your enemies are," Trustman said. "Got a pen and some paper? Good. Let's start thinking about the details. Have you ever been involved in an incident with a student before?"

"Verbal passes, but nothing like this."

"Ever had a situation where the student didn't understand and respect your saying no?"

Alexis shook her head.

"What kind of training were you given to handle situations like this?"

"Little to none. The school has a policy, but they don't do any training or workshops. And back in college... all they did was warn us."

"Are there any skeletons in your closet that are going to come out? Youthful arrests of any kind? Drugs or alcohol? Gossip or scandal? Anything of a sexual nature?"

When Alexis didn't answer, Trustman said, "We all like to think our private lives are just that—private. But in a case like this, if there's anything someone besides you knows, the police are likely to find it. When you're under suspicion, especially when the alleged wrong is of a sexual nature, they'll be particularly interested in invading your privacy. Better I should know, so I can be prepared."

Alexis looked up from studying her wrists. "I hate this."

"Love it, hate it, you've got no choice. What is it?"

"My husband. Micah. He was my professor. We had an affair. I didn't know he was married at the time. He lied to me. But that could be taken the wrong way. People could say, she gets seduced when she's a student, now she goes and seduces a student herself."

"They might. We haven't talked about your husband yet. Will he be supportive?"

She wanted her lawyer to see her as a strong woman, and here were those goddamned tears again. "I just found out he's doing it again. Having an affair with one of his students. This is the second time since we've been married."

The pain of this admission spiked like a dentist's drill hitting a nerve. "I just found out," she repeated, "and yet, Evan already knew my husband is being unfaithful. He said something about Micah not giving me what I need. He must have been spying on us. Following Micah."

Could Trustman understand how threatened she felt? "I can see how this reads," Alexis continued. "Husband gets it on with a student. Wife, in retaliation, gets in on with one of her students. The difference? Her student is only sixteen. Fifteen when it begins." She sat with that a minute, then exploded, "How can anyone believe such bullshit? Who on earth would be interested in sex with a fifteen-year-old? Who, in their right mind, would ever be interested in having sex again?"

Her lawyer ignored that. "You aren't going to like this, but I want to arrange a private polygraph test. Out of state. Something we do for our own information and peace of mind. Lie detector," she explained, seeing Alexis's confusion.

"That means you don't believe me? That you believe I could have...?" Her stomach had never hurt this much before. A bizarre thought popped into her mind. Was this a test of her dexterity—could she rub her stomach and her wrists at the same time? Resigned, she said, "If you think it's necessary."

"I do. And we should consider a private detective—I know a good one—to investigate Evan's background. What happened before he moved to Crawford Valley. Where he used to live. Things he's done since he's lived here. Anything helpful he may have said or done. I've got to be straight with you, Alexis. Fair or unfair, it doesn't matter. This will be expensive. It's not cheap to mount a defense to something like this. We haven't talked about a retainer, but I'll need one. Two thousand dollars, for starters."

For starters. She had about a thousand in savings, close to a thousand more in checking. She could probably borrow on the house but that would take time. At least she didn't need Micah to agree. Her mother had given them the down payment, and not trusting Micah, had insisted the house be in Alexis's name. She hated it when her mother was right. She could get a credit card advance. Over time, her salary would be adequate. Her needs were modest. And she could teach summer school. Assuming she was allowed to teach.

"What about my job? When they tried to get me to take a voluntary leave, I said I needed to know the procedures for an involuntary leave. Now I don't know what they can do."

"A voluntary leave might be better, at this point, since you could craft the terms. We can probably negotiate a leave with pay."

"Can we still do that? Huston did offer a paid leave. But that was before—"

"Let me talk with the administration and get back to you. One last question. Have you ever felt as if you were being watched? Ever wondered if someone had been in your house?"

"Someone *was* in our house. Last week." Alexis described coming home and finding the ladder and the mess in the storage space. "Because of what he's been saying, I wondered if it might have been Evan, but his car was in the lot when I left school."

"Ask around, see if anyone actually saw him at school that day. Or get someone to do that for you. One of your fellow teachers. Were things missing? Moved? Was this the only time?"

"Whoever it was didn't get into the house, only into the storage space over the garage. Moved boxes, spilled things. Old high school and college stuff. No way to tell if things were taken."

"What did you do?"

"What anyone would. Called the police. Collins came. He and my husband took down the ladder and put it in the garage."

The lawyer made a note. "Is this the only time you've suspected someone might have been in the house?"

It wasn't. "Sometimes I had the creepy feeling things were moved. But nothing much ever seemed to be missing. Just little things I might have misplaced. Like that lingerie." She described a time she thought she smelled aftershave. "I decided I was being paranoid. Now I'm flat-out scared."

"Got friends you can talk to who won't be intimidated by the accusation against you? Your arrest?"

Alexis nodded.

"Keep in touch with them. Use them. You need support right now. You have a cell phone?"

Alexis nodded again.

"Keep it charged and always keep it with you."

Trustman flipped the pages on her legal pad and stared across the desk. "The police are going to want another interview. I know I said you could talk with Dr. Huston without me. I don't want you doing that with the police. If they ask to interview you again, tell them you'll be glad to cooperate but only with your lawyer present. They might try to wiggle around that. Don't let them. Even if they threaten to arrest you again. They can't question you without me there."

"All right." Alexis pulled out her checkbook. "I can give you five hundred today and another thousand tomorrow."

"That's fine."

Alexis wrote the check, her writing shaky, and passed it across the desk.

Trustman wrote something and handed her a card. "My cell number. Don't be afraid to call if something happens or if you need an answer right away. I try to keep my work life nine to five, but I don't want you unprotected. If Collins shows up on your doorstep, you don't have to talk to him, no matter how intimidating he is, no matter what he says. He shows up, you call me. And call me if he shows up to search your house. Okay? And meanwhile, you might want to do a little vetting."

"Vetting?"

"Getting rid of things in the house you wouldn't want them to find."

Alexis put the card in her pocket and listened to a brief explanation of what would happen next. Trustman thought they might have a few days' grace before the next act. "What about work?"

"Unless you hear otherwise, you go to work, hard as that may be. Remember, you're innocent."

"Try telling them that," Alexis said grimly. "What about reporters?

Hovarth's been dogging me, and you saw the reporters at the courthouse. What do I do if they're outside my house?"

"You have a garage?"

Alexis nodded.

"Drive into your garage, close the door, and go straight inside. If they're blocking your way into the garage, or into your house, call the police. Being accused of a crime doesn't suspend your rights as a citizen. The police have to help you. If you have any trouble, call me. If Hovarth bothers you again, we can get a restraining order. Remember what I told you the other day. You don't deserve this. Don't let anyone treat you like you do. Don't treat yourself like you do."

"That's really hard to believe after today."

"That's why they do it."

Alexis shook her head. "They think I'm evil."

"Are you evil?"

"I don't know. I…"

"Alexis Jordan!" Trustman snapped. "Don't you dare go whiny and pathetic on me. It takes guts to defend yourself against something like this. You can't do it if you start doubting yourself, if you start thinking you must be bad because someone says you are. You've got guts and you know it."

She appreciated the pep talk, even if she couldn't respond with much pep. She felt like she'd swallowed a gallon of acid and her guts were on fire. She needed time and privacy to recover. Still, she straightened her shoulders and lifted her head. "Thank you. I'll do my best."

She was tempted to salute smartly and march out of the room but Trustman wouldn't appreciate the irony. She held her head high until she was alone in the privacy of the restroom.

She did not turn on the light but stood for a moment in the darkness. The way things were going, she was likely to be spending a lot of time in darkness. Metaphorical darkness, at least. Goddamn Evan Palmer. Goddamn him. *God damn him!*

"A dismal universal hiss, the sound
Of public scorn."
—John Milton, *Paradise Lost*: Book X

CHAPTER EIGHTEEN

From the end of her street, Alexis spotted two news vans parked at her house. She couldn't face that right now. She snapped off her turn signal and drove on, disappointment weighing her down. She was wounded and scared and longed to be at home. The word "home" had connotations of all the things she needed—warmth, safety, healing, privacy. But not when that home was under siege.

A few blocks away she pulled over and called to warn Micah. No answer in his office, at home, or on his cell, so she left messages. He'd be furious when—if—he came home but she'd done all she could except call his fluttery-voiced bimbo. Even if sending messages via telepathy worked, he wouldn't receive them. They weren't tuned to the same frequency.

She liked to think of herself as a strong woman, someone who'd left the pernicious influence of her narcissistic mother behind, but in these last two weeks, she'd become a wreck. A knot of barbed wire now resided in her stomach. The muscles in her neck and shoulders were taut as piano strings. She could go to a friend's—Lori's or Claire's, but that would mean conversation. What she needed now was solitude.

She drove aimlessly until her gas gauge neared empty, then filled the tank and went inside to pay. On the counter, the bold black headline of the *Crawford Journal* jumped at her: **High School in Uproar over Alleged Seduction**. With unsteady hands, she signed the credit slip and bought the paper.

Back in the Jeep, her eye was drawn to the photo.

They'd used a picture of her taken last May at the Crawford 5K road race. A cancer benefit run on a hot day. Wearing brief shorts and a running bra top, showing strong arms, strong abs, strong legs, smiling proudly, and holding up her medal for the camera. Sweaty and triumphant. Dressed not to look attractive but to move. Out of context and juxtaposed with the word "seduction," what was striking about this image was not her strength or her achievement at having run a great race, but how naked she looked.

She didn't need the byline to know it was Hovarth's doing. She slumped over the wheel, staring glumly at the picture, until a sharp horn blast reminded her someone wanted the pump. She started driving again. Random streets, random neighborhoods, random towns. Everything rushing past her in a blur until her need for a restroom forced her to pull off at an unfamiliar diner. It looked quiet and homey. Simple cars, compacts, and workmen's trucks, not the Crawford crowd's high-end SUVs.

She picked a booth toward the back and opened a menu with as many colorful pages as a little Golden Book. Everything looked delicious. She'd order, then hit the restroom.

She ordered the cheeseburger club special, medium, with fries, no onions. And a chocolate milkshake. Comfort food. Meat and chocolate. Cushy bun. Potatoes, grease, and salt. A dangerous combo, given the state of her stomach. But she needed it.

She stared, unseeing, out the window, limp as a wrung-out dishrag. Unexpectedly, her phone rang. She rarely used it. She wasn't one of those omnipresent phonophiles, glued to their instruments, loudly polluting every public place with their inane chatter, texting, and apps.

She stared at it, warily, then said a tentative "Hello?"

"Alexis! Where the hell are you?"

Not how she'd hoped to discuss this day with Micah. "In a diner somewhere. I don't know." She looked down at her place mat. "Eldon."

"What the hell are you doing in Eldon? Do you have any idea what I'm going through? Our house is surrounded by news vans. The phone keeps ringing. People are knocking on the door and ringing the bell. What am I supposed to do?"

Like she'd staged this to annoy him. Hot tears filled her eyes. In Micah's view, her getting arrested and heaped with shame and ignominy was one more inconvenience for him. The marks on her wrists and the welts on her soul didn't matter.

"Ignore them?" she suggested. "After a while, they'll give up and go away. I did leave messages to warn you. If they block your way or come on the property, my lawyer says to call the police."

"Oh, sure, Lex. The same police who arrested you are going to come and help me out?"

She heard something crash. Maybe a kitchen chair. He didn't mind damaging things he didn't care about and he'd never liked those chairs. A motley second-hand collection she had sanded, primed and painted blue and yellow and soft green to match the wallpaper.

So he knew about the arrest. She supposed the reporters would have waved it in his face. But he didn't offer a word of support or ask how she was doing. For richer, for poorer, in sickness and in health. But not in shame or suffering. Micah hated to be embarrassed. She was so habituated to his scorn, she almost apologized. "*You* weren't arrested," she said, lowering her voice so others couldn't hear. "Even if I'm a pariah, your situation hasn't changed."

"Of course, it's changed," he exploded. "We've got the same name. Everyone knows you're my wife." In a softer voice, he asked, "When are you coming home?"

"As soon as I've had something to eat. Or maybe I should wait until they've gone. I'm not up to facing them again. Could you call me when they've gone?"

"I don't think so." The softness was gone. Maybe she'd only imagined it. "I'm going out myself. There's nothing here to eat."

Nothing except several kinds of leftovers and a freezer filled with his favorite things. Nothing to eat that wouldn't require Prince Micah, who preferred to be waited on, to carry it to the microwave. She realized she couldn't face returning to an empty house. Humiliating herself, she said, "Micah, I need you. I'm so miserable. Please be there when I get home."

"You should have thought of that before you went out to dinner by yourself."

Like she was just larking about. "I was terribly upset," she said. "I'd been arrested, dragged out of school in handcuffs, and stuck in a jail cell. Then I had to go to court and then I had to see my lawyer. And then I saw that headline in the paper. That picture. And I spotted those vultures all around the house. Since then, I've just been driving randomly. Until I got so hungry…"

She broke off. "Can't you think of how this is for me?"

"We can talk tomorrow," he said. "Meet for lunch. Maybe that fish place at the Mall."

"Tomorrow I'll be at work."

He snorted derisively. "You don't seriously think you're not fired after this?"

"I didn't do anything wrong," she said.

"Maybe. But while all that's working itself out, they'll want to protect those high school kids from exposure to someone as dangerous as you."

It was a nasty thing to say, but she was stuck on his first word. "Maybe? What do you mean, maybe? You know I'm innocent."

The only answer on his end was a chair spinning across the floor.

She had the uncomfortable sense people were listening. She lowered her voice. "Micah? You *do* know I'm innocent?"

No response.

"Please don't break those chairs. I spent a lot of time on them."

She didn't want to talk about chairs. "I need advice, Micah. I need to know what to do."

"You could get a gun and shoot the little bastard." Then, "Alexis, I'm sorry, but I can't stand this."

"Micah, please be there when I get home. I need your help." She hated herself for begging. "Don't our years together mean a thing? You're throwing that away because some crazy high school boy developed an obsession and is getting even with me for rejecting him?"

"All right. All right." Petulant but sincere. "Eat your dinner and come home. I'll wait."

She ended the call and glanced around to see if anyone was staring. No one was. She went to the restroom and returned to find the burger had arrived. Hot, delicious and meaty. She lifted the bun and poured on ketchup, hoping to appease the tiger by feeding it. Slowly, she raised it to her mouth and bit. Perfectly pink on the inside. Grill-crisped on the outside. Something so fundamental about burgers and chocolate milkshakes. So American. So illicitly satisfying. She gobbled the first half and drank the milkshake.

She was dipping a fry in ketchup when she sensed movement behind her and Hovarth slid into her booth. "You can run," he said, setting a pad and pencil on the table, "but you can't hide."

She wanted to scream at him. Stab him with her knife. But he'd put it in the paper. "Mr. Hovarth, I want to be alone."

"That's not what I hear... unless you mean alone with young boys."

She looked around the room, hoping to find someone who could help, or to see her waitress to get a check. Saw a room full of strangers bent over their food. The waitress had disappeared. "Please leave," she said. "I don't want to talk to you."

"Evan says you loved having him go down on you because it's something your husband won't do. Did it give you a feeling of power, having a teenage sex slave to do your bidding?"

"You have a filthy mind, Mr. Hovarth. Perhaps Evan does, too. But that doesn't have anything to do with me. Now will you please leave?" She looked longingly at the rest of her burger.

"It amazes me that after being arrested for such a serious crime, you can still eat," he said. "But that's what they say about the guilty, isn't it? Only the innocent are nervous."

Still no sign of her waitress, or any server she might flag down. Maybe Hovarth bribed them to stay in the kitchen. That didn't mean she had to listen to his garbage. She'd wait at the register. If no one came to bring her a check, she'd go into the kitchen and ask for one.

She slid out of the booth, leaving the rest of her food untouched.

"He says you like to lie on your stomach with a pillow under your hips and be taken from behind. But he didn't tell me, Alexis," he paused insinuatingly on her name, as if he knew she hated people using her first name when they hadn't been invited to, "whether you like it the normal way or prefer taking him in the ass?" He raised his eyebrows, smirking, and waited.

She stood and tried to move past him. His hand shot out and grabbed her arm.

"Let go of me, Mr. Hovarth," she said, raising her voice, aware of people staring.

She seized the full glass of ice water from the table and dumped it in his lap. The second his grip slackened, she jerked free and stormed down the aisle. By the time she got to the register, an employee was there. "That man," she said, pointing at Hovarth, "sat down in my booth uninvited and refused to leave. Then he grabbed me and tried to force me to stay with him. His language is filthy. I would like to pay my check and leave."

The employee held out his hand. "Give me your check."

"The waitress didn't bring it yet."

"I'll get it." He disappeared into the kitchen and the door swung shut behind him.

Hovarth caught up with her, his face contorted with rage. "You're going to be sorry you did that, you castrating bitch."

The whole diner was now their audience. She was at the limits of her self-control, but she wasn't giving this hateful prick the satisfaction of tears. She raised her voice. "If you've been castrated by a glass of water, Mr. Hovarth, you must have been in pathetic shape to begin with. I should think a wordsmith like yourself could be a tad less clichéd. It really is tiresome the way some men, when they don't get their way, fall back on the tritest forms of criticism. Am I supposed to cower because you're an aggressive bully? Are your false, ugly insinuations supposed to move me to grant you an interview?"

She turned her back on him, staring stoically at the kitchen door. Where was her check? She couldn't imagine what could be happening in there to prolong this horror show.

Beside her, Hovarth said loudly, "I guess I just have a lot of trouble figuring out what kind of a woman seduces a fifteen-year-old boy."

She wanted to put her hands over her ears to drown out his vile words. It took incredible effort to keep her head turned away from him, her hands by her sides, and continue to look indifferent. The diner had gone silent, all ears bent to hear what he'd say next.

Hovarth played to his audience. "What was the attraction?" he continued. "You're a pretty woman. You could have any man you want. So why a boy? Why that boy?"

Was this how things would be? People not only staring at her and speculating in their minds, but openly accusing her of horrible acts and asking pointed questions about them? Not just the police but complete strangers? She heard Dan Morgan's quiet voice, warning her. Everything tainted. Maggie had to shop in the next town. In the end, they'd had to leave. She'd barely listened. Maybe such hostility was impossible to imagine until it happened. She looked down at a floor blurred by tears that wouldn't blink away.

Where was that man? Her waitress? Anyone? She couldn't leave without paying, that would compound her sins. Beside her, Hovarth heaped ugliness on ugliness, the words rasping like sandpaper over her wilting spirit.

Behind her, a man's voice addressed Hovarth, asking him to stop spewing filthy language in a family restaurant. Then the man addressed her by name. "Alexis, is this man bothering you?"

She looked around. Peter Everett. "Oh. Peter... yes. Yes. He is bothering me. He's crucifying me."

"Go outside and wait for me." Moving, as he spoke, so the vast wall of his body stood between her and Hovarth.

"Oh. Oh my God. Thank you." She shoved several bills in his hand. "For my check. They're supposed to be getting it." She pointed at the kitchen door, then sprinted for the exit.

She got to the Jeep so grateful for being rescued. Intending to speak to Peter. But Hovarth would come after her, make something vulgar out of Peter's rescue. And all those people were watching, no doubt, from the window.

Peter Everett came down the steps before she got the Jeep into gear, coming up to her, his face hard and angry. "I'm so sorry about that, Alexis. I..."

Hovarth paused at the door of the diner, camera in hand.

She had to get out of here.

"Peter. Thank you. But I'm sorry, I can't stay. You heard him in there?" Everett nodded. "I'm, it's been... today. So horrible. And he's got a camera." Tears she'd tried to suppress poured down her face. She squeezed his hand. "Another time, when I'm not so broken."

He looked tragic. But the last thing she needed was to linger here, talking with Peter, while Hovarth watched.

"I got arrested," she said, shoving the paper at him. "I didn't do this. I'm sorry."

Hovarth was raising his camera.

"I've got to go before he can do more harm."

She slammed into gear and peeled out of the lot.

"Meanwhile, as Nature wills, night bids us rest."
—John Milton, *Paradise Lost*: Book IV

CHAPTER NINETEEN

Perhaps, like Frost's character, she would become one acquainted with the night. In the dark, sitting here in her car, in the park where she ran every day, no one could see her tears or read the fear on her face. No one would see her shoulders drooping, or the bowing of her head. Listening to the night sounds, she was acutely aware of how easily the familiar became alien. So many years of doing the same things every day. Tomorrow would be different. It would take all her will power to get herself to work. Once she arrived, she was afraid to speculate on what would happen.

The voice in one part of her head snapped, "Oh, get over yourself," while another soothed that it was all right to feel hurt and afraid, that her hurt and fear were genuine. The first voice was her mother's voice, perfect in intonation and inflection. Alexis had been told to get over herself as long as she'd had feelings.

Her mother. Elsa Stewart Levine. Gordon Stewart, her father, had left. David Levine, her stepfather, had died. One paid liberally for his freedom. The other unable to take it with him.

She couldn't put it off. She had to call her mother. She needed money and money— however much the woman claimed poverty—was something her mother had plenty of. Alexis might as well compound the awfulness of this day by making the call. It was just before nine. Prime time for pouring salt in wounds.

She dug out her phone and dialed, waiting, muscles tensed. Three rings and her mother barked a sharp hello.

"Mother? It's Alexis."

"I hope you're calling to tell me I'm finally going to have a grandchild."

"I… we're… Well, no. Actually, it's not a very good time for that." Reduced by one sentence to a stammering idiot. She sucked in a breath. "I'm in a bit of a jam right now. I need some money."

"Oh, honey…" Her mother's voice was laden with sighs and reproaches. "What's the matter? Has that husband of yours gone and gotten himself into some legal pickle? Or is it just overspending? You know I've told you to keep him on a budget. It's always been clear to me that he can't hang on to a cent. Caviar tastes on a beer budget, that's Micah."

"It's not Micah. Well, it is a little, but this is really about… It's me."

"I can't believe that. You've always been so cautious with money. I give you a check to buy yourself something and you put it in the bank. You may not be ambitious, but at least you're thrifty. Did I tell you that I'm taking a trip to Europe in June? It's one of those cruises where all the rooms have balconies. I'll see ten cities and only unpack once. It sounds heavenly. My friend Lou and I are going. I told you about Louise, didn't I? Another lonely old widow like me."

Alexis *was* thrifty. She'd been saving for a baby, for being able to stop work for a while when a baby came. For the baby they were supposedly trying to have. It was like building sandcastles. Micah spent it as fast as she saved it. Probably a moot point, now.

"Mother, it's not about money. My problem, I mean. That is, I do need some money, but we're not having money troubles."

"That makes no sense, Alexis. If you need money, you are having money troubles, aren't you?" Her mother sighed. "I'm a little short right now, having to pay for the trip and all." The sound of a refrigerator opening and closing and the snap of a pop-top. Her mother drank five or six cans of Diet Coke a day. "What kind of trouble?"

"Legal trouble. I've been falsely accused. One of my students is claiming that I—" Just spit it out. It wouldn't get any easier to say. "He told his mother and the administration that I seduced him. That we've been having an affair."

"Oh." Her mother was silent for a moment. "Well, that's ridiculous.

Anyone who knows you knows you're far too serious about your job. I'm sure it will all blow over. Teenagers are so mercurial. So unstable. I remember how difficult you were. So damned secretive. Yes. It will all blow over. You'll see." Fingernails tapped against the metal can. "Now, what is it you need money for? You think if you buy yourself something nice, you'll feel better?"

"You're right about the accusation being ridiculous. But such a claim against any teacher is serious. I need money for a lawyer. And a private investigator. To defend myself."

"Oh, you don't need all that. Just explain to them that you didn't do it. I'm sure they'll understand. God knows you've worked for them long enough. Killing yourself at that dead-end job. They ought to know you by now. Maybe it's time to get out of there anyway. Maybe this is just a sign, Alexis. A blessing in disguise. Go back to school, get your MBA, and be a broker or something. That's where the money is. Think how much fun I'd have, introducing you as my daughter the broker. Lou's daughter Gail earned in the high six figures last year. Sure beats a teacher's salary. But of course, she has her MBA from Harvard. And Shirley's daughter, Anne, is making pots of money, being a realtor. Did you ever consider that?"

Her throat tightened. She was twelve years old again, trying to ask for her first bra. So awkward and embarrassing. Her mother wouldn't listen. Too busy for a trip to the mall, not interested in clothing a child who was fast becoming an attractive female, a threat to her own attractiveness. A child who outgrew her clothes too fast, it really was inconsiderate. Eventually, Alexis had given up and used her babysitting money. Gone with a friend. Then her mother had walked into her room, caught her wearing it—a cheap bra a size too small—and made fun of her.

"I was arrested today, charged with indecent assault and statutory rape. My lawyer needs a retainer and then there's the private investigator."

The fingernails drummed. Her mother sighed. "Why honey, you're serious, aren't you?"

No, Mom. I'm begging for money because I was bored with correcting papers and wanted to spice up the evening. Micah and I were having sex on the living room floor and as a lark, he suggested I call you and ask for

165

money. I saw these jewels in a store today. "Of course I'm serious. I'm in real trouble and I don't have any money and a good lawyer is critical in a case like this."

A brief silence on her mother's end. "Well, as I said, I'm a little short right now. I had to pay for the whole trip up front, you see. I saved almost a thousand dollars that way." A sigh. "How much do you need?"

Alexis understood this part. Her mother needed to feel important. Lady Bountiful. She needed Alexis to appreciate the extent of her sacrifice. How great a trial it was to have such an unsuccessful daughter. Nothing to brag to her friends about. The enormous inconvenience of having to write a check and carry it to the post office. The troubles involved in balancing a diminishing checking account. Especially when the expense involved an ungrateful daughter who wouldn't even produce a suitable grandchild whose pictures could be passed around at the pool.

She needed two thousand at this time, preferred the cushion of three. So to give her mother some nickel-and-diming room—the woman wasn't happy unless she thought she'd gotten a bargain—she had to ask for more. "I need five thousand dollars."

"Good Lord, Alexis. Have you gotten the most expensive lawyer in town?"

Her mother was one of those snobs who believed expensive was better, even if she did pride herself on being thrifty. "Yes, mother. I got the meanest, toughest, most experienced criminal lawyer I could find. And it will cost more. But I couldn't afford to look for a bargain. My future is at stake. Something like this, I could be sent to prison."

"Well, I'm glad to see that for once you're using your common sense, Alexis."

Her mother agreed with Micah about the painted chairs, about her rehabilitated thrift-store finds. Her mother's version of thrift was a Bloomingdale's sale. There was a rustling and the sound of a drawer being opened. Her mother flipping through a checkbook. "Five's a little much right now. I'll send you a check for four tomorrow and the rest next week. I'm sure your lawyer will understand if you give him this now and say the rest is coming."

Alexis felt the surprising heat and wet of tears on her cold cheeks. It was icy in the car without the engine on. She didn't correct her mother and say the lawyer was a woman. Her mother would have immediately assumed a female lawyer deserved a smaller retainer. Though her mother despised men and always treated them badly, she was conventional in expecting them to run the world, so long as they didn't run hers. A pretty woman with a heart of stone. For some reason, men found the combination irresistible.

"Thank you," Alexis said, trying to keep the tears from her voice. In her mother's book, emotion represented a lack of self-control. "Not having to worry about money will make it possible to focus on my defense."

"I should hope so. Tell your lawyer that since I'm paying, I'll expect to receive itemized bills. You have to watch them, Alexis, even the best of them. They'll bill you for time they spend on someone else's business. You've always been so unworldly. You've never understood about these things. But lawyers are society's biggest bloodsuckers."

David Levine, the second husband, had been an attorney. A gentle man, balding, stooped, peering at the world through slipping glasses, who had surrounded her mother with a downy cushion of cash. Alexis suspected her mother had nagged him about money until he'd taken refuge in the grave, the only place he could go where his wife's grating voice wouldn't find him. Alexis had been sorry when he died and cried hard tears. He had always been kind to her.

The drawer opened and closed again. "It seems like an awful lot of money. Defending you ought to be a romp in the park. It's not like you're the type to do something like this. Too much like your father. The dour Scot. You have his low thirst for living."

Rescue me, then give me a few whacks to be sure I know my place. Would her mother like her better if she engaged in bold things like seducing teenage boys? She'd long doubted anything she did would please her mother. Not even produce that much-desired grandchild. Its sex would be wrong. It wouldn't be adorable enough. It would have the wrong birthday, conflicting with tours and spa specials. And fail to be devoted to a cold grandmother whose idea of a relationship was to be adored.

167

"Maybe we could take a trip together," her mother was saying. "A girl thing. The two of us. I heard of a great spa in Mexico."

"By the time this is over, I'll need a spa," she said. If she wasn't in prison. Or working three jobs to pay her mother back. Or a cold day in hell unexpectedly arrived. She couldn't imagine anything less pleasant than vacationing with her mother, being told hourly, if not oftener, what a dismal failure she was, and the few simple steps she needed to take to shape up. She'd taken so many simple steps in her life with nothing to show for any of it but a bruised psyche and worn-out mental shoes.

"Honey, it's great talking to you, but my favorite program is starting in a few minutes. So, don't forget. Make your lawyer send me statements." And a click.

She was two for two, wasn't she? Micah and her mother, arguably the two people in the world who should be closest to her, hadn't asked how she was doing or offered any comfort or consolation. She must be some big dummy if she still had any expectations of being cared about after growing up in such a critical, loveless environment and choosing to continue to live in one. A big dummy and a slow learner. Or was she just asking too much? Micah said he'd wait for her to come home and make his supper. Her mother was sending a check.

Longing for a friendly voice, she called Lori but Ned answered and said Lori was busy with the baby. He didn't give her time to leave a message. Just hung up. She could have tried Claire but she was out of the energy for tries.

Sadness overwhelmed her. She bent over the steering wheel in her cold, dark car, tears running between her fingers and down her arms. She cried until her eyes ached and her chest and stomach were sore from sobbing. Fumbling tissues from the box she'd put on the seat beside her until she was surrounded by masses of crumpled white balls like tiny grief clouds.

She was reaching for the key when a police car, lights flashing, pulled in behind her. The officer got out. Not one she'd encountered earlier today, thank goodness. She dropped her hand and waited, rigid with fear, watching in her mirror as he went to the rear of her car and reached down. Then, holding something in his hand, he came up to her window.

The illumination from his flashlight gave his face a horror-film eeriness. She couldn't remember how to breathe.

He bent low, studying her. "Excuse me, ma'am. Are you all right?"

There was no denying the evidence of her puffy face, her red eyes, and the wads of tissue. "Just having a good cry, Officer." She barely kept herself from adding, "Is that a problem?" Her eyes fixed on her bruised wrists, a reminder that it would be unwise to do anything that could cause him to bring out handcuffs.

"Were you aware of this?" He handed her a square of cardboard, a pretty good imitation of a Massachusetts license plate. Her car had a vanity plate, a long-ago gift from Micah, that said, "TEACH." In its place, someone had affixed a cardboard one which read, "SCREW."

"I'm afraid not." Gingerly, she set it on the seat beside her. "It wasn't there this morning." She shrugged. "How often do people look at their license plates?"

"You're right about that," he said. "But you might want to start keeping an eye on things. Looks like someone's playing tricks on you."

Dirty tricks. "Thanks for bringing it to my attention." She started the engine. "Guess I'll head on home." It was time. The press might be gone. And Micah was waiting.

The officer's look was concerned. "Is that going to be okay?" His eyes dropped to the mock license plate. "This isn't some kind of threat?"

Oxygen began to flow again. A policeman who'd actually stopped to see if she was all right, seemed genuinely concerned that her home be a safe place to go to. She didn't know. Her home might still be surrounded by the ravening beasts of the press, but that wasn't his worry. She'd like to preserve this moment intact. A moment when the police were friends, not enemies. "Home is fine, thanks. I'm a teacher," she said. "That's probably some student prank. But I appreciate your concern."

"You take care." He stepped away from the car and snapped off his light. Alexis put the Jeep in gear.

The hungry beasts were still milling around. She parked on the next street and grabbed her bag, weaving her way between the houses to her backyard. As she slipped through the bushes between her yard and the next, she thought she heard someone moving. She froze. Were the press back here, too? Would they dare be that brazen?

Still as a statue, she held her breath and listened. She didn't hear anything. As her eyes adjusted to the dark, she couldn't see anything either. Still, she had the creepy feeling that someone was there.

She let herself in the back door, glad to see the shades drawn. The kitchen was dark except for a light over the stove. Automatically, she righted the two fallen chairs and swept some dirty dishes into the sink. She slipped through the dark living room and climbed the stairs, so glad to be home, so eager to be lying down.

"Oh, God, Micah, I can't believe they're still here," she said as she dropped her heavy bag by the bedroom door.

But Micah wasn't there. She went through the rest of the upstairs, then downstairs, looking through all the rooms, hoping to find him napping on the couch or snoozing in a chair. It was almost ten-thirty. Finally, because confirmation was different from knowing, she checked the garage. His car was gone.

What a hopelessly trusting fool she was. Trusting a kid to be a kid, a husband to be a husband. Heaviness returned to her chest as pain bloomed in her gut.

She pushed away thoughts she didn't have the energy for, turned off the stove light, and headed for the stairs. Someone banged on the front door and called her name. Across the room, the answering machine, a demented red eye in the darkness, blinked wildly.

She pressed the button. Messages from reporters, offering her the opportunity to tell her side. What was her side? That she was the true victim? That she'd been wrongly arrested, her car and her person battered? That she was being harassed by another reporter, one of their own? Would it help to choose one of the callers and get her own story out? But no. Her lawyer would kill her.

She let the strangers' voices pour over her, deleting them as she listened. What was she hoping for? Someone offering consolation? Fat chance of that. She was about to press stop when she heard Dan Morgan's voice. "Lex? I've called a dozen times and gotten the machine. I wasn't going to leave a message, but then I thought about what must be on here. Who has been calling you and I wanted to leave something good for you. You're probably feeling awfully alone and discouraged right now. Remember. You aren't alone. I know you're innocent and Maggie and I are here for you. Plenty of other teachers support you. So square those shoulders and keep your head up. Here's Maggie."

Alexis sat on her kitchen floor, leaning against the cupboard, as Maggie Morgan's soft voice filled the darkness. Maggie's message closed with what sounded like a biblical quotation. *"Now therefore keep thy sorrow to thyself and bear with a good courage that which hath befallen thee."* She'd forgotten Maggie was an ordained minister. After a brief silence, Maggie said, "I know it's the hardest thing, Lex. But you have to believe in yourself. Any time you need to, come cry on my shoulder. Because we absolutely know how you feel."

She undressed in the dark, and crawled into bed, floating in the land of crazy dreams. She woke at three, sweating and sickened from a dream world grueling in which Collins queried her on the most intimate details of her sex life.

She looked out her window. At last, the reporters were gone. In half an hour, it would be getting light. Unlikely they'd be back between four and five a.m. She found her running gear by touch and put it on. As she waited for daylight, she stumbled around the house, collecting everything she didn't want the police to find if they searched. She purged computer files, burned old notes, letters, even her sexiest underwear, in the fireplace.

When she was done, she sat back on her heels and faced another ugly fact in her increasingly ugly life. She now knew the source of the filth that Hovarth had spewed at her. The reason her innermost thoughts, her most intimate confessions, were coming back at her from the mouth of a stranger. One of her diaries was missing.

EVAN – SIX

He put the disk in the player, crossed the room, and slid under the covers. He loved violent, sexy movies. A little rape, a lot of violence. The way the women squirmed and begged and became compliant. Not easy to watch movies on weeknights. The Witch was always coming in and lecturing him about wasting his time. When he watched a violent movie, he liked to get naked under the covers, rub himself all over with her panties, and jerk off. These days, the cold metal of the stolen knife against his thigh made it even better.

The near certainty of a visit from The Witch put kind of a damper on his pleasure. Tonight, though, she'd gone out. When she got back, she'd go straight to bed. She always did when she was out late.

He wanted to watch a woman writhe and scream. He wanted to see her degraded and hurt. That's what he planned for Mrs. Jordan. He needed to see her punished for what she'd done to him. Sometimes, before he went to sleep, he'd play over in his mind the things he'd like to do to her, imagining the look on her face, her screams. Once, she had mattered a lot to him. Now he could cheerfully watch her be raped and dismembered— maybe even do it himself—and feel nothing but satisfaction.

The other night, talking to that reporter, Hovarth, he'd felt he was with a kindred spirit. More than anyone, Hovarth seemed to understand what a despicable person his teacher was. When he told the reporter about the times they'd been together, how she'd led him on, seducing him with hopes and expectations, then coldly dumping him, he'd thought the man was going to cry. That had made him feel better.

The police were okay, but they'd been cops, after all. Skeptical. Asking lots of questions to see if he was telling the truth. In the end, when he described her sheets, what was in her bedside tables, and told how she liked to have sex, they'd been convinced. Ha! And Mrs. Jordan thought he wasn't a good actor. He was good enough to fool her into spending all that time alone with him because he was so bad at his lines.

Those had been good times. He'd miss that. Now he saw those times as just another way she'd tricked him. Listening so intently. Pretending to be sympathetic. As if she cared his dad had deserted them and his mother was a witch. As if she understood.

Now she was the one who had to understand—about crossing him, about betrayal. She'd gotten her first taste of it yesterday. The look on her face when the cops put handcuffs on her and dragged her out the door. Pure shock and humiliation. Did she think only she got to humiliate, that it would never come back at her? She'd looked like she was gonna be sick when that big cop put her into the car. It sent him straight to the bathroom to jerk off.

She hadn't looked much better coming home tonight. Creeping through the bushes in the dark, like a thief, to sneak into her own house. Moving so quietly she'd almost tripped over him. That would have been bad. She might've told the cops. Even if they didn't believe her, it would have looked bad, him lurking outside her house.

Yeah. Mrs. Jordan had only had the first of many bad days. Which meant he'd had a pretty good one.

Smiling, he picked up the remote and started the movie.

> "Of an impulsive and passionate nature, she
> had fortified herself to encounter the stings
> and venomous stabs of public contumely..."
> —Nathaniel Hawthorne, *The Scarlet Letter*

CHAPTER TWENTY

She slipped her phone into a pocket, punched up a driving beat, and set out. The birds weren't even up. The world was a place of smudgy purple shadows and streaky sunlight creeping through the trees. The cool air smelled green and fresh. Her stomach didn't hurt. Her back didn't ache. It was heavenly to be so completely physical, so entirely alone. For this brief time, fooling herself that life was good.

If the vultures of the press were back when she finished running, she'd push through without comment. She couldn't go through another day without a run. Running kept her calm and sane, and it was increasingly important to be both. Bad as yesterday was, today could be worse.

She took a different route. Too many people knew the other one. She didn't want to meet Hovarth, or Collins, or Evan. Any one of them might be out there waiting for her.

Last night, she'd had the disturbing feeling she was being watched. It could be paranoia—her situation would make anyone paranoid—but her instincts had always been good. Like her instinct that Micah wouldn't be there when she got home, despite his promises. Or that today, the day after her arrest, would be another hellish day. Everything but the creep in the bushes was obvious. But the creep was scariest.

She got home without being ambushed, pumped with endorphins, and headed for the shower. She picked red satin underwear from the drawer, a set she couldn't bring herself to burn, as ideal for the alleged scarlet woman she was. She stared at her boring clothes in colors dull as dust. Yesterday, she'd gone marching out as herself and had cause to regret it. Today she was back to being queen of the frumps. She wound her hair in a tight chignon and put on a black turtleneck and jumper. Checked the mirror. And took them off again. Looking like the saggy-baggy elephant wouldn't change anyone's mind.

Playing their game all these years hadn't kept her out of this mess. Being good. Being responsible. Being endlessly careful. They thought she was an evil predator anyway. Predatrix?

She grabbed yesterday's black skirt, brushed off some leaves from her creep through the bushes, and put on a black ribbed sweater. Head to toe black. Mourning the death of truth and innocence. Likely the end of her marriage. Possibly the death of her career, though in that arena she'd hardly begun to fight. Only she would know that beneath her mourning lurked a sinful splash of red. Probably they didn't let you have nice underwear in prison.

That flippant thought sent a frisson of uneasiness through her. She'd always tried to face reality and act like a grown-up, but the reality of this situation overwhelmed her. She put on the small gold cross her father, the mostly absent Gordon Stewart, had sent her for her tenth birthday. Protection against vampires and soul suckers. Took a breath as she searched for an incantation against evil. If only the serenity prayer weren't so sappy. She could use some serenity. Today would be easy as walking barefoot on a row of broken light bulbs across a pool of barracuda.

She slipped quietly out the back door and through Mr. Lowden's yard, and drove off, relishing the emptiness of the roads. She zipped into Ollie's parking lot and dashed inside. Like the roads, the coffee shop was quiet. No one gave her dirty looks or muttered ugly things. She patted Mr. Riley's head and started to scoot her hand across little Emily's tray, but Emily's mother shot out a hand.

"Keep away from my child," she ordered. Emily's gummy smile, the opening act of so many of Alexis's days, crumpled into a wail. Her hat, fashioned like a daisy with a yellow crown and overlapping white petals, bobbed crazily.

Reddening, Alexis walked to the counter, cautiously raising her eyes to Ollie's face. Impassively, he bagged her muffin and snapped the lid on her coffee, setting them both on the counter without a word. Hearts don't really sink, but at this moment the sensation in her chest and stomach was pure desolation. Lowering her eyes, she fumbled money from her purse and held it out.

He clasped her outstretched hand between his rough warm ones and leaned forward confidentially. "I read that stuff about you in the paper," he said, his normally loud voice low, for her ears alone. "I don't believe a word of it. I know you are not what they say." He shook his head vehemently. "You would never do that."

Her legs felt weak and there were those damned tears again. She put her other hand on his. "Thank you, Ollie. You have no idea how much that means."

He shrugged. "I know something about troubles. Now you go along, before it gets too busy." The hands made shooing motions. She took her coffee and muffin and left.

A Crawford Valley cruiser was parked beside her Jeep, Officer Collins lounging against it. "You going to the high school?"

She nodded.

"Get your stuff and get in," he ordered, gesturing toward the cruiser door. "I'll give you a ride."

She rocked back on her heels. "Said the spider to the fly?"

"I'm not such a bad guy, you know."

There was no polite response to that.

"I'm only offering because all the reporters are gonna be out front, waiting for you. I could drive you around the back, you could slip in without the hassle."

"Maybe I'm missing something here," she said. "I should think subjecting me to the maximum amount of—what did you call it? Hassle?—would be exactly what you'd want."

He didn't respond.

"Thanks for the offer," she said, "but I'm going to have to run the gauntlet sometime. I may as well get used to it. Besides, I want my car there." She didn't add in case they threw her out on her ear. The last thing she needed was to be stuck without a ride, turfed out to be feasted on by a hungry press.

A passing car full of teenagers slowed down, blasting the horn as the occupants yelled obscenities. She knew them all. "Looks like it will be another fun day."

"I'd like you to get in the car," Collins said.

The human body can go from calm to jazzed up and ready for flight in seconds. Suddenly she was on her toes, leaning forward like a runner at the starting line, assessing her chances of escape. She glanced into her open purse, checking for her phone, feeling the electric surge of adrenaline. "Are you arresting me?"

"Just offering you a ride."

Just? Offering? The sun was reflecting off the glass, but she was sure the patrons in Ollie's were glued to the windows. Like yesterday. Alexis and the cops. A one-woman stand-up routine. All that was missing was the comedy.

If he wasn't arresting her, she wasn't getting in his car. "I'm overwhelmed."

Spoken as irony, felt as truth. He stayed planted between her and her car door. How could such a benign-looking man be so intimidating? What was that indescribable quality which gave him such authority? It would be handy to be able to exert that kind of control over an unruly classroom. Was it something taught? Innate? Did it happen only when Collins put on his uniform or did he have the same authority when he pranced around in his underwear?

Collins stood there, immovable as a rock. "You look different today."

She shrugged. "A field trip to hell will do that."

Who wouldn't be changed? Someone totally callous, indifferent to the world's opinions? Someone with an adoring spouse, a supportive parent, a cadre of kind friends? She'd be a long time recovering from this, and that was if nothing further happened.

"Yeah. I don't imagine yesterday was very pleasant for you," he said.

Alexis took her sunglasses out and put them on. She was gaining insight into why teenagers liked those hooded sweatshirts. Not only the anonymity of conformity but because you could pull your head in like a turtle and hide. She should have worn one. Arrived at school with the hood up and her shoulders hunched, like criminals on TV. Should have worn one yesterday. Good pictures for the news.

"You holding up okay?" he asked.

What the hell did he care? Was he trying to trick her with sympathy again? Better lay her cards on the table. She hated dishonesty and game-playing. "Perhaps I've misled you by standing here talking to you. Politeness is pretty deeply ingrained in me. That and the damned air of authority you have. Yesterday, I was helpless. I thought I had no choice about talking to you. Now I know that's not true. I can choose when, and under what circumstances I will answer your questions, beginning with not here and not now. And never again without my lawyer."

He started to say something, but she held up a hand. "Listen, I'm not trying to start an argument. You believe that I'm a bad person. A predator who has taken advantage of her position of trust to abuse an innocent boy. You probably think you know the truth, and your challenge is to get me to confess. But you're wrong about me. Totally wrong."

More words pushed against her throat, straining to escape. They got to accuse her, question her, humiliate her. She got to take it and keep her mouth shut. She wanted to have her say, assert her innocence. But she knew she wouldn't help her case with a passionate outburst to someone primed to disbelieve her. And she might inadvertently say the wrong thing. Anything she said could and would be used against her. She heard Trustman's warning: even things said in jest might be taken as true.

She dropped her eyes. Her hands were twisted together in a white-knuckled knot she was sure Collins hadn't missed. The blooming pain in her stomach said the best of the day was already over.

"Go on," he said, his voice soft and easy. Everything about him seemed easy. Everything but his steely eyes. They swept the passing landscape like searchlights.

She started to speak, then pulled back. She couldn't do herself any favors by saying anything more. "I've got to get to work," she said.

"But you don't look well."

"You'd look unwell too if you were the target of a diabolical, dishonest, dangerously obsessed sixteen-year-old out to ruin your life." As soon as the words were out, she regretted them. How often had she complained about her students' lack of impulse control? "I've got to go. I'd appreciate it if you'd move so I could get in my car."

Collin's duplicity scared the heck out of her. Why hadn't she called her lawyer like she was supposed to?

"Suit yourself." He stepped briskly to his driver's door, got in, and drove away.

She got in her own car and headed in the opposite direction.

She took the service road and parked in the back by the dumpsters. Walking the ten feet to the door, she was filled with an eerie sense of time suspended. What if they'd anticipated her? What if all this was a trap and the press was waiting inside? What if the door was locked and she'd have to go around the building?

Cautiously, she grabbed the handle, cold and slightly damp from the morning dew. Turned it. The knob clicked and rolled smoothly in her hand. She jerked it open and slipped inside. She stopped then, alone with the chessboard tile, the institutional smells and the harsh fluorescence. The corridor was empty.

She started to breathe again.

She heard the clatter of approaching feet and deep male voices, the words indistinguishable over the HVAC hum and the patchwork of other sounds. Whoever they were, she wouldn't be found huddling against the wall like some refugee. She straightened and started resolutely down the corridor.

With the teacher's room only steps away, Dr. Huston and Mark Clemente wheeled around the corner. They spotted her and squared off like gunslingers in the old west, Mark's hand poised on his cell phone, Huston's fat finger pointing.

The astonishment on Huston's face was almost laughable. "What in the hell do you think you're doing here?" he exploded, his face blooming heart-attack red. "I can't believe you'd have the nerve to show your face after what you did. Get out of this building. Get out right now!"

> "This person prefigured and represented in
> his aspect the whole dismal severity of the
> Puritanic code of law..."
> —Nathaniel Hawthorne, *The Scarlet Letter*

CHAPTER TWENTY-ONE

"I work here."

"Not anymore." The fat finger dropped. "Under the circumstances, I didn't think it necessary to call and tell you that. I assumed you'd understand."

He blustered to a halt, genuinely baffled. Another person who expected her to crawl under a rock and cower in shame when the only thing she might be ashamed of was not being more cautious. She'd worked here for six years. Six years of jumping through absurd procedural hoops and filing her life in triplicate because this fat little paper hoarder was so hung up on process. How dare he think he could dismiss her without even the courtesy of a phone call?

"What I understand is that I'm innocent, Dr. Huston. The last information I had was that you'd only begun your investigation, and either you or Mark would get back to me about the contract process for putting a teacher on leave. Is there something in my box that I might have missed because I had to leave early yesterday?"

"Leave early? Are you crazy? You were arrested, for gosh sakes. Arrested for molesting a student."

Curious students were gathering. "We should continue this discussion in your office," she said. "First I need to stop in the ladies' room. I'll be along shortly."

"Right. In my office." He wheeled and marched away, Mark on his heels like a smart little orderly. How had she ever thought Mark was a friend? He was a toad. A sycophantic toad.

She slipped into the teacher's bathroom and called Janice Trustman. The first number she'd ever programmed on autodial. Like it or not, she'd joined the modern age.

"It's Alexis Jordan," she said. "I'm sorry to bother you, but I need help."

"I told you to bother me. What's up?"

"I'm at the high school." Her voice faltered. "Dr. Huston says I don't work here anymore. There was no notice. Not even a phone call. He says I should have understood that I no longer work here. I'm mad as hell but I don't want to screw this up."

"Hold onto your temper, Alexis. You want to appear calm and reasonable as well as wronged. They're in a good position to force an involuntary leave. Our best strategy at this point is to negotiate a voluntary leave with pay. I'm six minutes away. Stall him 'til I get there."

"Will do." She wanted to tear Huston's limbs off and beat him with the bloody stumps. A predator's reaction, consistent with the monster people thought she was. She closed her eyes and took long, slow breaths, searching for calming words to keep her from saying or doing something foolish.

At times, she benefited from a childhood attending Sunday school— where her agnostic mother had sent her weekly to get rid of her. As she leaned against the gray cinder block walls in the school's unlovely bathroom, she found the words to steady herself: *Whatsoever things are true, whatsoever things are honest, whatsoever things are just, whatsoever things are pure, whatsoever things are lovely, whatsoever things are of good report; if there be any virtue, and if there be any praise, think on these things.*

Breathe in. Breathe out. Her tensed fingers unclenched. *True, honest, just, pure, and lovely. Think on these things. Think on these things.*

She tucked a few stray hairs into her chignon, put on some demure lip gloss, and checked her watch. Six minutes. She headed for the office, detouring to the English department to check her box in case they'd left something she needed to know about. Official notice that she'd been fired, for example. They were sneaky enough to do that. But the box was empty.

As she passed through the corridors, silence fell around her. Silence and stares, broken by the occasional kid who managed a normal greeting to which she responded politely. In her wake, the silence exploded into giggles and chatter. Her calming repetition of the passage carried her right past Evan, who'd positioned himself in her path, blunting the venom of his look, the naked hate on his face. *Whatsoever things are honest. Are just. Are true.*

Janice Trustman was waiting in the outer office, in a gray suit so smart and serious it looked like she'd anticipated this meeting. Her brown hair was crisp and impeccable. She wore simple gold earrings. Black shoes. Carried a black briefcase. Looking bright and tough.

She put her hand on Alexis's arm. "Let me do the talking. If there's something I want you to say, I'll ask. If there's something you think I need to know, tap your finger twice. Okay?"

Trustman turned to Huston's secretary. "We're ready."

Huston had seated himself at the head of the conference table, Mark on his right, an empty chair on his left. Two other chairs, obviously intended for them, were positioned eight feet down the table, eliminating any possibility of conversation unless they shouted.

Without comment, Trustman picked up her chair and set it down near Huston, remaining standing as Alexis parked her bag, moved her chair, and sat. A short man with a Hitler mustache and Groucho Marx hair bustled in and took the chair to Huston's left.

Trustman nodded at him. "Hello, Harry."

As if she had all the time in the world, Trustman opened her briefcase, took out a pad of paper, a pen, and a manila folder. Set them on the table. Got out a copy of Alexis's contract. Set that on the table. Got out a copy of the Crawford Valley Regional School District procedures manual and set that beside the contract. The last things out of her bag were a thick red volume of the Massachusetts General laws and a small recorder. From her pocket she took three crisp white business cards and slid them across the table.

KATE FLORA

"Janice Trustman, representing Mrs. Jordan," she said. Still standing, she snapped on the recorder. "Recording this meeting so I don't forget anything." When no one responded, she said, "And you are?"

"Attorney Harry Pringle, representing the school district," the newcomer said, and added, "Dr. Huston, principal, and Mark Clemente, vice-principal in charge of discipline."

Trustman sat down and picked up her pen. "Can you both spell your names for me?"

Harry Pringle answered for everyone.

She wrote that down, then asked, "And your phone numbers? And Harry, you've got a card?"

Indicating the papers spread out before her, she said, "Now, I think we all understand what this meeting is about. But to be sure we're all on the same page, I'd like to sum up the situation as my client and I understand it. Dr. Huston, you recently held a meeting with Ms. Jordan regarding a complaint by one of your students, a junior named Evan Palmer, concerning what he termed an inappropriate relationship between himself and Ms. Jordan, correct?"

"Yes."

Inside, Alexis cheered. As a seasoned Huston-watcher, she could tell he resented the way Trustman had taken over. He kept looking at Pringle like he wanted the man to intervene. Pringle was fussily sorting papers.

"Is your investigation ongoing or have you reached some conclusion?"

"Ongoing." Huston looked at his lawyer, who nodded. "Though, in light of present circumstances, we may suspend our efforts in deference to the subsequent police involvement."

Trustman flipped the contract open, scanned some underlined material, and reached for the procedures manual. "You have your own copies of these, of course, and are familiar with them, so perhaps you could show me where you're permitted unilaterally to suspend an investigation without reaching a conclusion, particularly in a matter such as this, where a teacher's professional reputation is under attack."

She didn't wait for Huston to respond. Instead, she pulled some papers from the manila folder and passed them across the table. "These are

184

the sections of your regulations and the teachers' contract regarding voluntary and involuntary leaves. Am I correct in understanding there is no paperwork in existence concerning either avenue with respect to Ms. Jordan?"

Huston was fuming. He hated to lose any contest involving power. But he should have anticipated this. Loving paperwork as he did, he or his lawyer ought to have papered this entire business with memos. To her. To himself. To the files. To the superintendent and the school board. Yet she had received nothing in writing since the notice of the meeting she'd attended with Claire.

"That would normally come from the Superintendent's Office," Huston said. "Unfortunately, he is out of state this week at a conference. We do, however, have this." He took the sheaf of papers Pringle was offering and passed them to Trustman.

She placed a hand on the papers. "Do you have another copy? I'm sure Ms. Jordan would like to see this."

Reluctantly, Pringle gave a second copy to Huston, who shoved it across the table. *Temper, temper,* Alexis thought. She lowered her eyes to the page. It was a notice placing her on involuntary leave immediately and barring her from setting foot on school property, pending the outcome of the legal process. Dated two days earlier. Before her arrest. She looked at the date, then at her lawyer. Trustman nodded.

"Ms. Jordan, was this paper putting you on leave, which is dated Monday, ever delivered to you?"

Alexis said, "No."

"Were you present at school in your capacity as a teacher on Monday?"

"Yes."

"Did either Dr. Huston or Mr. Clemente mention this? Suggest that you shouldn't be present or otherwise discuss anything with you regarding your teaching status?"

"No."

"What about yesterday? Did you receive a copy of this or have any discussion about it yesterday?"

Alexis shook her head.

"We need your voice for the recorder," Trustman said.

"No."

"So you were allowed to teach on two days subsequent to the date of this notice. Now, I understand that when you came to work this morning, Dr. Huston accosted you in the hallway and yelled at you in front of students, is that correct?"

"Yes."

"And as a professional, you were embarrassed and humiliated?"

"I was."

Janice Trustman tapped the paper with her finger, looking at Pringle. "I don't know what this is," she said, her voice calm, slightly puzzled. "Nor do I understand what you are trying to accomplish with it, since it so clearly fails to conform in every way, both in form and notice, with your own rules and regulations. Never mind any standard of due process, Harry."

She paused to let that register, then said, "My client and I appreciate your difficult position, balancing your perceived need to protect your student population with your equally strong obligation to avoid defaming Ms. Jordan while affording her all the rights and protections established by her contract and law. Correct?"

How could they disagree with that? Huston looked at his attorney, who elected not to respond.

"Since she appreciates the difficulty of your situation," Trustman continued, "and based on your last conversation with her, Ms. Jordan asked me to prepare this."

She slipped five copies of a page out of the manila folder and handed them around. "As you can see, this is a request for a voluntary leave of absence, with pay, for the balance of the school year." She sat quietly, giving them a chance to read the document.

Harry Pringle skimmed it and raised his head. "Things have changed considerably since this was discussed, Janice. Your client was arrested and charged with a felony."

"Charged, Harry. My client is innocent until proven guilty. This is only until the end of the year, by which time I'm sure she'll be fully vindicated, and puts everyone in the fairest position until things are resolved, don't you agree?"

Pringle cleared his throat. "I don't believe the school has any duty—"

Trustman passed him some papers. "I believe you'll find there *is* a duty, Harry. If you'd like to take the time to read these, I believe you'll have to agree that by continuing her salary and allowing Ms. Jordan a voluntary leave, all parties are best protected and the fairest result is achieved. In the event of an ultimate adverse decision, which we feel is highly unlikely under the circumstances, the school district will, of course, be able to terminate her."

Realization struck Alexis then like a knife in her heart. While she sat there like a child, being seen but not heard, they were negotiating away her job. Yes, she'd nodded when Trustman suggested it. But it hadn't felt real then. She tapped twice on the table. Her lawyer scribbled on a piece of paper and passed it to her. "Stay calm and please trust me."

Her lawyer was doing a masterful job, yet Alexis felt like her soul was being torn apart. *Whatsoever things are true, whatsoever things are honest, whatsoever things are just, whatsoever things are pure, whatsoever things are lovely, whatsoever things are of good report, if there be any virtue, and if there be any praise, think on these things.*

Do not think of the coil of barbed wire. Evan's vengeful face. Hovarth's filth. Emily's mother's horror this morning as Alexis approached her child. Officer Collins' duplicity. Do not think of the empty house. Of someone lurking in the bushes. Of that bag left in her car and or the broken window. Of the lascivious curiosity of the press. The humiliation of being arrested.

Voices rose and fell around her as they discussed the wording of her request for paid leave, the terms of her sentence into purgatory, the means by which the career that kept her grounded and vitally alive would be taken from her. Voices of others, with Trustman calmly crafting the language of what would appear in the leave request and what would exist in an entirely private agreement, with Pringle's reedy voice battling her at every step—the subject of their fight the details of Alexis's latest humiliation.

Their voices became nothing but a buzz as Alexis grew smaller and smaller, like Alice in Wonderland, but with no hole to disappear into. Oblivious to her surroundings, she saw only crazy blackness within.

She was jerked back by a strong hand on her shoulder and Trustman's sharp, "Alexis?" The voice dropped, close to her ear, soft yet fierce. "Dammit. Get a grip and hold on until we're out of here. We need to run the final language by you."

She listened as Trustman read her the agreed-on language. Suggested one change—that the salary continuation reflect not just the period of her leave but the balance of her contract for that year. Huston's face told her he'd hoped they wouldn't catch that. The pig. With that change, she indicated her assent.

"I'll leave now," she said, "and return after school to retrieve my things."

She recognized Huston's urge to say he didn't want her coming back for any reason—his feelings had always displayed themselves all over his face—but today everyone was pretending to be civilized, so he nodded.

Pretending. She felt as uncivilized as any of her ancestors who might have painted themselves blue, wrapped themselves in skins, and hurled themselves on their enemies.

"Thank you, gentlemen." Trustman gathered her papers. "I'll take this with me, make the revisions we've agreed on, and fax it over to you. Harry, your fax number is on your card? I'm sure it's understood by all that any public comment about Ms. Jordan's leave of absence will be confined to the terms of this document." A pause. "Without innuendo or editorializing? And that the faculty will be so advised?"

Mark and Dr. Huston would not have responded in any way if Trustman hadn't stood and waited until she had their assent as well as their lawyer's. "Thank you. I think this has been very productive. And just so we're clear—the fact that she's been accused of a crime doesn't strip my client of any of her rights under the law in either tort or contract. She can sue for breach of contract or defamation just like any other citizen."

Only then did Trustman retrieve the one thing remaining on the table. Her recorder.

"But what will not ambition and revenge
Descend to?"
—John Milton, *Paradise Lost*: Book IX

CHAPTER TWENTY-TWO

She looked through the school's front window at the group milling in the April sunshine, cameras and gear ready, sipping coffee from cardboard cups, so glad her car was in the back. The way they circled and bobbed their heads, they resembled a flock of pigeons waiting for someone to strew cracked corn. She was their cracked corn, their sustenance. Briefly, she thought about the machinery that might be used to crack corn, and that led to thinking about the machinery of the law that was being used to crack her. In the contest of *Commonwealth vs. Alexis Jordan*, their goal was to keep the pressure on until she broke down and admitted she'd done terrible things. Her goal was to resist. Resist until what? She cracked? No. Her role was to keep her kernel hard, tight, and intact around herself, as if her shell was designed like a turtle's.

"Janice, thank you. You were amazing," she said.

"You were very good in there yourself," Trustman said. "I was afraid…"

"That I'd zone out again? Lose it and say or do something incredibly stupid. I don't blame you for worrying, but I'm not stupid and I don't zone out unless I have a wicked headache. I know you have high standards. I appreciate it. It helps when I'm faltering. The fact is, though, that this is a completely abnormal situation. I'm not going to get through it without glitches."

She faced her lawyer in the hallway. There was much she wanted to say, but not here, with no privacy and with students watching. "What happened in that meeting? I'm only human, you know. Until today, that humanity has mainly taken the form of being the best damned teacher I know how to be. I love teaching. Since I was twenty-one, I've been pouring my life force into serving developing minds. In there you were working out the details of how to take that away."

Trustman walked her to the back door, where they paused. "Of course, I reacted," Alexis said. "It hurt too much. It overcame me. Maybe I'd be a better client if I were pliable and obedient. But I am who I am."

"I don't have a problem with that," Trustman said. "I like you like this. I was afraid you were going in a different direction. That you were falling apart." She took out her phone. "The detective is named George Bannerman. And since you find yourself free for the rest of the day?" She graciously didn't add week, month, forever, who knew? "Let's see if he can meet with you today."

She dialed the number. "Hey, George. Janice. Yes, it is a beautiful day, isn't it? Right. Yes." Her head bobbed. "Got a big, juicy problem that's right up your alley. Do you have time today when you could meet with a client of mine? This one's very time sensitive. Two o'clock? At my office?"

She put her phone away. "Can we meet around two, Alexis?"

What else could she possibly have planned for two o'clock on a school day? She nodded.

"In the meantime, you'll be okay?"

"I hope so. Right now I feel completely unpredictable, even to myself."

Trustman's eyes, like weakness-seeking lasers, performed a body scan. "This is going to be very stressful. But if you think you're losing it, we need to talk about that. Are you sleeping all right? Eating? Feeling reasonably healthy?"

"No. No. And no."

"Might not be a bad idea to ask your doctor about anti-anxiety meds. Something to help you sleep. You can expect to be in this situation for a while. In for the long haul, as they say. Over time, this level of stress is a killer. There's nothing shameful in getting some help."

"I've got help," Alexis said. "I've got you. I'll be okay."

"Just be sensible, Alexis."

Before they parted, she told her lawyer about Collins trying to get her into his cruiser. "Did he really think I'd forget about yesterday, and how he behaved? Does he think I'm stupid?"

"Lot of criminals *are* stupid," Trustman said. "But even people who aren't criminals or stupid, when scared, are pretty vulnerable, looking for a sympathetic ear. He was playing on that."

"Goddammit, Janice. This isn't a game. This is my life."

"This situation, Alexis? Yes. It's your life. But the game playing? That's his. So be careful out there. No candy from strangers or rides from cops unless you're under arrest. And don't give anything to reporters, no matter what they do or say."

Alexis watched Trustman walk away, fighting a childish desire to ask her lawyer to stay and watch over her. Living a life that changed hour by hour, she felt the ground crumbling under her feet. The only thing solid was Trustman. She'd never thought of lawyers as comforting before.

Somewhere along the way, she'd lost her coffee and muffin, so the demands of her empty stomach carried her back to Ollie's. Remembering Ollie's expression of support, she'd forgotten, for a foolish, careless minute, about her new state of notoriety, the stares and looks, the discomfort of waiting in line with an ugly buzz around her.

When it was her turn, Ollie gave her his usual morning assessment, as though they hadn't met and spoken earlier. "Never seen you around this time of day," he said. In a low voice, he asked, "What happened? You get fired?"

Matching her voice to his, she said, "Something like that."

"It'll work out okay," he said. "What do you need?"

She wanted to leap over the counter and hug him. "My usual. I lost it somewhere."

"Too bad." He fixed the coffee, bagged the muffin, and passed them across the counter. "That guy sittin' over there." He jerked his chin toward the window. "Lookin' at you like you broke his heart. You let me know if he gives you any trouble, okay?"

The guy over by the window was Peter Everett. He was looking at her, troubled, but hadn't gotten up or come over to say hello. Why would he, after he'd stepped in to help her last night and she'd run like a scared rabbit? It made her feel like a user. She hated users. "Thanks, Ollie. He's okay. Really. One of the few people, besides you, who's still nice to me. He's just shy."

She reached for the bag.

"You know, Red," Ollie said, "maybe, you not working, someday we might go fishing. What do you say, if the weather is good, we go Saturday?"

She hadn't been fishing in years. "I say that you are my hero, Ollie. My knight in shining armor. I'd love it." She smiled for the first time in she couldn't remember how long.

"Plan on it," he said and turned to the next customer.

She approached Peter's table. "May I sit down and apologize?"

He folded his newspaper and set it on the floor. Nodded at the chair without speaking. She sat down and reached to take the top off her coffee. In a moment of silence, she heard someone say, "Yes, the redhead, that's the one who's been screwing her students."

Her hand fumbled. The top flew off. The cup started to tip. He caught the cup and snapped the lid back on. "Come on," he said, shoving back his chair. "Let's take this outside."

She grabbed her muffin and followed him out, her face burning. He led her to a green van, opened the passenger door, and put a hand under her elbow to boost her up to the high seat. Then he set her coffee in a holder, went around to the driver's side, and started the engine, backing smoothly out and pulling onto the road.

"You got any problem with cemeteries?" he asked. "Real pretty at this time of year. If it bothers you, we could go somewhere else."

"Sounds like we'd have a good chance of being undisturbed."

She looked sideways at his fierce face, so much more handsome than it had been when she'd known him in high school. Back then, his features had seemed too big. He'd been shy and awkward and had lousy skin. She'd been drawn by his personality. Like now, he'd exuded a gentleness other boys lacked. He'd felt safe to be with at a time when other boys were jittery skins of hormones and dates were wrestling matches.

Five minutes later, they sat on a lichen-covered granite bench on a hilltop overlooking the river that wove its slow way through the center of town. "Nice," she said. "I've never been up here."

"I eat lunch here sometimes between jobs. Coffee?" he asked. He peeled back the little drinking slot and made sure it latched before handing it to her.

"About last night," she began.

He pried the lid off his own coffee. "I understand about last night, Alexis."

"You read that story?" He nodded. "And you heard what that reporter was saying? And you don't think I'm horrible?"

"Why would I think that?"

"Everyone else does." She shivered at the memory of Hovarth's ugly words. "They've made me out to be a monster. I've been suspended from my job. Yesterday, I got arrested. They came to school with handcuffs and took me away." She held out her hands, the marks from the cuffs still livid.

He took her hand, his square thumb running gently over the marks, and looked at her with solemn eyes. "Alexis, surely you don't think you deserved this."

She flashed back to that horrible moment when Kennedy snapped the cuffs on. Dr. Huston's surprise. Her stunned sense of disorientation, the rush of humiliation, her fleeting urge to run. The sharp pain of the cuffs was the only thing grounding her. Then the hammer starting up in her head. "Of course not. It's just…"

Just what? Just everything.

His warm hand transfused an energy that helped combat the chill. But she was confused. "I don't understand. You really don't know me, Peter. It's been years, yet you believe in me, while most of the people I've known and worked with, colleagues and friends, act like I'm foul and dirty. Capable of this. It makes me feel—"

She broke off. "I'm sorry. I meant to apologize, to thank you for rescuing me last night, and all I've done is talk about myself. I shouldn't burden you with all this."

"I don't know you?"

KATE FLORA

"We were juniors in high school. We went out a few times. Then you moved away." She gave a slight smile. "Left me abandoned and pining hopelessly."

"That's a good one," he said, his grin a little lopsided, as much pain at those high school memories as humor. "The prettiest girl in school pining for a loser like me."

"You were not a loser."

"I could have been the poster boy for Clearasil," he said.

Across the bridge of a decade, she remembered watching him work himself up to ask her to the prom. Knowing he was the date she wanted. Assiduously avoiding all the other boys who wanted to invite her until the time got so close she was convinced he'd never ask and she'd be home, alone and dateless, on prom night. She remembered deciding to take matters into her own hands. How she'd gotten a friend to drop her at the pizza place where he worked, late at night and miles from home, lingered until he got off work, then screwed up the courage to ask for a ride.

As if he read her mind, he said, "Our junior prom. God, what a crappy month. Every day I'd spend twenty minutes in front of my mirror, rehearsing what I'd say, and I'd get to school and see you and the words would fly right out of my head. I'd be sweating and shaking and a total idiot. I must have sweated through twenty shirts. That night you asked me for a ride I'd given up hope. Maybe that's why I wasn't nervous. I was so sure it was too late. I finally got up the nerve to ask you, knowing you must have had a date for ages. And then, when I blurted it out, you barely let me finish before you said 'yes.' I thought I'd pass out."

"Good thing you didn't," she said. "You were driving. Junior prom. I wore blue and you wore black and it turned out you could really dance. I think it was the best evening of my life."

"Me, too," he said. "You can't imagine what it was like for a guy like me to have a girl like you say 'yes.' No wonder I could dance that night. My feet never touched the floor." He hesitated, then said softly, "I always wondered if that's one reason my marriage never worked. You were a hell of a hard act to follow."

"Come on, Peter, I was a shy, gawky girl."

194

She *had* been a shy girl. Her mother's voice forever in the background, reciting the ways in which she didn't measure up. Those few weeks between the prom and summer had been so good, before he moved, before her mother packed her off to a summer program to get her out of the way. She'd felt safe with him. And special. And then he was gone.

Was it possible he'd been as smitten as she? That he'd nursed a tender place for her in his heart all these years? Ill-timed as it was, that someone could come forward now and offer her such a gift—the gift of faith in her fundamental goodness—was touching and almost miraculous.

"We're so hopeless at that age, aren't we?" she said. "I thought I was the loser. You thought you were the loser. Imagine what we might have discovered if we'd talked about it. If you hadn't left, we might have become the loves of each other's lives."

He set his coffee on the ground beside him, then set hers beside his. Slowly and cautiously, as if he were cradling something terribly fragile, he put an arm around her shoulders and pulled her against him. "I'm sorry to be saying this. Doing this. It's the last thing you need right now," he said. "But you were. I think you are."

She rested against him for a moment, speechless. What she'd so desperately longed for from Micah, not only coming home last night but throughout her ordeal, and before it, she was finding in the company of a high school boyfriend. She should jump up and demand that he take her back, even though she knew how much rejecting him after his confession would hurt him. One thing she couldn't handle right now was complications. Taking a risk like this.

She turned to explain and he bent down and kissed her. A careful, tender, almost chaste kiss.

At precisely that moment, Hovarth jumped up and snapped a picture.

"The lower still I fall, only supreme
In misery."
—John Milton, *Paradise Lost*: Book IV

CHAPTER TWENTY-THREE

So much for her lawyer's advice to stay out of trouble.

She took off after him, reaching the road just as his green Escort pulled away. She scooped up a softball-size rock and lobbed it, breaking his rear window.

"You sure don't throw like a girl," Peter said, emerging from the bushes behind her. "And boy are you fast."

"Not fast enough. He got away, didn't he?"

They hiked back uphill without speaking. He sat down on the bench, unwilling to look at her. "I'm sorry, Alexis. So damned sorry. The last thing I wanted was to make things worse."

"Hard to do that. If it wasn't this, it would be something else," she said. "I just wish it hadn't been Hovarth. He's a twisted man who's made me the target of his venom." What had Hovarth said? *You can run but you can't hide.* She didn't know who she was madder at—Hovarth or herself. He was vile and vindictive. She was intractably stupid.

The temporary repair Ollie and Peter had made to her spirits was undone. There was no place she could go that had any privacy, nowhere that felt safe, not even her home. Would she soon be bathing fully dressed, as she'd once heard that nuns did? How could she explain this screw up to her lawyer? Less than an hour ago, she'd promised to be careful.

"You shouldn't have to put up with that kind of thing," he said. "I wish there were something I could do to help. Something real, I mean, besides believing in you." He hunched like a kicked dog. "Although, given the success of my efforts so far, you're better off without me."

"You think believing in me doesn't help?" she said. "You heard those people at Ollie's. Anyone can say anything about me, in front of me or even to my face, and I'm not supposed to mind because I'm wearing this damned scarlet letter on my chest. Even my own husband—"

No. She wasn't spilling her guts in some pathetic, tell-all confession. She wasn't Peter's problem. He wanted to comfort her, but that would not happen. She might want his arm around her—as a human thing, not a sexual thing—but even that was impossible. She couldn't take chances. Evan might believe his revenge was moving slowly, but the list of things he was taking from her lengthened by the minute.

She ate her forgotten muffin. The morning's events had stolen her appetite, but like Trustman said, eating was essential to not falling apart. She crumpled up the bag and sat there, tossing it from one hand to the other. If she had two more, she could juggle. She felt as hopelessly bad at keeping her feelings balanced as she did at juggling. They skittered like quicksilver from calm to hysteria to rage to tears. Despite head up and shoulders squared, she wore a "kick me" sign visible to everyone but her.

"You'd better take me back to my car," she said. "I'm too deep into self-pity to be decent company. I've got to meet with my lawyer and her detective at two. Trying to keep from going to prison."

He looked like he carried the weight of the world on his shoulders. "Don't look so miserable," she said. "You were only trying to comfort me."

"I tried to kiss you. I wanted to kiss you."

He unlocked the truck and opened her door, once again placing that careful hand under her elbow. On the drive back, he asked, "I can see what your lawyer's for, but this detective, what's he supposed to do?"

"Look into Evan's past. See if we can get a handle on what makes him tick. Why he's doing this. Whether he's done anything like this before or has a psychiatric history. He and his mother have been here only two years. Maybe, where they lived before, things happened."

"This kid's how old? Sixteen? And he's claiming you two have been having an affair since he was fifteen?"

"It's absurd," she said wearily. "You saw that stuff in the paper. He's invented a whole relationship. He's concocted an entire fantasy about the night I'm supposed to have seduced him. Some of it is pretty creepy. I'm pretty sure he's been in my house when I wasn't there. He knows stuff about me. About my house. My things. And things are missing. He even gave the police some of my lingerie."

Maybe she shouldn't tell him this. Shouldn't tell anyone it really was her underwear. She thought she could trust Peter, but could she trust anyone anymore? Look at her "friend" Mark. At her husband. What if Peter Everett was a plant? If he and Hovarth were working together and that photograph was a set-up? She hasn't seen the man since high school yet suddenly he's everywhere. And so is Hovarth with his filthy questions and camera.

She was innocent. She hadn't done anything. She had no idea how to live defensively, what to do when being innocent wasn't enough. Maybe becoming a nun wouldn't be so bad. A secular nun. She'd simply avoid all contact with others. Never say anything to anyone. Or would becoming a nun look like an admission of guilt?

They were back at Ollie's. "Hold on," he said, as she reached for the door handle. He took a card from his wallet. "In case you need me for anything. My work number. Answering service. My cell phone. My home phone."

She opened the door.

"Alexis." Something in his voice made her pause. "I know I screwed things up for you today, but I want to help. You can call me for anything. Anytime. And I'll come."

"Peter. I can't."

"Day or night," he said. "If you just want to talk. If you think of something, anything I could do. Or if you need rescuing." There was something in his dark eyes, elemental and pleading, more eloquent than his words. If he was tricking her, he was a wonderful actor.

But Evan had been an awfully good actor. Maybe she was too easily fooled. Maybe all the certainties she'd had about herself were only self-deception. No. She had to stop thinking like this. It played right into

Evan's hands. She slid off the high seat.

"Thank you. It's good to know there's someone I can call."

She watched him drive off, thinking how pathetic that had sounded. As though she had no friends. She still had Dan and Maggie. And Claire. And Lori. And Ollie.

Only eleven. What was she going to do for the next three hours? For starters, she could try to get Evan's student file. Unless the administration had locked it up or turned it over to the police, Dan or Claire might be able to copy it.

She pulled into the parking lot of a strip mall and called the high school. She tried Claire first, since she often spent all three lunch periods sitting in her fishbowl, keeping an eagle eye on the computers. Lunch was prime time for porno-surfing.

"Claire? It's Alexis. I need some help."

"Don't I know it? What can I do? You want me to beat somebody up? I used to be pretty tough, back in the day."

"Janice is hiring a detective to look into Evan's past. It would help if we knew things like the name of his previous schools. His former address. All the stuff in his file."

"That shouldn't be too hard, Lex, if Huston hasn't locked it in his office. If he has, I'll just have to get out my lock picks." She heard a voice in the background and Claire responding. "Things are pretty quiet here right now and I just saw Huston drive off. I'll hop down to the office and see what I can find."

"Claire, you're an angel."

"Still trying to earn my wings. Not sure breaking the law is the way to do it."

Breaking the law. Student records and privacy. She'd always been such a stickler for rules. Now she was asking someone she cared about to break them for her. She brooded on that for maybe ten seconds. Given what Evan was doing to her, she couldn't worry about his privacy.

She owed Trustman a check, so she drove into Crawford center and parked behind the bank, looking around warily as she went up the steps into the back lobby. Was it paranoid to expect to find Evan watching her?

Hovarth? To expect a verbal attack from a stranger? She slid her card into the ATM and called up their savings account. Instead of the $1,200 she expected to find there, it showed a balance of less than $200.

She knew with sickening certainty what had happened. Twice in the past, she accumulated savings in their joint account only to have Micah spend them. Now he'd taken their joint money again. Money he knew she needed to pay her lawyer.

Just to be sure, she sat down with a bank officer. Sure enough, that morning, Micah had transferred the money into another account. The man wouldn't give her details, but it was obvious it was an account Alexis knew nothing about. Now he had $1000, and who knew how much more? And she had $200. This straw didn't break the camel's back, it strengthened it. She'd been a fool for love long enough. He'd now betrayed her sexually, emotionally, and financially.

When Alexis stepped out into the late morning sunshine, she was furious. There was no mystery about her next destination. Micah was lucky she carried neither a knife nor a gun, but she had her wits and her temper and was ready to use both.

The department secretary, Joanne, had been at the college for at least a hundred years and never aged a day. She smiled at Alexis. "Looking for your handsome husband?" She consulted a list. "He's over in Simmons 201. Got a class in ten minutes." No curious stares, wrinkled nose, or revulsion. Maybe Joanne didn't read the papers.

Down the stairs, across a lawn strewn with students spread out on the grass, catching some rays, and into Simmons. Here it felt like a spring day. Chat and laughter surged around her as she passed. She strode through it as if in combat boots. She might look normal, but mentally she was clad in fiery garments, a horned helmet on her bright hair, clutching a shiny sword.

Micah stood in the corridor surrounded by students vying for his attention. "Excuse us, please," she said to them. They milled and stared, impervious to nuance and subtlety. Not that she'd been subtle. The classroom behind him was empty. She led him in and closed the door.

"What the hell, Lex," he sputtered. "What's your problem?"

"I think you already know."

"Look, can we do this later?" He looked toward the closed door. "I've got a class."

"No, we can't. With you, there is no later. You're the man who said, 'I'll wait for you, Alexis. I'll be here,' last night, who was nowhere to be found. You're the man who's been keeping another woman on the side for months. You're the man who went to the bank this morning and took a thousand dollars of my money—money you know I need to pay my attorney—and moved it into a bank account I didn't even know existed."

He looked at her coldly. "*Our* money, Lex, not *your* money."

"If the money in *our* account is our money, then the money in *your* account is also our money. And I need it. I have to pay my lawyer a two thousand dollar retainer. What were you thinking?"

"I was thinking about protecting myself from this whole dirty business."

She fought the sting of *dirty business.* "Without a thought for what happens to me? You knew I needed the money. We talked about it. Lawyers are expensive, Micah."

"You should have thought of that before you got yourself into this mess."

"Got myself into what mess, Micah? This mess exists only in Evan's sick head."

"Oh, really?"

He tugged a manila envelope out of his briefcase, dumped three photographs out on the desk, and stepped back with a flourish. "Then what about these?"

She stared, first with astonishment, then with understanding. She picked up the envelope he'd dropped beside the pictures, addressed to him here at school.

"What am I supposed to think? You say it's all in his head. Then I see these?"

She picked up the first picture. Evan Palmer, a bath towel low on his hips, standing in their bathroom. Set it down and picked up the second. Evan Palmer's head on the pillow of what was unmistakably their bed.

The third was a picture of her, red hair, creamy skin, and a pale yellow bath towel. Hands poised to drop the towel, a sweetly seductive expression on her face.

She put two of them back in the envelope, tucked it under her arm, and held out the third. Handling it carefully, by the corner. Thinking about fingerprints. Already moving on. Away from this horror show and the agony of crash-and-burn feelings she didn't have time for. Secular nun. Avenging angel. It didn't matter. Neither avatar had time to wallow in personal feelings.

"Photoshop," she said scornfully. "Take another look, a good look, Micah, and use your brain this time. You really think that bath towel's draped on a six-foot-two, sixteen-year-old white male athlete? You're so goddamned ready to believe the worst of me that you ignore the evidence of your own eyes. That's a picture of you, you idiot, with Palmer's head. A picture I took myself. Same with the other picture. And that picture of me? You took it. Then I dropped the towel and you dropped the camera."

She grabbed a breath. "Pictures that were in the desk in our den. That you should recognize. Pictures that Evan stole." Like her missing diary.

So many years with this man. Had she ever known him? Was she such a terrible judge of character to have committed her life to him? Had she known him once but he changed? What had he said the other night? *There's no poetry any more. It's like we're just walking through it because it's easy and familiar, but we're not really connecting.* There was a vast distance between drifting apart and actively cheating on your spouse—cheating not just physically but emotionally and financially. A huge gap between not communicating and writing off without a qualm someone you once loved. A gulf between issues that needed to be discussed and readily believing the worst about someone.

Had he ever loved her? The question brought a pain that was breathtakingly real. She clutched her side. Pain that might not call for a cardiac specialist, but certainly involved her heart. Behind her, the door opened and students began filing in, filling the room with noise and clatter. Put her in a classroom blindfolded and she'd know from the noise alone where she was.

"Lex? Are you all right?"

She looked at her husband, who watched her with an unfathomable expression on his face. She patted her chest. "Broken heart," she said. "I was either naïve enough or romantic enough to think you believed in me." She took a breath, slammed by the pain of recognizing that what was between them was ended. "I'll get over it."

The doctored photographs were absurd. Could a man stare at a picture of his own body—even where the skin tone had been lightened—and not know he was looking at himself? Or see a photograph of his wife in an intimate pose and forget having taken it? Could he not only fail to recognize his own body with another's face on it, but then seethe with jealousy? She'd never thought him stupid. Not that it mattered. By tomorrow morning, Micah and the rest of the world would have a totally undoctored, compromising photograph to stare at.

She arrived at her Jeep with no memory of walking there. Maybe she should get in and drive off some bridge. End this now and avoid the next humiliation. She checked her watch. Did she have time for suicide now, or should she meet with Trustman first? She'd always been scrupulous about not keeping anyone waiting.

Her cell rang. Claire's voice held a happy note of triumph. "Mission accomplished. I've got to run out to the post office. Can you meet me there in ten?"

"It's right next to the police station. Is that wise?"

"Dry cleaner then. I've got Cal's shirts in the back. This is cool. I feel like a spy."

Suicide postponed. It wouldn't be fair to ask Claire to risk her job, then stand her up. Time for more deep breaths. Not enough oxygen in the atmosphere to calm her after Micah's last betrayal.

Nine minutes later, after a harrowing drive in which she obsessively checked her rearview mirror for the foul Hovarth, she zipped into the parking lot of a busy laundry and stopped beside Claire. A headline flickered through her brain: **Suburban teachers conspire to break student records law.**

Their transfer of the clandestine documents took place via a CVS pharmacy bag. Alexis looked in the bag and burst out laughing. Inside were an economy-sized box of minipads, a package of Midol, a copy of Glamour, and a half-eaten chocolate bar.

"They're in with the pads," Claire explained. Then her smile faded. "Lauren Findley came to see me this morning. She wanted to know if I thought it would be all right for her to call you at home. I said you were pretty busy right now." Claire glanced around the parking lot, as though she shared Alexis's paranoia. "She said it wasn't about her. It was about you. Something she wanted to warn you about. Well, she didn't say 'warn,' but that's the impression I got, so I told her to go ahead and call. If I see her again, is it okay to give her your cell number?"

"You have no idea what Lauren was worried about?"

"Not a clue. It's probably nothing. These kids can make mountains out of molehills."

Right, Alexis thought, *that's why I'm giving her my cell phone number.* Two weeks ago she wouldn't have thought twice about it.

"Sure. And one more thing?" Alexis pulled out the grocery bag stuffed with her old journals. "Can you keep this for me?"

"No problem."

Claire opened the rear door of the car, put in the shopping bag, and gathered an armload of shirts. "Guess I'd better get moving. Got a class at one-fifty. Let me know if there's anything else I can do."

"Claire?" But Alexis didn't know what she'd ask. Rescue me? Do you have hospitable friends in Brazil? Got a spare stiletto? "Thanks for everything."

"You're welcome. Now you be careful, okay?"

Alexis looked up at the beautiful arching blue of the sky. Bad things weren't supposed to happen on days like this. Bad things came on gloomy, lowering days when the sky was the pallid gray of cement. Today was the kind of spring day to feel gloriously lucky to be alive. Alexis did not feel lucky.

She watched Claire disappear through the door of the laundry, uneasiness about one more unknown sending a prickle across her skin. She had the absurd desire to run through the door, hurl herself into

Claire's arms, and beg the older woman to keep her safe. When the police aren't your friends, and your husband isn't your friend, when you don't want to impose on your other friends and you know the bad guy has been in your house, how in Heaven's name do you stay safe?

"Tomorrow would bring its own trial with it;
so would the next day, and so would the next..."
—Nathaniel Hawthorne, *The Scarlet Letter*

CHAPTER TWENTY-FOUR

Alexis felt as if she'd spent the last three hours in a rock tumbler. She struggled for the words to explain. "I'm afraid something's happened."

Janice Trustman cocked an eyebrow. "Yes?"

"Dave Hovarth took... that is, I didn't mean anything by it. It didn't mean anything, only it's going to look so awful."

"For heaven's sake, Alexis, spit it out!" Trustman snapped. "You're an English teacher. It can't be worse than listening to you beating around the damned bush." Her finger snapped the pen open and shut as she glanced at the clock.

But it could. Alexis took a deep breath. "I went back to Ollie's to get some coffee and a muffin. There was a man there. An electrician. Peter Everett. I used to know him in high school. No. Back up. Last night, after you got me released, when I tried to go home, the place was surrounded, so I just drove around."

The impatient finger clicked the pen again. She didn't expect warm and fuzzy but she needed a little patience. "Eventually I ended up at a diner in Eldon. Hovarth appeared from nowhere and sat down. He said filthy things, deeply disturbing things about my sexual preferences, loud enough for the whole restaurant to hear. I asked him to stop. He wouldn't. I asked him to leave. He wouldn't. When I tried to leave, he grabbed me, so I dumped my ice water in his lap."

Even the bare retelling, omitting his repulsive questions, was like being subjected to it again.

Trustman leaned forward. "That's the terrible thing? You poured water in his lap?"

"Oh, no. I'd do that again in a minute. I couldn't leave because I didn't have my check. I waited at the register and Hovarth kept saying awful things, sexual things about me and Evan Palmer. Everyone was listening. Suddenly someone's asking if I need help. It was Peter Everett. He lives in Eldon. I gave him the money for my check, left him to deal with Hovarth, and ran out."

Trustman's pen clicked.

"Today, when I went into Ollie's, Peter was there."

"This is a guy you knew in high school?" Trustman interrupted. "Boyfriend?"

"Briefly. Junior year. I was feeling awful about running out last night and leaving him to deal with things, so I went over to his table to apologize, but then someone was saying ugly things about me, so he suggested we take our coffee outside. We got in his van and drove to the cemetery."

She took a long, slow breath. Trustman had warned her she'd have to get used to this, her personal life open for public consumption. "We talked about our junior prom, what a great night it had been, and I jokingly said something like who knew, if he hadn't moved, we might have been the loves of each other's lives." Could Trustman understand how innocent it had been? "Then he said he thought I had been. Of his life, that is. And he kissed me. And that rat bastard Hovarth jumped out of the bushes and took our picture."

She felt like she'd ripped this damning confession out of her soul. Trustman only rolled her eyes. "I told you not to give them *anything*, Alexis."

"But I didn't know. I hadn't seen the guy in nearly ten years. Never imagined he might still care. Or that he'd do something like kiss me."

Trustman gave her an exasperated look.

"All right. I know. A woman in my circumstances shouldn't have been off alone with any man but her husband."

"It was goddamned stupid, that's all." The pen clicked. "What else?"

"I chased Hovarth and pitched a rock through his car window. I broke the glass." The lawyer bit her lip. "I don't imagine there's anything we can do about that picture."

"Maybe," Trustman said, half smiling. "Go on."

This was like rubbing herself with sandpaper. "This morning my husband went to the bank and withdrew a thousand dollars from our joint account, and transferred it to a secret account he has. He hasn't exactly said he's left me, but he's moved in with the student he's been screwing. Embarrassed about the charges, he says."

Gripping one hand with the other, she forced herself to continue. "When I went to see him at the college this morning, to ask about the money, about his plans, he said he had to protect himself from the mess I'd gotten myself in. Then he showed me these."

Holding the envelope she'd gotten from Micah carefully by the edges, she dumped the pictures out onto the desk, then offered the envelope. "I kept this. I thought it might be useful. Fingerprints, maybe, or handwriting."

Trustman looked at the pictures. "Tell me about these."

"This one here," she pointed at Evan in the bath towel, "is a picture I took of Micah, only it now has Evan's head. Wonderful what you can do with Photoshop." She teased out the second one. "And this is Micah in bed, same alteration. I mean, how could he miss this? Micah's slender, about five-foot-eight, Asian and Black, while Evan is six-foot-two, muscular, and white. The third is a picture Micah took of me, though he's totally forgotten. These must have been stolen from my house along with all that other stuff I told you about."

Trustman carefully lifted the picture of her in the bath towel and slid it into the envelope.

"There's more," Alexis said.

"More what?" her lawyer said sharply. "More compromising photographs?"

"Goddammit, Janice! They're fakes."

She'd hired this lawyer because the woman was tough, and she needed someone tough to protect her. If her lawyer snapped at her, she probably

TEACH HER A LESSON

deserved it. But she didn't deserve this mistrust. "I got up in the night," she said miserably. "I was thinking of what you'd said about the police searching the house. About all the personal things that I wouldn't want them to find. I purged computer files and burned everything I could in the fireplace."

"I hope you sifted the ashes and buried them in the yard."

Alexis flinched. "Are you serious?"

Trustman nodded.

"When I was collecting stuff to burn, I realized one of my diaries was missing. Not diaries. Journals. Extremely personal journals. That's when I understood how Hovarth could know such intimate things. Things Evan must have told him. Which means Evan has my missing journal. And since he must have gotten in my house, he probably read all the others. So maybe the ladder we found against the house last week was Evan's?"

"That ladder still in your garage?"

Alexis nodded.

"We'll see if George can pick it up." Trustman looked at her watch. "He'll be here soon." She made a note. "Evan Palmer's never been in the house by invitation?"

"I can't remember a time when I've had any students in the house. I always keep my home separate from my work."

"So if he has your diary, or anything else of yours, he broke in and stole it?"

Alexis nodded. "Like the set of my underwear that he gave the police."

"But you burned all the other diaries, which means we can't show similarities or a gap in the cycle and offer that as an alternative source of his knowledge." Trustman shook her head. "Bad move. You should have called me."

In the middle of the night? "But I didn't burn them."

"You said—"

"I was going to. Then I thought about what you just said. So I left them with a friend."

"Will she keep them safe?"

Alexis nodded. She reached into the CVS bag and pulled out the pads.

KATE FLORA

"I think these are for your detective, but you might want to look at them." Her face flamed as she realized what she was holding. This crazy mess was turning her into a full-fledged idiot. "Not the box. What's in the box." And that was stupid, too. Her life had become absurd. Kissing strangers in cemeteries. Juggling minipads in her lawyer's office. What would she do for an encore? She got to the bottom of the box and pulled out the folded papers. "Copies of Evan Palmer's school records."

Her lawyer looked at them and then at Alexis. "I think you'd better save those for George."

Another faux pas?

"Anything else?"

Alexis shook her head.

"Okay. By the time you leave today, you'll hate me. Believe me, I'm doing this for your defense." Trustman leaned forward, "Time for the truth, the whole truth, and nothing but the truth. You ever sleep with the kid?"

"Absolutely not."

She wasn't going to cry. She was going to get over the sick feeling in her stomach and the urge to run. She had to get tough and this was part of the program. The world Evan Palmer had inducted her into was full of people who would be nice in order to elicit confidences and trap her. Trustman was only trying to learn what she had to in order to help.

"You ever think about it? Ever look at him with lust in your heart?"

"Never."

"What about former students?"

"Never."

"Not even one delicious, irresistible adolescent male in six years?"

"I guess I prefer them seasoned."

"The men in your life? Tell me all about the skeletons in your closet."

"There's just my husband," she said. In a flat voice, she repeated what she'd told Trustman before. "I was his student. We had an affair. He told me he was single. When I found out he was lying, I stopped seeing him until he left his wife. I suppose I caused their divorce. If it hadn't been me, it would have been someone else. But that doesn't clear my slate, does it?"

"And this was when?"

"Seven years ago."

"And since then?"

"Since then, I have lived a blameless life with respect to sexual activity."

"Really?" Trustman's eyebrows rose. "And with respect to other activities?"

"I have been guilty of hubris. Overconfidence. Also, apparently, blindness."

"We'll come back to that. What else?"

"I told Mrs. Hirsh that if her dog pooped in my flower bed again I was going to spray its ass with turpentine. I harbor a secret wish to encourage my students to be rebellious. I sometimes give other drivers the finger. I have a tattoo."

She was being ridiculous, but it was the only way she could do this.

"A tattoo. Where?"

"Well... you know the advice about tattoos. Keep them small. And someplace where people see them only if you want them to. It's right here." She stabbed a spot a few inches below her navel. Formed her fingers into a circle. "About this big. It's the letter M, surrounded by decorations. Black and green and red." Something else from the advice about tattoos. Think twice. Tattoos last a lifetime, relationships often don't.

"Who knows about this?"

"Two girlfriends who were with me. Micah, of course. And my doctor."

"Anyone else?"

"I'm not in the habit of going around with my stomach bare."

"How did the police react to that?"

"I didn't tell them. I thought it might get back to Evan. If we're supposed to have had this wild sexual relationship, and according to Hovarth, we made love in every possible position and just about every place in town, then Evan would know about the tattoo. Is it a problem, not telling the police?"

"No. It was smart. Anything else? Secret piercings, anything like that?"

Alexis looked down at her lap, blushing. "I have a ring in my navel. It was another stupid thing to do. But I was visiting my mother and that always makes me crazy. Micah didn't come. I worried about what he was doing while I was gone. I was at the mall—my mother had sent me to get something fancy to wear to dinner with her friends at a swank restaurant—and saw this place that did piercing. Something came over me and I just marched in."

"Something came over you," the lawyer murmured. "But something like that didn't come over you with regard to Evan Palmer? You didn't simply stop fighting him off and do it? Just because you wanted to and the impulse overcame you? Because you were tired of being a good girl and wanted to have some fun? He's a very attractive boy. Or maybe you wanted to get back at your husband for what he was doing? He screws around so you screw around?"

"Yes, goddammit, yes. You're right, Janice. That is exactly what happened."

"...behold here the unhappy woman..."
—Nathaniel Hawthorne, *The Scarlet Letter*

CHAPTER TWENTY-FIVE

"Don't you ever do that again!"

Trustman's words exploded at her with such vehemence Alexis flinched. "What I was just taking you through was a rehearsal. That's what the cops are going to do to you. That's what the DA's gonna do. Reporters, if they get the chance. Over and over and over until you're rubbed raw. And you can't ever, ever, let down your guard and snap back with an affirmation like that. Because you're charged with a felony. Miranda is no joke. Interrogation is no joke. Anything you say *will* be used against you."

Trustman leaned forward, "Listen," she said fiercely, "you think you're playing some kind of verbal game. That sarcasm will be understood as part of the normal currency of social intercourse. They're looking for a confession, Alexis. An admission of guilt. In their minds, you've done something unspeakable and if you're a normal person with a conscience, it's weighing on you. A part of you longs to confess. The belief that confession is good for the soul is one of the underpinnings of police work. And don't think they're all going to come at you like mad dogs, either. A good cop can be very charming."

"Jesus, Janice. You scared the hell out of me."

"Better me than someone else. Listen, you're a smart woman," the lawyer said. "But you're just so damned naïve and trusting it scares me. I'm afraid you'll be frightened and needy and you'll confide in the wrong person or turn to the wrong person for help. When something like this happens, people you think are your friends often turn out not to be. You have to be suspicious to the point of paranoia, no matter how much it bothers you."

Alexis was paralyzed by the enormity of this thing. What it was asking of her, all the new life skills she needed to learn. She was a stroke victim, only she'd had a legal stroke. A stroke of bad luck. She had to learn to walk and talk and function all over again with a different set of rules. A new consciousness that required oversight over everything.

"Look. I'm sorry I have to do this but I don't do you any favors if I treat you with kid gloves. Your future depends on our ability to mount a successful defense."

She shoved back her chair and stood up. "Let's take a break and see if we can get you unwound." She walked to a filing cabinet and pulled out a file. "I don't know if Hovarth remembers that I have this." Smiling, she handed a photograph to Alexis.

It was a picture of Dave Hovarth, pants down around his knees, holding a sign in one hand that said, 'suck my dick' while holding his dick in the other, urinating on mail scattered on the steps around him. The focus was great. It was possible to read the house number and address on one of the packages.

Alexis stared at her lawyer. "Where did you get this?"

"The detective. George Bannerman. He's good. Mail tampering is a federal offense."

"Too bad you don't have a picture like that of Evan."

"Maybe we'll get one," Trustman said, and resumed her interrogation. "Are you eating?"

Alexis shook her head. Every time she tried to eat, something happened. Like Hovarth or Grant Collins or strangers wanting to discuss her sex life.

"You have to eat. Hunger makes you weak and weakness makes you vulnerable." The lawyer looked pointedly at her hands, which were pressed hard against her stomach. "It hurts?"

"All the time."

"What do you do to decompress?"

"I run."

Janice Trustman shook the pen impatiently, tossed it in the trash, and got another. "Okay. If you were the detective on this case, what would you do?"

"Three things," Alexis said, relieved to get the focus off her personal life. "First, I'd go back to the town Evan came from. See if he was in any kind of trouble there. If there was any episode, any event, something which triggered their leaving town. If I didn't find that, I'd look for smaller things. Signs that he wasn't quite right. Instances of violence or indifferent cruelty. False accusations. Inappropriate or obsessive behavior. I'd look into what was known about the family. What the gossip was. What the neighbors thought. Evan told me that when he was younger, he was abused by an uncle. That kind of thing's a trigger."

Trustman made some notes. "What else?"

"Look for signs of imbalance. The boy's mother is an icy, heartless woman. The kind who will move heaven and earth to secure any privilege or opportunity for her child, but will make him feel unloved, worthless and degraded. He's been raised to believe he's entitled to have whatever he wants, but there's been no model for empathy."

"How do you know this?"

"Evan told me. They need someone who listens. I try to be available if they're troubled. If it's serious or they need more than a listening ear, I'll refer them to a counselor. Evan's stuff came out gradually, over two years. I was being a caring teacher when he made his move. And that's how it felt, Janice, like a move. He'd planned it, worked himself up to it, until the day when he was perfectly ready. And he'd convinced himself it was a mutual thing. He had a whole construct in which I'd been sending him signals and he was just responding. It's a pretty sophisticated level of delusion."

She sighed. "I know it's his fantasy and not my reality, and yet I find I'm going back over everything I ever said or did and second guessing myself."

Janice Trustman raised an eyebrow. "You need to identify actions or words that could have been misleading, but don't start seeing things his way. It sounds to me... Look, to weather this, you need to stay strong.

Mentally. Emotionally. Physically. If I sound like a worried parent, it's because I've been here before and this is your first, and hopefully last, trip."

She rolled up her shirt sleeves. Brisk, neat, decisive motions. "When you say you're beginning to doubt yourself, I want to give you a shake. Yell 'get real' and scare you again. Because it's so easy for something like this to mess with your head and so hard to have faith in yourself when the whole world is trying to catch you out."

Trustman looked genuinely sorry. "Now, what you've said about Evan's version of events sounds like mental illness, or at least, mental unbalance. This didn't happen out here in our world. It happened inside his head. The reason he talks about it so well, so convincingly, is that for him it *is* real. In his fantastic construct, if you put your hand on his shoulder, it *was* purposeful. If you smiled in his direction, you smiled at him. If you expressed enthusiasm for his work, it wasn't because you were his teacher and were proud of him, it was because he was special and you wanted him to know it."

"That's exactly right," Alexis said. "Everything you said. That's what he's doing. How he sees it. How did you know?"

"He's not the first person to do this, Alexis, to get obsessed with someone. It's what drives a lot of stalkers. Often they're crazier or more obvious, less smart and good at it. But it happens. And the people it happens to tend to be like you. Generous, well-meaning people who have no idea ordinary gestures and good-hearted warmth and encouragement can be so completely misinterpreted. Our goal is to show how regular you are and how crazy he is."

Trustman gave a decisive nod. "Okay. What's the second?"

"Second is his interactions with his peers here. What he's saying. Whether he's bragged about things he's done or plans to do. Teenage boys do that. They talk. It would be helpful to know if he's been abusive toward girlfriends. Carrie Canavan is his latest. But there have been others. Megan Lauriat, very briefly, and Doreen Flanagan. One of them has talked to someone, I'm sure. I'd like to know if he was the one who vandalized my car."

"That sounds right. What's the third?"

"Find out if anyone's seen him around my house during the day. Are his fingerprints on that ladder? On the window of the crawl space or anywhere inside? Is his DNA on the baseball cap I found. Things like that. Stuff that will make him look sneaky and weird and explain how he knows the inside of my house and how he can describe my things. We need to find ways to start unraveling his story."

"That's a good start. Now…"

Start? Alexis felt like she'd been dragged over burning coals, and Trustman was just warming up? Trustman pulled out the list of times and places where Alexis and Evan had been together for various reasons. "Lex, did you keep a copy of this?"

She shook her head. "I didn't dare. In case the police searched my house."

"Right. But you need to have one so you can work on it. Because for every date, I want you to think who else was there. When we get Evan's version, you'll have to do the same with his dates. Go over Hovarth's story in the paper, see what you remember about the stuff alleged in there. Keep the list with you. If the cops come, stick it in your bra."

Trustman was pretty when she smiled. "Now, I need names and addresses. Your husband's office address and phone number. Same for your closest friends. Your doctor? The cops'll probably ask. Abortions, STDs. Anything sex-related. You ever seen a psychiatrist or therapist?"

"But that's all confidential."

"Doesn't mean they won't try, Alexis. So, I take it you have?"

"Years ago. I'll have to look that stuff up."

"Bad credit history?" She shook her head. "Bad driving record?" Another shake. "OUI?" She felt like a bobble-head doll. No criminal record. No prescription drugs.

"Do you do drugs?"

"For the last two years, I've been trying to get pregnant. Before that, we occasionally smoked pot. I never bought it. There's none that I know of in the house."

"You might check with your husband."

"Call him at his girlfriend's and ask if he has illegal drugs in the house?" But Trustman had a point. She'd vetted her things but not Micah's.

"Any dangerous hobbies or avocations? S&M? Pornography? Black belt in anything? A basement full of nunchucks? A collection of stilettos? You ever visit risqué internet chat rooms?"

"You're kidding. You mean they do that?"

"Have you been listening? Of course I'm not kidding. I'm surprised they haven't already searched your house. Anything else that might come around and bite you on the ass?"

"I burned Anais Nin. I never imagined..." But it was time to start imagining, wasn't it? "I belong to the National Abortion Rights Action League. I give money to Planned Parenthood. I used to study kick boxing. Once a month, I volunteer with battered women. During the holidays, I sing for senior citizens."

"Too squeaky clean for words."

"I sneaked into Walden Pond one night and went swimming. Didn't get caught. I stole a milk crate once. I ran a red light once in front of a cop. But he didn't give me a ticket."

"You give him a blow job?"

"Why, Janice," she said, "how did you know?"

"I think we're getting tired." Trustman set down her pen and pushed back her chair. "Let me start poking around. I'll be back at you with more questions. You keeping your cell phone charged? Keeping it with you?"

She nodded.

"Good. Keep doing that. And Lex, if a cop wants to talk to you, say you've got to call your lawyer? And if the cop wants a blow job? Don't."

"It was a joke."

"Like I said earlier. No jokes. Remember?" The phone rang. "George is here. He'll follow you home and get that ladder."

"My house is surrounded by the press."

"George won't care."

"Lucky George. I'm beginning to feel abraded." She thought of something. "There's an Hispanic janitor at the high school. Carlos. He's quiet. Mostly keeps to himself. I'll bet he notices things."

"Friend of yours?"

She nodded.

"Good idea."

She leaned back and closed her eyes. She felt like a ping pong ball after a match.

"Hey, are you falling asleep?" Trustman's voice was amused.

With an effort, Alexis pulled herself back. "Sarcasm alert, okay? You know how it is with the guilty. We sleep right through it."

"Innocence, that as a veil,
Had shadowed them from knowing ill, was gone"
—John Milton, *Paradise Lost*: Book IX

CHAPTER TWENTY-SIX

George Bannerman bounced into Trustman's office, wired and restless as a terrier, looking too young and too good to be a competent detective. He had bright eyes, a mop of curly, dark hair and an engaging, boyish grin. A nice change from Trustman's "buck-up-gal" severity. The last hour with Janice had left her rattled. He shook hands, exchanged some data with the lawyer, and followed Alexis down to the parking lot. He escorted her to his car. "Sit a minute," he said. "Put me in the picture."

She must have looked overwhelmed, because he added, "I don't mean the whole story. I talked with Janice. I mean about the ladder. And if there's anything else I should be looking for at your house."

She stared out the car window, feeling like some giant thumb had smeared her across the landscape. Bannerman's car had a big, plush front seat, so inviting she wanted to tell him to drive around, like a parent with a fretful toddler, while she curled up and slept. Instead, she told him about coming home and finding the ladder. Evan's knowledge of her house. The things that were missing.

"The kid's obsessed with you, right? A real looney tune?"

She nodded.

"Janice may already have told you this... but the longer you can hold out and stay strong, the more you push him toward the edge, the greater the likelihood he loses that golden boy cool. Starts acting out."

"Golden boy cool. That's a great description. Have you met Evan?"

"Saw him on the news. Damn, what a performance. Wide-eyed innocence. Genuine perplexity. He loved you. You used and discarded him. Oh, the pain, the pain. He probably had half the mothers in the Commonwealth in tears. Half the teenage girls getting wet at the idea they might console him. Excuse me. That was crude."

"George… Do you mind if I call you George?"

He shook his head.

"You say he'll start acting out. Acting out how?"

"Unravels until he stops thinking clearly and starts acting crazy and it becomes clear to everyone that he made it all up."

"Then he'll try to destroy me."

"I thought he already was."

"I mean something far worse than lies and slander. Than cops and handcuffs."

"Come on, Jordan. He's a sixteen-year-old kid."

"You sound like the rest of them. Fooled by, what did you call it? His golden boy looks. His air of injured innocence? Janice said you know about these people. Delusional people. How they think and act."

He considered what she said. "Maybe you're right. You know the boy. And you've had time to think about this." He seemed to reach a decision. "So you will start being very careful, and I'll start doing some detective work. How's that?"

"Maybe you'd like to sit on my steps with your pistol at the ready?"

"I don't think you can afford that much George Bannerman."

"You're expensive?" Dumb. Everything about this was expensive.

"I'm not cheap." He grinned. "But I'll give you my number, so if you need me to bring the pistol, you can call." He scribbled on a card and wrote her information in a notebook. "On to your house. How do we do this?"

"We'll both drive into the garage and close the door. Then you can look around. See the house. Load the ladder on your car and depart. And the press can go to hell."

"Good. Okay." He waved a hand toward the Jeep. "After you."

"My car goes on the right side," she said. "Yours on the left."

She thought about Evan spinning out of control, the press camped in her dooryard, the thousands of dollars Evan was costing her. She flipped on the CD player and music came on. Loud. What did women listen to when they went to war? What was the background music to frustration and rage? This whole process—formal complaints, hearings, arrest, warnings, forms, rights and obligations—was so controlled, so hedged about with rules. Underneath another battle raged. A primitive battle of the sexes in which a male strove to control a female, and, being thwarted, embarked on a course of destruction.

Evan's behavior was primitive in another way, too—the way of the very young child. Or the profoundly selfish and self-centered. If I can't have it, I'm going to make sure no one else can have it either. Alexis had seen that behavior in her own mother. When she was twelve, the kindly David Levine had come home on Valentine's Day with two elaborate gift boxes done up in deep purple paper with gauzy lavender ribbons and clusters of purple silk violets—the prettiest packages Alexis had ever seen. She received hers with eyes wide with wonder.

The three of them sat in the living room. She remembered the way the creamy white sofa set off the package that stayed on her lap, waiting for her mother to go first. Elsa Levine was a "me first" person. She waited as her mother undid the lovely ribbon, pushed aside the violets, and stripped off the shiny paper. Watched the scarlet-polished fingers pry the lid off the box and lifted the contents from their nest of white tissue. Her mother held up a soft, short-sleeved cashmere sweater in a delicate shade of peach that was perfect for her creamy skin and blonde hair. She had smiled up at her husband and mouthed her thanks. "Now let's see what you've got, Alexis."

She opened her own box. Very carefully, so that she wouldn't tear the ribbon or the paper, setting the ribbon aside along with the little flowers. Sliding her nail under the tape so the paper wouldn't rip. Folding it and setting it beside the ribbon. Prolonging the moment. Savoring it. With the box on her lap, she slowly lifted the lid and opened the tissue. She had a sweater, too. Angora. A pale, pale lilac with long sleeves and a turtleneck.

Fifteen years later, Alexis could still feel the pleasure as she'd lifted her gift from the box and held it up to her chest, her chin rubbing across its soft surface. Still smell the faint department store perfume. Still remember her mother crossing the room, snatching it out of her hands and holding it up to herself, discovering that it was a junior-sized sweater, too small for her own full figure. Flinging it on the floor, grinding it under her heel as she yelled at the perplexed David Levine, "I wanted that color, dammit!" Then balling up the carefully saved ribbon and wrapping, the tiny flowers, shoving them into the wastebasket, and storming from the room.

She still remembered crouching on the carpet, picking up the sweater and staring at the puncture wound where her mother's heel had ground right through it. Holding the poor ruined thing to her chest and burying her face in the soft angora fuzz. Later rescuing the ribbon and silk flowers from the trash.

What kind of music helped fuel your anger when life had habituated you to accept bad treatment and made you believe you were unworthy? She would not sit passively while Evan ground her under his heel, destroying everything she cherished.

She turned down her street and into her driveway, hitting the remote that opened the garage door, Bannerman right behind her. Reporters with their cameras and mikes swarmed toward her. She stared straight ahead as the creaky old door to finish its ascent, then drove into the garage, waited until he'd pulled in beside her. She got out of the Jeep, remote in hand. By now, reporters had come into her garage.

"I need to close the door," she said. She got a gaggle of voices, a swarm of mikes and questions. "Please," she said firmly, "get off my property."

Reluctantly, they edged out. She hit the button. The door descended, beheading them, then chopping off their shoulders, their torsos, their legs and finally, their feet.

"Which ladder?" he asked, getting right to business.

She pointed to the older, more battered one.

He photographed the ladder in place. "Got any bungee cords?"

"Is there a Pope?" She grabbed a handful. Micah loved bungee cords. It was a guy thing. Go to the hardware store and come home with products that piled up in garages and closets, stored until the day that product might be needed. One week, it was bungee cords. Another week glue or sanding sponges or a staple gun. There were going to be no more such weeks with Micah. The irony was that Alexis did all the repairs.

"Great," he said, grunting as he lifted the ladder. "Want to give me a hand here?"

Together, touching it carefully with gloves Bannerman produced like a magician from his pocket, they hoisted the ladder onto his roof and secured it with the cords. "Come on inside," she said. "I'll give you the grand tour."

He followed her into the house, noting the drawn blinds, surveying the rooms with an eye not for décor but for what could be seen from outside. Taking the occasional picture. In the living room, he knelt by the fireplace and poked the ashes. "You stash these in a bag, I'll take them with me." Then they went upstairs.

"Evan knows the layout of my bathroom. The color of my sheets. The contents of my bedside drawers."

"The storage space where your burglar was, does that connect to the house?"

She pointed to the small door in the wall. "Through here."

"You always keep it locked?"

"Now we do. Before, I'm sure we occasionally left it open. Just like I'm sure we occasionally left a window unlocked. It always felt like such a safe neighborhood."

Standing together in the upstairs hall, looking out the window, he asked her the names of the neighbors and made a little sketch.

"The one right across the street is empty. They're renting for six months while it's being renovated. Otherwise, they've been here for years."

"Maybe some of the workmen saw something," Bannerman said. "I'll check that out."

She could see the reporters standing numb as sheep outside the garage. Did they think she'd brought home a man? Were they salivating over another hot story?

"You want me to shoo them away when I leave?" he asked. "Do what I can to keep you from going out there on an impulse and talking to them."

"I've had Janice's lecture on impulse control, George." She looked toward the window and back at him. "Yet here I am, standing in my window with a strange man, with the press in my yard. I doubt Janice would consider that circumspect."

Another news van came down the street. Bannerman, looking grave, checked his watch. "Something's about to happen."

"Probably the cops coming to toss my house in time for the six o'clock news."

"Which means that ladder and I better vamoose," he said. "You've got my numbers. Office. Home. Cell. Program them into your phone and don't—seriously, don't— hesitate to call. I'll come with my gun, if that's what you need. And if you hear anything or want to know anything, call anytime." He headed for the stairs. "If you do talk to the press, remember. No irony. No jokes. No nothing."

"I'll be good."

His eyes twinkled, as though he wanted to comment on that. Instead, he said, "Something you could do for me. Get me a set of Palmer's fingerprints. Coke can, sports drink, whatever your pals can do."

She followed him back to the garage door, her stomach already clenched with anxiety at the idea that they might be coming to search her house.

Before he left, he said, "You got an iPad and headphones? Because if the cops do come, they'll try and push every button you've got. There's nothing more offensive than a bunch of strangers rooting through your house. I suggest you find yourself a quiet corner and listen to loud music. Take some pleasure in driving them nuts while they're trying to drive you nuts."

She was changing into jeans when she remembered something Janice had said. Did Micah have anything around that she might not want the cops to find? She opened his dresser drawers and started feeling around among his clothes.

*   *   *

Half an hour later, when the police rang her doorbell, she had flushed four joints and half-a-dozen colorful condoms down the toilet. A packet of graphic love letters from Yvonne and a few other former students, torn into shreds, now moldered in the kitchen trash under spoiled gravy, coffee grounds, and other random items from her fridge. She had asked Dan Morgan to get Evan's fingerprints and had programmed Bannerman's number, and Peter Everett's, into her phone.

Her old friend Officer Collins personally presented the warrant with full cop formality. Asking her to identify herself. Asking if anyone else was at home. If anyone else shared ownership of the home. Asking if she would consent to the search. She said no.

He stood by politely while she read the warrant. "This is my copy to keep, right?"

He nodded.

"I have no experience with searches. May I ask you not to be too messy or destructive?"

"We're not here to harass you, ma'am. We're here to search for evidence."

Ma'am. Like they'd never met before, he didn't know her name, and hadn't tried his sweet-talking tricks on her. Lying to her like she was born yesterday. They made her so tired. She walked into the kitchen, a police officer following, watching as she grabbed her cell. When Janice answered, she said, "Collins is here with a bunch of Crawford officers, preparing to search my house."

She carried the phone into the living room and held it out to Collins. "Janice Trustman would like to talk with you." Officers were already going through drawers and pulling books off the shelves. It was too painful to watch.

She was cold, so she got a sweater and went back to the kitchen. She took out the book of poetry she'd carried off so optimistically in the morning, fixed herself seltzer with ice, and opened a can of smoked almonds. The almonds tasted wrong. The drink made her colder. She put water on for tea.

She read, "He sang his didn't he danced his did…" Would her students have liked it? She might never know. "Doomsday is the eighth day of the week." What day was this? The longest? The worst? Perhaps the worst was yet to come. She turned to something older, seeking comfort in cadence, wisdom in the judicious choice of words. Seeking food for her anger and solace for her soul.

When the kettle whistled, she made ginger tea. Good for her stomach. However calm she tried to be, however much she tried to think tranquil thoughts, her gut churned and writhed like a sack full of snakes. All around her, as she slowly turned the pages, Collins and his brethren turned out her drawers and her closets. Rooted through her books and her underwear. Dug beneath the sinks and read through her papers. Piled up financial records and check registers and credit card bills. Sifted through her flour and sugar and looked in the freezer.

She read Yeat's poem, "Into the Twilight." Too close for comfort on a night like this. Turned the pages looking for something more soothing. Longfellow? No one read Longfellow anymore. The tea made her hot. She took off the sweater.

"Excuse me, ma'am?"

Kennedy loomed over her. Instinctively, she pulled her hands away and put them under the table, safely away from him. Did it please him to know he'd hurt her?

"Would you have a couple of plastic bags we could put things in?"

You come to collect evidence and don't bring your own bags? The request was probably to rub her nose in the search. "Under the sink," she said. In her lap, her hands were shaking.

"Did you know you have to erase a computer file five times before it's gone?" he said.

"About all I know is how to send e-mail and move text around. My husband's the techie." He knelt down to get the trash bags and she turned the page, exposing the ugly grooves in her wrists. What the hell. He might as well get a good look. She draped the sweater over her shoulders.

"Did I do that?" he asked.

"Spare me," she said. "You know you did and I know it was deliberate."

"Hey. I asked you if..."

"Your reputation has preceded you," she said. "You knew what you were doing. If you meant to hurt me, you succeeded. It's not difficult to bruise someone with skin like mine. Now, if you'll excuse me, I've had enough pretense, lying, and manipulation for one day."

"You're a fine one to talk about lying." His jaw jutted aggressively, but she saw hurt. God. Beneath that commanding exterior, he was probably younger than she was.

"If it wasn't deliberate," she said quietly, "you should make a point of checking them yourself. Asking questions, under those circumstances, is unfair. No sense getting a reputation for brutality if you don't deserve it."

She felt feverish. A headache was building behind her eyes. She pressed an icy hand against her forehead. Time to take some aspirin and lie down. It was all of what, eight? But she was short on sleep and the last thing she needed was to get sick. She closed the book and got up. Her legs felt unsteady.

"Ms. Jordan?" Kennedy at her elbow, ready to serve and protect. "Are you all right?"

The overhead lights bored into her skull. She waved him away, checked her pocket for her phone, and walked out of the kitchen. Collins was presiding over a small mound of household items, entering things on a list. "I'm going to lie down," she said. "You should lock up when you go. You'll leave me a list of what you take, right?"

He looked like he wanted to say something, but only nodded.

The staircase felt like Everest. Her lovely, peaceful bedroom looked like a bomb had exploded. At least she wouldn't have to wonder about what to do tomorrow. Wearily, she retucked the covers on her bed, head pounding when she bent over, got some soft old sweats, and changed. With arms almost too heavy to lift, she braided her hair and took some aspirin.

Sitting on the edge of the tub, she considered the trajectory of her day, more EKG than meteoric, a series of such intense ups and downs it was no wonder she was exhausted. But the chills and fever, the headache and surging body pain said this wasn't exhaustion. It was flu. She wanted to lie on the cool tile floor and proceed directly to death. No passing Go or collecting $200.

She wanted to ignore the commotion downstairs, burrow into her pillow and give herself up to sleep, but she didn't trust them to lock the house. The press was still out there. And worse, Evan, who liked to creep in through unlocked doors.

EVAN — SEVEN

That damned ladder, locked up in her garage with his fingerprints all over it, haunted him. He had to get it back. Sooner or later, The Witch would notice it gone. He could think of something to tell her. Lying to The Witch was easy as breathing. But he didn't like that it was in HER garage.

Right now, things were cool. The cops believed him. She'd been arrested. She'd been fired, thrown out on her ear in the middle of the morning, fat Huston waddling after her like he was afraid she wouldn't go. But what if she got someone to believe her? What if the cops came and got the ladder and they found his fingerprints? How would he explain that? And there was his hat, somewhere in the crawl space. Hat. Hairs. Forensics. He watched all that stuff on TV.

Ordinarily, he'd go by when she was at work and get the ladder. But now she didn't work. And the house was surrounded by reporters. He'd driven past an hour ago and the street was crawling with media, that cold bastard Collins standing on her steps, talking to the press. He'd have to wait until later, when everyone had gone home and she was asleep. If he couldn't get in, he had something else in mind. It wouldn't get the ladder back, but it would take care of fingerprints.

He smiled with satisfaction, thinking of Mrs. Jordan going up against Officer Collins. Collins was a sneaky bastard. He could be so damned nice until he got you to say what he wanted, and then he was down your throat and all cop attitude. She'd have a tough time with that. She wasn't a pushover about papers and things, but you could get to her, because she cared. Some of those scraggy old biddies didn't care if you were dying, you had to get those papers in on time and they never read 'em anyway. Mrs. Jordan read everything.

Tricky, getting out without waking The Witch. Lately, she was always watching him. Since she'd found him jerking off to that movie, she'd been weird. Not that The Witch hadn't always been weird, especially about sex. But this was different. Maybe she was worried that this teacher business had unleashed some hidden vileness in him, triggered psychosis or something. That her poor boy, having been seduced by that terrible woman, would become a predator, too. That happened to abused kids.

Even though she was easy to fool, The Witch wasn't stupid. After she walked out of his room with that cock-withering look, she'd come back and gone through his stack of videos. She hadn't missed the subject matter. At dinner tonight, she quizzed him about girlfriends. Who was he seeing? Was it serious? Did he have enough money for dates and clothes? Need a bigger allowance? Like she was afraid he'd attack some dumbass high school girl because of what Mrs. Jordan had done. How fucking likely was that?

The Witch was right, of course. He did want to attack someone. But it was no pathetic, inexperienced high school girl. And it wouldn't be some passion-driven, out-of-control thing, either. He was already planning it. Imagining the fear on her face. Her disbelief. She'd probably fight. She was strong even if she was small, and that would be part of the fun. Smacking her down until she cried and cringed and let him do what he wanted. Or until he'd done what he wanted, whether she let him or not. Just thinking about it made him so stiff. Every day the urge got stronger. He didn't know how long he could wait.

"Thither, full fraught with mischievous revenge,
Accursed, and in a cursed hour, he hies."
—John Milton, *Paradise Lost*: Book II

CHAPTER TWENTY-SEVEN

The symptoms came on fast. Soon, she couldn't tell dream from reality. She felt as if people stood over her, talking, but she couldn't swim up from the depths. She imagined someone putting cold cloths on her forehead and taking her temperature, but when she forced her gummy eyes open, squinting against the stabbing bedroom lights, she was alone.

She dropped back into a swirling black hole, trying to get away from something but making no progress. Her attempts felt like swimming through molasses. She was so hot. She threw off the covers. Nightmares now. People chasing her with knives, her blood gushing everywhere. She shivered with cold.

Her screams woke her, her throat raw and sore. Not an inch of her that didn't ache. And now she was going to be sick. She pushed back the covers and stood. Floor, walls and stomach swooped and danced. The carpet tilted to meet her.

With shaky hands, she lit the candle on the back of the toilet. Some soothing aromatherapy thing Micah had bought. The gentler light didn't hurt so much. She huddled on the cold tile floor, and let her flu move through its next act. While pondering on the imminence of death, she fell asleep on the floor.

It could have been minutes or hours before she woke, icy and stiff, at the sound of breaking glass. The candle had snuffed itself out, leaving the air redolent with eucalyptus. She listened. All quiet. No wind. No dogs.

No house sounds. Somewhere a car started and drove off. Her watch said 2:36.

Carefully, she pushed herself upright and sat in the deep gray darkness, arms around her knees and back against the tub, gearing herself for the journey back to bed. Over the soothing eucalyptus there was a bitter scent. She took a deep breath, filled her lungs with air, and got a jolt of recognition. Smoke! A sudden adrenaline rush pulled her to her feet. She stumbled into the bedroom, put her phone in her pocket, and started searching for the source.

She checked the living room, the study, the dining room. The smoky smell grew stronger, but she saw no signs of fire. In the kitchen, the air was hazy. She turned on the basement light and peered down. Quiet, cobwebby, musty.

When she opened the door to the garage, smoke billowed into the kitchen. Oh, no. Her car! She grabbed her bag off the counter, jabbing her thumb onto the garage door opener as she fished for her keys. The garage was full of smoke. She dashed into the smoke, jammed the key in the ignition, and slammed it into gear, tires squealing on cement as she backed into the street.

Leaving her bag in the car, she ran back up the driveway and into the garage. Saw flames licking the outside garage wall. Something exploded. A burning sensation on her arm. She hurried into the kitchen, slamming the door behind her. The smoke in the house was thicker now and she had to fight to breathe.

She found the landline phone by the blinking message light, sinking to the floor as she peered through the smoke and punched in 9-1-1 with clumsy fingers. She croaked, "My house is on fire," into the phone. Then "Jordan." Coughing. Her lungs were on fire. What was her address?

From the garage, another explosion. Glass in a window shattered. "Woodmere." She had a number. "1001." A palindrome. The dispatcher was still talking but she dropped the phone.

Crawl into the living room. Less smoke there. Creeping along on her sore belly, she felt the bump of the threshold and then the smoothness of the hardwood floor. Find the edge of the rug. It would lead her to fresh air. She found the edge. Crawled to the door. But it was the wrong door.

Back to the corner and turn. That would lead her out. But she had to rest. Her head hurt. She couldn't breathe. A little rest and she'd go on. She crawled some more. Her little living room seemed the size of a gym. She rested her head on the soft wool carpet.

*   *   *

"Alexis." The man's voice low and insistent, close to her ear. "Why did you set your house on fire?" With her eyes closed she sensed, rather than saw, the questioner moving away. Then the voice, louder and sharper, from a distance. "Why, Alexis? Why?"

There'd been a fire. That was why her lungs felt singed and everything smelled smoky and her arm hurt. Raising her eyelids took too much effort and would expose her stinging eyes to the light, so she didn't bother. She loved her house. Half its value was her own sweat equity. Damn Collins. He'd been there when the house had been violated the first time. Seen how upset she was.

But his voice went on, badgering her with its certainty, with its contempt, with base insinuations and unrelenting interrogation. "What did you think you might accomplish? Win some sympathy? Divert attention from yourself?" Then the voice moved close to her ear again. "Maybe there was something we missed? Something you were desperate to hide. Is that it?"

As her hands clenched into fists, another man's gentle voice murmured, "Hey, hey. Take it easy there. Stay still."

Not Collins. He didn't want her comforted.

Her brain remembered he wasn't allowed to do this and that he knew it. She only had to remind him he couldn't question her without her lawyer present and he'd have to stop. But her throat had been scrubbed with sandpaper. Her lungs hurt. Her right arm throbbed. She was pinned to what she assumed was a stretcher by a weariness someplace beyond exhaustion.

Hot tears slid down her face, running into her ears and into her hair. The hand she directed to wipe them away remained stubbornly at her side. She realized they were giving her oxygen. Maybe in a while the smoke would clear. Finally she summoned the strength for speech. Tore "Stop!" out of her wounded throat.

"Welcome back, Alexis." Collins bent over her with a mean smile. "I was wondering when you'd be rejoining us. And since you *can* talk, maybe you could clear up a few things for me, like where you got the bright idea to use charcoal? Did you honestly think we'd miss that?"

She tried to lift an arm to ward him off, but the EMT, who was wrapping it in gauze from wrist to elbow, put a restraining hand on her and said, "Stay still." Then, to Collins, "I have to ask you to step outside for a few minutes, Officer, so I can work."

Collins grunted and moved grudgingly away.

"Hey, Alexis, do you know where you are?" the EMT asked. She knew he was an EMT because a quick blink revealed he wore a label on his uniform. She shook her head, a minimalist form of denial.

"You're in an ambulance. There was a fire in your house. Do you remember what happened?"

She remembered smelling smoke. Running out in her socks to save her car. Calling 9-1-1. She shrugged.

"You remember some things?" Nod. "Does it hurt to talk?" Another nod. It hurt to nod, too. "You inhaled a lot of smoke," he said. "We're giving you oxygen."

"Water?"

"Slow and easy, now." He gave her a couple of sips through a straw.

"Collins," she said. "Please. Keep him away."

He patted her shoulder. "I'm sure his questions can wait. Is there someone I should call for you? Do you have someplace to go?"

In response to a kind voice and a human touch, she wanted to whimper and squirm like a happy puppy. So grateful for a respite from the vile Collins.

"Go?"

"A friend to stay with? You can't go back to your house tonight." She blinked back tears as he explained, "It's a mess. Still full of smoke."

Her nice house? Would it be all black and sooty? "My phone?"

"It's right here."

She couldn't manage it. "Call Peter Everett. Tell him what happened." Even those few words made her throat feel like she'd swallowed a red-hot poker.

She could have called Dan, but he had his hands full with three babies. Or Lori. Lori would take her in but that might expose little Emma to the flu, though it felt like the flu had done its damage and gone. Claire would have come, but she'd already done so much. Peter had the qualities she needed most right now. He was quiet, kind, safe. He didn't live in Crawford. He would take care of her. Even if her lawyer took her head off in the morning, right now she desperately needed taking care of.

She heard the EMT make the call, apologizing for the ungodly hour, and explaining the situation. "He'll come pick you up. He's on his way." He bent to work on her arm again. It felt hot and angry.

"One more call. Bannerman. George."

She waited until he'd connected and handed her the phone. "George? Alexis Jordan. Someone set my house on fire." Her voice had such an ethereal lightness she wondered that he could hear it at all. But it was the best she could do. "I'm okay. Sort of. Inhaled smoke? Collins thinks I did it. Call Janice for me?"

She held the phone out to the EMT. "Tell him... I can't talk."

Collins returned and talked at her some more. The man must have memorized an encyclopedia of sexual terms. New questions about her alleged sexual misadventures, relentlessly trying to get her to confess to things she hadn't done. She moved his voice to the edge of her consciousness like the buzzing of an annoying fly.

She would certainly confess to impaired judgment. To deep gratitude for the fireman who'd broken through her door, scooped her up, and carried her out into the fresh air. Maybe that she desperately needed a bath. But Collins knew that anyway, since he'd gotten himself pretty up close and personal. Finally Collins muttered, "Blood from a fuckin' stone," and slammed noisily out of the ambulance.

The EMT gave her more water. "You had a close call tonight," he said.

"Give yourself a couple days, take it easy, and you'll be good as new."

She wondered if she'd ever be good as new. Whether, even with a successful outcome in her criminal case, she'd ever be anything like her old self again. "My house, is it bad?"

"I don't know. Want me to see what I can find out?"

If he left, Collins would begin picking at her again. "Please. No. Don't leave me."

He squeezed her hand. "Hey. You'll be okay. Really. Are you scared?"

"Somebody set my house on fire. I could have died. Of course I'm scared."

The EMT held her hand. Time passed.

Finally, Peter came, bringing an aura of reassurance into the ambulance. She felt absurdly safe with him there. The possibility that she could put herself into some else's hands and let go was heavenly. Peter held a whispered colloquy with the EMT, then touched a warm hand to her grimy cheek. She wrapped her hand around his. "Peter?"

He held a finger to his lips. "Don't talk."

He looked fierce and sinister, his face creased with worry. Cheeks dark with what? Four a.m. shadow? "It's okay, Alexis," he said softly. "Whatever it is, you can tell me later. This guy says you shouldn't be talking. Told me about your arm. Let's just get you home to bed."

"My bag, Jeep?"

"Don't talk, Alexis, please. Got my marching orders. Lots of liquids. Aspirin. TLC. I'll get your bag and we'll go."

The EMT helped her up from the stretcher and guided her tottering progress to the ambulance door and down to the ground. "Easy does it. There you go." He set her on her feet, steadied her, and handed her off to Peter. Peter let her try two faltering steps before sweeping her into his arms. She was ready to sleep for a thousand years.

Collins blocked their way. "Where the hell do you think you're going?"

"Taking her home."

"This is her home," Collins grunted. "And I'm not done with her."

"I think you are," Everett said. "What can you accomplish tonight, other than more bullying?"

"I'm trying to get some goddamned answers."

"She's not supposed to talk. Guy says her throat feels like strep, plus inhaling smoke like that." Peter sounded unflappable, though Alexis, pressed up against his chest, felt the tension in his body.

"She can talk just fine," Collins said. "Called you, didn't she?"

"No. The EMT called me."

"Why? You're not her fuckin' next of kin. Woman's got a husband."

"That's right. Where is he, anyway?" He took another step toward the truck, and another, Collins coming right along beside them.

"Who the hell do you think you are?" Collins demanded. "Where are you taking her?"

Peter balanced her with one arm, as easily as if she were a child, while he fished in his pocket for a card.

This had gone on long enough. "Officer Collins." Dragging the words through her ravaged throat. It was worth any amount of pain to shut him up. "I said this before, and I'm saying it again. I will not... speak with you... without my lawyer."

She expected him to interrupt, but maybe he was tired of his own game.

"Tomorrow," Collins grunted. "Tomorrow morning. At the station. With your lawyer."

It was already morning. So did he mean today or tomorrow? She really didn't care. Yesterday, this was when she'd gone out running. That seemed a long time ago.

Peter cradled her against his chest while he opened the door, lifted her carefully onto the seat, and leaned past her to fasten her seat belt. She had a dark moment, remembering Kennedy doing the same thing. But Peter Everett wasn't here to bully her or hurt her or play mind games. For now—likely a pretty short now if Collins had his way—she was safe from hateful people asking intrusive questions.

She only half woke when he carried her into his house. Obeyed like a sleepy child his commands to hold up her hands as he pulled off her smoky sweatshirt and to lift her bottom as he pulled off the filthy pants. Too tired to give a damn that he was seeing her in her underwear. Then she lay on soft, cool sheets, blankets tucked up around her. His lips brushed her forehead, he whispered 'good night' and was gone.

She fell into a black hole and this time, into a sleep mercifully without dreams.

"Oh sun! to tell thee how I hate thy beams,
That bring to my remembrance from what state
I fell..."
—John Milton, *Paradise Lost*: Book IV

CHAPTER TWENTY-EIGHT

She woke to the distant buzz of conversation. Usually it was quiet in the morning, with Micah still asleep. They rarely crossed paths on weekday mornings. But if Micah was home, who was he talking to? She looked toward the window, studying the light, the position of the sun. She was late for school. Terribly late. In all her years of teaching, she'd never overslept.

She sat up in bed, ready to bound downstairs and ask why he hadn't woken her, and realized she wore only her underwear. This wasn't her bedroom. Her lungs burned. Her arm was on fire and wrapped in gauze. She smelled like a campfire.

Where was she? Where were her clothes?

The room was pale grayish blue with a barren dresser top, a neat row of three closed doors and a wooden rocking chair. She was in a queen-sized cherry spindle bed. Clean white sheets and a chambray blue comforter. Plain hardwood floor. Empty bedside tables, except for a few books and a lamp. No pictures. No clutter. And no clues.

What had happened? Why was she in this strange place? She held her poor fuzzy head gently in her cold hands, hoping that if she stayed very still, the circuits would reset. She was dirty, mostly naked, and bruised. Her throat burned and she had a pounding headache. How or where had she injured her arm? She knew she wasn't in jail or in a hospital, but it was clear something bad had happened.

She needed a bathroom, soap, and hot water. Three sides of this room had windows. The fourth wall had three doors. One for the lady. One for the tiger. Maybe the third was the bathroom?

To find out, she'd have to walk. Walking meant getting upright and that would make her dizzy. She might fall down. If she fell, someone might come to see if she was all right. Did she want to be found in her underwear? Did she care? As her need for the bathroom became more urgent, would her priorities change? Write a five-paragraph essay on the dilemma of finding yourself in a strange place in your underwear.

That phrase "five-paragraph essay" banged against an earlier thought. Late for work. The collision triggered the return of memory. She wasn't late for work—she no longer had a job. She didn't have a job because of Evan Palmer.

Last night's awfulness flooded back. She was weak and shaky because she'd been sick. She was bruised and dirty because of the fire. Her throat hurt because of the smoke. She was in a strange place because she'd been burned out of her house. Now she was mostly naked in Peter Everett's bed, oh dear Jesus, God, because she'd been weak enough to ask him for help.

Time to find him, get her clothes, and get herself out of here. Too late for damage control. And she didn't have a car.

She stood, taking baby steps. The first door was a closet. She took a neat blue shirt from its hanger and put it on. It came nearly to her knees. Door number three led to a small hall, and she found the bathroom. She was filthy, and the tub beckoned, but she had no clothes. She attended to basics, gulped a handful of painkillers from the medicine chest, and headed toward the voices.

George Bannerman spotted her first. "Afternoon, Jordan," he called cheerfully.

Janice Trustman sat at the table. She nodded but didn't speak. There was no sign of Peter.

Carefully, she walked to the table and sat. Her lawyer's cold silence continued.

"You're mad at me," she croaked.

"You bet I'm mad at you. First you get a compromising picture taken with Peter Everett, which I had to do some serious arm-twisting to get squelched. Then you spend the night with him. I can do a lot for you, Alexis, but I'm not a miracle worker."

Would she never get the chance to heal? As fast as her wounds scabbed over, the scabs got torn off. The last thing she remembered was that pit bull Collins gnawing on her. Now, her eyes barely open, it was starting all over again, and from someone who was supposed to be on her side.

She felt too awful for this. She turned away. "I have to go lie down."

"Sit down, dammit! We have work to do."

"Janice, take it easy," Bannerman soothed. "The kid has had a rocky twenty-four hours."

"She's going to have a rocky twenty-four years if we don't get on top of this. Look, Alexis, I'm sure you could use some warm and fuzzy right now. But you didn't hire me to hold your hand, you hired me to save your ass."

Alexis made a shaky time-out sign. "Let me... find some tea and toast... and you can jump in with both feet."

"I'm on it." Bannerman smiled at Alexis. "Regular or herbal? Buttered or plain?"

"Peppermint? Buttered?"

"Want anything, Janice?"

The lawyer continued to stare at Alexis. "I want straight answers."

"Right," he said. "Tear off a limb and beat her with it. It's the least you can do."

Alexis planted her elbows on the table to support her wobbly head. "What are you so pissed off about?"

"You mean aside from the obvious stupidity of spending the night with a man who isn't your husband and letting the cop who wants your head on a pole know you're doing it? This guy you knew briefly in high school shows up again and suddenly he's your new best friend? Why didn't you go to a friend's house—a female friend? Or a hotel?"

"It was four in the morning. I'd been sick with a fever and the flu, even before the fire. I inhaled a lot of smoke. I couldn't walk or talk or open my eyes. I certainly couldn't drive. Of my two closest female friends, one had to get up soon to teach, the other has a small child. Same with my good, married male friend, only he has three small children. None of them needed me around, dirty, smelly and bringing the flu. Collins was in my face and he wouldn't stop. I was desperate. Peter felt safe. I knew he'd come."

"You didn't call *me*." The lawyer rolled her eyes. "How can I help you, Alexis, if you won't listen? I said do nothing controversial, nothing the press can get its hands on. Maybe your gentle giant seems like a knight on a white horse to you, but to a world eagerly scrutinizing your morality, he's the drop-dead handsome old boyfriend who's been waiting for his chance, and you're a sexual opportunist who moves without hesitation from one man to the next. Did you consider that before you called him?"

"I didn't consider anything, Janice. I was scared and I was desperate. Collins was spewing his endless litany of filth and his insinuating questions. Someone had just tried to burn down my house with me in it. I could have died. I was practically delusional and I needed a place to go."

"Well, you didn't help matters any. Let me explain one more time, since you don't seem to have gotten it yet. We—meaning you and I—are engaged in a game of Truth or Consequences. You tell me the truth, and I use that information to craft a strategy to protect you from consequences. Right?"

Her throat was still raw. Her eyes stung from the smoke, from weeping and weariness, and the lingering effects of the flu. The sunlight in Peter's living room was piercing and painful. She put up a hand to shield her eyes. "Right. But I have never lied to you, so I don't understand what you're so upset about."

"Besides what I've already said? I'm upset when I hear that there are witnesses who can put you in your car with Evan, with your arm around him, when you tell me there was no relationship between you other than teacher and student. I'm upset when I hear Evan's version of how the affair began… that you invited him back to your house to help you move some furniture, when you tell me Evan has never been in your house.

When I learn that others can corroborate his stories."

Alexis wanted to crawl back into bed and pull the comforter over her head. But she couldn't hide. She heard the lawyer's pen click. Click. Click.

"Janice." There was a whiskey and cigarettes rasp to her voice. It really hurt to talk. "There has never been any improper relationship between me and Evan. The thing in the car? It was nothing. Nothing. No normal kid would read anything into it. The other one... the furniture moving? That's when he said it started? I completely forgot about that."

"The thing with the ice cream was in the paper, Alexis. Weren't you supposed to go over that article and start thinking?" Trustman slammed her palm down hard on the table. "When are you going to stop calling this Everett guy to come and rescue you and start rescuing yourself?"

"Ice cream?" Alexis said.

There was the sharp sound as Janice inhaled. "And just how many other goddamned things are you going to remember, Alexis? Do you have any idea how this looks? For you? For me? Maybe you cherish some absurd notion you can lie your way out of this. If so, forget it. You're a hopelessly bad liar. You'll get all tangled up and trip over your own lies. I suggest you take some time, search through your memory more carefully, and figure out what else you've 'forgotten to tell me' that could make us both look like lying asses. Then I can figure out if I'm still representing you, and how in hell I go about it. Okay?"

You get sick, you get burned, cops search your house and someone tries to burn it down, you pass out from smoke inhalation, and in a few hours you'd better be back on your feet. Otherwise you're off the team.

"Right," Alexis said, "I get it. Shape up or I'm bounced back down to JV."

"Alexis, this is no joke."

She jumped up. "Goddammit! You think I don't know that? You think having Collins and Hovarth whispering every filthy thing a man ever said to a woman everywhere I go is funny? You think I like being in a public place and asked if Evan's taken me in the ass? That shit in my car is funny? That someone trying to burn down my house while I'm asleep is a joke? That I think these things don't matter? That it isn't beyond painful when someone sets my house on fire with me in it, Collins doesn't think arson, he thinks Alexis did this?"

Oh no. She'd forgotten slow and easy. The chair and the table were wobbling. She tried to sit, missed the chair, and landed hard on the floor. She pulled her knees in to her chest and wrapped her arms around them. "Collins accused me of setting my own house on fire."

After a moment, ignoring the burning in her throat, she said, "About Evan and the furniture. Micah and I were out getting ice cream. Evan said, "Hello, Mrs. Jordan." We had this loveseat that needed to be moved upstairs, too heavy for the two of us. Micah saw a big, strong boy and asked if I thought Evan might help. I asked. Evan said he'd come by in a while. We went home. Then Micah went out. When Evan showed up, I apologized that Micah was gone. He said maybe another day. I said thanks for coming and he left. I was dressed. He was dressed. He was in my front hall less than two minutes. End of story."

Janice Trustman stood over her, a hand outstretched to help her up.

"I'm fine down here."

"You make me feel like a bully."

"You *are* a bully."

"I'm trying…"

"Janice, I *know* what you're trying to do. And I'm grateful. But if you're going to yell at me every time Evan finds another way to make me look like a liar, you'll do a whole lot of yelling. He's put a lot of thought into making me look guilty. I know I'm doing a crummy job of defending myself, but I'm used to *being* innocent. I've probably done several things that in hindsight are going to look incriminating, but everything was innocent and well-intentioned."

She swallowed. "You want to hear about the time in the car?"

George Bannerman came in behind her, carrying a tray. He set the tray on the coffee table, pulled her up, and steered her to the couch. "You'll be more comfortable here," he said.

"Comfortable isn't in my vocabulary today."

"Don't know about that," he said, "but unclean and unkempt certainly are."

"Thanks a million. Why aren't you out there ferreting out the truth about Evan?"

"Got one of my best people on it. We're working on the local angle."

"You have people? I thought it would be you."

"It had to be you," he sang, with a Groucho Marx waggling of his eyebrows.

"George," Trustman's voice was sharp. "We're trying to work."

"Me, too, boss," he said. "Bucking up the poor invalid so we can get her story."

The poor invalid slumped on the couch. It didn't do any good to pull herself together. She'd get herself organized into some kind of coherent whole, chug forward a few feet, someone or something would trip her, and she'd fall apart again, like a jalopy held together with paperclips and chewing gum.

Bannerman handed her toast. "Eat, eat," he urged. "You need to build up your strength."

"It's not funny," she said. "I feel like a dishrag."

"And a bowl full of warm, soapy water would be a good place for you."

"About Evan and the car. Last fall there was an important soccer game. Evan had told me how much he wanted his mother to come and see him play. He said she never came to his games, but he'd made a point of telling her how much this mattered. I love soccer, so I was there. And he played a beautiful game. He has a spark that can ignite a team. They were losing until he decided he wasn't letting that happen, and almost single-handedly went out and won it."

She looked at Trustman's suspicious face. "Look, back then, he was just one of my kids. When the boys headed back to the gym, I was sitting in my car. As he passed, I leaned out the window and said, 'You played an incredible game, Evan,' because I knew what it meant to him. He looked at me. Instead of triumph on his face, there was heartbreak. I said, 'What's the matter?' He got in—I didn't invite him—and he said, 'drive me up to the gym, would you' and just slumped over in the seat. He said, 'She didn't come. I played the best goddamned game of my life for her, and she didn't come.' Without thinking, I said I was sorry and gave him a hug."

Alexis wrapped her arms around her body. "So shoot me, okay. I'm probably too damned stupid to be a high school teacher. I sometimes make the mistake of showing the kids I understand how they feel. I know what it's like to play your heart out and be ignored. If I just listened to the deadheads and the burnouts on the faculty and took their advice, this never would have happened. Because I never would have done anything that mattered."

She hugged her arms tighter, trying to hold herself together. "So I'm sorry that I've done dumb things like accidentally let my students know I care. And if that means you can't represent me, so be it. Because it's too late to change the past." She reached for her tea, because she was shivering again, and thirsty, but her hand was too shaky. She pulled it back.

"Alexis want a sippy cup?" Bannerman said.

"Fuck you, George."

"Highly unlikely," he said, "despite your lurid reputation. I'll go make more toast."

She grabbed the tea, cradling the warm cup in two hands and shifted her gaze back to the lawyer. "Like Popeye says, I yam what I yam. A hopelessly flawed human being. Emphasis on human, as good as fired from her job, abandoned by her husband, and most likely burned out of her home. So if you want to make that dumped by her lawyer, too, go ahead and play pile on the pig. It's probably good for my character to see how many hits I can take and keep standing."

"Oh fleeting joys
Of paradise, dear bought with lasting woes!"
—John Milton, *Paradise Lost*: Book IX

CHAPTER TWENTY-NINE

Trustman looked at her watch. "You better get cleaned up. It's almost one-thirty. Collins wants to see you... us... at three. He wanted to see you this morning but I told him that wasn't happening."

"Does that mean you aren't quitting?"

"For the moment."

"No," Alexis said.

Her lawyer's head came up, wary and a little disdainful, like a horse flaring its nostrils.

"I appreciate the difficulty of your position. If you want to represent me, I'm grateful, and if you want to quit, I'll be distressed, but you can't play I will, I won't, I will, I won't, until you scramble the inside of my head like a pan full of eggs. I spent eighteen years playing 'mother, may I?' with a woman who never gave clear signals and couldn't be pleased. That doesn't work for me. I need to know where I stand."

She didn't give Trustman a chance to speak before she rushed on. "What does Collins want and why do we have to do this today? Last night, Collins was crawling down my throat because he knew I was helpless. The man's a big prick and right now, I can't swallow that."

Her face flamed the color of her hair as she realized what she said. From the doorway, Bannerman said, "Colorful, Jordan. Very colorful."

Ignoring him, she asked, "Do we know anything about the fire?" she said. "It was arson, right? Are things at my house very bad? And where's Ev?"

"You mean Peter?" Trustman said. "He went out, muttering something about getting you clothes, and making sure your house was secure, and that there were people he had to see. Didn't say when he'd be back. I hope it's before three. I'm not keen on taking you to the police department like that. You smell like a bonfire and look like a chimney sweep, Cinderella, and there's the matter of shoes."

"I think it's cute," Bannerman said. "There's a certain urchin charm. Too bad Collins is impervious to charm." He checked his watch. "School's out soon. Must be on my way. People to see. Questions to ask. Pictures to take. Who knows? Today I may get that perfect picture of Palmer doing something naughty."

"Dan Morgan's working on getting us Evan's fingerprints," Alexis said. "I gave him your name. Told him you might be coming around."

Bannerman shrugged. "Some people have been hoping for years that I'll come around."

"Anyone know where Peter put my stuff?" Alexis asked.

"I think your bag is in the kitchen."

She pulled herself up and went to the kitchen, still keeping a steadying hand on the furniture and walls. Giving her to Collins today would be like putting a lamb in a lion's den. At least she'd have Janice. She found her things folded on a chair, the bag on top. Her phone was in the bag. There were three new messages. She returned to the living room where she sat and listened.

First was a girl's voice, coming at her in an incomprehensible rush. Lauren Findley, trying to dictate a garbled message. The second was Dan Morgan, announcing, "We have lift off. Or at least the potential for lift off. Call me." Then Lauren again, giving her home phone number, she'd be home by two, and begging Alexis to call.

It wasn't yet two. She might as well take that bath. Her skin felt greasy and grimy and so did her hair. Her lawyer was on the phone, so she just pointed toward the hallway and made scrubbing motions. Trustman nodded.

She was wrapped in a towel, struggling to comb the knotted mass of her hair when Peter knocked on the bathroom door. "I've got your clothes," he said.

She opened the door. He held a suitcase, which he set on the floor. Then he turned to her, filling the small space. "I fixed your front door, so the house is secure. Boarded up the door to the garage and garage windows. The upstairs isn't too bad. Downstairs?" He shrugged. "It's kind of a mess."

"You didn't have to do all that." She struggled with the tangles. Her burned arm made everything harder.

"I wanted to." He took in the comb and her drooping shoulders. "I'll be right back."

He returned with a kitchen stool and held out his hand for the comb. "Sit down."

Tears filled her eyes as she perched on the stool. He was just so damned nice to her. She wasn't used to this much kindness, even less to being around someone observant. Very carefully, he started on her hair, teasing out the snarls. She flashed back to her old Nana Stewart, combing her hair after a bath and crooning, "Pretty girl, pretty, pretty girl." Nana Stewart had departed along with her fleeing father.

"Your lawyer explained about the trouble I'm causing," he said. "You know I only ever wanted to help you, not to make things worse, but I understand how... well, how it looks."

Something husky had crept into his voice, making her aware that she was naked under the towel. What was it Janice had said to her recently? That she was too damned naïve? Maybe it was true. Only a hopelessly naïve woman or one on the make would be with a man she knew was attracted to her, wearing nothing but a towel, pretending that a man combing her hair wasn't erotic.

He set down the comb and reached for the hair dryer.

"Peter, I don't think we..."

But he was in the middle of voicing a thought. "When it's between a man and a woman, it's never completely innocent. But I'd never do anything you didn't want me to. I'll stay away from you, Alexis, if that's the best thing. But please, if you need me for anything, an errand, a lightbulb, call me. I'd do anything for you. Maybe, when this is over..."

"When this is over," she echoed. Maybe he could visit her in prison.

He switched on the dryer and soothing currents of warm air blew over her. She was battered and naked. He was shy and tender. She was married and up to her neck in trouble. He made her feel like a princess.

She wanted what he was offering her. She wanted comfort and safety. She wanted to look into a face that glowed when it saw her, to enjoy the image of her that was reflected back. She wanted to be cherished and special instead of cheated on, lied about, and judged. Who wouldn't? She even wanted the sex that shimmered between them, unspoken but tangible. Loving sex could be so good and healing, and her life was so utterly bad and damaged.

"Done." He set the dryer down and turned to go.

She bit back words that would hold him. Kept her arms down so they would not reach out.

Then he turned and opened his arms and she stepped forward into them. His warm hand started at her shoulder and traveled down her back as slowly as if she were written in Braille and he was just learning to read. Reading her need and her hunger. His hands pressed her against him as he mumbled things into her hair, a litany of confession that wasn't so much words as a vibrating hum that caused a matching vibration deep in her belly.

The bathroom door was open. Janice Trustman steps away in the living room. As suddenly as the impulse had come, it fled, leaving them shaken. He released her, then gently touched her cheek. "I want you as much as any man has ever wanted a woman," he said.

His words curled inside her, leaving her breathless.

"Someday," he said. "Meanwhile, if you need me, I'm here." And he walked out.

She closed the door behind him, knelt by the open suitcase, and started to dress. How odd to have a man, almost a stranger, picking her clothes. Underwear. Socks and shoes. When she emerged from the bathroom, there was no sign of Peter.

"He left," Trustman said, shrugging.

Alexis called Lauren Findley's number. Likely more bad news, but abandoning an upset student wasn't in her rulebook, especially one willing to call her when, to the rest of the world, she was a pariah. Lauren answered on the first ring.

"Oh, hi. Thank you so much, Mrs. Jordan. I was afraid you wouldn't call me back." Something edgy in Lauren's voice. "I've been worrying until I can't stand it. I didn't want to make a nuisance of myself, calling you, but I'd never forgive myself if I didn't tell you."

"Didn't Mrs. Simkoff tell you it was okay to call?"

"Well, yes, but when you didn't call me back, I wasn't sure."

"I didn't call you back last night because I had a fire at my house. What's up?"

"Yes. Well. I mean, you know, I'm like the last person who'd be gossiping or anything, like you do know that's not me."

"That's not you," Alexis agreed, forcing a patience she didn't have.

"But it's, like, if I don't tell you this I'll never forgive myself. So, I'll just say it and get off the phone and I'm sorry I bothered you and everything… with all that's going on."

"If you thought it was important enough to call, it probably was." Trying to be reassuring. Letting Lauren work herself up to this.

"You're always so nice," Lauren said. "That's why it bothered me so much."

"What? What have you heard?" Keep calm, she reminded herself, though Lauren's words grazed her panic button. Her stomach tensed with the agony of waiting. Tea and toast were not much of a panacea against sickness and terror.

"And you can't ever say you heard it from me, because, like I have to live with these girls, don't I?"

Alexis murmured an assent.

"Okay, so, like I overheard it in a conversation between Carrie Canavan and Shireen O'Reilly. I mean, they were talking right in front of me, so it wasn't exactly overheard or anything. Something Evan is supposed to have said. They could be making this up. You know how they both hate you."

Some well-deserved correction and discipline didn't merit anything as strong as hate. But passion ran high in these kids, while perspective didn't. "What did you hear?"

"Maybe he didn't mean it. Maybe he was only joking around. You know how guys are. All big talk and posing."

Her patience ran out. "Lauren, what did Evan say?"

"I... I don't know. I mean, now that I've probably gotten you all upset and everything, it's pretty hard to say. I didn't think I'd have trouble but..." Silence, then what sounded like a sob.

Would they ever get through this game of twenty questions? Hadn't Evan done enough harm? Would he never be satisfied? She couldn't consider that now. She had to talk Lauren through her embarrassment and find out what Evan was planning. This is was what the insanity of her life had come to—using her teaching skills to coax out an ugly threat against herself. "Lauren, is this hard because it's something Evan wants to do to me?"

"Yes. Something Evan wants to do to you. They said that he said... oh, Mrs. Jordan, I'm sorry." While Lauren pulled herself together, Alexis filled the silence with terrifying possibilities. "He said it's gonna be like 'Resident Evil' or 'God of War' or something. One of those violent video games the guys like. What he's going to do to you, that is, so you'll understand how violated and awful he feels. And he's got a great big knife."

Rape, Alexis thought. *Torture. Dismemberment.* Her stomach flipped. There was a long silence, the explosion of exhaled breath. "I'm sorry, Mrs. Jordan. I hope he doesn't mean it. But I had to tell you."

"You did the right thing." She hoped Lauren couldn't hear the quaver in her voice.

She took her own deep breath. Lauren was just a kid caught between loyalty to peers and trying to do the right thing, a hard place for any teenager. Hard for any young woman to have information about something so violent and brutal as the horrors of a video game directed at someone in the real world. Alexis could deal with her own crisis later. First, she had to take care of Lauren. "Is your mother home?"

"Sure."

"It's your decision, but I think you ought to tell her what you just told me. It's a pretty big burden for someone your age to be carrying. It's serious, scary stuff. It would be good to have a grownup to share it with."

"My mom's kind of a stiff."

"She's also your mom, and she really cares about you. She wants you to be happy and untroubled. I think sharing this, your struggle to do the right thing and your worries about betraying your friends, would be a good idea."

Lauren uttered a relieved, "All right," and hung up.

Alexis put her phone away and went to tell Trustman. The minute she came into the room, her lawyer was alert. "What's wrong? What's happened now?"

"Don't we have to go?"

"Okay. You can tell me on the way. Bring your stuff and I'll drop you at your house afterward."

"Right."

She got her suitcase and followed her lawyer out.

When they were on the road, Trustman said, "You look sick."

"I am sick." Sick at heart. Sick in her soul. Sick of this whole, ugly, disturbing business. But she didn't want anyone's goddamned sympathy.

"What is it this time?"

"This time? You sound as if I'm a hypochondriac."

"I meant who was on the phone and what did they say that turned you green."

Green, huh? Great with her hair. People always had such positive responses to red and green. "One of my students. Lauren Findley. Remember when I first told you about Evan, I said I was afraid of him? Of what he might do?"

"You were worried that he might become violent."

"Lauren says she overheard two girls talking. She says that Evan wants to hurt me."

"Hurt you how?"

She forced the words out. "I don't know. He mentioned imitating some violent video games where women are raped and tortured, so that I can understand his humiliation and feel what it's like to be on the powerless end of a relationship. She says he has a big knife."

She gripped the door handle. "Stop the car. Please."

Even before Janice's car stopped rolling, Alexis bolted out and gave up her tea and toast. She stood by the roadside, gasping, her eyes streaming and her heart pounding, aware of the passing cars and how this must look.

She was homeless. Unemployed. An outcast. None of it was enough for Evan.

"For never can true reconcilement grow
Where wounds of deadly hate have pierced so deep."
—John Milton, *Paradise Lost*: Book IV

CHAPTER THIRTY

When this was over, she could make her fortune marketing the Evan Palmer Stress and Terror Diet. Perfect for talk shows and the shopping channels. Begin each day with a generous serving of ignominy, mix with humiliation. For lunch, threats and rumors, spiced with bold and curious glances, with a julienne of courage. Dinner was accusations and slander, or humble pie, followed by cold desertion. Then a bedtime snack of violence. In only weeks, you, too, could become a shadow of your former self.

As Alexis got in the car again, Janice handed her scented alcohol wipes and a bottle of water, staying silent while Alexis composed herself. "I'm sorry. I couldn't help it."

"You think I'm heartless, don't you?"

"It's not you. I'm not used to being out of control like this. It frightens me. One of the many things that frighten me."

Trustman put the car in gear. "You need to find someplace to stay, Alexis. Somewhere you'll be safe."

"I know. I don't see the Crawford Valley police department being very helpful about this."

"Is there somewhere you can go?"

"I'll call my best friend, Lori. We used to teach together. I'm sure she'll take me in."

"Why don't you call her now?"

She punched in Lori's number, exchanged pleasantries, and listened to her friend's babble of sympathy, Baby Emma's more cheerful babble in the background. "Yes. It's been horrible. Look, you heard about the fire, right? My place is a mess. I need someplace to stay tonight. Just for tonight. Could I stay with you?"

She got silence. Then Lori said, "Lex? I'm not sure. I'm afraid Ned... well, you know what he's like these days. I mean, I guess if you really need a place."

What had someone said? Your friends won't be your friends? "I really do. It's just tonight, Lori, until I get things cleaned up."

The silence persisted.

"If you can't, I'll understand."

Like hell she would. She was sick of people who expected *her* to be understanding. Dr. Huston expected her to understand that it would inappropriate for her to be teaching adolescents in her current tainted state. Mark expected her to understand that he could be a sponging, needy friend until it became inconvenient for him, then she was *persona non grata*. Micah expected her to understand that he could have affairs, but couldn't bear her humiliation or disgrace.

"Well, it might be better... you know how Ned can be." Lori twisted her words around a little, trying to wheedle some forgiveness.

Lori hesitated because Ned wouldn't like it? Whatever happened to Lori the forthright and courageous teacher? Was this an example of love for Ned conquers all, including kindness, generosity and friendship?

"Right." Alexis wished her lawyer weren't there hearing this. "I've been fired from my job, arrested, burned out of my house. My husband's left me. I've got cops breathing down my neck and reporters on my lawn. Why should I expect my best friend to help?"

"Oh, Lex. Come on. It's not fair to lump me with those people."

Weren't some of "those people" also friends? And family? Since everyone broke down into pro- and anti-Alexis these days, what the hell did pro-Alexis mean if not help and support?

"You're making me feel awful, Lex."

Well sorry, but she wanted Lori to feel bad.

She couldn't talk around the lump in her throat, so she pushed "End."

Lori called right back. "I'm so sorry, Lex." Her voice choked like she was crying. "I'm a total jerk. You ask for help and what do I do? Please come. Ned won't be here. He's working late. We can have pizza and wine. Rent a movie. A regular girl's night. Long time since I've had one of those. I'll leave the door open. Emma usually goes down around seven, so if I don't answer, it's because I'm with her. Okay?"

"Okay. Thanks." She hung up before she said something mean.

Alexis stared out at the passing scene, the blue of the sky, the flowering shrubs, people in spring clothes. Everything looked so ordinary and unchanged. Life went on, the routines were the same, people lived the same lives, while hers was irrevocably changed. She studied her hand, feeling that even her skin must reflect this change. Saw fading bruises from the arrest, the thick bandage, what seemed a permanent case of the shakes. What was coming wouldn't help.

"What should I be prepared for with Collins?"

"He'll probably have an assistant D.A. with him," Trustman said. "You'll answer the questions you can answer, but look at me first. I'll tell you whether it's okay. If you don't know, don't answer. Don't speculate. Don't agree with anything he says, no matter how reasonable it sounds. Always give dates as approximate. You know what a snake he is. This is an opportunity to learn what they're thinking."

"I know what they're thinking. Collins has been whispering it in my ear for days."

"Well, now he'll have to say it for my ears, too. And I think, whatever he wants, that we'll keep it brief. You're not up for a long interrogation today. We're just trying to look cooperative."

"I don't feel cooperative."

"Then act. And if you think you're going to be sick again, ask for a ladies room."

Collins was waiting in an interview room like the one she was in before, only larger, with a big man in a bad suit, introduced as Karl Berger. Big as in stout. Berger had receding hair, a high red forehead, and belligerent chins. He greeted Trustman coldly, shoved her card in his pocket without a glance, and looked at Alexis like she was something found on his shoe. In the room less than two minutes, she hated Berger as much as she did Collins. She laced her fingers over her tender stomach and waited.

"For the record," Berger began, "we are conducting this interview at the Crawford police department, and the parties present are…"

What came first was a whole series of questions about her background and education, which Trustman let her answer. These were followed by some questions about her marriage. Her husband's name and occupation. How long she'd been married. Then the first zinger.

"Mrs. Jordan, are you and your husband currently living together?"

Did a few nights apart constitute a separation? She felt separated, but was it any of their business? "My husband and I have been living at the 1001 Windmere address for the past five years."

"Isn't it true that you and your husband are separated and he is living at Hamden House apartments, Unit 9-C?"

Her lawyer had said don't guess. She and Micah hadn't discussed a separation and she had no idea where Yvonne lived, so Alexis simply sat and waited for the next question.

"Isn't it true, Mrs. Jordan, that your husband is currently living with a woman named Yvonne LaCroix at the Hamden House apartments?"

She didn't respond.

"Isn't it true, Mrs. Jordan, that your husband is having a sexual relationship with Yvonne LaCroix, that Ms. LaCroix is one of his students, and that this relationship has been going on since last fall?"

"That's three questions, Karl," Trustman said.

"You want me to break them down?" he said. "Okay. Mrs. Jordan, is your husband having a sexual relationship with Yvonne LaCroix?"

"I don't know," Alexis said. "You'd have to ask him."

"Is Yvonne LaCroix one of your husband's students?"

"You'd have to ask him."

Berger shrugged. "Mrs. Jordan, to your knowledge, has your husband ever been unfaithful to you?"

"I've had my suspicions. I don't know that I've ever had actual knowledge, whatever that means."

"Isn't it true, Mrs. Jordan, that at the time your own relationship with your husband began, he was married to another woman?"

"At the time our relationship began, he told me he was single."

"But subsequently, you learned that he was married?"

"Yes."

"But you continued the relationship?"

"No. I discontinued the relationship and refused to see him as long as he remained married." She was puzzled. This didn't seem relevant to anything. She looked at Trustman, but her lawyer's face was impassive.

"Do you recall an occasion a few years ago, when you screamed at your husband in a restaurant that if he didn't stop having affairs, you would start having them, too?"

It could have happened. Micah's conduct had occasionally made her utterly furious, and on those rare occasions when she lost her temper, she really lost it. But she didn't remember the incident. "I don't recall such an occasion."

Berger went on for what felt like hours asking her questions about her relationship with Micah. She realized Micah must have given them this information. His sexual and financial infidelity wounded her. But betraying the secrets and confidences of their marriage was like tearing the wounds open and pouring salt in. She pictured Micah holding forth. "Alexis has always been rather insecure about her abilities as a teacher... blah, blah, blah." The more Berger asked about her private life—her fears, her insecurities, her job worries, difficulties with her mother—the clearer the depths of Micah's betrayal became. She wanted to deal with the terrible pain of his betrayal, but she had to stay focused.

"Do you recall telling your husband, early in your teaching career, that you weren't sure you'd ever get used to the boys staring at you and didn't know if you could handle it?"

"It was a little unnerving at first. I was only four years older than the seniors were. It's part of the learning process. No one starts any career aware of all the challenges ahead and how to handle them."

"Mrs. Jordan, isn't it true that you've chosen to dress in loose and baggy clothes because you find your body unattractive and want to disguise it?"

"I choose to wear unrevealing clothes because high school students have enough distractions. I want my students to be listening to what I say, not noticing how I look."

She looked at Trustman. When was her lawyer going to make this stop? If Trustman didn't intervene soon, she'd stop it herself. Enough was enough.

Berger went on, all his questions prying and personal. She did her best to follow her lawyer's instructions and playact as he continued to reveal the extent of Micah's betrayal, all the half-truths and lies. Her innocence, her insecurities, her hopes, and dreams—all the things she'd confided to her husband as her companion and lover—coughed up and given to strangers to use against her. She felt as if something fragile had shattered inside her and was stabbing her with its sharp edges.

"Isn't it true, Mrs. Jordan, that you once told your husband you could understand why he had trouble resisting his students' flirtations because your own were so attractive?"

The room was very cold. Maybe another of Collins' ploys. He knew she'd be vulnerable. The more Berger talked, the colder she got. She touched her cheek. Her hand was frigid. If Evan's wound was causing a spreading and insidious infection, Micah's had gone straight to her heart. Maybe that sharp, broken thing inside was causing internal bleeding and she was slowly going into shock.

How would she endure months of this? Like a cornered animal. An explosive, frustrated, exquisitely fragile animal. Berger's exposed, flabby throat was looking quite tempting.

"Cold in here, isn't it?" her lawyer remarked. "Alexis, you have a sweater in the car, don't you? Why don't you go get it?"

"I can send—" Collins began.

"And Grant, maybe you could scare up a cup of tea?"

Nicely done. Alexis took the keys and headed for the door, Collins right on her heels. She steeled herself for one of his nasty remarks, but all he said was, "Milk or sugar?"

"Both. Please." Her effort to look normal as she descended the stairs and crossed the lot was like she imagined walking a straight line was for a drunk. She unlocked Janice's car, seized by the urge to jump in and take off. Hit the highway and keep going until she found someplace peaceful and soothing, somewhere she could rest and get her perspective back. Right now, she was a ping pong ball and everyone else owned the paddles. But running wouldn't be understood as a panicked and exhausted act. It would be seen as guilt. And there was also the small matter of stealing her lawyer's car.

She lifted her suitcase onto the back seat, her skin pricking with an eerie sense of being watched. Looking around, she saw nothing out of the ordinary. But that was how the world looked these days—ordinary— when she knew that wasn't true.

She put on the sweater, knowing neither tea nor warmth would restore her. Every word she spoke felt like someone was running a file up and down her throat. Might as well go back and tell them she was done. What did she care how they reacted? She already knew what they thought of her. She locked the car and retraced her steps, moving with the stunned slowness of the badly wounded.

She slid into her seat and wrapped her cold fingers around the teacup. Before she could speak, Berger jumped in with another question. "Mrs. Jordan, is it true that for the past two years, you've been trying to have a child?"

"On and off."

"Do you recall telling your husband that if he was unwilling to have a child with you, you would find someone else who would?"

"No." It was a possibility she'd barely admitted to herself. She'd hoped Micah would resolve his ambivalence and come around. As he had, periodically, though no pregnancy had resulted.

"Mrs. Jordan." Berger paused, as if he could sense her thoughts drifting. "Wasn't one reason you initiated a sexual relationship with Evan Palmer so that you might become pregnant?"

She almost laughed out loud. Pick out a likely stud from the healthy crop at the high school? If that was her plan, wouldn't she choose a closer match to her husband? She shook her head. "There has never been any relationship between me and Evan Palmer other than that of teacher and student, within the appropriate boundaries of such relationships."

Berger looked down at the sheet of paper he was using to craft his questions, then over at Collins, telegraphing a none-too-subtle "watch this." Collins acknowledged with a slight nod. "Mrs. Jordan, are you aware that your husband has had a vasectomy?"

Alexis stared at the cup in her hands, seeing neither cup nor hands. There was a black rushing in her head. The sound of the breaking cup, the splash of hot liquid, happened out on the fringes of perception. She had no memory of getting up or leaving the room until she found herself in the parking lot, leaning against the car.

Trustman unlocked the doors, took Alexis by the elbow, and steered her into the car.

"How could he do that, after all we've..."

"Your husband is an idiot. These days, an affair with a student is a firing offense. He knows it. Berger and Collins know it. I expect they leaned on him a little and next thing you know, he's telling them anything they want to save his own ass."

"Speaking of ass, I feel like one. Trying to get pregnant by a man who never bothered to tell me he had a vasectomy."

"You didn't know?"

"I had no idea. None. He even acted sorrowful along with me when I got my period. Like Evan told the cops... there are condoms in the table beside the bed. For when he seemed to get ambivalent about having a baby. So either Micah is lying now, or he was lying then—and playing me for the complete fool I am." This latest humiliation was such a deep betrayal. It was so intimate.

As she stared through the car windows through a blur of tears, she had a clear vision of Micah's next move, and something hardened inside her. A hard core surrounded by a dead numbness. "Janice, tomorrow morning, I want to file for divorce. And is there some way you can get a paper, an injunction or whatever you call it, to keep him from taking things out of the house and our accounts until we can sit down with our lawyers and sort this out? Because once he realizes I know what he's done—the big lies, the little lies, all his deceptions—he's going to be there with a U-Haul, looting the place."

True, she'd been building toward this for days, but making the decision was an admission to herself of something irrevocably broken. The pain was almost unbearable. "Please," she said, "can you take me home now."

EVAN – EIGHT

He found the picture in a manila envelope under the wiper of his car. Scrawled on the envelope, in sloppy black writing: "Bitch doesn't waste any time, does she?"

Carrie, who'd wheedled a ride home from school, was hopping around, trying to snatch the envelope. "Come on, Evan, let me see. What is it? What's in the envelope and why was it on your windshield?"

He wanted to open it in privacy. It felt like something significant, something he needed to deal with, without her yapping in his ear like a Chihuahua. He held the envelope out of reach. "Come on, Carrie, back off. It's private, okay?"

"Oh, private. Probably a picture of some slut you've slept with, isn't it? Who? Come on, Evan, let me see."

He couldn't stand it another minute. She thought she was so damned cute with all that fucking bouncing and noise. She never paid attention to what he said, to what mood he was in. Now that he was no longer eager to get into her pants, he realized Carrie reminded him of The Witch. She was nosy, self-centered, and critical of him in lots of the same ways. What a stomach-turning thought—sleeping with a girl who was like your mother.

While he processed those thoughts, she grabbed the envelope and raced off across the parking lot, shrieking with laughter. As she ran, she tore the envelope open, then stopped beside Mr. Morgan's truck and pulled out its contents. She was staring at the picture when he came up and snatched it from her hand.

"Looks like your lover-girl's got herself a new man," she said. "Big guy, too. I wonder if it's true what they say about big guys?"

He felt a surge of righteous anger as he stared at the photograph of Mrs. Jordan in the cemetery, kissing a man he didn't recognize. He could tell from the season, her clothes, her hair, all the things he'd carefully studied about her, that the photo was recent. It made her rejection of him that much more painful, his anger that much more righteous. She didn't shoot him down because she was a faithful wife and an honorable teacher, like she said. She rejected him for some other guy. He'd never felt regret for how he was punishing her. He'd known all along she deserved it. But now he felt even more justified, his anger fueled afresh.

He felt a powerful urge to hurt her. Do the things to her he'd been dreaming about, that had to be done to really punish her. Time to stop thinking about it and do it. He crumpled the photo between his fingers. Soon it would be Mrs. Jordan between his fingers. Begging for mercy. How he was going to love that—Mrs. Jordan begging for something from him instead of telling him what to do.

Carrie's infuriating noise continued in his ear. "Will you shut the fuck up!" he said.

She planted her hands on her hips and flipped her head back and forth. "No, Mr. Big Shot, I will NOT shut up. Jeez. You're so goddamned controlling, you know? And it's always about you, isn't it? How I feel, what I want, that doesn't matter at all. And you know I hate it when you use the word 'fuck.'"

"I'll say fuck as much as I please."

"Oh. Right. Go ahead. Say it all you want. You're just mad because your love object, Mrs. Jordan, won't fuck you because she wants a mature man instead of a pimple-faced high school boy."

He looked down into her pale face, her twisted, purple-painted mouth, dumb plucked eyebrows rising like puzzled moons above her eyes, and he hit her, watching with immense satisfaction as she went sliding down the side of the truck and landed with a thud on her twitchy little ass. She stared up at him in complete astonishment, a trickle of blood starting at the corner of her mouth. Then her face crumpled and she began to cry.

That was his cue. He was supposed to help her up, fawn over her, apologize a thousand times. Then, satisfied that he must love her, she'd let him take her home and fuck her.

But he had something else in mind. He was saving himself. Leaving her sitting there, he strode back to his car, the crumpled picture fluttering in his hand.

"The scarlet letter was her passport into regions where other women dared not tread. Shame, Despair, Solitude! These had been her teachers,—stern and wild ones,—and they had made her strong."
—Nathaniel Hawthorne, *The Scarlet Letter*

CHAPTER THIRTY-ONE

When they stopped in her driveway—no press, at least, perhaps they knew the house was uninhabitable—Trustman got out her notebook. "Let me get some basic information. I'll file your divorce complaint in the morning. If you're sure."

"Absolutely sure." Numbly, Alexis gave the necessary data. The lawyer looked sad, as though, tough as she was, she felt genuinely sorry about what was happening. She also wrote down Lori's number, then put the notebook away. "I'm going to sound a whole lot like a mom, but I wish there were a way I could make things better."

"Gonna take more than a kiss and a lollipop to fix this boo-boo."

"I'm afraid so. Still, let's hope that while you were being tortured at the PD, George was out scaring up ammunition. He's really good at what he does, and with a kid like Palmer, there's usually something. They rarely progress to this level without some preliminary signs. I'll call you if there's anything new."

"Janice, did you mention Evan's threat to Collins?"

"He dismissed it. Swagger, he said. Bravado and wounded pride. Sometimes even the smartest people can be blind. Collins, as much as I dislike his tactics, is an able cop. But they're really all the same. If it quacks like a duck and walks like a duck, they're not likely to look further. He did offer to have patrol keep an extra eye on your place."

"Even when you told him about the knife?"

Trustman shrugged. "I'm glad you're not sleeping at home. Meanwhile, try to put it out of your mind. Go to your friend's house and have a good time."

Alexis felt far removed from good times. She collected the mail, sorting through it until she found the check from her mother. Then, gearing herself up to face the damage, she headed for the house. Standing on the steps, breathing in damp smoke and ash, she almost couldn't go in.

She looked back at her suitcase, sitting forlornly in the driveway, and at her Jeep, the only car on the street. At her blackened garage and her yard and gardens, trampled by firefighters and the press. She felt scorched and trampled herself. It was too late in the day to open a bank account and deposit the check and too early to head over to Lori's. She would have gone running, but her lungs and throat still hurt. She might as well assess the damage and make a cleanup plan.

Seeing the unnecessary messes made by the cops and even the necessary one made by the firefighters almost broke her heart. Much of the downstairs was coated with smoky residue and grime. The air was thick and acrid with smoke and burning and the scent of damp. So many of these things were her thrift store treasures, restored to life and beauty though hours of sanding, scrubbing and painting.

The kitchen was the worst. There wasn't a pot or pan or dish or glass that didn't need washing, and every inch of counter, shelf, and wall need scrubbing. She couldn't face any of it right now.

Too tired to work, too restless to do nothing. A practical use of the time would be to get new running shoes. She lugged the suitcase inside, then went out to the Jeep. In last night's confusion, she hadn't locked it. On the passenger seat lay a small piece of paper, anchored by a stone. She recognized her handwriting. A scrap from her missing diary. It said, "… *sometimes Micah says he fantasizes about tying me to the bed and having rough sex until I beg him to stop. He gets excited just talking about it. It's fun to share our fantasies but I wonder if he'd really do all those things, if he really wants to? I find the idea of being helpless very frightening.*"

She drove to the mall, trying some loud music therapy to see if she could chase away her demons. How do you run away from something invisible? Protect yourself from a danger others refuse to believe existed? She flew into the first available parking space and practically ran to the mall door. An hour later, she hurried back across the parking lot carrying her new shoes, socks, jog bra and running tights. A person more susceptible to shopping as therapy might have been healed. She felt clumsily held together with Band-Aids, which gave way when she saw another paper under her wiper.

"It disturbed me last night when Micah said he sometimes dreams of raping me, of grabbing me suddenly and forcing me to do exactly what he wants. No love. No reciprocity. Just pure sex... He says most men fantasize about rape. It's one way they get excited..."

She scanned the lot. Evan didn't show himself, but she knew he was watching.

Shopping was a great way to kill time. She had to hurry home and grab her suitcase or she'd be late. An evening of pizza and girl talk would be fun. As she ducked in her house to grab the suitcase, something rustled under her shoe. Holding her breath, she switched on the light. This time, he'd used a hi-liter, her own words illuminated in bold yellow: *"Sometimes, when he says he's working, he's looking at pornography, and the things he likes to look at turn my stomach. Bondage and S&M. Whips and chains and obscene positions and women being penetrated in awful ways. It makes me sick to think I'm having sex with a man who entertains himself like that."*

She looked nervously around the silent house, then shoved the paper in her pocket with the others and hurried to the car, haunted by the feeling he was watching.

*   *   *

She'd been there only fifteen minutes, and Lori was pouring their first glasses of wine, when Ned came home early. He stopped inside the door like he'd been frozen by a stun gun, stared at her, then turned on his wife. "Lori, I cannot believe you did this. You allowed this woman into our home."

"Ned, listen to yourself! Alexis is my best friend. Of course I allow her into my home. She's staying here tonight. Has to. She had a fire at her house." Her words were bold, but Lori cringed slightly, like a dog expecting to be kicked.

"Over my dead body!" he roared.

Lori stared at him as though his Jekyll-Hyde transformation baffled her as much as it did Alexis. "Please lower your voice," she said. "Emma is sleeping."

"Emma is an innocent child," he said, raising his voice. "And I will not have someone like her," he stabbed a belligerent finger at Alexis, "a child molester, in my house or anywhere near my daughter."

"I don't believe any of that, Ned. I know the boy and he's dangerously unbalanced. Besides, Alexis is my friend," Lori repeated. "She needs our help."

"She needs more help than we can give," he said. "I don't know how to make this any clearer. I will not have that woman in my home. I will not have her near my daughter."

"Neddy, I..."

Lori stared miserably from one of them to the other. "Alexis, I don't know what to say. I don't know what's going on here. I never would've invited you if I thought he could be so rude, so terrible to you, when you've been through so much."

"Don't apologize for me," he said, still addressing only his wife. "Making judgments about someone's immoral behavior is a perfectly acceptable thing for any adult to do. She cheated on her husband, seduced a fifteen-year-old boy. A child, Lori. You used to be teacher. How can you stand by someone who would behave like that?"

"I still *am* a teacher, Ned," she said quietly. "And I repeat... I don't believe for a second that Alexis did those things. I know the boy, remember?"

"If you would think with your head instead of your heart." He turned to face Alexis. No longer the dull, self-centered, slightly supercilious man she knew but some stranger ferocious with anger. "Lori and I need to discuss this matter in private," he said. "Please get your things and go."

"Ned! She can't!" Lori wailed.

"She damned well can!" He slammed his fist on the counter. Emma began to wail.

Lori gave her a helpless look. "I've got to see to her."

"I'll come with you." Alexis wasn't staying alone with him. She'd rather face a classroom of out-of-control teenagers than one self-righteous suburban husband with at least two scotches under his belt and his own private domain to oversee and dominate.

"Don't you dare—" he began pompously.

"Don't be an ass," Lori snapped. "She's got to get her things."

Sulkily, he stumped to the cupboard, got out a glass, and poured himself a generous measure of wine. Alexis followed Lori up the stairs.

"Oh, Lex, I am so sorry. I never know when he's… what will set him off." She paused outside the room where her baby was screaming. "Let's just say, you aren't the only one with husband problems."

Alexis tried to compose herself. Her heart was racing. In the soft light of the guest room's bedside lamp, the blond wood bed with its cheerful quilt was so inviting. She'd been looking forward to crawling into it. Instead, she grabbed her suitcase and her bag and headed for the stairs.

Lori, with Emma over one shoulder, held out a hastily wrapped package. "Here," she said. "Put this in your bag. A little something I want you to have. And don't, whatever you do, unwrap it until you get home."

She drove through the empty darkness consumed by a terrible sadness. Light rain floated down. She parked on the next street again and let herself in the back door, making sure it locked behind her. Then she carried her things upstairs. Peter said it was better up there. She should call Trustman and let her know what had happened. Go to a motel. She was too tired to bother.

She turned on the bedroom light, illuminating her unmade bed and the mess the police had left. She couldn't face tonight in the bed she'd shared with Micah.

She went into the guest room—what would, she thought ironically, have been the baby's room—and set down her bags. Sitting on the edge of the creaky double bed, she pulled out the package Lori had given her and stripped off the happy birthday wrapping.

Many happy returns of the day, she thought, as she opened the small case and stared at the dainty little handgun. A loaded gun. Feeling a whole lot more like Calamity Jane than Annie Oakley, she put on a sleeveless pink nightgown, tucked the gun under her pillow, and tried to sleep.

"Regions of sorrow, doleful shades, where peace and rest can never dwell, hope never comes."
—John Milton, *Paradise Lost*: Book I

CHAPTER THIRTY-TWO

A swarm of harpies were gathered around her bed, wings folded and claws in their laps, like matrons at a tea party, discussing her as though she wasn't there. Their voices created a distant cacophony. Their black feathers rustled like stiff taffeta as they turned and chatted, and a foul, smoky scent rose from them. Once or twice, one of them stretched out a claw and patted Alexis in a manner almost maternal, as if to say, "Well, dearie, in your present state, if you crave comfort, this is what you get."

Harpies. Fabulous monsters. Rapacious and filthy. Welcoming her into their number. She struggled to wake and send them packing, but weariness lay so heavily on her she couldn't make it to the surface. They smiled at her efforts, smiles only half malicious, as though recognizing a kindred spirit. She fought to rise up, deny the connection, and chase them out of her head, but she was imprisoned in the dream.

What brought her to the surface with no memory of waking or getting out of bed, was the unmistakable crackle of breaking glass.

She grabbed the throw from the foot of the bed, wrapped it around herself, and crossed to the window, expecting to see her empty street and silent darkness. Instead, it looked like a football rally. Cars and SUVs lined the street and crowds of teenagers, many clustered under umbrellas, milled about before her house, drinking from paper cups, occasionally yelling encouragement as someone threw something else at her house. The trees and bushes were strung with toilet paper streamers, her lawn littered with papers and spilled trash. Someone had started a small, smoky bonfire in her driveway. One boy was urinating on her azalea bush.

She ran into the bedroom, dialed 9-1-1, and told the dispatcher what was happening, making no effort to control her hysteria. He said they'd already had a call and cars were on the way. As she went back to the upstairs hall to watch for the police, a rock burst through the window, showering her with glass.

Good sense said run to the back of the house, to the master bedroom, away from the street. A furious sense of violation kept her by the window, surveying the crowd, well-illuminated by a streetlight and their own car headlights, making a mental list of those she recognized. Laurie Kaplan, capering like a demented pixie, snapped pictures like she was recording the event for the school paper. Three tall boys who appeared to be the leaders were Evan's friends, Jason Rogers, Luke Barton, and Billy Staples. As she watched, they launched a fusillade of rocks that thudded against her house.

She looked at her pillow, where Lori's gun lay. For one terrible moment, she considered going forth like a homesteader in the Old West, armed to defend her property. But thrilling though the impulse was, countering their violence with worse violence would bring her down to their level, making her as much a thug as those undisciplined adolescents out there indulging in unspeakable destruction as entertainment.

They'd just broken a third window when the first patrol car rolled up. Without getting out of the car, he made a loud announcement, ordering everyone to clear out and go home. A second car pulled up behind the first. That officer got out, went over to the window of the first car. Together they watched the crowd of teenagers disperse.

The assault on her property ended like a spring party, with everyone slowly furling their umbrellas, drifting to their cars, and driving off.

Clutching the blanket around her, she stood in her dark upstairs hall, cold rain drifting in, curtains billowing, glass sharp under her bare feet, enveloped by helplessness and desolation. Her lawyer had said she was entitled to the same rights and protections as other citizens. From the actions of the Crawford Valley police, it seemed she was entitled to none. The practice in Crawford was to look lightly on teenage hijinks, to disperse crowds rather than make arrests. But this was no prank, this was mob mentality vandalism, just like the out-of-control party at the Rinaldis' that ended in looting and vandalism. Condoning it sent the message that such destructive behavior was acceptable.

No one came to the door to see if she was all right. One cruiser flicked its lights and sounded the siren briefly. Then they drove away, leaving her shivering in her violated house with shattered glass and rain coming in, her vandalized yard rank with garbage.

She should call her lawyer, or George or Peter. Get someone over to help. But she was tired of laying her unremitting troubles before her paid friends, and she'd been instructed to stay away from Peter. Instead, she went onto adrenaline-fueled autopilot. Like a zombie, she went to work trying to repair the damage and restore order.

She swept up the glass, then got a roll of plastic from the basement and covered the broken windows. This was trash night, and it looked as though they'd dumped all the trash from the neighborhood in her yard. Oblivious to the rain, barefoot and in her nightgown, she went out to move it off the few flowerbeds that weren't already ruined.

She padded back and forth across the yard, gathering the bags and dragging them to the driveway. Aching, drenched, and blue with cold, she trudged. The sodden strands of toilet paper she pulled from the bushes clung to her arms like spider webs. She got trash bags to collect the loose stuff the rain was matting against the ground. Slimy, stinking garbage that would reek when day came and it warmed up. Coffee grounds and orange peels and bloody meat wrappers and chicken bones and vegetable peelings. Rancid lunch meat. Dirty diapers.

She never heard his car, never saw him approach until Collins was beside her, yelling in her ear, "Alexis, stop it. Stop it! You'll make yourself sick." He put a hand on her arm.

She slapped it away. "Stay the fuck away from me."

When he didn't budge, she picked up the closest thing, a gristly beef bone, and threw it at him, missing by a mile. "You heard me. Go away. Get in that joke of a police car and drive away like your buddies did.

Serve and protect, my ass! No one questioned, no names taken, no arrests made. Just roll up and disperse the crowd like it was a fucking picnic."

She heaved a soda can at him. "Whatever happened to the fucking presumption of innocence, huh? The rights of citizenship?" The can clattered noisily onto the sidewalk behind him.

"Look at this place... at this... this... Jesus Christ, Collins. This is my home! Even if you don't care about me, it affects the whole neighborhood, you know. The way it will stink."

Her voice faltered like a badly tuned engine, returning as a ragged scream that hurt her throat. "Arson. Vandalism. Destruction. This is my home, goddammit. They've turned it into a garbage dump. How on earth will I...? You want to know who did this? I can give you names. Not that you care. All the time in the world to harass one small woman. No time to stop the rampaging mob or its ringleaders, the teenagers who are terrorizing our town. No wonder Evan thinks he can do whatever the hell he wants."

He was talking, but she couldn't hear over the furious pounding of her heart, the wild pumping of blood in her head. "You know why they think it's okay to do this? Because your department lets them. Jason Rogers. Billy Staples. Luke Barton. Evan's buddies. Along with an admiring crowd you are teaching to watch destruction as entertainment. First the Rinaldis, then this."

"Calm down and come inside," he said. "You're making yourself sick."

"*You* make me sick. And what the hell do you care anyway?"

She grabbed a rotten orange and pitched it at his head. Nothing hit. Nothing stuck. "Will you please go away and leave me alone. What the fuck are you doing here, anyway? You stop by for some entertainment? Think maybe you've finally found the perfect time to come and pick my bones, you insatiable vulture? You think you've finally broken me enough so I'll answer your filthy questions and confess? Did you fucking *plan* this?"

She picked up a spongy eggplant and hurled it in his general direction. Staggering with exhaustion. Her aim getting worse and worse. Her voice a jagged rasp. "Well, I am ready to confess. I am. I confess to having been stupid enough and soft-hearted enough to care about my students. To listen to their troubles and to want to make their high school lives go a little better. If I had it to do over, I might make those same mistakes again. Though after tonight, I wonder how I gave six years of my life to that pack of animals."

She searched for something else to throw, while Collins stood a little distance off, continuing to talk in a soothing voice. Probably trying to talk her down. But she was so wound up she felt she would burst right out of her skin.

"Yes," she rasped, "I confess! I confess to being a damned fool in just about every arena of my life. I never slept with Evan, and the way things look right now, I may never sleep with any man ever again. Fucking assholes, the whole lot of you! And that's all I have to confess to, so get the fuck out of here and leave me alone."

Turning away, she slipped on the muddy ground. The hand she put out to brace herself sank into the spongy soil. Getting up was too much trouble, so she stayed where she was, on her hands and knees, one hand buried in the mud. Collins could go to hell. They could all go to hell. The whole world could go to hell. Looking around, she thought it already had.

She crouched there, breathless and still charged with rage, and watched Collins walk back to his car. The air was rank with garbage. Her hands lacerated and filthy. Her throat raw from screaming. She swayed like a flower wilting on its stem, and buried her other hand in the mud to keep herself upright. Rage and adrenaline had kept her going. With Collins' departure, there was nothing left to push against.

She looked at her star-shaped porch light, the wondrous shape and yellow warmth that had welcomed her home so many times, amazed the mob hadn't broken it. She was less than ten feet from her front steps. For all the strength she had left, it might have been miles.

Like a hunter trapping a wary animal, he sneaked up behind her, threw the blanket around her, and lifted her into the air. She fought like a cat in a sack, flailing at her attacker with her pinioned arms and legs, cursing like a fishwife, as he carried her inside.

EVAN – NINE

Hiding at the edge of Mrs. Jordan's yard, Evan had fun watching her picking up all that crap. He was as cold and wet as she was, but he didn't mind. He got a down and dirty thrill seeing her get colder and wetter and dirtier and more miserable with every sack of trash she lugged. She'd been cocky for too long. Finally, she was beginning to look beaten. And he sure didn't mind the way the rain plastered her nightgown to her body like another skin. She might as well have been naked for all it concealed, clinging to her nipples as they hardened in the cold and to the crack of her nice, tight butt. He'd waited a long time to see her naked. He wouldn't have to wait much longer.

He hadn't planned to make his move tonight. He wanted to toy with her a while longer, leaving those little notes. Torturing her with her own words was a fine touch. He was proud of himself for thinking of it. He had one in his pocket he planned to slip under the door tonight, a second to leave on her car tomorrow. But if circumstances meant for him to take her now, he was ready. He had the rope and the knife in his car.

Tonight she'd be too exhausted to fight him and that would make everything so much easier. Mrs. Jordan was tough. He'd always expected to have to work pretty hard to reduce her to the state he wanted her in— begging for mercy, offering to be his slave, willing to do whatever he wanted if he'd only spare her pathetic little life.

He was enjoying watching her drooping progress across the yard when that asshole Collins drove up. Fuck it. What was he doing here? Weren't cops supposed to work shifts? Wasn't he supposed to be home in bed? The guy must never sleep. The other cops who'd showed hardly bothered to get out of their cars. Just sent the kiddies home to bed and drove off.

Those dumb cops hadn't even noticed his car, still parked down the street. Lazy fuckin' slobs. Just how he wanted it. Now that he's about to grab Mrs. Jordan, drag her inside, and have his own private party—and got this monster boner just thinking about it—that asshole Collins shows up and ruins everything.

Well, there was always tomorrow. And he'd enjoyed a hell of a good show, especially watching Collins talking nice and calm and Mrs. Jordan going totally apeshit. Then Collins gets that blanket and throws it over her and drags her into the house. God, he wanted to be in Collins' shoes right now. What the hell was Collins going to do with her, anyway? Too damned tight-assed to think of having fun. Probably wouldn't even feel her up. What the hell could she do about it anyway? And Collins had handcuffs. Man, that would be so cool.

Might as well get going. It was cold and wet out here and he sure wouldn't want to miss school tomorrow. He slipped out of the bushes, stuck a note in her back door, another on her car, and left.

"Whatever her sins, they were not sins of intention,
but of inadvertence, and why should she have
been punished so persistently?"
—Thomas Hardy, *Tess of the D'Urbervilles*

CHAPTER THIRTY-THREE

Collins lugged her up the stairs and into the bathroom, holding her twisting and squirming with one arm while he jerked the shower door open, turned on the water, and dumped her onto the shower floor.

She couldn't even summon the energy to be outraged. Water sluiced over her, swirling in muddy eddies as it ran down the drain. She was a detached observer, watching her strong, resilient body go completely out of control, flailing limbs rattling and banging like a dancing skeleton.

Collins didn't speak, or touch her, or try to interfere. He only thrust in a quick hand and made the water hotter.

A long time later, she struggled to a sitting position and wrestled off the nightgown. It had been a favorite, but after tonight she'd never wear it again. Another eon passed before she clawed her way up the wall and reached for the soap. The gauze on her burned arm drooped like The Mummy in a rainstorm. Her eyes were at half-mast, her arms too heavy to lift. It took both her hands to turn off the water and she had to put her shoulder against the door to push it open.

Collins waited with a large towel. He wrapped it around her, scooped her off her feet, and carried her to bed.

She slept the drugged sleep of total exhaustion, too far gone to care that Collins, her archenemy, had seen her naked. Cops see lots of bodies. She didn't even care that he'd slung her around like a sack, or that she'd thrown things at a police officer or screamed in public like a brawling drunk. She cared only that the bed was warm and her body was horizontal. For the rest of the night, no windows broke and there were no fires or Harpies. She woke to soft snoring—Collins, dozing in a chair—and sun filtering in the window.

Asleep, Collins looked pleasant, almost human, the hard edges and dogged determination gone from his face. She felt a twinge of satisfaction that his clothes were spotted with mud. Then the mud brought it all back.

She couldn't face thinking about last night. Instead, she concentrated on the practical. Find someone to fix her windows. Clean up her house. Deposit her mother's check. Call her insurance company. See her lawyer. Tangible, keep-busy, physical actions to hold the escalating deterioration of her life at bay. Soon enough, Collins would wake. Her body clenched in anticipation of more questions, vulgar insinuation, and obscene prying.

How would she ever explain this to Trustman? Alexis had no idea how long she'd toiled in the rain, but she recalled with vivid mortification swearing and throwing things at Collins. Less than two weeks of unrelenting pressure and she'd cracked.

Was it too much to hope that while Alexis was being reduced to a state of total humiliation, George and Janice had actually accomplished something? Then, if her lawyer didn't quit after learning that Alexis had made a screaming ass of herself—culminating in getting naked with Collins—it could be a good day after all.

She felt around under the covers, found the damp towel, and wrapped herself in it. Clutching the towel, she crossed the room on stinging, lacerated feet and quietly opened her underwear drawer, willing the weary Collins to stay asleep. No such luck. His eyes popped open, he took a second to orient himself, then stretched and smiled, as easy as if he woke in strange women's bedrooms every day.

"Feeling better?" he asked.

"Embarrassed as can be, and like I've been beaten with a rubber hose. But calmer."

"You were provoked," he said.

She glanced at the chaos in the room left by the police search. "Don't start that being nice crap again. I've got you in the sneaky bastard/ manipulative asshole niche, and you're staying there."

"I could make some coffee."

"Have you seen my kitchen?"

"I guess you're right," he said, getting to his feet. "Wanna ride over to Ollie's and get something?"

Like there was no history between them? "Even if I could eat undisturbed in public places, which I can't, I'd rather be shot than be seen with you. I might have lost my temper last night, Officer Collins, and my self-control, but I haven't lost my memory. Despite my current state of informality," she turned pink with a blush from her toes to her head, "I do recall the underlying basis for our relationship, and it hardly suggests a friendly tete-a-tete at Ollie's."

Standing in her bedroom, wearing a towel, talking to the goddamned police officer who'd dedicated his life to destroying her, while he wore the genial smile of a man making small talk to a pretty girl. Could her life get crazier? At that moment, it did.

In the guest room, her cell phone rang. She limped off to answer it, checking her watch as she went. Almost eleven. Plenty of beauty sleep. No doubt she looked beautiful, too, with a rat's nest of uncombed hair and swollen, lacerated hands.

"I've got your papers ready to sign and file and got a restraining order so he can't take anything out of the house," Trustman said. "Can you be here at two? We've found some important stuff. And your electrician friend has dug up some interesting witnesses. It's time to go on the offensive. I've announced a press conference for tomorrow at three. You up for that?"

"For going on the offensive? You bet. A bunch of Palmer's friends showed up here last night. They threw rocks at my house. Dumped garbage in the yard. Broke some windows."

"You called the police?"

"They dispersed the crowd and left. No questions, no names taken, no arrests."

"That's outrageous, Alexis. Did you get the responding officers' names? Badge numbers?"

"Janice, the police never even came to the door."

She heard voices downstairs. One of the voices was Micah's. The high, girlish voice must be Yvonne. How dare he bring that woman into her house?

"Look, someone's here. I'd better go. See you at two."

"What on earth happened here?" the girl's voice asked.

"I don't know," Micah said. "It looks like a fire, and who knows what else?"

"Won't that mess things up? I mean, the things we want for our new place?"

Like what had happened to her lovely little house didn't matter at all. Like anything in the house was theirs for the taking. Her blood pressure and temper skyrocketed. She called Trustman back. "Janice, Micah's here with his bimbo. They've come to take stuff out of the house. What do I do?"

"Tell him not to touch anything. I'll be right over."

She limped back into the bedroom, wincing with every step. "Looks like my husband's here. Micah and his girlfriend. You two have met, of course." She grabbed some jeans and a jersey, and went into the bathroom. Her hands were a mass of tiny cuts and bruises. It felt like her feet were, too. What she got for wandering barefoot and gloveless amidst the glass and trash. But who thinks of that during a meltdown?

She dressed quickly and grabbed a pair of socks, every step reminding her of the sharp slivers in her feet. Cinderella after everything crashed and burned, nothing left of the glass slippers but pain and slivers. Her mirror suggested the best solution to this bad hair day would be a crew cut. She gathered it into a clumsy braid, and went downstairs.

She found Micah and a buxom brunette in the living room, picking up CDs where the cops had dumped them and busily packing them into boxes, the girl reading the titles aloud and announcing, "Oh, we have to have this one." Seven in a row, all belonging to Alexis, like it was open season on her property. Micah hadn't once said no.

Why was she surprised? He'd already demonstrated his willingness to steal from her, hadn't he? Cheat, lie, steal. She folded her arms. "Micah, what are you doing?"

The girl gave a surprised squeal and dropped the CD she was holding. Micah looked up from the box he was packing. "Just getting some of my things."

"*Your* things?"

"Of course, my things." He straightened up, sweeping a hand toward the girl. "Yvonne LaCroix, my... uh...wife, Alexis."

Alexis folded her arms. "I'd say 'pleased to meet you' but it would be a lie. And I think," she looked at her husband again, "one liar per family is enough."

"Hey, look," Yvonne was all hand-on-hip and shoulder-twitching adolescent attitude, "I never..."

Alexis gave the girl a teacherly 'sit down and shut up' look. "Don't even start." She knelt by the box, a painful shifting of stiff muscles, and flipped through the CDs, picking out hers. "Guess he kind of forgot it's *our* house." She started on the second box. He'd worked fast. Man would make a hell of a burglar.

"Lex," he said, belligerent at being embarrassed in front of his girlfriend, "are you going to question everything I want to take?"

"Other than your clothes? Yes." She kept her tone light. Let him pick the fight.

"Look." He leaned in so she could smell the aftershave she'd bought him. "I don't want to fight about this, but Yvonne and I have rented a bigger apartment and we need furniture. I'm taking whatever I want and you can't stop me."

"I'm not sure that's right, Micah. Most of the things in this house are things we bought together. Or things I've repaired and refinished. If we're splitting up, *we* have to decide *together* how we're going to divide them." Putting special emphasis on "together" and "we."

"Come on, Lex. The mess you're in? You're lucky I don't make you move out so I can have the house, but I figured you'd have a hard time finding anywhere else to live." Skirting the fact that her mother had provided the down payment and insisted that the house belong to Alexis. "Puts a man in a terrible bind when his wife's all over the papers as a child rapist, you know."

KATE FLORA

"I wouldn't know, would I? I always thought, if the situation were reversed, that I'd be singing 'Stand by Your Man.' How old is Yvonne, anyway? And aren't there rules about relationships with students?" She put the CDs back on the depleted shelf.

Micah stormed across the room. "At least you can't complain about me taking my clothes. Come on, Yvonne."

There was a knock at the door. "Micah, you want to get that?" she called, like it was a normal day and they were a normal couple.

Alexis watched as he jerked the door open and Janice Trustman, taller than he in her smart heels, stepped into the hallway. "Micah Jordan?" she asked. "I'm Janice Trustman, your wife's attorney. The one whose phone calls you haven't returned? You'll be getting a set of these served on you, but as a courtesy I brought you copies."

She thrust an envelope into Micah's outstretched hand, then looked past him at Alexis. "George is taking pictures. What a mess. I'm so sorry."

Micah opened the envelope. "Alexis," he mumbled, "what the hell is this?"

"You're standing in *our* house with *your* girlfriend, putting *my* things into boxes to furnish an apartment you two have rented, and you don't understand what this is about?"

"Not the divorce, goddammit, this thing!" He waved a paper. "This restraining thing. How dare you try and stop me from taking things out of my own house."

"Maybe you should read it," Alexis said.

"I did read it. It says I can take my fucking clothes, Alexis. Everything else has to be agreed on by the two of us through our lawyers."

"Sounds right to me."

"Goddammit!" He picked up a vase from the bookcase and smashed it onto the floor.

"I think," Trustman said, "you will see the restraining order says you shall not 'remove, donate, give away, sell, encumber, damage or destroy' any property."

"Oh, fuck!" Under stress, the man could be so eloquent. "Come on, Yvonne." He stomped up the stairs.

Alexis dropped onto the couch, feeling immensely weary. "Sorry I had to get you over here for that." She shrugged. "Seems like I'm turning into a full-time job for you."

"Don't apologize." Trustman looked at the emptied shelves and the boxes on the floor. "Looks like you called it just right. I ought to be used to it, but sometimes the things people do to each other still amaze me. Was that Collins' car outside?"

"I don't know."

Trustman caught the hesitation. "Was he here?"

Alexis nodded.

"What did he want?"

"I don't know. I'm afraid I've made a total ass of myself again."

"Oh, Alexis." Trustman rolled her eyes. "Don't tell me you slept with him?"

She jumped to her feet, outraged. "Slept with him? Slept with that manipulative, piece of shit, fiend from hell? Is that what you really think I'm capable of? Are you crazy?"

Collins, listening from the doorway, cleared his throat. "Jeez, Alexis," he said. "I didn't think I was that bad." He started toward her, a small piece of paper with bold yellow streaks fluttering in his fingers. "What the hell is this? I found it stuck in your back door."

Stomach clutching, she took it from him.

> *"...there was a time when I felt so guilty about what I'd done that I wanted to die. I'm better now, but sometimes despair still reaches up its dark tentacles and pulls me back down and I stare at my wrists and think it wouldn't take long, or hurt too much, and then I'd be free forever of this tainted, unworthy feeling."*

It was an entry she'd written after a painful encounter with Micah's ex-wife. The woman had been so kind. And so terribly hurt. Alexis had felt incredible guilt even though the hurt she'd inflicted had been inadvertent.

Evan couldn't get much clearer, could he? "It's another message from

KATE FLORA

Evan," she said, handing the paper to her lawyer. She pulled the other three pieces of paper from her jeans pocket and threw them into her lawyer's lap.

She looked at Collins. "Not that you'll believe me, but these notes? They're Evan's game plan. Rape me, torture me, maybe kill me."

The stuff she'd tried to keep at bay roared back. She couldn't breathe. Couldn't endure their staring eyes, the immense pressure of her exploding fear, the crushing sense of menace, her certainty that nowhere was safe.

She walked out of the room, wincing on her wounded feet, and out the back door. Raising her head, she screamed her desperation at the sky.

"Assaying by his devilish art to reach
The organs of her fancy, and with them forge
Illusions..."
—John Milton, *Paradise Lost*: Book IV

CHAPTER THIRTY-FOUR

Like someone waking from coma, she found herself in the middle of her back yard, Collins's arm around her shoulders. "Hey, now," he soothed. "Take it easy. It's okay. Take it easy." His words were gentle but his arm firm, as though he sensed her instinct to bolt and run.

She attempted to twist free but his grip tightened. "Come on inside now." His "come inside" was not a request.

"Has Micah gone?"

He shook his head.

"Then I'm not coming in."

How could he say anything was okay? Or urge her with a straight face to take it easy. Take what easy? Evan's threats? All the random violence and vandalism? Seems everyone had more confidence in how much humiliation she could handle than she did.

"Come along." His arm pressed insistently.

"Or what? You'll use handcuffs again? You think I care?"

"Alexis, come on. Jesus. I'm trying to help you."

"One of the three big lies."

"What? Oh."

He spotted the chairs and table on her back deck. "Will you sit here? And promise not to run away while I make some tea?"

Where could she run to? If she *could* have run on her damaged feet.

She just wanted a day without calumny heaped on her head, without some confrontation that made her nerves go taut. She wanted a day without cops and lawyers, fires and vandals. Without blood-chilling threats.

It was emblematic of her newly insane life that the person looking after her was practically her worst enemy. A man whose moves had to be constantly watched. The person least likely to understand that what scared her most was not arrest, trial, and the possibility of incarceration, but that Evan would grow frustrated with the slowness of his revenge—these kids lived in an instant gratification world—and do unspeakable things to her.

"You want to fix me tea?" she said. "You are just so fucking nurturing. If you really want to help, get my husband and his bimbo out of this house."

"If I do that, will you sit here like a good little girl and get yourself back under control?"

"I am under control."

"And I'm the Good Humor man."

"I wonder how I missed that."

He marched her over to a chair and waited until she'd dropped sullenly into it. She wanted to stick out her tongue, say mean, provocative things. But it would be wasted on Collins. He didn't care what she called him so long as he got results. The cops wanted her cooperative, obedient, and scared out of her mind. That last, at least, they were getting.

She leaned back in the chair and closed her eyes, feeling the warm sun caress her face as she listened to the thud of his departing feet, the closing of the door.

"That great acting or are you really losing it?" Bannerman asked. He was leaning over the rail, camera in hand, looking tougher than she'd remembered.

"Guess," she said, keeping her eyes closed.

"Losing it. I hope for all our sakes this is over soon. Managing a client using a net and a spear has never been my idea of a good time."

"Am I that bad?"

"I've seen worse. It's the wild-eyed edginess I'm concerned about. The air of incipient explosion. The increasing use of profanity. You got any Valium?"

"Incipient?" But she was too tired for word games. "Micah does. Up in the medicine cabinet."

"I'm going to get you some," he said. "I didn't know you then, but I'll bet, before this began, you were controlled, self-contained, and extremely cautious about language. You don't do yourself any good screaming in public or mouthing off to Collins. Mistakes happen too easily."

"I don't mean to keep making an ass of myself. It's just... a lot of bad things keep happening."

The door slammed and angry footsteps came at her. She knew which of the testosterone trio it would be. "I thought you'd gone," she said, not opening her eyes.

"Goddammit, Lex..."

"Don't swear at me, Micah."

He kicked the table leg. "That damned cop is trying to throw me out of my own house. My own goddamned house! What'd you do, Lex? You fuck him, too?"

"You'll never get it, will you?" It was hopeless. Hopeless. How could she have loved this man so much?

She opened her eyes, but she couldn't look at him. "It's hopelessly old-fashioned, I know, but for years I've been trying to make up for the sin of sleeping with you while you were still married by being the most faithful wife a man could have. To make up for *my* transgression, I mean. You don't understand the concept."

She had to say this, even if it was foolish to waste truth on a man who didn't listen. "The only man I've ever slept with is you. I overlooked your infidelities, hoping with all my heart that you'd realize how much I loved you. Trying to be everything *you* wanted. I am finally realizing I can't change in whatever way would make you love me better, because what you love is variety. Your reflection in a new set of admiring eyes."

She studied the face she knew so well and saw nothing.

"Some guys are upstairs, looking through the medicine cabinet for Valium."

"Did you tell them where it is?"

"Two of them looking at me like they're hawks and I'm a mouse, I had a choice?"

"One of those guys is the cop you talked to about me. You told him quite a lot."

"Well, hell, Lex. What could I do? He's a cop."

"You didn't have to say anything, Micah. You're my husband."

"Yeah? And how would that have looked?"

"Loyal," she said. "Honorable. Decent. Words you don't know the meaning of." She could hardly bring herself to ask, but she needed to hear this from him. "Did you really have a vasectomy?"

He looked everywhere but at her. "Yes."

She thought she was done being angry, but his careless 'yes' triggered a small explosion. "When? Back when you were with your first wife?"

"Two years ago."

About the time they'd agreed to start a family. She'd started watching what she ate and drank, enduring headaches and bad colds and aches and pains without medication because each month she hoped she was going to be pregnant. Enduring the ups and downs of his yes, no, I'm not sure. The joyous couplings when she was sure they had started a baby. The sad times when he still pretended he wasn't sure and insisted on a condom. All a sham. "All that time, letting me hope I'd get pregnant, when you knew it couldn't happen. Why?"

"It kept you happy, didn't it?"

He could say that with a straight face?

"Look," he said, "I need to finish packing. I can't leave Yvonne up there waiting."

"How long does it take? Or were you going through my things, too?"

"You haven't got anything anyone would want."

What about the CDs they'd been packing? The money he'd taken from their account? "Go away, Micah," she said. "Not upstairs, out of here. Out of the house."

"I'll be back." He stomped away.

No doubt he would, this man who'd watched Evan's destruction of her life without a word of comfort. Who'd perpetrated a deception of almost ungraspable magnitude. How could a supposedly intelligent woman be so utterly blind?

The kitchen door opened. Collins and Bannerman moved toward her purposefully, Collins with tea, Bannerman with a pill bottle and a glass of water.

"Your husband's gone," Collins reported.

That was breaking news. "Not before sticking his knife in and twisting it."

The policeman looked her over carefully. Searching for blood, maybe? "Not literally," she said. "But even if he'd stabbed me with a knife instead of actions, what would you care? You could write 'case closed' and move on to the next suspected pervert."

"Alexis" George said in a warning voice. "Be a good girl and take your medicine."

Wasn't that exactly what she'd been doing? Being a good girl and taking her medicine? Bannerman uncurled her fingers and put a small white pill in her palm.

Collins smiled wearily and headed for the steps. "I'm going home to shower and get some lunch. Catch you later."

"Coming from you," she said, "that is not good news."

"I'm off, too," Bannerman said. "Gotta polish my magnifying glass and brush off my deerstalker, get ready for our press conference."

"But I'm hungry," she said, realizing that she was. It had been a long time since her last meal.

"If you were a helpless girl, I'd probably try to find you something to eat. But you hate being helpless or called a girl. You spit on sympathy and thrive on abuse. So fend for yourself."

"I thrive on abuse? George. Please." She tapped her chest lightly, certain he'd overheard her talking to Micah. Information gathering was his business, after all. "I'm wounded."

"Right," he said. He disappeared into the kitchen, popping out a minute later with a bowl of cereal. "Don't say I never gave you anything. Now eat this and then take a nice nap. I'll be back to get you around 1:45.

And Jordan? Your husband, pardon me, but what an asshole."

She stayed in the chair, overwhelmed by all she'd have to do when she got up, watching Mr. Lowden, her elderly backyard neighbor, puttering in his garden. A widower, he fussed over his roses like they were children, never let a weed near his vegetables. Occasionally, he brought her a bouquet or a zucchini. If she baked, she'd make a small loaf of bread or a pie for him. As if sensing her eyes on him, he waved, then made his way across the lawn. Although he didn't have a hat, the way he stood and held his hands suggested a shy man twisting his hat brim.

"Been reading about your troubles," he said. She tensed. "My nephew Darren's in the glass business. You want someone who'll fix your windows quick, and who's honest, I could give him a call."

"Would you, Mr. Lowden? I'd be so grateful. I'm feeling a little overwhelmed."

"Be glad to," he said.

As he was turning away, she thought of something. "Mr. Lowden, I was wondering, you're home during the day, aren't you?"

He smiled. "Retired ten years now."

"You ever see anyone snooping around while I'm at work? Young guy, blond, tall?"

He considered. "I dunno," he said. "Few times I've seen a guy, looked like a workman doing an appraisal or something... going around checking your windows and doors. First time, I figured it was business, you'd called him. Second time, I came over and stood right there watching him." He pointed to a gap in the shrubs. "He gave me a dirty look, then took off."

"Just those two times?"

"Maybe three. In the winter I'm not out much, and I was away a month, visiting my son."

"You ever see him go into the house?"

"No. But a coupla times, coming into the neighborhood, I saw a truck driven by a guy looked like him heading away."

"Think you'd recognize a picture?"

"Well, I'll tell you. My eyesight's not what it used to be. I could try."

"Wait right here." What felt like a dozen splinters stabbed her feet. She got the yearbook and found a picture of the soccer team. "Was it any of these boys?"

He studied the page, then pointed at Evan. "That's the one, there. He had the same look he does in that picture. Bold like, and rude. Looked right at me and stuck up his middle finger. In my day, a boy wouldn't do that to an old man." Holding her breath, she found the lacrosse team. He picked out Evan again. "That boy there."

He would have been mortified if she hugged him. She settled for an effusive thank you. "Would you be willing to talk with my lawyer, if she thinks it's necessary?"

"Would it help you?"

"It would show how he might have known about my house, my furniture, what's inside. And the fact that he was sneaking around looks suspicious. And that he was driving a truck."

"You're right about that." He nodded. "Sure. Have her call me. What's her name?"

"Trustman. Janice Trustman."

"Oh. Janice. Used to know her father," he said. "Good man. I hear she takes after him." He ducked his head politely. "I'll be getting back to my roses. And I'll give my nephew a call."

Alexis watched him slowly cross the yard and disappear through the bushes. When she looked down at Evan's team picture, it was blurred by tears.

She was still standing there, holding the yearbook and pitying her wounded feet, when Dan Morgan's wife Maggie came through the kitchen door. "Sorry to barge in like this," she said. "I knocked... but the front door was open, so I just walked in. I've come to apologize for being so remiss."

She took Alexis's hand between hers. "Nobody knows what you're going through like Dan and me, but I've been so wrapped up in my babies I haven't been here for you. Not when you were arrested and not when you had your fire, and I'm ashamed. When Dan told me about the vandalism, I couldn't sit on my hands any longer. I drove the babies to my mother's. How can I help?"

"Are you any good at splinters? I think I've got glass in my foot. Feet."

"Got some tweezers?"

"Upstairs in the medicine cabinet. If Micah didn't take them to his girlfriend's house."

Maggie raised her eyebrows. "Oh dear."

"My whole life's an oh dear these days."

"Believe me, I can imagine. I'll be right back."

"I'll come with you," Alexis said. "I need to lie down." She followed Maggie, wondering what she'd find upstairs. Had Micah taken his things and left, or indulged his bad mood by leaving a mess? A quick glance answered her question. It looked like a whirlwind had gone through the room. Drawers and doors were open, piles of hangers and discarded items everywhere. As a parting gesture, he'd taken the bedspread. Fine with her. She'd been thinking about burning it.

"Take off your socks and lie down," Maggie ordered, smoothing the bed.

It was nice to have a woman helping. Maggie would let her have her emotional storms and understand. Maggie knew what it was like to be stared at and gossiped about, the helpless feeling of being unjustly accused. Maggie would not tell her to be a good little girl. Right now she didn't feel like she could "be" anything.

After setting some things on the table, Maggie said, "Okay, Lex, here we go." She slid Alexis's feet onto her lap and went to work.

"They gave me Valium," Alexis said. "They thought I was losing control."

"Who wouldn't, after what you've been through?" There was a prick in the sole of her foot. "Hold on. I think I've got it." A sharper prick. Another. And another. "What did you do? Dance on light bulbs?"

"I went a little crazy last night, cleaning up the trash."

Maggie bent to her task again. "This is a real mess. Got a magnifying glass?"

"Down in the living room in the desk."

Many minutes and many pieces of glass later, Maggie started on the second foot. "It's going to be a while before you're running again."

"I haven't been running much anyway. Not with reporters jumping out of bushes, Evan chasing me with his car, and the press camped on my doorstep."

"That was the thing that drove Dan crazy. Everywhere he went, it was right there in his face. But at least we had each other. The way Micah's behaving... it's so hurtful."

"People haven't been very nice."

"Only too ready to believe the worst, aren't they? But you have a lot of friends you don't even know about. People who may be shy about coming forward. You'll see."

"Thanks, Maggie."

Despite the painful pricks in her feet, Alexis couldn't keep her eyes open.

When she woke, it was late afternoon. There were voices in the kitchen and loud music. She struggled out of bed, the Valium making her feel like someone had tied a plastic bag over her head. Her bandaged feet felt like chopped steak.

There were four other women in the kitchen, women from her church, done up in rubber gloves and aprons, systematically scrubbing everything to a driving Bob Seeger beat.

"Oh, Maggie... all of you... you didn't have to do this."

The Reverend Maggie Morgan smiled benevolently. "It's our own 21st century version of a barn-raising." The teakettle whistled. Maggie snapped off the burner, and asked, "Want some tea?"

She nodded, struggling to get oriented. "I was supposed to meet my lawyer and I slept right through it."

"It's okay. That investigator came by. George? When we couldn't wake you, he said it was better to let you sleep." Maggie poured hot water into a row of mugs. "He seems nice."

The other women came and collected their mugs, each pausing to pat her shoulder or give her a hug, making her feel teary. "I can't believe this. I was... I don't know... beginning to believe I was a pariah, I guess."

"That's what it does to you," Maggie agreed. "We're trying to turn that around."

KATE FLORA

Alexis sat on a chair amidst their bustle, remembering something Bannerman had said earlier—that she wasn't a helpless girl. She'd been acting helpless. Letting this thing cow her while she waited for her lawyer, or George, or Peter—for someone else—to rescue her. It was time she started rescuing herself.

"Revenge, at first though sweet,
Bitter ere long, back on itself recoils."
—John Milton, *Paradise Lost*: Book IX

CHAPTER THIRTY-FIVE

She still had Evan's school records, tucked away in that box of mini pads. She'd forgotten to give them to Bannerman. Left in her car in their off-putting feminine container, they'd escaped notice. Now she was going to act on them.

Once Maggie and the others were gone, she pulled them out, plotted her course, threw some things into a suitcase, and jumped in her car. A few hours later, she drove her Jeep into the Connecticut town where Evan had last lived. She located the high school, ate comfort food at a cozy local restaurant, and found a bed and breakfast. Then, though it was early and she'd already slept much of the day, she went to bed.

After a night without crowds or fires, breaking glass or damning accusations, she woke to a sunny day. She pinned up her hair and put on teacherly clothes, ate the offered plate of bacon and eggs and toast, and paged through a decorating magazine, imagining a fresh new bedspread to replace the one Micah had taken. Different paint. Sheets he'd never slept on.

Then she headed for the high school.

She almost couldn't get through its front door. The design was different from Crawford Valley High's, but everything else was painfully the same. Having been barred from teaching less than a week, she was swept with such a wave of nostalgia and regret it stopped her in her tracks. She skipped the office, a too-vivid reminder of Dr. Huston and

Mark, and followed signs to the library. Librarians were great sources of information of both the reference and social kind.

The slim blonde at the desk had a friendly face. When she asked how she could help, Alexis abandoned all her carefully prepared phrases and dove right in. "I'm looking for information about a former student here. Evan Palmer."

The woman literally backed away from the desk. The way she said, "I'm sorry. I'm afraid I can't help you," told Alexis she'd scored a direct hit.

"I think you can," Alexis said. "You obviously know who I'm talking about."

"Sorry. I suggest you go to the office," the woman said and turned away.

"I really need your help," Alexis told the rigid back. "Please. He's trying to destroy me."

"You can inquire about former students at the office."

She had to make this woman talk to her. She knew she'd be stonewalled if she went to the office. "Until a week ago," she said, "I was Evan's teacher at the high school in the town he and his mother moved to two years ago. Until he tried to destroy my life. Until he lied and claimed I'd seduced him. Until he got me fired. And arrested."

Were those shoulders wavering? Willing the woman to care, to respond, she said, "Because Evan didn't get what he wanted, I was dragged out of my class in handcuffs and thrown in a jail cell. Someone tried to burn down my house. With me in it." *Turn around*, she thought. *Don't make me say this to an unfeeling back.* "A gang of students broke my windows and filled my yard with garbage. I've lost my job. My husband has left me. I came here hoping to find someone who knew about Evan's behavior while he lived here."

Her voice wavered unsteadily. "Something I could use in my defense."

The woman hadn't turned, but she was listening, her hands frozen in mid-air. Alexis forced herself to go on. "I'm trying to show he has a pattern of destructive behavior. I'm trying to save my life. Please. I think you know something that can help."

So much for big, brave Alexis rescuing herself. Her eyes were full of those stupid tears again. She dug in her bag for a tissue.

The woman turned, plucked one from a box, and handed it to her. "We're not supposed to discuss former students. But that boy has done enough harm. Give me a minute. I'll find someone to cover the desk."

Alexis followed the woman into an empty office. When the door was closed, the librarian said, "I'm Sally Carter. Tell me again. What brought you here?"

"Alexis Jordan. I'm an English teacher at Evan's new high school. Crawford Valley in Massachusetts. Evan was one of my students. One day, out of the blue, he made a pass at me." She wasn't sure how much to tell. "I tried to set him straight... but it turned out he'd constructed an entire fantasy in which I'd encouraged him to believe his advances were welcome. When I ultimately convinced him there was no possibility of a relationship, he swore he'd make me sorry."

Sally Carter looked receptive, but would anyone believe this?

"Evan went to my principal, claiming I'd seduced him. That we'd been having an affair. When I wasn't fired, he took his story to the police. And the newspaper." It was hard to talk around the lump in her throat.

"This sounds crazy, I know, but somehow he got into my house. Stole things. My underwear and other things he's using to support his lies. I'm asking a lot, when you don't know me from Adam, but I don't know where else to turn. The whole town thinks Evan is a victim. No one listens when I say he's dangerous. I'm looking for something... anything... to show he's told lies before. Done vicious things to retaliate when he hasn't gotten his way. That I'm not the first person he's tried to destroy."

This was so much harder than she'd imagined. She studied the woman's face, hoping for understanding. For charity. "You seem to recognize what I'm saying."

"It's not me you need to talk to," the woman said, reaching for the office phone. "If she's willing, you need to see Pat Coleman. Evan did terrible things to them. I don't know if she'll want to talk about it, though. It might be you'll need to see our local police."

Police. Alexis hoped her panic didn't show. She wasn't supposed to leave the state. She folded her hands in her lap, trying to look calm as the woman dialed.

"Pat? Sally Carter at the high school. I've got a woman here who teaches at Evan Palmer's new school. It looks like he's at it again." She listened. "Well, he's gotten her fired and she's been arrested. I know it's a hard thing to ask, but it sounds like she really needs your help. Do you think you could talk to her?" She listened. Nodded. "I know. I understand. I said you might not want to."

Alexis wanted to snatch the phone and beg this Pat Coleman to see her, but Sally held up a warning hand. She listened again, then wrote something on a sheet of paper. "That's good of you, Pat, because this woman is in serious trouble. I'll send her right over."

She handed Alexis the paper. "Pat Coleman knows precisely what you're going through. She can tell you what happened when he lived here."

Sally shook her head. "It's criminal, really. The Palmers move away and he gets to leave his whole dirty past behind. Nothing in his records. No warning to the people where he's going. Just a nice clean slate, like all the harm he did doesn't matter."

Alexis didn't feel triumphant. A layer of dread and discomfort made her wish she didn't need to do this. She didn't want to hear the ugly things she expected she was about to hear, or cause people pain by reviving old hurts. She hoped Pat Coleman, whatever her story, would see them as sisters in the struggle to stop Evan before he hurt someone else.

The directions took her to a modest suburban house and up a bluestone walk lined with spring bulbs. The woman who answered the door had the spare frame and clipped hair of a marathon runner. She was dressed like one, too. Black running tights and a trim black top along with a pair of industrial-strength trail runners. She had the gaunt look of someone recovering from an illness.

"You're Alexis Jordan?"

When Alexis nodded, the woman stepped back to admit her, then looked carefully up and down the street before closing the door. "Come back into the kitchen. That's where I've laid out all the stuff."

She headed that way, leaving Alexis to follow. "You want coffee?"

"Tea, if it's no trouble." She was jumpy enough. Beyond Coleman, in a cheery kitchen, papers were spread out on the table.

"Sit down. I'll put the water on." The woman touched the back of a chair, then whisked the kettle off the stove and filled it at the sink, her movements quick and economical. "Sally says you lost your job because of Evan?"

Alexis repeated her story. "I'm on leave right now, but they tried to fire me, and because I was arrested, it may only be a matter of time. I want my job back. At least, I think I do, but that's not why I'm here."

"Why are you here?" The woman's tone was flat and uninflected. Behind it, Alexis sensed such a reservoir of caution she was surprised Coleman had agreed to this meeting. But she had, and the papers on the table said she was willing to share what she knew. Maybe it was simply the caution of one who'd been badly burned.

Would she, too, become taut and watchful and joyless?

She looked down at her clenched hands. "I'm here because I'm afraid of him," she said. "Not of losing my job or having to go to court, or the risks of being convicted, though all that does scare me. I'm here because I'm afraid public humiliation and an eventual trial won't be enough for Evan."

She swallowed hard against the persistent lump in her throat. It felt like she was trying to choke down a rock. "I'm afraid..." Her fingers knotted into a tight ball. "...afraid of what he's going to do. His threats. He wants to punish me himself and I don't know how to stop him."

"What about getting the police involved?"

"They believe him." Alexis met Coleman's skeptical gaze. "They won't protect me. They think I'm a child seducer. When we—when my lawyer—told them about his plans for punishing me, things he's told other students, even when we told them he'd been showing a big knife around, the investigator said it was just an adolescent blowing off steam. But I know Evan's capable of real violence."

Pat Coleman stared out her kitchen window, silent for an excruciatingly long time. "I hoped I'd never have to talk about Evan Palmer again. About the things he does." She waved a thin hand over the papers on the table. "I'm trying, my daughter Bethany and I are both trying, to put the whole ugly mess behind us."

A quick flick toward her running gear. "You're a runner. I can see that, so you'll understand. I still do ten miles a day. It takes that long to work him out of my system. He's like a chronic disease, some toxic poison that reproduces in my body. After I told Sally you could come over, I..."

Her voice faltered. "I don't think I can do this." She wrapped her arms around herself and turned away again. "Bringing it all back. It hurts too much."

"I'm so sorry, Mrs. Coleman," Alexis said. "I know this isn't your problem. I'm just..." Her voice caught. "I'm desperate. I didn't know what else to do. I thought if I could find someone who understood about Evan... that he isn't some innocent golden child. That his threats of violence are real."

Guilt warred with desperation. Badly as she needed this woman's story, she couldn't stand inflicting this much pain. It was like doing Evan's evil work for him.

She picked up her purse. "I'm sorry. I'll go. It's not fair to put you through this. It's just that I'm afraid he's going to kill me."

She wondered, as her battered feet carried her away, whether she'd have the courage to see the local police instead.

"Wait," Pat Coleman called. "Wait. How can I not help, when I know what you're up against?"

When Alexis was back at the table, Coleman told her story. "I used to be a librarian at the high school," she said. "I lost my job because of Evan. It was a very different situation from yours. In our case, the person he'd fixated on was my daughter, Bethany. But once Bethany stopped going out with him, once he couldn't have her, couldn't control her, he set about trying to destroy both of us."

He would have been a high school freshman. A ninth grader. He should have been a child still, not a diabolical monster.

Coleman set the tea on the table and sat across from her. "It started so innocently," she said. "Evan was Bethany's first boyfriend. Soccer star. Cute boy. She was the envy of all the girls in the class. Then he started to control who she could talk to. Which friends she could hang around with. Wanting her home every evening in case he called. She wasn't ready for that. We decided she had to explain to him that it wasn't healthy for one person in a relationship to be so controlling."

Coleman gripped her mug like it was a lifeline. "It never occurred to me he'd be anything but reasonable. She went out for the evening in a lovely blue dress with a bright smile. She came home with her dress torn and filthy. With a black eye and a split lip and her sense of safety shattered. We called the police. They were very good. Very gentle with her and supportive. But the cops didn't want him to have a record, a boy that young, so all Evan got was a slap on the wrist."

There was a sharp crack as Coleman's mug handle broke.

"A few weeks later, he showed up on the doorstep with roses and a written apology and demanded to see Bethany. We had a restraining order. He wasn't supposed to come near her. But he wouldn't leave. It was like he heard only what he wanted to hear. We finally called the police and they took him away, but that didn't end it. Everywhere she went—to the movies or out for pizza or to the mall—he'd show up with his friends. Staring at her. Sitting in the row behind her. Phone calls at all hours—until we got an unlisted number—whispering about what he was going to do to her. Bethany was terrified."

Coleman jumped up, dumped her tea, and threw the mug violently into the trash. "We went back to the police and told them what was going on. The detective we dealt with had a girl in Bethany's class and he could see how she was being affected. My daughter had gone from being a sunny girl to a jumpy wraith. It was the detective's idea to wire her, like on some TV cop show, and tape what Evan was saying, so they could show he was violating the restraining order."

She shook her head. "After that, he switched his focus to me, getting back at her that way. He and his friends used to come into the library and hang around where they were sure I could hear them say filthy things about her. Spreading ugly rumors. Even passing around ugly pictures they claimed were her. One day, I couldn't stand it anymore. I got right into Evan's face and told him it was slander and if he didn't stop, we'd take him back to court. He just stood there with this arrogant smile on his face and told me how much fun he and his friends had the time Bethany gave them all blow jobs. How she'd let two of them fuck her while the other two sucked her tits. How she had a vagina that smelled like bad fish... and someday soon he was going to stick dynamite up there and make the world a cleaner place."

Coleman shoved back her chair, a hand over her mouth. "Excuse me." From the small powder room off the kitchen, Alexis heard her being sick. After a long while, she returned, her face pale.

"As I said... he's like a poison in the system." She grabbed a handful of tissues and blotted her eyes. "I yelled at him to shut his filthy mouth, then slapped him as hard as I could. He smiled like he'd just won a prize, thanked me, and I lost my job for hitting a student."

Alexis thought she might be sick, too. "His mother knew about all this?"

"Dinah Palmer knows only what she wants to know. She's content to believe that her son is a misunderstood boy who attracts girls who are slightly unbalanced. He told his mother Bethany was a vindictive, seductive girl who'd led him on, then tried to get him in trouble." Coleman shook her head. "Mrs. Palmer clung to that lie even after Bethany testified in court, and she heard Evan's recorded voice saying those vile things."

"But they left," Alexis said. "They moved away."

"He kept after Bethany, or his friends did, until the police finally sat both Palmers down and explained they had two choices. Move, or have Evan go to jail."

"And now, he's doing it again," Alexis said. "And because I'm an adult, they believe I seduced him."

"We weren't even the first," Pat Coleman said. "Once the police started looking at Evan, they went back to where he'd lived before. I hate to say it about another human being, but I think it's possible Evan was born bad."

She passed some papers across the table. "Take a look at this."

"Your change approaches, when all these delights
Will vanish, and deliver ye to woe…"
—John Milton, *Paradise Lost*: Book IV

CHAPTER THIRTY-SIX

It was an affidavit from a man named Thomas Brownell of Irvington, Pennsylvania. "One of our local detectives went down there. Spoke with this man and with their local police. When we decided to bring a civil suit against the Palmers, our lawyer got this affidavit, and a statement from the local police chief. Read it," Pat said. "It will sound chillingly familiar."

Alexis pressed her hand against her stomach, willing it to settle. Outside, it was a sunny day. In here, there was darkness, as though a cloud surrounded them. The fear they shared as they discussed Evan was tangible.

The affidavit began: *My name is Thomas Brownell. When my son David was in fifth grade, I coached his Little League team. On that same team was a boy named Evan Palmer.*

Alexis lowered the page. She'd come for this, but anticipation is different from reality.

"Read it," Pat commanded. "You need to know."

> *Evan Palmer lived with his mother, who worked, and so he was primarily under the care of a housekeeper. There was no father in the house. During the course of the baseball season, Evan developed an attachment to me and began spending time at my home with my two sons,*

> *David and Ian. He frequently invited himself for dinner
> and tried to be included on family expeditions. I was
> willing to welcome Evan on an occasional basis; however,
> he became a frequent visitor, and increasingly he began to
> pick on my younger son, Ian. On one occasion, Evan was
> inappropriately rough with Ian. I had to reprimand him
> and send him home.*

Alexis looked at Pat, wanting to ask about the outcome, but Pat was studying another paper. *Subsequently, I received an irate phone call from Mrs. Palmer, complaining about how unkind I'd been to her poor fatherless boy.*

"You get to the part yet where Dinah Palmer calls to complain?" Pat asked. "I spoke to Tom Brownell. He said that never once, over the weeks Evan had been visiting their home, had she reciprocated with a meal or a pizza or an invitation to his sons. Yet she was so quick to perceive a slight. You know what makes monsters like Evan? Mothers like that. Brownell was kind of a saint, as you will see. Proof that no good deed goes unpunished."

> *I explained to Mrs. Palmer about Evan's bullying behavior,
> and told her that Evan would be welcome if he could play
> nicely with my children. The next day, Evan returned, but
> he was no gentler or nicer. I had to speak to him several
> times and explained it was the last time he'd be invited to
> play if he couldn't behave. At that point, I had to go into
> the house to prepare dinner. When it was ready, I called
> the boys. David and Evan showed up, but Ian was missing.*

Alexis shivered. "Pat, I have to know. Is Ian going to be all right?'
"I had exactly that reaction when the policeman who interviewed Brownell came to talk to us. I had to leave the room and let him speak with my husband." She set her own icy hand over Alexis's. "Nobody dies, okay."

I asked the boys where Ian was. David said while he was working on his bike, Evan and Ian headed off into the woods. Evan said that he and Ian had walked a little way together and then Ian had run off and wouldn't come back. Knowing that Ian was timid and also that he'd been told on many occasions not to go into the woods alone, I was skeptical about Evan's story. I set off into the woods with Evan, asking him to lead me to the place where he'd last seen Ian. Evan wandered around for a while acting confused, then blurted out that he had to go home and ran off. I searched for another forty-five minutes, eventually finding Ian tied to a tree. Ian reported that Evan had tied him up, telling him it was part of a game, and then left.

I took Ian home, and after dinner, I called our local police chief, reported the incident, and asked for his advice. He sent an officer over to take a report. The officer interviewed me, David and Ian. I assumed this would be the end of things and I would handle Evan Palmer by ending his visits to my home. Knowing that Mrs. Palmer had reacted badly to my previous call concerning Evan, I had the officer stand by while I called her. I told her that Evan was not welcome to visit anymore. Once again, she refused to acknowledge the validity of my concerns about her son, and accused me of being insensitive and overreacting

Pat was watching closely, as though she could tell what part of the affidavit Alexis was reading. "Tom Brownell said the police chief told him they liked to get reports of incidents like that. That they watched children like Evan in case this was the beginning of a series of escalating events," she said. "What happened next surprised them all, according to Brownell, but I guessed even before my lawyer told me."

"I don't think I want to know."

"Well, you have to," she said. "Because it's terribly relevant to your own circumstances. You came here to find out about Evan's past, right?" The woman's brave voice stumbled. She was still too close to the pain. "This is what you came for."

"I think I'm going to be sick."

"Be my guest. I call it the Evan Palmer purge. But then you've got to read the rest."

Alexis was willing to bet that Pat Coleman had once been a warmer, gentler person. This was what Evan did. *What doesn't kill you makes you strong*? It was a barren, agonizing kind of strength. She went into the slightly sour-smelling bathroom, and followed her hostess's example, remembering how she'd joked to herself about the Evan Palmer diet.

> *The next morning, the police chief called to inform me that Dinah Palmer had come into the station and filed a complaint alleging that I had abused her son, taking advantage of my position as his coach to touch him in inappropriate ways. Subsequently, Mrs. Palmer hired a lawyer and attempted to have me removed as a coach and fired from my job as an elementary school teacher. A psychiatrist who evaluated Evan described him as showing signs of an attachment disorder and lacking in empathy. A thorough police investigation exonerated me. As a result of his behavior, and his mother's, people weren't comfortable having Evan around their children. He was uncomfortable in the schools and had difficulty making friends. Eventually, they moved away.*

"I don't get it," Alexis said. "Why would Dinah Palmer do that? What did she hope to accomplish? How was destroying someone else supposed to help her child?"

"I doubt if she was thinking about that," Pat said. "Mothers like that don't model appropriate behavior for their kids, because they don't know how kids are supposed to behave. They've made their own way through life by a process of angry bullying and they make their kids' ways by the same means. The message the kids get is that they're entitled to have their wishes and desires, however inappropriate, satisfied, and any means are fair to achieve that. Other people simply don't matter."

"That sure sounds like Evan. Can I get a copy of this?"

Pat had selected a small stack of papers. "You want copies of all of these. There's the Pennsylvania police chief's letter, and the coach's report, and Dinah Palmer's complaint, and the investigation report exonerating the coach. There's a copy of Bethany's affidavit. The restraining order. The judge's order finding Evan had violated the restraining order. Actually, there are several of those. The complaint in our own civil suit against Evan and his mother, and a transcript of the tape that Bethany made of Evan's threats."

She hesitated. "I'll come with you. We haven't seen or heard from this monster since he left town, but as long as he's alive, I'll always be expecting him. Bethany's getting better, but she'll never be the same. Sometimes, ugly as it is, I wish I'd had a gun so that I could have shot that boy instead of slapping him."

She snatched her purse off the counter. "Maybe I sound paranoid, but I want you to make two copies of everything and mail one of them to your attorney. There's a post office next to the copy shop."

Everything Coleman said and did validated her own fears about Evan, the deeper ones no one would take seriously. "I'm very grateful to you for sharing this," Alexis said. "I know how much it hurts."

"But you don't feel relieved."

"It's incredibly helpful to my defense to be able to show Evan has a pattern of this kind of behavior. But..." Could she say it, even to this woman who knew what he was like? She didn't need to. Pat Coleman said it for her.

"But you're not sure you'll live long enough to benefit from the information."

Like a fist in the gut, but true. Alexis nodded. It was a dreadful sisterhood they shared.

They took a circuitous route through a shopping center parking lot, around behind some buildings, and through a tunnel under the road, ending up in a restaurant parking lot behind the copy shop. "Just because you're paranoid," Pat said, "doesn't mean they aren't out to get you."

"Do you always do this?" Alexis asked. "Driving like you're trying to lose a tail? Checking the street when you leave your house?"

"I always check the street. I don't usually take driving precautions. But Evan is two years older and two years crazier and craftier. I assume he's also two years taller and stronger. Because he's locked onto you now, it's reasonable to think he might have followed you."

Alexis wanted her life back. She didn't want to become like Pat, always checking, forced to run ten miles instead of five. Worn to the point of emaciation by a constant sense of danger. "I was careful."

"So were we."

In the end, Pat's paranoia, added to her own, was so infectious Alexis made three copies. One to carry. One to mail, and a third to hide in the car. She thought about writing on the envelope: TO BE OPENED IN THE EVENT OF MY DEATH, but her hand was too shaky to write "death." She had enough trouble writing her lawyer's address.

Silently, the two women drove back to where they'd started. The route Pat took back was entirely different. Then Alexis started home, doing a little bobbing and weaving herself before she parked behind a Toys "R" Us and stowed the spare set of documents. Then she called Trustman's office.

"Where the hell are you?" her lawyer demanded. "I've called your house and your cell a dozen times. We've got a press conference today at three. Did you forget?"

Forget? Had she ever known? The last twenty-four hours were a blur. It was eleven, and she was three hours away. "Can we meet beforehand to discuss it? I've got some important things I'd like you to see."

"More dirty pictures or more bruises?"

"How about evidence that Evan has done things like this twice before?"

"Where are you?"

"In Connecticut."

She pictured her lawyer biting back criticism of her latest folly. "You'll be here at two?"

"Yes." Just like the little engine that could. Barring traffic jams, traffic stops, or Evan suddenly looming up on her tail.

*   *   *

The black Volvo appeared just as she came through the tolls onto the Massachusetts Turnpike. At first she dismissed it as one of those idiotic drivers who thought they owned the road, but when she moved into the middle lane to let it pass, it moved into the lane behind her.

The program on NPR was about the monarch butterfly. She was thinking about butterflies, about how, in kindergarten, they'd found monarch caterpillars on milkweed and brought them into the classroom to hatch. She was so interested in the story she was caught unaware when the Volvo suddenly pulled out to pass her, coming so close she had to swerve to avoid being hit, then pulling in so close she had to hit the brakes. Then it sped up and zoomed off.

She uttered a few profane comments and moved into the right lane to let her adrenaline rush subside. Thinking ahead to her meeting with Janice and wondering what George had dug up, she didn't notice the black Volvo in the breakdown lane until she was almost on it. By then, she was trapped. There was a truck beside her and another behind. She hit the gas, pulling past the Volvo just as it darted out at her.

In her mirror, she saw it jerk back into the breakdown lane as the truck blew past, horn blaring. That's when it registered, slamming into her like a body blow. Evan's buddy Jason had a Volvo. Despite her precautions, someone, Evan or one of his friends had followed her and was here on the highway trying to hurt her.

Fifty miles more. Fifty long miles of not knowing when or where they might strike again. She realized that once she'd put her foot on the gas, she'd kept it there. Now she was in the fast lane, doing between eighty and ninety, a speed at which she felt wildly out of control. When, these days, didn't she feel that way? *Get a grip*, she told herself. The last thing she needed was to get stopped by the cops. She eased off the gas and moved over, hoping to lose herself among the trucks.

She drove at the speed limit, in the middle lane where no one could jump at her, constantly checking her mirrors and counting off the miles. The truck that had blasted its horn at the Volvo was still behind her, right through the tolls and onto 290 toward Worcester. Gradually, as the miles ticked off, she eased her frantic grip on the wheel.

They get you when you let your guard down. Out of the corner of her eye, she saw a dark car, going like a bat out of hell, weaving in and out of the lanes until it was beside her on her left. The Volvo again. It stayed there, menacingly close, matching its speed exactly to hers. Just enough over the white line so the two cars were only inches apart. The tinted glass was so dark she couldn't see who was inside.

Her idea of hiding among the trucks had trapped her here, with a semi looming on her bumper and another on her right. It would only take a sharp twist of the wheel to knock her into the truck beside her. She was so scared she couldn't breathe.

A sudden sharp horn blast from the truck on her right almost made her lose control. She glanced up, saw the trucker gesturing at her. Then he slowed so she could move in front of him. She swung the wheel sharply and zipped into the space. As the Volvo veered to follow, the driver of the truck that had been behind her leaned on his horn and blasted forward, nosing out the Volvo and neatly filling the space beside her. She'd never thought of truckers as guardian angels before, but that's what was happening. Like whales, they were using their size to protect her. She raised a hand to acknowledge them.

They stayed with her for the next twenty miles. Shortly before her exit, she put on her blinker and pulled into the breakdown lane. Both trucks managed to stop a little beyond her. She got out of the Jeep and stood on the grass, well away from traffic, watching the truckers approach. The one who'd made the space for her was a massive man, easily 6' 6", with a long black ponytail. The other, small and wiry, looked like someone's grandfather.

"Hey, there, little lady," the grandfatherly one said. "You okay? You looked pretty darn scared." He smelled of tobacco and fast food.

When Officer Kennedy had used the word "lady" she'd felt patronized and demeaned, yet with this man she wanted to throw herself into his arms and weep. "I *was* scared," she said. "I don't know what he might have done if you two hadn't rescued me."

In a surprisingly gentle voice, the big man asked, "That jerkoff your boyfriend or husband?"

"One of my high school students," she said.

"You're kidding. What did you do, give him a bad grade?"

Embarrassed, she stared down at her shoes. "Told him I wouldn't sleep with him."

"Can you believe it?" the older man said. "What's the world coming to, a kid makes a pass at his teacher, then tries to run her off the road when she shoots him down?"

"Wish I'd run him off the road," the big man said. "Little bastard." He stuck out a hand the size of an Easter ham. "Name's Buck Pawling."

She met his eyes. "Alexis Jordan."

"I'm Earl Barker." Barker's grip was gentle and warm. He studied her with sharp blue eyes. "You going to be okay? This guy gonna keep bothering you?"

She shrugged. "I don't know."

Barker looked at Buck Pawling. "You want us to talk to anyone, your local cops or whatever, let us know. No one ought to get away with stuff like that." He took a paper from his pocket, scribbled on it, then looked at Pawling. "You want to give the lady your number?" Pawling did. Barker handed her the paper. "I wrote the license plate, too, so's they can run a check if they want." He looked uncertain whether it was all right to leave her. "We gotta get on. But I'm worried about you, little lady. You got people lookin' after you?"

"Yes. Thanks. I do. And thanks so much for rescuing me. I sure did need it."

"All right then." They turned to go, then Pawling swung around again. "You watch yourself now. Kid that crazy, who knows what he might do. I was you, I'd call the cops when I got home, tell 'em the whole story."

Been there. Done that. A voice crying in the wilderness. "Thanks," she said. "I will."

"While I abroad through all the coasts
of dark destruction seek deliverance…"
—John Milton, *Paradise Lost*: Book IX

CHAPTER THIRTY-SEVEN

By the time she reached Trustman's office, the stress of confronting Evan's past and the adrenaline rush from that terrifying highway chase had done her in. All her injuries seemed magnified. Her lacerated hands stung, her burned arm stung, her tender feet reminded her she'd recently been dancing on glass. She limped into the room and dumped the papers she'd gotten from Pat Coleman on the desk in front of Janice and George.

"What's this?" Trustman asked. For once, her lawyer looked relaxed and happy.

"Stuff I got from a woman named Pat Coleman down in Connecticut. Where the Palmers used to live. Her daughter Bethany was one of Evan's victims."

"You know you weren't supposed to leave the state."

"I couldn't just sit around waiting for Evan's next move." Alexis perched on her chair, ready for a good fight, as her "team" read through the papers.

"This is great, Alexis. Just great," Trustman said. "George will have to do some follow-up, but this is exactly what we need."

"Great for us," Alexis agreed. "But it's so sad, what he did to that little boy. And Bethany and her mother are scarred forever. Why didn't Mrs. Palmer catch on to her son's behavior? Stop him? Get him some help?"

"She doesn't believe there's anything wrong with him," Bannerman said. "She proves she's a good mother, when she's actually a sick, twisted bitch, by winning for him. Dinah Palmer is all about winning. She has no idea what Evan is really like because she won't let that information in."

"How do you know?" Alexis asked.

"I met the lady," he said. "And interviewed her own former co-workers and employees. Of course, the kid arrived here with a clean slate. Nothing about his history, because juvenile records are confidential."

Alexis thought about Evan's school records. Silent about Bethany or Pat Coleman or restraining orders. She looked at Trustman. "Now that we know this, what do we do with it?"

"We'll get to that, Alexis," Trustman said, "but we've got more."

"We've got Evan's fingerprints off that ladder," Bannerman said.

"And we solved the mystery of that note you supposedly wrote to Evan," Trustman said. "The one in your handwriting? Your friend Peter Everett explained it."

Recognition dawned. "It's the note I wrote to Peter the day after our prom. We never called him Peter. That was his dad's name, so he was Everett, or Ev."

"A note he sent back to you with flowers, and a pencil message of his own, which someone tried to erase. Evan altered the note."

"Isn't he supposed to be here?" Bannerman said. "Peter Everett," he explained, catching her worried look.

"He's coming." Trustman smiled. "I know I yelled at you about him, Alexis, but he's working incredibly hard on your behalf. I think he's tracked down every subcontractor who's worked on the empty house across from yours over the past six months, which gives us a pretty good record of Evan Palmer's comings and goings while you were at work."

"My backyard neighbor can testify to that, too," Alexis said. "He identified Evan from his yearbook photo." Moving on, she said, "This press conference? What's it all about? What am I supposed to do?"

"It's our defense strategy," Trustman said. "The best defense often is a good offense. Until now, we've been getting a sense of their case against you and doing our own investigation. Your impression of the situation has been confirmed by everything we've learned. We're dealing with a boy with a pattern of false accusations and obsessive, vindictive behavior, who's been protected by his mother's intervention and the legal system's unwillingness to penalize a young boy."

She leaned forward. "Look what happened in Connecticut. There was a restraining order, but despite the persistence and ugliness of his behavior, the cops weren't aggressive about enforcing it. He kept bothering that girl until her parents filed a civil suit against both Evan and his mother which was settled only by their moving to Massachusetts."

Trustman looked pleased. "George learned that since they've been here, there have been two complaints against Evan by former girlfriends alleging physical abuse. Both times the girls recanted. Now that we know of the threats that happened before, we can imagine why. We've got the golden boy athlete who commits violent acts against women and who keeps being given second and third chances."

Alexis was about to ask why, when the police had evidence that Evan was violent, they'd refused to take her concerns for her safety seriously. But Trustman was already explaining that. "Of course they'll argue that accusing a teacher of seducing him is different from beating up his girlfriends, but it's just another form of destructive retaliation. In Evan's mind, anything that doesn't give him what he wants deserves to be destroyed. The teachers and administration and police who are aware of the problem and don't act reinforce that behavior."

The lawyer nodded at Bannerman. "Tell Alexis what you learned."

"I'm lucky I didn't get arrested for loitering around the school yard," he said. "We can thank your friend Claire. She hooked me up with people who gave me these." He waved some papers.

"Affidavits," Trustman explained, "from some of Evan's former girlfriends. As you know, George can be very persuasive."

"And this." Bannerman passed Alexis an envelope.

She studied the photographs. Evan and Carrie Canavan arguing. Evan hitting her. Carrie knocked back against a truck, shock and pain on her face, blood running from her mouth. Evan walking away, leaving her stunned and bleeding. Beautiful quality pictures. Shatteringly clear. And deeply disturbing.

"You took them?"

He nodded.

She put them back in their envelope and returned them to Bannerman. "Excuse me." She ran from the room.

In the bathroom, she clutched the sink. She was supposed to be happy. She'd taken steps to rescue herself, showing that Evan Palmer was dishonest, manipulative, dangerously unbalanced. But uppermost in her mind were George's photographs, the righteous certainty on Evan's face and no sign of regret.

Trustman was geared for battle. Her immediate focus was the press conference and going on the offensive. Casting Alexis as the true victim would be good for her criminal case, and in retooling her image in the public eye. But removing the legal stigma was only part of the problem. Despite Bannerman's pictures, Bethany's story, and what Evan had done to little Ian, Alexis was terrified of the downside: Evan would be unraveling. Unless he was locked up or forced to move far away, she would never be safe.

When she returned to Trustman's office, Peter Everett had joined them, and the room seemed crowded. He stood when she entered, rocking slightly on his feet, looking like a boy dressed for church in jacket and tie.

She smiled. "I hear you've been playing detective." Her voice still had a rasp. The lingering effects of smoke, screaming, the constrictive power of fear.

He shrugged. "Doing what I can, Alexis." He looked as tired as she felt. Even from across the room, she knew he wanted to touch her, to affirm that she was okay, but was obeying Trustman's order to keep away.

"Okay, people," Trustman said. "It's almost time. Alexis, I know you're dying to tell your side of the story. You'll hate me for this, but all I want you to do is introduce yourself, explain how hard this has been, and then, unless I ask a specific question, say what you've said all along: there has never been any relationship between you and Evan except the relationship of teacher and student within the appropriate boundaries of such a relationship. Got that?"

Panic seized her. She'd have to stand before reporters, all those judging eyes and vulgar questions. Did she have the courage for this? Did they understand how fragile her control was? They hadn't seen her out in the rain, covered in filth and mud, screaming at Collins. Or out on the highway, bug-eyed with fear and clenching the wheel. She nodded.

"Good. Now, I know you've been concerned about what you perceive as a lack of support from your friends and colleagues," Trustman held up her hand, warding off protests, "so I've asked a few people to come today to lend their support."

A small and solemn procession, the four of them went down the stairs of the office building and through the doors into the blinding sunshine. Into crowds and noise and confusion. She grabbed George's arm.

"Just keep breathing," he said. "You'll be fine."

They approached a row of mikes set up facing a mass of people. On their side of the mikes, Dan Morgan and other teachers from the high school. Women from church. Her neighbors. Ollie and some of the regulars. Smiling groups of high school students. Senior citizens from the center where she sang. Maggie Morgan in full ministerial regalia, turning to embrace her. She felt her throat tighten. The swell of tears. George's voice in her ear, "See. You aren't alone."

With Trustman beside her, she stepped up to the mikes, dizzy from so many days of holding her breath, stunned by the possibility of rescue. "First, I'd like to thank everyone for coming out today to lend their support. You can't know what it means to me to have you all here. I'd been feeling very much alone with this."

Her voice faltered and George passed her his handkerchief. "The past weeks have been a terrible ordeal. I had to go on leave from my job... and for a teacher who loves what she does as much as I do... that is very painful. I was arrested. Taken out of school in handcuffs. I was interrogated, humiliated and vilified, to my face and in the press. My car was vandalized, my house set afire. Two nights ago, a mob of students smashed my windows and filled my yard with trash while the Crawford Valley police stood by and did nothing."

She looked at the sea of reporters, cameras, and curiosity seekers, daunted by this voracious crowd, before all the eyes undressing her and putting her in bed with Evan. The reporters were scribbling but barely listening, their mouths poised to bombard her questions. The people who really mattered stood behind her.

"I'll leave it to my lawyer to explain the purpose of this news conference," she said. "I'll save any speeches for the day I finally put all of this behind me. For now, I will say only this—" The crowd had begun murmuring, and she gave a 'settle down' look. "The only relationship I have ever had with Evan Palmer has been that of teacher and student. Any other claims he has made are pure fiction."

The words had barely left her mouth before the questions started. She bowed her head, clasping her hands like a penitent. "My attorney, Janice Trustman, will address your questions." She moved back as her supporters surged around her.

Maggie Morgan, tall, imposing, and ministerial, standing behind her. Alexis admired the way Janice had staged this. The theater of it. Did she look as diminished as she felt? Was she supposed to?

At the back of the crowd, Evan and Jason and Luke and Billy, boys who had nothing to be proud of, stood tall and defiant. Listening as her lawyer spelled out her case as if she was speaking to a jury. What the allegations were, and how she would disprove them. Calmly and eloquently laying it out for Evan. For the police chief. For Collins and Hovarth.

Alexis watched Evan's expression of malicious triumph morph into uncertainty, then uneasiness, finally contorting with furious disbelief. Had he thought his history of bad behavior would never catch up with him? That he'd be allowed to sow ruin again and again, never accepting that what he did was wrong? He probably had.

It should have been a moment of triumph, but fear eclipsed her hope. Just like with Mr. Brownell and Bethany, if Evan couldn't get what he wanted one way, he'd try another. He wanted Alexis punished for the crime of rejecting him. He wanted her to suffer. She watched him stalk away, trailed by his friends. Thought of Pat Coleman, still taking circuitous routes and obsessively checking her mirrors. George Bannerman's half-joking advice, echoed by the kindly truck drivers.

"Watch yourself, little lady."

It was no joke.

> "Waited with hellish rancor imminent
> To intercept thy way, or send thee back
> Despoiled of innocence, of faith, of bliss!"
> —John Milton, *Paradise Lost*: Book IX

CHAPTER THIRTY-EIGHT

It was over. Janice walking away from the microphones, Peter hovering protectively by her side as people surrounded her, as she smiled and shook hands and murmured her thanks and appreciation. Over and over and over, as they slowly made their way through the crowd to the door.

She paused to give Ollie a hug.

"How about tomorrow we go fishing," he suggested. "I'll pick you up between nine-thirty and ten and bring us some lunch, okay, Red?"

An oasis on her horizon. The insurance guy was coming at eight, then fishing with Ollie. Peace and quiet. Murmuring water. No cops or bad guys. No lying, cheating husbands or struggling with her damaged house.

"That would be great, Ollie." She gave him her address and cell number, waved one last farewell, like some celebrity, and disappeared into the relative calm and quiet of the building.

Trustman stood behind her desk, cheeks flushed and eyes shining, accepting congratulations from Peter and George, from Claire and Dan and Maggie Morgan, who'd come upstairs with them. "Thanks," she said. "Thanks. I thought it went pretty well."

Alexis searched for words to express her appreciation for what had been an extraordinary effort made on her behalf. She was still processing the message she'd seen on Evan's face.

"It's time we all went home," Janice said, finally. "Alexis, you need a good dinner and a night's rest. Call me tomorrow and we'll set up a time to talk about this."

She felt a surge of panic. "But… I can't go home. And Janice, I… there's something else I have to tell you. Coming back from Connecticut this afternoon someone in a black Volvo convertible, just like Evan's friend Jason drives, tried to run me off the road." She pulled out the scrap of paper and pushed it across the desk. "I was rescued by these two guys. Truck drivers. They wrote down their numbers, and the license number of the Volvo, in case…" Her voice faltered. "In case I want to report it to the police."

"Check this out, will you, George?" Her lawyer handed the paper to Bannerman. "Home to get your stuff, I meant. You're going to Claire's. Tomorrow afternoon we'll meet and we can work on a longer-term plan, but for tonight, just get some rest."

She read Alexis's hesitation. "I know you're worried about safety. Peter will see that you get some dinner, and stay with you until you get to Claire's."

"I'm supposed to stay away from Peter."

Trustman shrugged, like that didn't matter anymore. "George is busy and I want someone with you."

It sounded like a bad idea, but she was supposed to take her lawyer's advice, so Peter followed her to Claire's. She left her car there and joined him in the van.

As soon as her seatbelt was fastened, he started driving. And talking, sounding so serious she knew he wasn't going to talk about food. "I'm gonna make a complete hash of this, so I want to say that right up front." He stared straight ahead, eyes on the road.

"A hash of what?"

"My big speech. Alexis, I…" He took the turn onto the highway, heading west.

"Where are we going?"

"Someplace nobody knows us. Where there's no Collins, Hovarth, or Evan. Look, maybe I sound ridiculous, but I've got to say this. Finding you again seemed like a miracle. The other night, when the EMT called me, I was so happy I was the one you picked. Ever since, I've been building castles in the air. So I—I don't know, wanted to get that out on the table so there were no secrets between us. I didn't want to go falling crazy in love with you if you're looking at me like some good old buddy."

Classic guy timing. He not only picked a time when her whole life was in chaos, he picked tonight, when she was almost incapable of coherent thought.

"Peter," she said, "about something between us. My feelings aren't old buddy, okay? But this is such a bad time. I just filed for divorce. And Evan's manipulations have me so strung out my mind's like scrambled eggs."

He ducked his head. "I'm being a big jerk, putting you through this now," he said. "I just, you know, it was on my mind and I wanted to tell you."

His hand rested on his knee. She put hers over it, flashing back to that moment when his hands were touching her in his bathroom. "Part of me would like nothing better than to fall into your safe, comfortable embrace," she said. "But me and relationships? Not so good. And I've got to deal with this other stuff first."

"You haven't changed much," he said.

"What? You mean I'm still as gooney and confused as a high school girl?"

"I mean you're still as honest and direct and decent as you were then."

"Don't," she said. "A comment like that. You see, I'm…"

"Vulnerable?" he suggested.

"Uh-huh. Wounded. Broken."

He made a sound, like it hurt him, too.

They drove a while in silence. Then he said, "You called me. I was surprised. As surprised as that time before the prom when you showed up at work and hung around so I'd give you a ride home."

"This really isn't the time to talk about this, okay?"

It was dim in the van, and there was something peaceful and unthreatening about driving and talking. It reminded her of their dates in high school. She used to feel like she could say anything and he would understand. "I don't want a relationship based on gratitude or a need for safety. I don't want to be taken care of. I'm not a pet. I'm a woman. I want someone who needs me. Who'll be crazy in love with me. I want to laugh together. Build something. I want a cat and a dog. Kids."

"Big dog or little dog?" he asked.

"Medium. Mutt. But it has to like to run."

"How many kids?"

"Two."

"Would you consider three?"

"Peter, stop."

She stared at the oncoming cars, half-expecting one of them to drive straight at them, or to be rammed from behind. Talking with him made her feel normal. But her life wasn't normal.

"I'm in mourning for my life," she said. "My job. Even—not for Micah, but for my failed marriage. Got so many things to resolve before I can begin to look forward. That was a press conference, not a vindication. You'd have to be prepared to wait a long time and be awfully patient."

"Been waiting a long time," he said. "And I'm very patient."

They rode a while in silence. Then he asked what kind of food she wanted for dinner. "I don't want dinner," she said. "I want ice cream. Chocolate ice cream with hot fudge. On a brownie."

"Whatever makes you happy." They pulled into the lot of a busy ice cream stand. "I'll get it," he said. "You wait in the van."

"Whipped cream," she called to him through the open window, "and nuts."

She watched him thread his way among the cars and get into line, a head taller than everyone around him. For the past weeks, she'd been discovering what it was like to stand out in a crowd.

She leaned against the door, watching people line up for this annual ritual, which signaled the beginning of the summer season, then closed her eyes, practicing an observation exercise she assigned to her creative writing students. Sit somewhere and use only one of your senses to record what's going on around you. She listened to car engines, the loudspeaker calling numbers, scraps of music, giggles, mumbles, bits of conversations.

Behind it all, the night sounds of amphibians with mating on their minds.

And the sound of a thump nearby, something banging against the van. A car door opening too wide, or someone's arm. The overwhelming scent of aftershave destroyed the single sensory experience. Evan.

"Enjoying yourself, Mrs. J?"

"Get away from me, Evan. I have nothing to say to you."

"I never enjoy myself anymore, not since you ended our relationship." Leaning against the van like they were old friends. Peter was across the lot. At the order window.

"You have to stop pretending, Evan. We've never had a relationship."

"That was quite a show your lawyer put on today." He craned his neck around, imitating her. "Your boyfriend's kinda busy right now. Gives us a chance to talk." His voice dropped. "It's been hard to get near you lately. I've missed it."

She turned away from him.

"You know it's not over, don't you, Mrs. J? Not until *I* decide it's over."

"I know who you are, Evan. I know what you've done to people. I know why your mother keeps moving. And I know how you've treated Carrie. Sooner or later the world will find out, too. You're sick, Evan. Sick and evil."

"This from the woman who used to put her hand on my arm and murmur, 'Poor Evan' while accidentally bumping my shoulder with her breast? Oh please. You wanted me and you're going to get me."

His voice was low and insinuating. "I'm not going away. I said I wanted to be somebody special to you. And I will be. I'm going to be very special, Mrs. J. We're going to be together, and when we're done, you'll never be able to forget me."

She thought he'd gone, but when she turned, he was still there. "You're going to be watching all the time, Mrs. J. Night and day. And when you least expect it," he snapped his fingers, "there I'll be." He reached in the window and ran his hand lightly over her breasts, his smile holding more malice than a sixteen-year-old ought to possess. "There I'll be." He disappeared into the night.

"Abide with me, fast falls the eventide,
the darkness deepens..."
—Henry Francis Lyte

CHAPTER THIRTY-NINE

When Peter returned with the sundae and two spoons, she was cowering against the seat, the windows rolled up and the doors locked. He had to bang on the window before she'd let him in.

"What happened?" he demanded, putting the sundae on the dash. "What's wrong?"

"He was here," she said. "Evan Palmer."

"Here? What did he do? Are you all right?"

Everything normal had been destroyed by a few words. "I really don't want to talk about it."

"What did he do?" Peter persisted. "You've got to tell me, Alexis."

"He said—" She dropped to a whisper, uttering words too harsh and dangerous to be spoken aloud. "He said he was going to be someone special to me. That we were going to be together and when he was done..." She was stammering, and furious with herself for conceding the boy so much power. "Oh, Peter. I can't say it."

He grabbed her arm. "Dammit, Alexis, tell me!"

She stared at the hand that gripped her. "Now you're going to start, too?"

His hand dropped like he'd touched something hot. "Alexis. Oh, Alexis, no. I'm so sorry. I didn't mean... I would never want you to think I'm anything like him."

She was crouched against the door, arms wrapped tightly around her body to hold herself together.

"You're shaking." He removed his jacket and wrapped it around her, then very slowly pulled her toward him.

"I'm scared, Peter. More scared than after the fire. Than when I was arrested." Someone had fastened iron bands around her chest. Her heart was hammering.

He stroked her hair, a steady, soothing rhythm. "Tell me what he said. What he did."

"He said we were going to be together. That he'd leave his mark on me and when he was done, I'd never be able to forget him."

A gulf existed between her and the rest of the world. There, things went on as usual. For her, nowhere was safe. The darkness harbored evils and danger, a bogeyman under her bed, a monster in her closet. She couldn't stay with friends and be guarded forever. Despite Peter's arm around her, she felt completely vulnerable.

"There's more," she said. Why was this so hard? After the last weeks, when the words "have you touched his genitals?" had become as commonplace as "please pass the salt," she should be used to discussing intimate touches. "He touched my breasts and smiled this awful smile, and said, 'and there I'll be,' and walked away. He has absolutely no fear."

"Which is why Janice didn't want you home alone."

"But for how long? He'll wait as long as necessary. He wants me always looking over my shoulder. He wants to take delight in my fear and suffering. After two years, the woman in Connecticut still looks over hers."

"Where is the little bastard?" he said.

"Gone. But going after him doesn't work. It plays into his fantasy as the victim. You pick a fight with him, he thinks, first Mrs. Jordan seduces and abandons me, then her new boyfriend beats me up. With emphasis on 'new boyfriend' as well as on his victimhood. He's this young boy, and you're a big, strong man." She shrugged. It didn't need explaining.

"You still want this ice cream?"

Strangely, though the circumstance ought to have stolen her appetite, she did.

Then he took her back to Claire's. He walked her to the door, wanting to kiss her, she knew, and holding back. Janice Trustman's image and Hovarth's camera invisible chaperones between them. "Night, Alexis," he said. "You have my numbers?"

"Yes." She couldn't resist a smile. "I think I've got your number."

"I could stay with you," he said. "Or you could stay with me. I'd sleep on the couch."

"Hovarth would find us. Or Janice would kill us."

"Chin up," he said. "It's going to be okay."

What everyone said. What only a fool believed.

*   *   *

"Your room will make you feel about twelve years old," Claire said, opening a door. "I hope you don't have a stuffed animal phobia."

"Only an Evan Palmer phobia."

"I think a phobia is an irrational fear. Yours, my dear, is perfectly rational."

The room had pink wallpaper, a white twin bed with a canopy. Shaggy pink wall-to-wall carpeting. A large pink panda lounging against the pillow. And posters of female athletes. "Jackie chose this all herself. Frankly, it's so girly it turns my stomach, but that's how it is with kids. When she was seven and eight, she wore a tutu every second she wasn't in school. She wore a tutu to soccer practice. That was a hoot. Pink tutu, pink shoes, pink hair ribbons, and with her strong legs from all that ballet, she could kick better than the boys. Maybe, having brothers, pink was her way of staking out her territory. Now she's six foot two and playing college ball, and won't let me redecorate."

"It's a lot harder to imagine bad guys, bogeymen and Evan crouching on pink carpet under a white eyelet bedspread."

"Bathroom's next door," Claire said. "The pink towels are yours. Need anything else?"

"Bodyguard with a shotgun?"

"If you want, Rory can sleep with you." Claire stuck her head out the door and called, "Rory, here boy!" There was the skittering of toenails and an enormous black dog appeared. "He's as gentle as a lamb, but he looks plenty fierce, and if anyone comes near the house, he'll bark his head off."

Alexis looked at the dog. "I think I'd like that." When she got in bed, Rory curled up on the floor beside her, settling in with some circling, snuffling and a sigh.

All night long, when every moving branch and gust of wind and creak of the house woke her, tense and breathless, those soulful dark dog eyes stared up at her. She woke the dog a dozen times; he woke her only once. She'd finally fallen into a fairly deep sleep and the dog became suddenly alert and growling. By the time she figured out what was happening, he'd dashed down the stairs and was whining at the front door. She heard Claire's voice, the door opened and closed, and then Rory was rushing around the yard, barking. If Evan was out there, she hoped he was afraid of dogs.

*   *   *

"Lex, time to wake up." Claire was shaking her shoulder.

She opened her eyes to the pink extravaganza and pushed back the covers, almost tripping over the dog. "How much time do I have?"

"Time for a shower or coffee. Not both if you want to keep that appointment with your insurance guy. I let you sleep as long as I could."

"Coffee," she said. "I'll be right down." Hastily, she made the bed, brushed her teeth and hair, and threw her things back into her bag. Getting through another whole night without a disaster made the day seem more promising.

In the kitchen, Claire inspected her, then passed her a mug. "Cream and sugar, right? You sleep okay?"

"Like a baby."

"That's a myth, you know. Babies never sleep."

"Then I definitely slept like one."

Claire grabbed her bag and a sweater. "Gotta roll. County computer conference today. Got any big plans after the insurance guy?"

"Ollie's taking me fishing. Then later, Trustman wants to get together to work on a longer-term plan to keep me safe."

"Ollie? That loud man from the coffee shop?"

She nodded. "I think this is recreation therapy. You know. A field trip."

"Better take some bug spray."

"Good idea." She gathered up her stuff and followed Claire out, pausing on the walk to look up and down the street. More like Pat Coleman every day. "Macbeth does murder sleep," she murmured.

"What?"

"Wondering if I'll ever go anywhere again without looking over my shoulder."

"What do you expect to find there?"

"Evan. He knows if I call the cops, they won't care."

"You're welcome to stay tonight," Claire said. "For as many nights as you want."

"I appreciate the offer. But I like being at home. I've got a lot of straightening up to do."

"But you have to take his threats seriously."

"Would you let Evan drive you out of your house?"

Claire shrugged. "I might. You know the old motto... you can be dead right and still be dead." She clapped a hand over her mouth. "Forget I said that, okay? Mike says I suffer from hoof in mouth disease."

She and Claire got in their cars, and she headed cautiously home.

It was hard to think of menace and lurking danger when the birds were singing and the trees were leafing out in their amazing array of soft, new greens. When azaleas were bursting with flowers. Alexis longed to try out her new running shoes. She hadn't run for days and hated the sluggish way that made her feel. But her feet needed another day.

She went up the walk and unlocked the door, her whole body tensed, afraid some nasty surprise was waiting. But everything was fine. Maggie and the others had done wonders. No one had trashed the rooms or set any fires. Things were back on the shelves. Micah hadn't taken the furniture away. There were no notes.

It was almost time for the insurance man. She went into the kitchen and pressed the message button on the machine. A lot of junk, yesterday's increasingly irritated messages from her lawyer, and Mr. Lowden saying his nephew would be coming to look at the windows around nine. She didn't have to be home. He'd figure it out and leave her an estimate.

The doorbell rang. Her insurance man looked nervous. Evidently, he believed what he'd read in the papers. He held his clipboard like a shield between them. What was he afraid she'd do, seduce him? Wasn't that what every man dreamed of, that he'd ring the doorbell of some suburban house and the woman would drag him inside and ravish him?

She walked him around the inside and then to the garage, keeping a careful distance, making her voice deliberately soft and low so she wouldn't spook him. He was in and out and promised to call her with an estimate in no time. Dashing to his car with more alacrity than he'd shown in all the years they'd been doing business. Afraid he'd catch cooties or something.

She locked the door on his retreating back and went upstairs to figure out what to wear fishing. Jeans and a tank-top and a denim shirt. She dumped them on the bathroom floor, turned on the shower, and pulled off her dress. Someone knocked on the door.

Mr. Lowden's nephew. She could see the truck in the driveway. Living with plastic over the windows was like living in a cave. The sooner he could fix them, the better. She turned the water off, pulled on the jeans and tank top, and rushed downstairs. She pulled open the door, saying, "Your uncle told me you'd be coming."

"Morning, Mrs. J." Evan Palmer, a massive knife shining in his hand, a black duffel bag over his shoulder, shoved her back inside, followed her in, and slammed the door.

"…he shall hear
Infernal thunder, and for lightning see
Black fire and horror shot with equal rage…"
—John Milton, *Paradise Lost*: Book II

CHAPTER FORTY

"You look surprised," he said. "I thought you'd be expecting me."

"Evan, this is a bad idea," she said, stepping backwards into the living room, her eyes glued to the gleaming knife. "Maybe you think by doing this, by hurting me you'll feel better, but think about your own life. The harm you'll do yourself."

"Oh, don't worry about me, Mrs. J. They'll understand why I did it, that I had to do it. Worst thing that'll happen to me is a little therapy." He shrugged. "I can bullshit my way through that easy. Whereas, the worst thing that'll happen to you? Well, I really don't know yet. We'll see. Why don't we…" He looked around. "Go upstairs where we'll be more comfortable." He gestured with the knife.

The nearest phone was in the kitchen. She made a dash for it, her lacerated feet clumsy on the wood floor. She was no match for a bigger, fitter athlete. He caught her at the door, wrapping one arm around her waist, holding the knife against her throat, the blade cold and lethal against her skin. "Oh, come on. What's the matter? Aren't you glad to see me?"

"Evan. Please. Put the knife down." She tried to keep fear out of her voice. Where was her bag? Her cell phone? Upstairs on the bed? That made two phones up there. Two chances to dial 911. Would they come if she did? She didn't have much faith in the Crawford police, but they couldn't ignore 9-1-1, could they?

"Okay, Evan. I'll go upstairs with you. Just put the knife down."

The knife moved a few inches away. She felt her airways open again, gulping in air as he turned her, still with an arm around her waist, and headed toward the stairs. "No tricks, now," he said. "When I said we were going to play games, I meant *I* was going to play games. With you. You are going to do what I say, or you'll be punished. Understand?"

"Evan, why are you doing this?"

The knife snugged up against her throat again. She felt sharp pain and then the warm sensation of blood running over her collarbone. "Do you understand?" he repeated.

"I understand."

Could she last until Ollie came? Or Mr. Lowden's nephew? Would the nephew worry when she didn't answer the door? Wonder about the truck? Would he call for help and if he did, would it come in time? It wasn't yet nine. The earliest she could expect Ollie was nine-thirty. A half hour that would be an eternity.

He lowered the knife and shoved her toward the stairs. "Go on."

She climbed the stairs slowly, aware with each step of the knife resting against her spine, the small pricks on her skin. "I think we'll go in your bedroom," he said. "I've thought about being there with you so many times."

When she reached the middle of the room, he said, "Stop."

She stopped. The bag with her phone only four feet away. The phone beside the bed maybe eight feet. She only needed enough time to dial three numbers. 9-1-1. Visualized where they were on the receiver. Three quick punches. Lower right corner, upper left. 9-1-1. Felt her finger pressing invisible buttons in the air. Intensely aware of everything. The softness of the flokati rug under her bare toes. The citrus of his aftershave. The heat from his looming body. His panting breath. Her weak knees. He wasn't any more at ease about this than she was. But he had the knife.

"Now, turn toward me," he said. Slowly, she turned. Raised her eyes to his face. He had a look of excited anticipation. His cheeks slightly pink. Lips parted. Eyes shining. "I have waited so long for this," he said. "So long. Now, I want you to take off your jeans. For now, just your jeans. Nice and slowly. Like I'm your lover and I enjoy watching you undress. And take that thing out of your hair."

She unfastened the barrette. Sturdy metal. Shaped like a feather. It would have made a good weapon if he hadn't had a knife. Keeping her options open, she dropped it on the floor at her feet. Hope is a feather. More scared than she'd ever been in her life. She couldn't give in to it. Fear, like Evan, was her enemy. And menacing as he was, he was only sixteen. She shook her hair loose and undid the button on her pants. Slowly slid down the zipper. Slowly, slowly, trying to remember what underwear she was wearing. Trying to stay alive.

She could feel the heat of his eyes as she slipped her fingers into the waistband and slowly eased the denim over her hips. Remembering the occasional striptease she'd done for Micah. Willing this to have a different result. Would she have sex with this boy to save her life? Would she be forced to? Would it save her life? Would anything?

Currents of fear tripped down her spine. Her fingers, resting against her hips, were icy.

"Hey. Stop it right there," he ordered. She stopped and stood, still as a statue as he reached out, using the knife tip like a surrogate finger, and tapped lightly on the small blue stone in her navel.

"Neat." He smiled with boyish pleasure, like she'd done it just for him. "Go on."

Another inch and he'd see the tattoo. She slid the pants lower, shifting her hands to the back to begin easing them over her butt. Another inch and another, keeping her eyes on the floor, not wanting to see the lust on his face, the eagerness, the malice. They cleared her hips and began their descent down her thighs. Her underpants were powder blue lace with a small satin bow a few inches below her navel. Her thighs were milky white. They looked strong and vulnerable. Slowly down past her knees, the stiff denim piling over her feet, stacking on her calves. Not the best fabric for this kind of performance. She bent down and slowly tugged the first foot free. Bent her knee, freed the second foot, balling up the pants and hurling them into his face.

She raced for the phone, snatched it off the cradle, and punched 9-1-1. He dove across the bed, wrenched it out of her hand, and slammed it back on the cradle. Then he shoved her to the floor, pinning her there with one knee as he drew back his hand and smashed it into her face. Once. Twice. Three times. Her cheekbones stung, her lip split, her nose began to bleed.

"Goddammit!" he yelled. "Goddammit. I told you. Do exactly as you're told or you'll be punished. Didn't I tell you that?"

He drew back his hand again and waited.

"Yes, you did. You told me, Evan." Making her voice soft. Breathy. Feminine. Trying to play to his fantasy.

"Then what the fuck was that all about?" His hand poised, trembling. He wanted to hit her again.

Give him something, she thought. A victory. Feed his ego. Get him talking. Use up time. Every second he talked, she got closer to the possibility of rescue, to the chance she might think of some way to end all this. "I was scared," she said. "I am scared."

"Thought you weren't scared of anything, Mrs. J."

She was lying on her bedroom floor in her underwear, bleeding, facing a crazy man with a big knife and she wasn't supposed to be scared? "Everyone's scared of something, Evan. I try not to be, but I'm only human. Have you ever been on the pointed end of a knife?"

"No."

"But you've imagined this, haven't you? How you'd feel, holding it, how I'd feel facing it?"

He nodded.

"You want…" she swallowed, "… a report from the other side?"

"Sure." He actually looked curious, like this was a natural thing, a teacher conveying information. That was what teachers did.

"Could you hand me some of those tissues."

He looked from her to the box, sitting on the nightstand next to the phone, then back at her. "Promise you won't try anything?"

"I promise."

Did he seriously think any promise under these circumstances was valid? She tried to make her face blank as she waited. He grabbed a fistful of tissues and shoved them into her hand. She mopped some of the blood off her face, then held them against her nose. "About the knife," she said.

He gestured toward the bathroom door. "Get in there and clean yourself up. You look disgusting."

And what, she wondered, *you only rape women if they look lovely? You punch someone in the face and expect it to make no difference?* She could understand if he watched violence only in the movies because actors recovered from such violence in an absurdly short time. But Evan beat up women in real life. He had to know that hitting drew blood and was followed by bruises and swelling. Maybe, since she was a fantasy object, she ought to behave like a movie character.

"Then could you move your knee?"

She didn't know how he wanted her to be. The message of his words was that he wanted her compliant. But in his fantasy, she was a seductress. She was the aggressor. The one who'd come after him. Enticed him into all this. Maybe part of his rage was because she was acting scared. Because his paramount fantasy was still about being wanted. He pulled back his knee and stood, towering over her, holding the knife out in front of him. A none-too-subtle phallic symbol.

She rose slowly to her feet and walked into the bathroom. Acutely aware of how bare she was, of where this was sure to lead. Where this had been heading since the moment in that room off the library when he'd put his hand on her arm and declared his intention to be something special to her.

He hovered behind her as she bent over the sink, rinsed her face with cold water, dried it on a towel, and put cream on her split lip. She turned and faced him, planting her hands on the edge of the sink, shoulders back, lifting her chest. Sleazy pin-up girl posing, the skimpy tank showing cleavage. "About the knife," she said, making her voice lower, fear making it husky. "The way I see it? It looks big…" She flicked out her tongue, licked the welling blood off her lip. Brought her hands up and held them about twelve inches apart. "About this big. And when you hold it out there in front of you? It's all I can see."

"Come back in the bedroom," he said. Now his voice was getting husky, too. He followed her closely. She walked past the bed, to the middle of the room. "Stop right there... and turn around." She turned. "Now take off that top."

If only she'd worn more clothes. That would have prolonged this. Once she got the tank top off, there really wasn't anything left except two blue wisps. And how long would it take to get them off? If only she'd anticipated a daytime attack. She could have put on layers of clothing. She felt a hysterical giggle rising and squelched it. If she laughed, no matter what the reason, he would think she was laughing at him.

She took a step backward. He was so close she felt the heat rising off his body, smelled how his nervous hormonal sweat overpowered the aftershave. Not enough Right Guard on the planet to keep him cool and fresh through torture and rape, to keep him from sweating with pleasure as he anticipated violence. She crossed her arms, grabbed the hem of her top, and slowly pulled it up over her head, dropping it on the floor by her feet.

He pointed at the tattoo with his knife. "What's that about?"

"Celtic design around the letter 'M'," she said. "M for Micah. My husband. Learn from my mistake. If you're ever tempted to get a tattoo, don't get one that's too personal."

"Yeah." Evan nodded. "He's a real asshole, isn't he? That girlfriend he's got? She's not half as pretty as you are. And she's fat. Maybe he likes big tits?"

His eyes shifted to her breasts and he lifted the knife.

Fear slid like an icicle along her spine, reverberating through her abdomen like shock waves. He had threatened to leave his mark in a way that she'd never forget. She wanted to cross her arms protectively over her chest. She wanted to beg him not to hurt her. Feared that weakness might backfire, that cringing or begging would make him want to hurt her more.

Smirking, he slipped the knife blade under one of her bra straps and sliced through it, watched it sag limply over her breasts, then did the same on the other side. Reached out with the knife tip and traced it lightly across her skin above the bra's top, watching as a thin line of bright blood appeared.

He looked down at the shiny blade. "Big, huh? So big you can't see anything else?" He smoothed a hand across the front of his nylon shorts, and smiled with satisfaction. Pleasantly aroused by their foreplay with knife.

"Maybe," he said, pointing with his knife, his hot eyes on her ruined bra, on the seeping blood, "it's time to take that thing off and get down to business."

She reached behind her and found the hooks, ignoring the pain from stretching her lacerated skin. Then she hesitated. "Evan?"

"What?" He was rubbing a hand across his crotch, a slightly absent look on his face.

"Maybe it would be better if we went in the guest room? I was thinking—I know you wanted this to be a special time—and I've been with Micah in here so many times. But in there I've never been with anyone."

She lowered her eyes demurely, leaving it up to him. Waiting as she watched her blood trickle down her chest.

"The guest room? Why not? I am a guest, aren't I?" He gestured with the knife. "After you." She took a step toward the door. Heard a quick step behind her, then his arm snaked around her waist, dragging her back against him, the knife at her throat again. "No tricks. Understand?"

Every trick in the book, asshole Had he read her mind, known she planned to hurl herself down the stairs and run out the front door, not too proud to have the world see her in her underwear, or what was left of it. Anything to avoid what was coming. "No tricks," she agreed. "Did you want a condom or did you bring one?" She felt his hesitation. "You know where they are, don't you?"

He turned her around and propelled her back across the bedroom, swinging her to the side, the knife biting into her skin as he leaned down and opened the drawer.

"Evan," she gasped. "My throat."

The hand relaxed. Looking down, she saw two small rivulets of blood rolling toward her breasts to join the others. He pulled a handful of condoms out of the drawer, shoved them in his pocket, then spun her around and frog-marched her across the room and out into the hall. The hand that had been at her waist dropped down and came to rest between her legs. "Party time," he whispered.

She flung herself sideways, ducking under the arm that held the knife and down the stairs, stumbling sideways, bouncing off the wall, catching at the banister to arrest her fall. But her feet slipped. She missed a few steps, lost her grip, bounced off the wall again and landed in a tumbled heap at the foot of the stairs.

He was right behind her as she scrambled to her feet, catching her by the hair, jerking her head back, and slapping her until she was too dizzy to see. Then he grabbed her arm and dragged her back upstairs. Hauled her through the guest room door and threw her down on the bed. With one knee across her chest so that she could barely breathe, he hit her a few more times in the face, then punched her ribs and stomach, turned her roughly over, unhooked the bra, jerking it off and dumping it on the floor. He rolled her onto her back and picked up the knife, poking the tip of the blade very deliberately into one breast.

"One more trick and I cut it off," he said. "Stay still. This is going to hurt." As though nothing else had. He bent over her, pinning her to the bed with his knee, poised the knife over her stomach, and sliced. "I thought an E to go with that M."

She squeezed her eyes shut and tried not to scream.

Just one slice and he stopped.

"What am I thinking? This can wait. I don't want to fuck you if you're all bloody." She felt the weight of his knee lift, the shifting of the springs as he got off the bed. "I'm getting undressed. Take off those panties and just lie there, very still, until I tell you what to do next."

With fumbling hands, she worked her underpants down over her hips. Seeing that she was cooperating, he reached down to pull off his shirt. As soon as it was over his head, she stuck her hand under the pillow and pulled out the gun. She rolled off the bed, crouching, her back against the wall, and pointed it at his chest. Steadied it with two very unsteady hands. Loaded and with the safety off, just the way she'd left it.

Downstairs, the doorbell rang, then someone pounded on the door and yelled. She kept the gun pointed at him. Watched him reach for the knife. "Stop!" she yelled. "Don't touch that. Don't make me shoot you, Evan. Don't make me do it."

"You wouldn't shoot me, Mrs. J.," he said, picking up the knife, hefting it, smiling down at her where she crouched between the bed and the wall.

There was the sound of splintering wood and the loud crash of the front door slamming into the wall. Feet thundered on the stairs. A voice yelling, "Police!"

"It's over, Evan," she said.

He lunged at her, knife flailing.

She closed her eyes and squeezed the trigger.

"And that must end us, that must be our cure,
To be no more..."
—John Milton, *Paradise Lost*: Book II

CHAPTER FORTY-ONE

She lay in the lounge chair feeling the hot Florida sun beating down on her, soothing her damaged body, drawing pain out like a poultice. Alone on the beach except for some children far away splashing at the water's edge. Good that they couldn't see her. She shouldn't be wearing this bikini. She was monstrous, her skin marbled with bruises in a dozen colors mixed with the scabs of healing cuts. Too hideous even for her to look at. But it was the only bathing suit she had. She closed her eyes and immediately opened them again. The images inside her head were worse.

If she lived a thousand years she'd never forget Evan towering over her with his knife slashing through the air, bright and lethal and stained with her blood, his face twisted with rage. The sudden wet sound when his head exploded and showered her with a spray of blood and bone and chunks of brain. The way he fell forward, landing on top of her, his ruined head resting on her already bleeding chest. It happened lightning fast, but her memory played it in slow motion. Deafening gunfire. The exploding head. The brilliant red spray of blood filling the air. The wet, smacking thud as he fell against her.

She'd started screaming then, or maybe she'd been screaming all along. And she had screamed and cried, tears and blood mixing, unable to stop, her own voice rising and falling in her ears like a distant siren. Not stopping even when the two officers who'd come in with Collins pulled Evan's body off her, and Collins wrapped her in a blanket and carried her from the room.

Her memories of what happened after that had the dim quality of a smoky room. There had been too much going on with her. Thoughts raced and yawed, stammered and stuttered as she tried desperately to make sense out of what had happened and to simultaneously cover it over with blackness and forget it. A deep, husky voice sounded in the background, rasping out her horror, while some diligent filing system tried to assemble her jumbled impressions into a coherent version of the story, and Evan's head exploded over and over and over, spraying her with gore.

Interfering with the logical progression of thought was the utter agony of her torn body. Someday, in a few centuries when she calmed down, she'd probably experience some deep embarrassment at having been pulled stark naked from underneath a dead body. But that would be far in the future, after years of intensive therapy and her stint as a hermit, when her mutilated soul began to recover. In the immediately foreseeable future, all she wanted was oblivion. She wished for some benevolent person to stick a needle in her arm and put her out of her misery.

She'd been told that after Collins carried her from the room, she had huddled in the arms of the enemy, sticky with her own blood and Evan's, wracked with the breathless, unstoppable sobs of an exhausted child. Swaddled tightly in a blanket, her eyes squeezed shut, body clenched into a small, tight ball. The incomprehensible Collins had gripped her firmly— as though he understood his grip was all that held her together—and sat in her rocking chair and rocked. Rocked. Rocked. Sometimes she'd have a particularly violent spasm and he'd tighten his grip until it passed. Sometimes he talked to her—or she processed as talk the vibrations from his chest that might have been words. Her hearing had been wrecked by the gunshots.

People came and went, asking questions. Medical people tried to take her from the cocoon of Collins' arms but she fought them off, cowering deeper into her blanket. Finally they'd taken her arm, swabbed it with icy alcohol, and mercifully stabbed her with a needle. Only then did her outraged body relax, falling down, down, down into a bottomless black hole.

In the hospital, she hadn't wanted visitors. Not that she could have seen them anyway. In his final fury, Evan had blackened both her eyes and broken her nose. She'd woken with eyes swollen shut, a nose that wouldn't breathe and a body that couldn't tolerate being moved. Her restless, always active self suddenly stilled. No yearning to be up and doing, to be heading out for a run. She'd been listless. Indifferent. Spent.

Yet visitors did come. Came and stood by her bed, murmuring at her unless stilled into silence by her appearance and her unresponsiveness. Her lawyer. Bannerman. Maggie and Dan Morgan. Claire. But not Peter Everett. Maybe he'd finally come to his senses and realized she was more trouble than he needed. Thankfully, Micah had *not* come.

Unexpectedly, arriving in a commotion of demands and complaints, her mother appeared, as unrestful a presence as was ever placed on this earth. Her mother fussed over her, griped at her, tugged at her and talked at her until the doctor finally banished her from the room.

The only constant, the only person she could bear to have around her, was Collins. Comfort from the enemy. She didn't know why he wasn't at work. Maybe she'd been declared a full-time job, though it was a little late for a bodyguard and he no longer needed a confession. All she knew was that whenever she woke he was there, as steady and silent a presence as Poe's raven. When she had bad dreams, he held her hand. When she was thirsty, he gave her water. He was the one who told her she hadn't shot Evan. To let go of that thought. That in time, it would get better.

It was Collins, not her lawyer, who told her all the charges had been dropped and she could have her job back. Who told her he'd let the Colemans know what had happened. He who fed her Jell-O and comforted her when the doctor said she had to leave her safe bed in the hospital.

She hadn't known where to go or what to do. Sat numb and helpless through the hospital's *pro forma* discharge planning. Tiresome bullshit. She couldn't have planned her way to the bathroom. Something as basic as brushing her teeth took too much effort and hurt far too much. How could she find herself refuge? It was Collins who took her out of the hospital through a back door, tucked her into his car, and drove her to a hotel. Understanding without needing to be told that she couldn't go home, that she wasn't ready to face her friends. Some kind of understanding existed between them despite her never voicing anything. A woman who cherished language reduced to monosyllables.

Though her mother arranged the tickets and transportation to her condo on the Gulf Coast of Florida, it was Collins who packed her suitcase and drove her to the airport. Refusing to let her go home. He told her what he was doing, and Alexis, who despised passivity in herself and others, sat in her armchair in the dim hotel room and nodded. She gave no directions, made no demands, and asked no questions. The next day, he came with a suitcase, took her to his car, drove her to the plane, and walked her on board.

He installed her in first class her seat—courtesy of her mother—like someone's feeble grandmother. Stuffed her suitcase in the overhead bin, instructed the hovering flight attendant that she was not allowed to lift it down herself, and handed her a tote bag. "Music. Paperback novel. Sweater. Chocolate. Lip gloss. Sunscreen. Hat. Sunglasses. I forget anything?"

She shook her head, a minute gesture. Any form of movement hurt.

He held out his hand, a small recorder in his palm. "Recognize this?"

"Evan Palmer's initial proposition," she said, painstakingly stringing her first sentence together.

"Found it in your pocket when we searched your place. Took me a few days to get around to listening to it." He shrugged. "All these years. So much experience. I thought I knew what I was doing."

"Me, too."

He put a hand over hers. "You take care. I'll be calling you. Checking up. You don't have to talk. Yes, no, fine, will do." He stood, then, and pulled a card from his pocket. "But if you need to talk, you can always find me at one of these numbers." He straightened, turned, and walked off the plane.

She had managed to get herself and her suitcase to a cab. Gotten from the cab to the condo. Found tea and soup in the cupboard. And slept. She'd been here five days and all she'd done was sleep. Sleep and sit in the sun. She hadn't opened a book. Made a phone call. Spoken to a single human being except Collins, who called her nightly. She was running low on soup. It seemed like a lot of work to get herself more.

She watched the kids splashing and yelling at the edge of the water and wondered if her energy would ever return. How long a wound this big would take to heal? Her stomach rumbled. Nearly time to go upstairs and open that last can. Nasty cream of mushroom. But if she went out, she'd have to call a cab, and they'd stare at her still swollen face, the mottled, hard-boiled egg yellow under her eyes. Maybe she was almost ready to get something delivered. To try chewing a pizza.

She looked at the path that led up from the beach to the building. A man was coming down it. A very big man, looking hot and uncomfortable in pants and a long-sleeved shirt. Carrying a suitcase. Heading toward her as purposefully as a Fuller Brush salesman. Hastily, she pulled a towel over herself, covering the worst of it. He didn't wave or pause. Just walked until he stood beside her chair and looked down at her, his face set and determined. The look of a man with something to say who wasn't going to be deterred until he'd said it.

"I've come to take care of you," Peter Everett said. "And I'm not going away, no matter what you say. No matter what you do. I know you. I know you think you have to do this by yourself. That you deserve to be shut up in solitary for the sin of being too good, too careless, and too trusting. For having made the mistake of being too human. Too bad for you."

He plunked himself down on the sand beside her. Heavily. Wearily. As though he'd walked all the way to Florida. He might have driven. He looked road-worn and ragged. Needed a shave and a shower. A good night's sleep.

"How did you find me?" she asked. Then, answering her own question, "Collins, right?"

"Right. Man can be a real bastard and the man can be a saint. I stayed away while you were in the hospital. I knew you didn't need bothering. Well—" He ducked his head. "I was there, but I didn't talk to you. I was so mad at myself for letting you down. For letting this happen. I thought I should have done something—anything—to protect you. Every time I looked at you, lying there so terribly hurt, I felt…"

"Peter, it wasn't your fault. Don't—"

He held up a hand to stop her. "And then you disappeared. I went to see Collins and… I don't know. I guess he took pity on me. He told me where you were." He shrugged helplessly. "I followed you here and now you have to keep me."

"Peter… I can't." She stuck her hand out defensively, trying to stop him. It fell back into her lap. Too much work to argue. Too much trouble.

"Don't talk," he said. "Don't argue. I didn't come to make trouble for you. Think of me as your servant and general gofer guy. Tea and toast. Soup and sandwiches. I'm your man. Look." He grabbed his suitcase—heavy, solid, elephant-proof luggage—and laid it flat on the sand. Unsnapped the latches and flipped it open. In one half was a meager bundle of clothes, held in place by elastic straps. It was the other half that lifted her bruised and swollen face in a smile. Her first smile in a long time.

Eagerly, he reached in and held up the first item. "Tomato soup," he said. "Canned tuna. Peanut butter and jelly. Yucky boxed macaroni and cheese. Chef Boyardee ravioli. Instant cocoa. Oreos. Graham crackers, Hershey bars and marshmallows. Jell-O. Microwave popcorn."

He picked up a bag and rattled it like a maraca. "Cool ranch Doritos. I brought you a second childhood. A junk food extravaganza. So please don't send me away. You will never find another man like me. And I ask nothing in return."

Like everything else in life right now, it overwhelmed her. She leaned back in the chair and closed her eyes. "I can't, Ev… not now. Not yet."

"Look. I can go away. Find a motel. Come again in a few days. If you need more time. I just…"

He sighed. Closed up the suitcase. She heard the sounds of him getting up off the sand and felt his shadow as he rose and stood over her. "Alexis… can I… may I… at least fix you some lunch before I go?"

She opened her eyes and looked up at him. He wore a hat now. Maybe it had come out of the suitcase. A shabby baseball cap. Under it, he looked tired. As desperately sad and as much like a castaway as she felt. But handsome.

"I can make your favorite," he said. "Tuna and chopped pickle."

With an effort, she held out a hand. "Help me up," she said.

He stretched out his own and gently pulled her up. Her towel fell away, revealing her savaged body. He pulled her very carefully against him. She rested there, the touch of his hands on her back soft as clouds. This was a man whose every gesture said he wouldn't hurt her for the world. At sixteen, Evan Palmer's age, Peter Everett had already made her feel valued and special.

"That's what I'm here for, to help you," he said, offering her his sweetly sad smile, the one that hoped she'd say 'yes' but would never dare to presume. He'd come all this way just in case. "To look after you. Fix you tuna and pickle. Offer a shoulder to cry on or a listening ear. Someone who believes in you even when you've lost faith in yourself. A man who still knows how lucky he is that he got to date the prettiest girl in the class because she turned out to be both beautiful and good. A friend for life, if it turns out that way. Otherwise, a friend for now. No demands. No pressure. Just lunch."

"Tuna and pickle? Honest?" she mumbled into the tired smelling shirt.

"Honest."

He dropped his arms, retrieved her towel, and waited while she slowly tied it around herself. Then he lifted his suitcase and followed her up the path.

ABOUT THE AUTHOR

Maine native **Kate Flora**'s fascination with people's criminal tendencies began in the Maine attorney general's office. Deadbeat dads, people who hurt their kids, and employers' discrimination aroused her curiosity about human behavior. The author of twenty-four books and many short stories, Flora's been a finalist for the Edgar, Agatha, Anthony, and Derringer awards. She won the Public Safety Writers Association award for nonfiction and twice won the Maine Literary Award for crime fiction. Her most recent Thea Kozak mystery is *Death Sends a Message*; her most recent Joe Burgess novel is *A World of Deceit*. Her crime story collection is entitled, *Careful What You Wish For: Stories of Revenge, Retribution, and the World Made Right*.

Flora is a founding member of the New England Crime Bake and the Maine Crime Wave and runs the blog, Maine Crime Writers, https://mainecrimewriters.com. Flora's nonfiction focuses on aspects of the public safety officers' experience. She divides her time between

Massachusetts and Maine, where she gardens and cooks and watches the clouds when she's not imagining her characters' dark deeds. She occasionally swims in the shark-filled sea. She's been married for decades to an excellent man. Her sons edit films and hang out in research labs. Visit www.kateclarkflora.com for more information and the latest news.

CPSIA information can be obtained
at www.ICGtesting.com
Printed in the USA
BVHW042028260423
663101BV00002B/4

9 781645 994381